Reviews for Ian Rankin

A QUESTION OF BLOOD

'He writes with a natural rhythm which exerts an almost hypnotic effect.'
Independent

'Exemplifies the enhanced craftmanship of the author's recent work; the sheer number of handicaps Rebus overcomes and of the puzzles he solves evinces a relishable virtuosity.'
Sunday Times

'A rich absorbing narrative in which the focus is not on who did it – that we know – but why. Artful, moving and entertaining.'
Observer

'An exceptionally well-plotted book, which is guaranteed to hook you and keep you hooked.'
Sunday Telegraph

'Recent crime writers . . . have at their disposal all the opening for alienation afforded by the modern world – and, if one of them has to be singled out as being especially attuned to contemporary murder and social malaise, it is Ian Rankin.'
Times Literary Supplement

RESURRECTION MEN

'What is impressive in *Resurrection Men* is not just the deftness of the links between disparate crimes, but the fluency of the fugue-like counterpoint between investigations . . . On this form, nothing is beyond him.'
Sunday Times

'Rankin's Rebus novels should be required reading for anyone whose knowledge of Edinburgh has been derived from visits to the festival . . . Rankin conveys the visceral fears and hatreds lurking just below the smart Georgian surface of the "you'll have your tea" New Town.'
Sunday Telegraph

'Bears all the qualities that have established Rankin as one of Britain's leading novelists in any genre: a powerful sense of place; a redefinition of Scotland and its past; persuasive characters and a growing compassion among its characters.'

THE FALLS

'Rankin masterfully pulls his fascinating plot together, and his sense of place casts a powerful shadow over this subtle tale of the recurrence of evil.'

Guardian

'*The Falls* pulses with vitality. Suspense vigorously propels you through its pages. Rankin's prose is crisp, laconic and witty. So is his tangy dialogue.'

Sunday Times

'An extraordinarily rich addition to crime literature.'

Independent on Sunday

'*The Falls* is an inventive and absorbing book which lives up to the technical term of a rebus as an enigmatic puzzle.' *Scotsman*

'*The Falls*, the 12th full-length Inspector Rebus story, finds his creator, Ian Rankin, at his brilliant, mordant best, with the dark heart of the city featuring almost as strongly as Rebus himself.' *Sunday Telegraph*

SET IN DARKNESS

'Rankin is a master of his craft, handling each twist and turn of the plot with consummate skill as he takes us by the hand and leads us from the sparkling edifices of New Labour-controlled Scotland to the misty, mysterious Edinburgh alleyways, and from hip and trendy restaurants to dank pubs and bars without missing a step . . . Rankin is streets ahead in the British procedural writing field . . . our top crime writer.' *Independent on Sunday*

'The book sets off at a cracking rate, with bodies piling up in the first few chapters . . . Running parallel to the excellently paced plot is the theme of Scotland's national identity, its past and future, its regeneration and re-evaluation . . . *Set in Darkness* sees Rankin in impeccable form and will undoubtedly please his legions of fans and increase his appeal even further.' *The List*

'This is, astonishingly, the eleventh Inspector Rebus novel by a writer who is still not yet 40, but whose consistent level of excellence is unmatched in the field of British crime fiction.'   Marcel Berlins, *The Times*

'Rankin's particular skill is in producing a highly complex plot whose different strands cleverly come together at the end, a setting which brings to life the grim back streets of Edinburgh and a well-drawn cast of characters.'
                                                    Sunday Telegraph

DEAD SOULS

'Rebus resurgent . . . A brilliantly meshed plot which delivers on every count on its way to a conclusion as unexpected as it is inevitable.'   *Literary Review*

'Rankin weaves his plot with a menacing ease . . . His prose is understated, yet his canvas of Scotland's criminal underclass has a panoramic breadth. His ear for dialogue is as sharp as a switchblade. This is, quite simply, crime writing of the highest order.'   *Daily Express*

'A series that shows no sign of flagging ... Assured, sympathetic to contemporary foibles, humanistic, this is more than just a police procedural as the character of Rebus grows in moral stature . . . Rankin is the head capo of the MacMafia.'   *Time Out*

'An atmospheric and cleverly plotted tale well up to Rankin's CWA Gold Dagger standard.'   *Books Magazine*

'My favourite gritty page-turner was Ian Rankin's *Dead Souls*.'
                                        Lisa Appignanesi, *Independent*

'No one captures the noirish edge of the city as well as Rankin.'
                                                    Daily Telegraph

'His fiction buzzes with energy . . . His prose is as vivid and terse as the next man's yet its flexibility and rhythm give it potential for lyrical expression which is distinctively Rankin's own.'   *Scotland on Sunday*

'Rankin strips Edinburgh's polite façade to its gritty skeleton.'   *The Times*

Also by Ian Rankin

Ian Rankin

Fleshmarket Close

ORION

First published in Great Britain in 2004 by Orion Books
an imprint of The Orion Publishing Group
Orion House, 5 Upper St Martin's Lane, London WC2H 9EA

A CIP catalogue record for this book is available
from the British Library

ISBN (hardback) 0 75285 112 8
ISBN (trade paperback) 0 75285 113 6

Typeset by Deltaype Ltd, Birkenhead, Merseyside

Printed in Great Britain by
Clays Ltd, St Ives plc

In memory of two friends, Fiona and Annie, much missed.

It is to Scotland that we look for our idea of civilisation.

(Voltaire)

The climate of Edinburgh is such that the weak succumb young
. . . and the strong envy them.

(Dr Johnson to Boswell)

Acknowledgements

My thanks to Senay Boztas and all the other journalists who helped me research the issues of asylum-seekers and immigration, and to Robina Qureshi of Positive Action In Housing (PAIH) for information on the plight of asylum-seekers in Glasgow and in the Dungavel detention centre.

The village of Banehall doesn't exist, so please don't pore over maps looking for it. Nor will you find a detention centre called Whitemire in any part of West Lothian, or an estate called Knoxland on the western outskirts of Edinburgh. In fact, I stole my fictitious estate from my friend, the writer Brian McCabe. He once wrote a brilliant short story called 'Knoxland'.

For further information on some of the issues in this book, see the following:

www.paih.org
www.closedungavelnow.com
www.scottishrefugeecouncil.org.uk
www.amnesty.org.uk/scotland

DAY ONE

Monday

1

'I'm not supposed to be here,' Detective Inspector John Rebus said. Not that anyone was listening.

Knoxland was a housing scheme on the western edge of Edinburgh, off Rebus's patch. He was there because the West End guys were short-handed. He was also there because his own bosses couldn't think what to do with him. It was a rainy Monday afternoon, and nothing about the day so far boded anything but ill for the rest of the working week.

Rebus's old police station, his happy hunting ground these past eight or so years, had seen itself reorganised. As a result, it no longer boasted a CID office, meaning Rebus and his fellow detectives had been cast adrift, shipped out to other stations. He'd ended up at Gayfield Square, just off Leith Walk: a cushy number, according to some. Gayfield Square was on the periphery of the elegant New Town, behind whose eighteenth- and nineteenth-century façades anything could be happening without those outside being any the wiser. It certainly felt a long way from Knoxland, further than the three factual miles. It was another culture, another country.

Knoxland had been built in the 1960s, apparently from papier mâché and balsa wood. Walls so thin you could hear the neighbours cutting their toenails and smell their dinner on the stove. Patches of damp bloomed on its grey concrete walls. Graffiti had turned the place into 'Hard Knox'. Other embellishments warned the 'Pakis' to 'Get Out', while a scrawl that was probably only an hour or so old bore the legend 'One Less'.

What shops there were had resorted to metal grilles on windows and doors, not even bothering to remove them during opening hours. The place itself was contained, hemmed in by dual carriage-ways to north and west. The bright-eyed developers had scooped out subways beneath the roads. Probably in their original draw-ings, these had been clean, well-lit spaces where neighbours would stop to chat about the weather and the new curtains in the window of number 42. In reality, they'd become no-go areas for everyone but the foolhardy and suicidal, even in daytime. Rebus was forever seeing reports of bag-snatchings and muggings.

It was probably those same bright-eyed developers who'd had the idea of naming the estate's various high-rise blocks after Scottish writers, and appending each with the word 'House', serving merely to rub in that these were nothing like real houses.

Barrie House.

Stevenson House.

Scott House.

Burns House.

Reaching skywards with all the subtlety of single-digit salutes.

He looked around for somewhere to deposit his half-empty coffee cup. He'd stopped at a baker's on Gorgie Road, knowing that the further from the city centre he drove, the less likely he would be to find anything remotely drinkable. Not a good choice: the coffee had been scalding at first, quickly turning tepid, which only served to highlight its lack of anything resembling flavour. There were no bins nearby; no bins at all, in fact. The pavements and grass verges, however, were doing their best to oblige, so Rebus added his litter to the mosaic, then straightened up and pushed his hands deep into his coat pockets. He could see his breath in the air.

'Papers are going to have a field day with this,' someone was muttering. There were a dozen figures shuffling around in the covered walkway between two of the high-rise blocks. The place smelled faintly of urine, human or otherwise. Plenty of dogs in the vicinity, one or two even wearing collars. They would come sniffing at the entrance to the walkway, until chased off by one of the uniforms. Crime-scene tape now blocked both ends of the passage. Kids on bikes were craning their necks for a look. Police photogra-phers were gathering evidence, vying for space with the forensic team. They were dressed in white overalls, heads covered. An anonymous grey van was parked alongside the police cars on the muddy play area outside. Its driver had complained to Rebus that some kids had demanded money from him to keep an eye on it.

'Bloody sharks.'

Soon, this driver would take the body to the mortuary, where the

post-mortem examination would take place. But already they knew
they were dealing with homicide. Multiple stab wounds, including
one to the throat. The trail of blood showed that the victim had
been attacked ten or twelve feet further into the passage. He'd
probably tried to get away, crawling towards the light, his attacker
making more lunges as he faltered and fell.

'Nothing in the pockets except some loose change,' another
detective was saying. 'Let's hope someone knows who he is . . .'

Rebus didn't know who he was, but he knew what he was: he was
a case, a statistic. More than that, he was a story, and even now the
city's journalists would be scenting it, for all the world like a pack
sensing its quarry. Knoxland was not a popular estate. It tended to
attract only the desperate and those with no choice in the matter.
In the past, it had been used as a dumping ground for tenants the
council found hard to house elsewhere: addicts and the unhinged.
More recently, immigrants had been catapulted into its dankest,
least welcoming corners. Asylum-seekers, refugees. People nobody
really wanted to think about or have to deal with. Looking around,
Rebus realised that the poor bastards must be left feeling like mice
in a maze. The difference being that in laboratories, there were few
predators, while out here in the real world, they were everywhere.

They carried knives. They roamed at will. They ran the streets.

And now they had killed.

Another car drew up, a figure emerging from it. Rebus knew the
face: Steve Holly, local hack for a Glasgow tabloid. Overweight and
bustling, hair gelled into spikes. Before locking his car, Holly
tucked his laptop under his arm, ready to bring it with him. Street-
savvy, that was Steve Holly. He nodded at Rebus.

'Got anything for me?'

Rebus shook his head, and Holly started looking around for other
more likely sources. 'Heard you'd been kicked out of St Leonard's,'
he said, as if making conversation, eyes everywhere but on Rebus.
'Don't tell me they've dumped you out here?'

Rebus knew better than to rise to it, but Holly was beginning to
enjoy himself. 'Dumping ground just about sums this place up.
School of hard knocks, eh?' Holly started to light a cigarette, and
Rebus knew he was thinking of the story he'd be writing later on:
dreaming up punning sentences and scraps of twopenny philosophy.

'Asian bloke, I heard,' the journalist said at last, blowing smoke
and offering the packet to Rebus.

'We don't know yet,' Rebus admitted: his words the price of a

5

cigarette. Holly lit it for him. 'Tan-skinned . . . could be from anywhere.'

'Anywhere except Scotland,' Holly said with a smile. 'Race crime though, got to be. Only a matter of time before *we* had one.' Rebus knew why he stressed the 'we': he meant Edinburgh. Glasgow had had at least one race murder, an asylum-seeker trying to live his life on one of that city's thick-skinned estates. Stabbed to death, just like the victim in front of them here, who, searched and studied and photographed, was now being placed in a body-bag. There was silence during the procedure: a momentary mark of respect by professionals who would thereafter get on with the job of finding the killer. The bag was lifted on to a trolley, then wheeled beneath the cordon and past Rebus and Holly.

'You in charge?' Holly asked quietly. Rebus shook his head again, watching the body being loaded into the van. 'Give me a clue then – who is it I should be speaking to?'

'I shouldn't even be here,' Rebus said, turning away to make for the relative safety of his car.

I'm one of the lucky ones, Detective Sergeant Siobhan Clarke was thinking to herself, by which she meant that she at least had been given a desk of her own. John Rebus – senior in rank to her – hadn't been so fortunate. Not that fortune, good or bad, had had anything to do with it. She knew Rebus saw it as a sign from on high: we've no place for you; time you thought of chucking it in. He'd be on the full police pension by now – officers younger than him, with fewer years on the force, were throwing in their cards and readying to cash their chips. He'd known exactly the message the bosses had wanted him to take. So had Siobhan, who'd offered him her own desk. He'd refused, of course, said he was happy to share whatever space was available, which came to mean a table by the photocopier, where mugs, coffee and sugar were kept. The kettle was on the adjacent windowledge. There was a box of copier paper under the table, and a broken-backed chair which creaked in complaint when sat upon. No telephone, not even a wall-socket for one. No computer.

'Temporary, of course,' Detective Chief Inspector James Macrae had explained. 'Not easy, trying to make space for new bodies . . .'

To which Rebus had responded with a smile and a shrug, Siobhan realising that he daren't speak: Rebus's own particular form of anger management. Bottle it all up for later. The same issues of space explained why her desk was in with the detective constables. There was a separate office for the detective sergeants, who shared with the clerical assistant, but no room there for Siobhan or Rebus. The Detective Inspector, meantime, had a small office of his own, between the two. Ah, there was the rub: Gayfield already had a DI; had no need of another. His name was Derek Starr, and he was tall, blond and good-looking. Problem was, he knew it. One lunchtime, he'd taken Siobhan for a meal at his club. It was called The Hallion and was a five-minute walk away. She hadn't dared ask how much it cost to join. Turned out he'd taken Rebus there, too.

'Because he can,' had been Rebus's summing up. Starr was on the way up, and wanted both new arrivals to know it.

Her own desk was fine. She did have a computer, which Rebus was welcome to use whenever he liked. And she had a phone. Across the aisle from her sat Detective Constable Phyllida Hawes. They'd worked together on a couple of cases, even though they'd been in different divisions. Siobhan was ten years Hawes's junior, but senior to her in rank. So far, this hadn't seemed an issue, and Siobhan was hoping it would stay that way. There was another DC in the room. His name was Colin Tibbet: mid-twenties, Siobhan reckoned, which made him a few years younger than her. Nice smile which often showed a row of smallish, rounded teeth. Hawes had already accused her of fancying him, couching it in jokey terms, but only just.

'I'm not in the baby-snatching business,' Siobhan had responded.

'So you like the more mature man?' Hawes had teased, glancing in the direction of the photocopier.

'Don't be daft,' Siobhan had said, knowing she was meaning Rebus. At the end of a case a few months back, Siobhan had found herself in Rebus's arms, being kissed by him. Nobody else knew, and it had never been discussed between them. Yet it hung over them whenever they were alone together. Well . . . hung over *her* anyway; you could never tell with John Rebus.

Phyllida Hawes was walking to the photocopier now, asking where DI Rebus had disappeared to.

'Got a call,' Siobhan answered. It was as much as she knew, but the look Hawes gave indicated that she thought Siobhan was holding back. Tibbet cleared his throat.

'There's a body been found in Knoxland. It's just come up on the computer.' He tapped his screen as if to confirm this. 'Here's hoping it's not a turf war.'

Siobhan nodded slowly. Less than a year back, a drugs gang had

7

tried muscling in on the estate, leading to a series of stabbings, abductions and reprisals. The incomers had been from Northern Ireland, rumours of paramilitary connections. Most of them were in jail now.

'Not our problem, is it?' Hawes was saying. 'One of the few things we've got going for us here . . . no schemes like Knoxland in the vicinity.'

Which was true enough. Gayfield Square was mostly a city centre operation: shoplifters and troublemakers on Princes Street; Saturday-night drunks; break-ins in the New Town.

'Bit like a holiday for you, eh, Siobhan?' Hawes added with a grin.

'St Leonard's had its moments,' Siobhan was forced to agree. Back when the move was announced, word was she'd end up at HQ. She didn't know how that rumour had started, but after a week or so it had begun to feel real. But then Detective Chief Superintendent Gill Templer had asked to see her, and suddenly she was going to Gayfield Square. She'd tried not to feel it as a blow, but that was what it had been. Templer herself, on the other hand, *was* bound for HQ. Others were dispersed as far afield as Balerno and East Lothian, a few opting for retirement. Only Siobhan and Rebus would be moving to Gayfield Square.

'And just when we were getting the hang of the job,' Rebus had complained, emptying the contents of his desk drawers into a large cardboard box. 'Still, look on the bright side: longer lies for you in the morning.'

True, her flat was five minutes' walk away. No more rush-hour drives through the centre of town. It was one of the few bonuses she could think of . . . maybe even the only one. They'd been a team at St Leonard's, and the building had been in much better shape than the current drab edifice. The CID room had been larger and brighter, and here there was a . . . She breathed in deeply through her nostrils. Well, a *smell*. She couldn't quite place it. It wasn't body odour or the packet of cheese and pickle sandwiches Tibbet brought to work with him each day. It seemed to be coming from the building itself. One morning, alone in the room, she'd even placed her nose to the walls and floor, but there seemed no specific source for the smell. There were even times when it vanished altogether, only to reappear by degrees. The radiators? The insulation? She'd given up trying to explain it, and hadn't said anything to anyone, not even Rebus.

Her phone rang, and she picked it up. 'CID,' she said into the mouthpiece.

'Front desk here. Got a couple who'd like a word with DS Clarke.'

Siobhan frowned. 'Asked for me specifically?'

'That's right.'

'What are their names?' She reached for a notepad and pen.

'Mr and Mrs Jardine. They said to tell you they're from Banehall.'

Siobhan stopped writing. She knew who they were. 'Tell them I'll be right there.' She ended the call and lifted her jacket from the back of her chair.

'Another deserter?' Hawes said. 'Anybody'd think our company wasn't wanted, Col.' She winked at Tibbet.

'Visitors to see me,' Siobhan explained.

'Bring them in,' Hawes invited, opening her arms wide. 'More the merrier.'

'I'll see,' Siobhan said. As she left the room, Hawes was stabbing the photocopier button again, Tibbet reading something on his computer screen, lips moving silently. No way she was bringing the Jardines in here. That background odour, and the mustiness, and the view over the car park . . . the Jardines deserved something better.

Me too, she couldn't help thinking.

It was three years since she'd seen them. They hadn't aged well. John Jardine's hair was almost all gone, and what little was left was salt-and-pepper grey. His wife Alice had some grey in her hair, too. It was tied behind her, making her face seem large and stern. She'd put on some weight, and her clothes looked as if she'd chosen them at random: a long brown corduroy skirt with dark-blue tights and green shoes; checked blouse with a red checked coat thrown over the whole. John Jardine had made a bit more effort: suit and tie, and a shirt which had seen an ironing board in recent memory. He held out his hand for Siobhan to take.

'Mr Jardine,' she said. 'Still got the cats, I see.' She plucked a couple of hairs from his lapel.

He gave a short, nervous laugh, shuffling to one side so his wife could step in and shake hands with Siobhan. But instead of shaking, she squeezed Siobhan's hand and held it quite still in her own. Her eyes were reddened, and Siobhan felt there was something the woman was hoping she'd read in them.

'They tell us you're a sergeant now,' John Jardine was saying.

'Detective sergeant, yes.' Siobhan was still holding Alice Jardine's stare.

'Congratulations on that. We went to your old place first, and they told us to come here. Something about CID being reorganised . . .?' He was rubbing his hands together as though washing them. Siobhan knew he was in his mid-forties, but he looked ten years older, as did his wife. Three years ago, Siobhan had suggested family therapy. If they'd taken her advice, it hadn't worked. They were still in shock, still dazed and confused and in mourning.

'We've lost one daughter,' Alice Jardine said quietly, finally releasing her grip. 'We don't want to lose another . . . that's why we need your help.'

Siobhan looked from wife to husband and back again. She was aware that the Desk Sergeant was watching; aware, too, of the peeling paint on the walls, the scored graffiti and Wanted posters.

'How about a coffee?' she said with a smile. 'There's a place just round the corner.'

So that was where they went. A café which doubled as a restaurant at lunchtime. A businessman was seated at one of the window tables, finishing a late meal while talking into his mobile phone and sifting through paperwork in his briefcase. Siobhan led the couple to a booth, not too near the wall-mounted speakers. It was instrumental music, background pap to fill the silence. Probably meant to be vaguely Italian. The waiter, however, was one hundred per cent local.

'Anythin' to eat wi' that?' His vowels were flat and nasal, and there was a venerable dollop of bolognese sauce on the belly of his short-sleeved white shirt. His arms were thick and showed fading tattoos of thistles and saltires.

'Just the coffees,' Siobhan said. 'Unless . . .?' She looked at the couple seated opposite her, but they shook their heads. The waiter headed off in the direction of the espresso machine, only to be diverted by the businessman, who also wanted something and obviously merited a level of service which an order of three coffees couldn't hope to match. Well, it wasn't as if Siobhan was in any great rush to return to her desk, though she wasn't sure she was going to take much pleasure from the conversation ahead.

'So how are things with you?' she felt obliged to ask.

The couple looked at one another before replying. 'Difficult,' Mr Jardine said. 'Things have been . . . difficult.'

'Yes, I'm sure.'

Alice Jardine leaned forward across the table. 'It's not Tracy. I mean, we still miss her . . .' She lowered her eyes. 'Of course we do. But it's Ishbel we're worried about.'

'Worried sick,' her husband added.

'Because she's gone, you see. And we don't know why or where.'
Mrs Jardine burst into tears. Siobhan looked towards the businessman, but he wasn't paying attention to anything other than his own
existence. The waiter, however, had paused by the espresso
machine. Siobhan glared at him, hoping he'd take the hint and
hurry up with their drinks. John Jardine had an arm around his
wife's shoulders, and it was this which took Siobhan back three
years, to an almost identical scene: the terraced house in the West
Lothian village of Banehall, and John Jardine comforting his wife
as best he knew how. The house was neat and tidy, a place its
owners could take pride in, having used the right-to-purchase
scheme to buy it from the local council. Streets of near-identical
houses all around, but you could tell the ones in private ownership:
new doors and windows, tidied gardens with new fencing and
wrought-iron gates. At one time, Banehall had thrived on coal-
mining, but that industry was long gone, and with it much of the
town's spirit. Driving down Main Street for the first time, Siobhan
had been aware of boarded-up shops and For Sale signs; people
moving slowly under the weight of carrier bags; kids hanging
around the war memorial, aiming playful high kicks at each other.

John Jardine worked as a delivery driver; Alice was on the
production line at an electronics factory on the outskirts of
Livingston. Striving to do well for themselves and their two
daughters. But one of those daughters had been attacked during a
night out in Edinburgh. Her name was Tracy. She'd been drinking
and dancing with a gang of friends. Towards the end of the evening,
they'd piled into taxis to go to some party. But Tracy had been a
straggler, and the address of the party had slipped her mind during
the wait for a cab. The battery on her mobile was flat, so she went
back inside, asked one of the lads she'd been up for a dance with if
he'd lend her his. He went outside with her, started walking with
her, telling her the party wasn't that far.

Started kissing her; not taking no for an answer. Slapped her and
punched her, dragged her into an alley and raped her.

All of this Siobhan had already known as she'd sat in the house
in Banehall. She'd worked the case, spoken with the victim and the
parents. The attacker hadn't been hard to find: he was from
Banehall himself, lived only three or four roads away, the other
side of Main Street. Tracy had known him at school. His defence
was fairly typical: too much drink, couldn't remember . . . and she'd
been willing enough anyway. Rape always made for a tough
prosecution, but to Siobhan's relief, Donald Cruikshank, known to

11

his friends as Donny, face permanently scarred by the raking of his victim's fingernails, had been found guilty and sentenced to five years.

Which should have been the end of Siobhan's involvement with the family, except that a few weeks after the trial had ended had come news of Tracy's suicide, her life ending at nineteen years of age. An overdose of pills, found in her bedroom by her sister Ishbel, four years younger than her.

Siobhan had visited the parents, all too aware that nothing she could say would change anything, but still feeling the need to say *something*. They had been failed, not so much by the system as by life itself. The one thing Siobhan hadn't done – the thing she'd had to grit her teeth to stop herself doing – was visit Cruikshank in jail. She'd wanted him to feel her anger. She remembered the way Tracy had given evidence in court, her voice fading away to nothing as the phrases stuttered out; not looking at anyone; almost ashamed to be there. Unwilling to touch the bagged exhibits: her torn dress and underwear. Wiping silent tears away. The judge had been sympathetic, the defendant trying not to look shamefaced, playing the role of the real victim: wounded, a large muslin patch covering one cheek; shaking his head in disbelief, raising his eyes to heaven.

And afterwards, the verdict delivered, the jury had been allowed to hear of his previous convictions: two for assault, one for attempted rape. Donny Cruikshank was nineteen years old.

'Bastard's got his whole life ahead of him,' John Jardine had told Siobhan as they left the cemetery. Alice had both arms around her surviving daughter. Ishbel was crying into her mother's shoulder. Alice looking straight ahead, something dying behind her eyes . . .

The coffees came, jarring Siobhan back to the present. She waited until the waiter had gone, off to fetch the businessman's bill.

'So tell me what's happened,' she said.

John Jardine poured a sachet of sugar into his cup and started stirring. 'Ishbel left school last year. We wanted her to go to college, get some kind of qualification. But she had her heart set on hairdressing.'

'Of course, you need a qualification to do that, too,' his wife interrupted. 'She's going part-time to the college in Livingston.'

Siobhan just nodded.

'Well, she was until she disappeared,' John Jardine stated quietly.

'When was this?'

'A week ago today.'

'She just upped and went?'

'We thought she'd gone to work as usual – she's at the salon on Main Street. But they phoned to see if she was sick. Some of her clothes had gone, enough to fill a backpack. Money, cards, mobile . . .'

'We've tried phoning it umpteen times,' his wife added, 'but it's always switched off.'

'Have you spoken to anyone apart from me?' Siobhan asked, lifting her cup to her lips.

'Everyone we could think of – her pals, old schoolfriends, the girls she worked with.'

'College?'

Alice Jardine nodded. 'They've not seen her either.'

'We went to the police station in Livingston,' John Jardine said. He was still stirring the contents of his cup, showed no inclination to drink it. 'They said she's eighteen, so she's not breaking the law. Packed a bag, so it's not like she was abducted.'

'That's true, I'm afraid.' There was more Siobhan could have added: that she saw runaways all the time; that if she herself lived in Banehall, maybe she would run away, too . . . 'There hadn't been any fights at home?'

Mr Jardine shook his head. 'She was saving for a flat . . . already making lists of the stuff she'd buy for it.'

'Any boyfriends?'

'There was one until a couple of months back. The split was . . .' Mr Jardine couldn't find the word he was looking for. 'They were still friends.'

'It was amicable?' Siobhan suggested. He smiled and nodded: she'd found his word for him.

'We just want to know what's going on,' Alice Jardine said.

'I'm sure you do, and there are people who can help . . . agencies who look out for people like Ishbel who've left home for whatever reason.' Siobhan realised that the words were coming too easily: she'd said them so many times to anxious parents. Alice was looking to her husband.

'Tell her what Susie told you,' she said.

He nodded, finally placing the spoon back on its saucer. 'Susie works with Ishbel at the salon. She told me she'd seen Ishbel getting into a flash car . . . she thought it might be a BMW or something.'

'When was this?'

'A couple of times . . . the car was always parked a bit further

13

down the street. Older guy driving.' He paused. 'Well, my age at least.'

'Did Susie ask Ishbel who he was?'

He nodded. 'But Ishbel wouldn't say.'

'So maybe she's gone to stay with this friend of hers.' Siobhan had finished her coffee but didn't want another.

'But why not tell us?' Alice asked plaintively.

'I'm not sure I can help you answer that.'

'Susie mentioned something else,' John Jardine said, lowering his voice still further. 'She said this man . . . she told us he looked a bit shady.'

'Shady?'

'What she actually said was, he looked like a pimp.' He glanced up at Siobhan. 'You know, like off the films and TV: sunglasses and a leather jacket . . . flash car.'

'I'm not sure that gets us any further,' Siobhan said, immediately regretting the use of 'us', tying her to their cause.

'Ishbel's a real beauty,' Alice said. 'You know that yourself. Why would she just run off like that without telling us? Why did she keep this man a secret from us?' She shook her head slowly. 'No, there's got to be more to it.'

Silence fell on the table for a few moments. The businessman's phone was ringing again as the waiter held the door open for him. The waiter even gave a little bow: either the man was a regular, or a decent tip had changed hands. Now there were only three customers left in the place, not the most thrilling prospect.

'I can't see any way of helping you,' Siobhan told the Jardines. 'You know I would if I could . . .'

John Jardine had taken his wife's hand. 'You were very good to us, Siobhan. Sympathetic and all that. We appreciated it at the time, and so did Ishbel . . . That's why we thought of you.' He fixed her with his milky eyes. 'We've already lost Tracy. Ishbel's all we've got left.'

'Look . . .' Siobhan took a deep breath. 'I can maybe put her name into circulation, see if she turns up anywhere.'

His face softened. 'That'd be great.'

'"Great" is an exaggeration, but I'll do what I can.' She saw that Alice Jardine was about to reach out for her hand again, so started to rise from the table, checking her watch as if she had some pressing appointment awaiting her at the station. The waiter came over, John Jardine insisting on paying. As they finally made to leave, the waiter was nowhere to be seen. Siobhan pulled open the door.

'Sometimes people just need a bit of time to themselves. You're sure she hadn't been having any problems?'

Husband and wife looked at one another. It was Alice who spoke up. 'He's out, you know. Back in Banehall, bold as brass. Maybe that's got something to do with it.'

'Who?'

'Cruikshank. Three years, that's all he served. I saw him one day when I was at the shops. I had to go down a side street so I could throw up.'

'Did you speak to him?'

'I wouldn't even spit on him.'

Siobhan looked to John Jardine, but he was shaking his head.

'I'd kill him,' he said. 'If I ever met him, I'd have to kill him.'

'Careful who you say that to, Mr Jardine.' Siobhan thought for a moment. 'Ishbel knew this? Knew he was out, I mean?'

'Whole town knew. And you know what it's like: hairdressers are first with the gossip.'

Siobhan nodded slowly. 'Well . . . like I said, I'll make a few phone calls. A photo of Ishbel might help.'

Mrs Jardine dug in her handbag and brought out a folded sheet of paper. It was a picture blown up on to a sheet of A4 paper, printed from a computer. Ishbel on a sofa, a drink in her hand, cheeks ruddy with alcohol.

'That's Susie from the salon next to her,' Alice Jardine said. 'John took it at a party we had three weeks ago. It was my birthday.'

Siobhan nodded. Ishbel had changed since she'd last seen her: allowed her hair to grow and dyed it blonde. More make-up, too, and a hardening around the eyes, despite the grin. The hint of a double chin developing. The hair was centre-parted. It took Siobhan a second to realise who she reminded her of. It was Tracy: the long blonde hair, that parting, the blue eyeliner.

She looked just like her dead sister.

'Thanks,' she said, placing the photo in her pocket.

Siobhan checked that they were still at the same telephone number. John Jardine nodded. 'We moved one street away, but didn't need to change numbers.'

Of course they'd moved. How could they have gone on living in that house, the house where Tracy had taken the overdose? Fifteen

15

Ishbel had been when she'd found the lifeless body. The sister she'd doted on, idolised. Her role model.

'I'll be in touch then,' Siobhan said, turning and walking away.

2

'So what were you up to all afternoon?' Siobhan asked, placing the pint of IPA in front of Rebus. As she sat down opposite, he blew some cigarette smoke ceilingwards: his idea of a concession to any non-smoking companion. They were in the back room of the Oxford Bar, and every table was filled with office workers stopping to refuel before the trek home. Siobhan hadn't been back in the office long when Rebus's text message had appeared on her mobile:

fancy a drink i am in the ox

He'd finally mastered the sending and receiving of texts, but had yet to work out how to add punctuation.

Or capitals.

'Out at Knoxland,' he said now.

'Col told me there'd been a body found.'

'Homicide,' Rebus stated. He took a gulp from his drink, frowning at Siobhan's slender non-alcoholic glass of lime with soda.

'So how come you ended up out there?' she asked.

'Got a call. Someone at HQ had alerted West End to the fact that I'm surplus to requirements at Gayfield Square.'

Siobhan put down her glass. 'They didn't say that?'

'You don't need a magnifying glass to read between the lines, Shiv.'

Siobhan had long since given up trying to get people to use her full name rather than this shortened form. Likewise, Phyllida Hawes was 'Phyl', and Colin Tibbet 'Col'. Apparently, Derek Starr could sometimes be referred to as 'Deek', but she'd never heard it used. Even DCI James Macrae had asked her to call him 'Jim', unless they were in some formal meeting. But John Rebus . . . for as long as she'd known him, he'd been 'John': not Jock or Johnny. It was as if people knew, just by looking at him, that he wasn't the sort to endure a nickname. Nicknames made you seem friendly, more approachable, more likely to play along. When DCI Macrae said something like, 'Shiv, have you got a minute?' it meant he had some favour to ask. If this became, 'Siobhan, my office, please', then she was no longer in his good books; some misdemeanour had occurred.

'Penny for them,' Rebus said now. He'd already demolished most of the pint she'd just bought him.

She shook her head. 'Just wondering about the victim.'

Rebus shrugged. 'Asian-looking, or whatever the politically correct term of the week is.' He stubbed out his cigarette. 'Could have been Mediterranean or Arabic . . . I didn't really get that close. Surplus to requirements again.' He shook his cigarette packet. Finding it empty, he crushed it and finished his beer. 'Same again?' he said, rising to his feet.

'I've hardly started this one.'

'Then put it to one side and have a proper drink. Not got anything else on tonight, have you?'

'Doesn't mean I'm ready to spend the evening helping you get hammered.' He stood his ground, giving her time to reconsider. 'Go on then: gin and tonic.'

Rebus seemed satisfied with this, and headed out of the room. She could hear voices from the bar, greeting his arrival there.

'What're you doing hiding upstairs?' one of them asked. She couldn't hear an answer, but knew it anyway. The front bar was Rebus's domain, a place where he could hold court with his fellow drinkers – all of them men. But this part of his life had to remain distinct from any other – Siobhan wasn't sure why, it was just something he was unwilling to share. The back room was for meetings and 'guests'. She sat back and thought of the Jardines, and whether she was really willing to become involved in their search. They belonged to her past, and past cases seldom reappeared so tangibly. It was in the nature of the job that you became involved in people's lives intimately – more intimately than many of them would like – but for a brief time only. Rebus had let slip to her once that he felt surrounded by ghosts: lapsed friendships and relationships, plus all those victims whose lives had ended before his interest in them had begun.

It can play havoc with you, Shiv . . .

She'd never forgotten those words; *in vino veritas* and all that. She could hear a mobile phone ringing in the front room. It

18

prompted her to take out her own, checking for messages. But there was no signal, something she'd forgotten about this place. The Oxford Bar was only a minute's walk from the city-centre shops, yet somehow you could never pick up a signal in the back room. The bar was tucked away down a narrow lane, offices and flats above. Thick stone walls, built to survive the centuries. She angled the handset different ways, but the on-screen message remained a defiant 'No Signal'. But now Rebus himself was in the doorway, no drinks in his hands. Instead, waving his own mobile at her.

'We're wanted,' he said.

'Where?'

He ignored her question. 'You got your car?'

She nodded.

'Better let you drive then. Lucky you stuck to the soft stuff, eh?'

She put her jacket back on and picked up her bag. Rebus was purchasing cigarettes and mints from behind the bar. He popped one of the mints into his mouth.

'So is this to be a mystery tour or what?' Siobhan asked.

He shook his head, crunching down with his teeth. 'Fleshmarket Close,' he told her. 'Couple of bodies we might be interested in.' He pulled open the door to the outside world. 'Only not quite as fresh as the one in Knoxland . . .'

Fleshmarket Close was a narrow, pedestrian-only lane connecting the High Street to Cockburn Street. The High Street entrance was flanked by a bar and a photographic shop. There were no parking spaces left, so Siobhan turned into Cockburn Street itself, parking outside the arcade. They crossed the road and headed into Fleshmarket Close. This end, its entrance boasted a bookmaker's one side, and a shop opposite selling crystals and 'dream-catchers': old and new Edinburgh, Rebus thought to himself. The Cockburn Street end of the close was open to the elements, while the other half was covered over by five floors of what he assumed to be flats, their unlit windows casting baleful looks on the goings-on below.

There were several doorways in the lane itself. One would lead to the flats, and one, directly opposite, to the bodies. Rebus saw some of the same faces from the crime scene at Knoxland: white-suited SOCOs and police photographers. The doorway was narrow and low, dating back a few hundred years to when the locals had been a great deal shorter. Rebus ducked as he entered, Siobhan right behind him. Lighting, provided by a meagre forty-watt bulb in the

19

ceiling, was in the process of being augmented by an arc lamp, as soon as a cable could be found to stretch to the nearest socket.

Rebus hesitated on the periphery, until one of the SOCOs told him it was all right.

'Bodies've been here a while; not much chance of us disturbing any evidence.'

Rebus nodded and approached the tight circle made up of white suits. There was a scuffed concrete floor under their feet. A pickaxe lay nearby. There was still dust in the air, clinging to the back of Rebus's throat.

'The concrete was being taken up,' someone was explaining. 'Doesn't look as if it's been there too long, but they wanted to lower the floor for some reason.'

'What is this place?' Rebus asked, looking around. There were packing cases, shelves filled with more boxes. Old barrels and advertising signs for beers and spirits.

'Belongs to the pub upstairs. They've been using it for storage. Cellar's just through that wall.' A gloved hand pointed to the shelves. Rebus could hear floorboards creaking above them, and muffled sounds from a jukebox or TV set. 'Workman starts breaking the stuff up, and here's what he finds . . .'

Rebus turned and looked down. He was staring at a skull. There were other bones, too, and he didn't doubt they would make up an entire skeleton, once the rest of the concrete had been removed.

'Might have been here a while,' the scene-of-crime officer offered. 'Going to be a sod of a job for somebody.'

Rebus and Siobhan shared a look. In the car, she'd wondered aloud why the call had come to them, and not to Hawes or Tibbet. Rebus raised an eyebrow, indicating that he felt she now had her answer.

'A proper pig of a job,' the SOCO reiterated.

'That's why we're here,' Rebus said quietly, gaining a wry smile from Siobhan – more than one meaning to his words. 'Where's the owner of the pickaxe?'

'Upstairs. He said a snifter might help revive him.' The SOCO twitched his nose, as if only now catching a hint of mint in the stale air.

'Suppose we better have a word with him then,' Rebus said.

'I thought it was bodies plural?' Siobhan queried.

The SOCO nodded towards a white polythene carrier bag lying on the floor, next to the broken-up concrete. One of his colleagues raised the bag a few inches. Siobhan sucked in her breath. There was another skeleton there, hardly any size at all. She let out a hiss.

'It was the only thing we had to hand,' the SOCO apologised. He meant the carrier bag. Rebus, too, was staring down at the tiny remains.

'Mother and baby?' he guessed.

'I'd leave that sort of speculation to the professionals,' a new voice stated. Rebus turned and found himself shaking hands with the pathologist, Dr Curt. 'Christ, John, are you still around? I heard they were kicking you into touch.'

'You're very much my role model, Doc. When you go, I go.'

'And the rejoicing shall be long and heartfelt. Good evening to you, Siobhan.' Curt tipped his head forwards slightly. If he'd been wearing a hat, Rebus didn't doubt he'd have removed it in a lady's presence. He seemed to belong to another age, with his immaculate dark suit and polished brogues, the stiff shirt and striped tie, this last probably denoting membership of some venerable Edinburgh institution. His hair was grey, but this only served to make him appear even more distinguished. It was combed back from the forehead, not a strand out of place. He peered at the skeletons.

'The Prof will have a field day,' he muttered. 'He does like these little puzzles.' He straightened up, examining his surroundings. 'And his history, too.'

'You think they've been here a while then?' Siobhan made the mistake of asking. Curt's eyes twinkled.

'Certainly they were here before the concrete was laid ... but probably not too long before. People don't tend to pour fresh concrete over bodies without good reason.'

'Yes, of course.' Siobhan's blushes would have been spared had not the arc lamp suddenly lit the scene blazingly, casting huge shadows up the walls and across the low ceiling.

'That's better,' the SOCO said.

Siobhan looked to Rebus and saw that he was rubbing his cheeks, as if she needed telling that her own face had reddened.

'I should probably get the Prof down here,' Curt was saying to himself. 'I think he'd want to see them *in situ* ...' He reached into an inside pocket for his mobile. 'Pity to disturb the old boy when he's heading out to the opera, but duty calls, does it not?' He winked at Rebus, who responded with a smile.

'Absolutely, Doc.'

The Prof was Professor Sandy Gates, Curt's colleague and

immediate boss. Both men worked at the university, teaching pathology, but were constantly on call to attend scenes of crime.

'You heard we had a stabbing in Knoxland?' Rebus asked, as Curt pushed the buttons on his phone.

'I heard,' Curt replied. 'We'll probably take a look at him tomorrow morning. Not sure yet that our clients here demand any such urgency.' He looked again at the adult skeleton. The infant had been re-covered, not by a bag this time but by Siobhan's own jacket, which she'd placed over the remains with the utmost care.

'Wish you hadn't done that,' Curt muttered, holding the phone to his ear. 'Means we have to hang on to your coat so we can match it against any fibres we find.'

Rebus couldn't stand to watch Siobhan start blushing again. Instead, he gestured towards the door. As they made their exit, Curt could be heard talking to Professor Gates.

'Are you all gussied up in tails and cummerbund, Sandy? Because if you're not – and even if you are – I think I may have an alternative entertainment for you *ce soir* . . .'

Instead of heading up the lane, towards the pub, Siobhan started heading down.

'Where you off to?' Rebus asked.

'I've got a windcheater in the car,' she explained. By the time she returned, Rebus had lit a cigarette.

'Good to see you with some colour in your cheeks,' he told her.

'Gosh, did you think that up all by yourself?' She made an exasperated sound and leaned against the wall next to him, arms folded. 'I just wish he wasn't so . . .'

'What?' Rebus was examining the glowing tip of his cigarette.

'I don't know . . .' She looked around, as if for inspiration. Revellers were on the street, weaving their way to the next hostelry. Tourists were photographing each other outside Starbuck's, with the climb to the Castle as backdrop. Old and new, Rebus thought again.

'It just seems like a game to him,' Siobhan said at last. 'That's not what I mean exactly, but it'll have to do.'

'He's one of the most serious men I know,' Rebus told her. 'It's a way of dealing with it, that's all. We all do it in our different ways, don't we?'

'Do we?' She looked at him. 'I suppose your way involves quantities of nicotine and alcohol?'

'It never does to mess with a winning combination.'

'Even if it's a killing combination?'

'Remember the story of that old king? Took a little bit of poison every day to make himself immune?' Rebus blew smoke into the bruise-coloured evening sky. 'Think about it. And while you're thinking, I'll be buying a workman a drink . . . and maybe having one myself.' He pushed open the door to the bar, let it swing shut after him. Siobhan stood there for a few moments longer before joining him.

'Didn't that king end up being killed anyway?' she asked, as they moved through the bar's interior.

The place was called The Warlock, and it looked geared to foot-weary tourists. One wall was covered in a mural which told the story of Major Weir, who, back in the seventeenth century, had confessed to witchcraft, identifying his own sister as accomplice. The pair had been executed on Calton Hill.

'Nice,' was Siobhan's only comment.

Rebus gestured towards a fruit machine, which was being played by a heavy-set man in dusty blue overalls. An empty brandy glass was perched on top of the machine.

'Get you another?' Rebus asked the man. The face which turned towards him was as spectral as Major Weir's in the mural, the thick dark hair peppered with plaster. 'I'm DI Rebus, by the way. Hoping you might answer a few questions. This is my colleague, DS Clarke. Now, about that drink – brandy, am I right?'

The man nodded. 'I've got the van though . . . it's got to go back to the yard.'

'We'll get someone to drive you, don't worry.' Rebus turned to Siobhan. 'Usual for me, large brandy for Mr . . .'

'Evans. Joe Evans.'

Siobhan left without a fuss. 'Having any luck?' Rebus asked. Evans looked at the fruit machine's four unforgiving wheels.

'I'm down three quid.'

'Not your day, is it?'

The man smiled. 'I got the shock of my bloody life. First thought was, they're Roman or something. Or maybe some old burying ground.'

'You've changed your mind?'

'Whoever laid that concrete must've known they were there.'

'You'd make a good detective, Mr Evans.' Rebus glanced towards the bar, where Siobhan was being served. 'How long have you been working down there?'

'Just started this week.'

'Using a pickaxe rather than a drill?'

'Can't use a drill in a space like that.'

Rebus nodded as if he understood perfectly. 'Doing the work by yourself?'

'Reckoned one man would do it.'

'Been down there before?'

Evans shook his head. Almost without thinking, he'd slid another coin into the machine, pushed the start button. Plenty of flashing lights and sound effects, but no pay-out. He hit the button again.

'Any idea who laid the concrete?'

Another shake of the head; another coin deposited in the slot. 'Owners should have a record.' He paused. 'I don't mean a criminal record – a note of who did the work, an invoice or something.'

'Good point,' Rebus said. Siobhan returned with the drinks, handed them out. She was back on the lime and soda.

'Spoke to the barman,' she said. 'It's a tied pub.' Meaning it was owned by one of the breweries. 'Landlord's been out to a cash-and-carry, but he's on his way back.'

'He knows what's happened?'

She nodded. 'Barman called him. Should be here in a few minutes.'

'Anything else you want to tell us, Mr Evans?'

'Just that you should bring in the Fraud Squad. This machine's robbing me blind.'

'There are some crimes we're powerless to prevent.' Rebus thought for a moment. 'Any idea why the landlord wanted the floor dug up in the first place?'

'He'll tell you himself,' Evans said, draining his glass. 'That's him just coming in now.' The landlord had seen them and was making his way towards the machine. He had his hands buried deep in the pockets of a full-length black leather coat. A cream-coloured V-neck jumper left his throat bare, displaying a single medallion on a thin gold chain. His hair was short, spiked with gel at the front. He was wearing spectacles with rectangular orange lenses.

'You all right, Joe?' he asked, squeezing Evans's arm.

'Bearing up, Mr Mangold. These two are detectives.'

'I'm the landlord here. Name's Ray Mangold.' Rebus and Siobhan introduced themselves. 'So far, I'm a bit in the dark, officers. Skeletons in the cellar – can't decide if that's good for business or not.' He gave a grin, showing too-white teeth.

'I'm sure the victims would be touched by your concern, sir.' Rebus wasn't sure why he'd taken against the man so rapidly. Maybe it was the tinted glasses. He didn't like it when he couldn't see someone's eyes. As if reading his thoughts, Mangold slipped the glasses from his nose and started cleaning them with a white handkerchief.

'Sorry if I sounded a bit callous, Inspector. It's just a bit much to take in.'

'I'm sure it is, sir. Have you been the landlord here for long?'

'First anniversary coming up.' He'd narrowed his eyes to slits.

'Do you remember the floor being laid?'

Mangold thought for a moment, then nodded. 'I think it was going in just as I was taking over.'

'Where were you before?'

'I had a club in Falkirk.'

'Went bust, did it?'

Mangold shook his head. 'Just got fed up with the hassle: staff problems, local gangs trying to rip the place up . . .'

'Too many responsibilities?' Rebus suggested.

Mangold put the glasses back on again. 'I suppose that's what it boils down to. The glasses aren't just for show, by the way.' Again it was as if he could read Rebus's thoughts. 'My retinas are over-sensitive; can't take the bright lights.'

'Is that why you started a club in Falkirk?'

Mangold grinned, showing more teeth. Rebus considered getting some of those orange glasses for himself. Right then, he thought, if you can read my mind, ask me if I'd like a drink.

But the barman called over, something he needed his boss to deal with. Evans checked the time and said he'd be going, if there were no more questions. Rebus asked if he needed a driver, but he declined.

'DS Clarke will just take your details then, in case we need to get in touch.' While Siobhan rummaged in her bag for a notebook, Rebus walked over to where Mangold was leaning over the bar, so that the barman didn't have to raise his voice. A party of four – American tourists, Rebus guessed – was standing in the middle of the room, beaming over-friendly smiles. Otherwise the place was dead. Before Rebus had reached him, Mangold ended his conversation: eyes in the back of his head, perhaps, to go with the telepathy.

'We hadn't quite finished,' was all Rebus said, resting his elbows against the bar.

'I thought we had.'

'Sorry if I gave that impression. I wanted to ask about the work in the cellar. What's it for exactly?'

'The plan is to open it up as an extension to this place.'

'It's tiny.'

'That's the point: give people a taste of what Edinburgh's traditional drinking dens used to be like. It'll be snug and cosy, a few squashy seats . . . no music or anything, the dimmest lighting we can get. I did think about candles, but Health and Safety snuffed that idea out.' He smiled at his own joke. 'Available for private hire: like having your own period apartment in the heart of the Old Town.'

'Was this your own idea, or the brewery's?'

'All my own work.' Mangold almost gave a little bow.

'And you hired Mr Evans?'

'He's a good worker. I've used him before.'

'What about the concrete floor: any idea who laid that?'

'As I said, it was all in hand before I moved in.'

'But completed after you arrived – that's what you said, isn't it? Which means you'll have some documentation somewhere . . . an invoice at the very least?' Rebus offered a smile of his own. 'Or was it cash in hand and no questions asked?'

Mangold bristled. 'There'll be paperwork, yes.' He paused. 'Of course, it might have been thrown out, or the brewery could have filed it away somewhere . . .'

'And who was in charge here before you took over, Mr Mangold?'

'I can't remember.'

'He didn't show you the ropes? I thought there was usually a crossover period?'

'There probably was . . . I just can't recall his name.'

'I'm sure it'll come back to you, with a bit of effort.' He took out one of his business cards from the breast-pocket of his jacket. 'And you'll give me a call when it does.'

'Fair enough.' Mangold accepted the card and made a show of studying it. Rebus saw that Evans was leaving.

'One last thing for the moment, Mr Mangold . . .?'

'Yes, Detective Inspector?'

Siobhan was now standing by Rebus's side. 'I just wondered what the name of your club was.'

'My club?'

'The one in Falkirk . . . unless you had more than one?'

'It was called Albatross. After the Fleetwood Mac song.'

'You didn't know the poem then?' Siobhan asked.

'Not until later,' Mangold said through gritted teeth.

Rebus thanked him, but didn't shake hands. Outside, he looked up and down the street, as if debating where to have his next drink. 'What poem?' he asked.

'*Rime of the Ancient Mariner*. The sailor shoots an albatross, and it puts a curse on the boat.'

Rebus nodded slowly. 'Like an albatross around your neck?'

'I suppose so . . .' Her voice tailed off. 'What did you think of him?'

'Fancies himself.'

'Reckon he was trying for a *Matrix* look with that coat?'

'God knows. But we need to keep hassling him. I want to know who laid that concrete and when.'

'It couldn't be a set-up, could it? To get some publicity for the bar?'

'Planned well in advance if it is.'

'Maybe the concrete's not as old as anyone says.'

Rebus stared at her. 'Been reading any good conspiracy thrillers lately? The Royals bumping off Princess Di? The mafia and JFK . . .?'

'Who let Mr Grumpy out to play?'

His face was just beginning to soften when he heard a roar from Fleshmarket Close. A uniform had been posted to stop any passers-by using the passage. But he knew Rebus and Siobhan and nodded them through. As Rebus went to step over the threshold into the cellar, a figure barged into him from within. It was dressed in a lounge suit and bow tie.

'Evening, Professor Gates,' Rebus said, once he'd caught his breath. The pathologist stopped and scowled. It was the sort of look which could shrivel an undergraduate at twenty paces, but Rebus was made of stronger stuff.

'John . . .' Finally recognising him. 'Are you part of this bloody charade?'

'I will be, once you tell me what it is.'

Dr Curt was angling his body sheepishly into the passageway.

'This bugger,' Gates glowered, indicating his colleague, 'has made me miss the first act of *La Bohème* – and all for some bloody student prank!'

Rebus looked to Curt for an explanation.

'They're fake?' Siobhan guessed.

'That they are,' Gates said, calming by degrees. 'No doubt my esteemed friend here will fill you in on the details . . . unless that, too, proves beyond him. Now, if you'll excuse me . . .' He marched to the top of the passageway, the uniform at the top giving him all the room he needed. Curt gestured for Rebus and Siobhan to follow him back into the cellar. A couple of the SOCOs were still there, trying to hide their embarrassment.

'If we're looking for excuses,' Curt began, 'we might mention the initial inadequate lighting. Or the fact that we were dealing with skeletons rather than flesh and blood, the latter potentially far more interesting . . .'

'What's with the "we"?' Rebus teased. 'So are they plastic or what?' He crouched down by the skeletons. Siobhan's jacket had been tossed aside by the Professor. Rebus handed it back to her.

'The infant is, yes. Plastic or some kind of composite. I'd have noticed the moment I touched any part of it.'

'Course you would,' Rebus said. He saw that Siobhan was trying to show not the least scintilla of pleasure at Curt's downfall.

'The adult, on the other hand, is an actual skeleton,' Curt continued. 'But probably very old, and used for teaching purposes.' The pathologist crouched down beside Rebus, Siobhan joining them.

'How do you mean?'

'Holes drilled in the bones . . . do you see them?'

'Not easy, even in this light.'

'Quite.'

'And the point of the holes is . . . ?'

'There would have been connecting devices of some kind, screws or wires. To join one bone to its neighbour.' He lifted a femur and pointed to the two neatly drilled holes. 'You find them in museum exhibits.'

'Or teaching hospitals?' Siobhan guessed.

'Quite right, DS Clarke. It's a lost art these days. Used to be done by specialists called articulators.' Curt got to his feet, brushing his hands together as though to wipe away all trace of his earlier mistake. 'We used to use them a lot with students. Not so much now. Certainly not real ones. Skeletons can be realistic without being real.'

'As has just been demonstrated,' Rebus couldn't help saying. 'So where does that leave us? You reckon the Prof's right, it's some sort of practical joke?'

'If so, someone's gone to an inordinate amount of trouble. Removing the screws and any bits of wire and the like would have taken hours.'

'Has anyone reported skeletons going missing from the university?' Siobhan asked.

Curt seemed to hesitate. 'Not that I'm aware.'

'But they're a specialist item, right? You don't just walk into your local Safeway and pick one up?'

'I would presume that to be the case ... I've not been to a Safeway recently.'

'Bloody weird all the same,' Rebus muttered, standing up. Siobhan, however, stayed crouched over the infant.

'It's sick,' she said.

'Maybe you were right, Shiv.' Rebus turned to Curt. 'Only five minutes ago, she was wondering if it might be a publicity stunt.'

Siobhan shook her head. 'But like you said, it's a lot of trouble to take. There's got to be more to it.' She was clutching her coat to her, as though cradling a baby. 'Any chance you could examine the adult skeleton?' She stared up at Curt, who offered a shrug.

'Looking for what, exactly?'

'Anything that might give us a clue who it is, where it came from ... some idea of how old it is.'

'To what end?' Curt had narrowed his eyes, showing he was intrigued.

Siobhan stood up. 'Maybe Professor Gates isn't the only one who likes a puzzle with a bit of history attached.'

'You'd best give in, Doc,' Rebus said with a smile. 'It's the only way to shake her off.'

Curt looked at him. 'Now who does that remind me of?'

Rebus opened his arms wide and gave a shrug.

DAY TWO

Tuesday

3

For want of anything better to do, Rebus found himself at the mortuary next morning, where the autopsy of the as yet unidentified Knoxland corpse was already underway. The viewing gallery comprised three tiers of benches, separated by a wall of glass from the autopsy suite. The place made some visitors queasy. Maybe it was the clinical efficiency of it all: the stainless-steel tables with their drainage outlets; the jars and specimen bottles. Or the way the entire operation resembled too closely the skills seen in any butcher's shop – the carving and filleting by men in aprons and wellingtons. A reminder not only of mortality but of the body's animal engineering, the human spirit reduced to meat on a slab.

There were two other spectators present – a man and a woman. They nodded a greeting at Rebus, the woman shifting slightly as he sat down next to her.

'Morning,' he said, waving through the glass to where Curt and Gates were busy at work. The rules of corroboration meant that two pathologists had to attend every autopsy, stretching a service that was already past snapping point.

'What brings you here?' the man asked. His name was Hugh Davidson, known to all by the nickname 'Shug'. He was a detective inspector at the West End police station in Torphichen Place.

'Apparently you do, Shug. Something to do with a shortage of high-flying officers.'

Davidson's face twitched in what might have been a smile. 'And when did you get your pilot's licence, John?'

Rebus ignored this, choosing to focus on Davidson's companion instead. 'Haven't seen you in a while, Ellen.'

Ellen Wylie was a detective sergeant, Davidson her boss. She had a box file open on her lap. It looked brand new, and contained only a few sheets of paper as yet. A case number was written at the top of the first page. Rebus knew that it would soon swell to bursting with reports, photographs, lists of staff rotas. It was the Murder Book: the 'bible' for the forthcoming investigation.

'I heard you were out at Knoxland yesterday,' Wylie said, eyes fixed ahead of her as if watching a film which would stop making sense the moment her attention lapsed. 'Having a nice long chat with a representative from the fourth estate.'

'And for the benefit of our English-speaking viewers . . .?'

'Steve Holly,' she stated. 'And in the context of this current inquiry, the phrase "English-speaking" could be construed as racist.'

'That's because everything's racist or sexist these days, sweetheart.' Rebus paused for a reaction, but she wasn't about to oblige. 'Last I heard, we're not allowed to say "accident blackspot" or "Indian summer".'

'Or "manhole cover",' Davidson added, leaning forward to make eye contact with Rebus, who shook his head at the madness of it all before sitting back to take in the scene through the glass.

'So how's Gayfield Square?' Wylie asked.

'Moments away from having its name changed for being politically incorrect.'

This got a laugh from Davidson, loud enough to have the faces through the glass turning towards him. He held up a hand in apology, covering his mouth with the other one. Wylie scribbled something into the Murder Book.

'Looks like detention for you, Shug,' Rebus offered. 'So how are things shaping up? Got any idea who he is yet?'

It was Wylie who answered. 'Loose change in his pockets . . . not even so much as a set of house keys.'

'And nobody coming forward to claim him,' Davidson added.

'Door-to-door?'

'John, this is Knoxland we're talking about.' Meaning no one was talking. It was a tribal thing, handed down from parent to child. Whatever happened, you didn't give the police anything.

'And the media?'

Davidson handed Rebus a folded tabloid. The killing hadn't made the front page; the by-line on page five was Steve Holly's: ASYLUM DEATH RIDDLE. As Rebus skimmed down the paragraphs, Wylie turned to him.

'I wonder who it was that mentioned asylum-seekers.'

'Not me,' Rebus answered. 'Holly just makes this stuff up. "Sources close to the investigation".' He snorted. 'Which one of you does he mean by that? Or maybe he means both?'

'You're not making any friends here, John.'

Rebus handed back the newspaper. 'How many warm bodies have you got working the case?'

'Not enough,' Davidson conceded.

'Yourself and Ellen?'

'Plus Charlie Reynolds.'

'And yourself apparently,' Wylie added.

'I'm not sure I like the odds.'

'There are some keen uniforms working door-to-door,' Davidson said, defensively.

'No problem then – case solved.' Rebus saw that the autopsy was reaching its conclusion. The corpse would be sewn back together by one of the assistants. Curt motioned that he'd meet the detectives downstairs, then disappeared through a door to change out of his scrubs.

The pathologists had no office of their own. Curt was waiting in a gloomy corridor. There were sounds from inside the staff room: a kettle coming to the boil, a game of cards reaching some sort of climax.

'The Prof's done a runner?' Rebus guessed.

'He has a class in ten minutes.'

'So what have you got for us, Doctor?' Ellen Wylie asked. If she'd ever possessed a gift for small talk, it had been annihilated some time ago.

'Twelve separate wounds in total, almost certainly the work of the same blade. A kitchen knife perhaps, serrated edge, only a centimetre wide. Deepest penetration was five centimetres.' He paused, as if to allow for any lewd jokes in the vicinity. Wylie cleared her throat in warning. 'The one to the throat probably ended his life. Nicked the carotid artery. Blood in the lungs suggests he may have choked on the stuff.'

'Any defence wounds?' Davidson asked.

Curt nodded. 'Palm, fingertips and wrists. Whoever they were, he was fighting them off.'

'But you think just the one attacker?'

'Just the one knife,' Curt corrected Davidson. 'Not quite the same thing.'

'Time of death?' Wylie asked. She was jotting down as much information as she could.

'Deep-body temperature was taken at the scene. He probably died half an hour before you were alerted.'

'Incidentally,' Rebus asked, 'just who did alert us?'

'Anonymous call at thirteen fifty,' Wylie replied.

'Or ten to two in old money. Male caller?'

Wylie shook her head. 'Female, calling from a phone box.'

'And we've got the number?'

More nodding. 'Plus the conversation was recorded. We'll trace the caller, given time.'

Curt studied his watch, wanting to be on his way.

'Anything else you can tell us, Doctor?' Davidson asked.

'Victim seems to have been in general good health. Slightly undernourished, but with good teeth – either didn't grow up here or never succumbed to the Scottish diet. A specimen of the stomach contents – what there was of it – will go to the lab today. His last meal would seem to have been less than hearty: mostly rice and veg.'

'Any idea of his race?'

'I'm not an expert.'

'We appreciate that, but all the same . . .'

'Middle Eastern? Mediterranean . . . ?' Curt's voice drifted off.

'Well, that narrows things down,' Rebus said.

'No tattoos or distinguishing features?' Wylie asked, still writing furiously.

'None.' Curt paused. 'This will all be typed up for you, DS Wylie.'

'Just gives us something to work with in the interim, sir.'

'Such dedication is rare these days.' Curt offered her a smile. It did not fit well on his gaunt face. 'You know where to find me if any other questions arise . . .'

'Thank you, Doctor,' Davidson said. Curt turned towards Rebus.

'John, a quick word if I may . . . ?' His eyes met Davidson's. 'Personal rather than business,' he explained. He steered Rebus by the elbow towards the far door, and through it into the mortuary's main holding area. There was no one around; at least, no one with a pulse. A wall of metal drawers faced them; opposite it was the loading bay where the fleet of grey vans would drop off the unceasing roll-call of the dead. The only sound was the background hum of refrigeration. Despite this, Curt looked to left and right, as if fearing they might be overheard.

'About Siobhan's little request,' he said.

'Yes?'

'Perhaps you could let her know that I'm willing to accede.' Curt's face came close to Rebus's. 'But only on the understanding that Gates never finds out.'

'Reckon he's got too much ammo on you as it is?'

A nerve twitched in Curt's left eye. 'I'm sure he's already blurted out the story to anyone who'll listen.'

'We were all taken in by those bones, Doc. It wasn't just you.'

But Curt seemed lost. 'Look, just tell Siobhan it's being done on the quiet. I'm the only one she should talk to about it, understood?'

'It'll be our secret,' Rebus assured him, placing a hand on his shoulder. Curt stared at the hand forlornly.

'Why is it you remind me of one of Job's comforters?'

'I hear what you're saying, Doc.'

Curt looked at him. 'But you don't understand a word, am I right?'

'Right as usual, Doc. Right as usual.'

Siobhan realised that she'd been staring at her computer screen for the past few minutes, without really seeing what was written there. She got up and walked over to the table with the kettle on it, the one where Rebus should have been sitting. DCI Macrae had been into the room a couple of times, on both occasions seeming almost satisfied that Rebus was nowhere to be seen. Derek Starr was in his own office, discussing a case with someone from the Procurator Fiscal's department.

'Want a coffee, Col?' Siobhan asked.

'No thanks,' Tibbet replied. He was stroking his throat, fingers lingering on what looked like a patch of razor-burn. His eyes never left his computer screen, and his voice when he'd spoken had been otherworldly, as though he were barely connected to the here and now.

'Anything interesting?'

'Not really. Trying to work out if there's any connection between recent shoplifting sprees. I reckon they might tie in with train times . . .'

'How?'

He realised he'd said too much. If you wanted to be sure of grabbing all the glory, you had to keep information to yourself. It was the bane of Siobhan's working life. Cops were loath to share; any cooperation was usually accompanied by mistrust. Tibbet was ignoring her question. She tapped the coffee spoon against her teeth.

'Let me guess,' she said. 'A spree probably means one or more organised gangs ... The fact that you're looking at train times suggests they're coming in from outside the city ... So the spree can't start until the train arrives, and it'll stop as soon as they head back home?' She nodded to herself. 'How am I doing?'

'It's where they're coming *from* that's important,' Tibbet said testily.

'Newcastle?' Siobhan guessed. Tibbet's body language told her she'd scored a bull and won the match. The kettle boiled and she filled her mug, taking it back to her desk.

'Newcastle,' she repeated, sitting back down.

'At least I'm doing something constructive – not just surfing the Web.'

'Is that what you think I'm doing?'

'It's what it *looks* like you're doing.'

'Well, for your information I'm working a missing person ... accessing any sites that might help.'

'I don't remember a MisPer coming in.'

Siobhan gave a silent curse: she'd fallen into her own trap, coaxed into saying too much.

'Well, I'm working it anyway. And can I just remind you that I'm the ranking officer here?'

'You're telling me to mind my own business?'

'That's right, DC Tibbet, I am. And don't worry – Newcastle's yours and yours alone.'

'I might need to talk to the CID down there, see what they've got on the local gangs.'

Siobhan nodded. 'Do whatever you need to do, Col.'

'Fair enough, Shiv. Thanks.'

'And never call me that again or I'll rip your head off.'

'Everyone else calls you Shiv,' Tibbet protested.

'That's true, but you're going to break the pattern. You're going to call me Siobhan.'

Tibbet was quiet for a moment, and Siobhan thought he'd gone back to testing his timetable theory. But then he spoke again.

'You don't like being called Shiv ... but you've never told anyone. Interesting ...'

Siobhan wanted to ask him what he meant, but decided it would only prolong the conflict. She reckoned she knew anyway: as far as Tibbet was concerned, this fresh information gave him some power: a little incendiary he could tuck away for later. No use worrying about it until the time came. She concentrated on her screen, deciding on a fresh search. She'd been visiting sites maintained by groups who looked out for missing persons. Often these MisPers didn't want to be found by their immediate families, but wanted nevertheless for them to know they were fine. Messages could be exchanged with the groups as intermediaries. Siobhan had a text which she'd worked out over the course of three drafts, and had now sent to the various noticeboards.

Ishbel – Mum and Dad miss you, and so do the girls at the salon. Get in touch to let us know you're all right. We need you to know that we love you and miss you.

Siobhan reckoned this would do. It was neither too impersonal nor too gushingly frantic. It didn't hint that someone from outside Ishbel's immediate circle was doing the seeking. And even if the Jardines had been lying and there *had* been friction at home, the mention of the girls at the salon might make Ishbel feel guilty about having cast off friends such as Susie. Siobhan had placed the photo next to her keyboard.

'Friends of yours?' Tibbet had asked earlier, sounding interested. They were good-looking girls, fun at parties and in the pub. Life a bit of a laugh for them . . . Siobhan knew she could never hope to understand what might motivate them, but that wouldn't stop her trying. She sent more e-mails: to police divisions this time. She knew detectives in Dundee and Glasgow, and flagged Ishbel up for them – just the name and general description, along with a note saying she'd owe them big time if they were able to help. Almost immediately, her mobile sounded. It was Liz Hetherington, her contact in Dundee, a detective sergeant with Tayside Police.

'Long time no hear,' Hetherington said. 'What's so special about this one?'

'I know the family,' Siobhan said. There was no way she could keep her voice quiet enough for Tibbet not to hear, so she rose from her desk and went out into the hallway. The odour was out here, too, as if the station was rotting from within. 'They live in a village in West Lothian.'

'Well, I'll circulate the details. What makes you think she'd head this way?'

'Call it an exercise in straw-grasping. I promised her parents I'd do what I could.'

'You don't think she could have gone on the game?'

'What makes you say that?'

'Girl leaves village, heads for the bright lights . . . you'd be surprised.'

'She's a hairdresser.'

'Plenty of vacancies for those,' Hetherington conceded. 'It's almost as portable a career as street-walking.'

'It's funny though,' Siobhan said. 'There was some guy she'd been seeing. One of her friends said he looked like a pimp.'

'There you are then. Has she any friends she could be crashing with?'

'I've not got that far yet.'

'Well, if any of them live up this way, let me know and I'll pay a visit.'

'Thanks, Liz.'

'And come see us some time, Siobhan. I'll show you Dundee's not the ghetto you southerners think it is.'

'One of these weekends, Liz.'

'Promise?'

'Promise.' Siobhan ended the conversation. Yes, she'd go to Dundee . . . when it appealed more than a weekend slouched on the sofa, chocolate and old movies for company; breakfast in bed with a good book and Goldfrapp's first album on the hi-fi . . . lunch out, and then maybe a film at the Dominion or the Filmhouse, a bottle of cold white wine waiting for her at home.

She found herself standing by her desk. Tibbet was looking up at her.

'I've got to go out,' she said.

He glanced at his watch, as if about to make a note of her time of departure. 'Any idea how long you'll be?'

'Couple of hours, if that's all right with you, DC Tibbet.'

'Just in case anyone asks,' he explained sniffily.

'Right then,' Siobhan said, picking up jacket and bag. 'There's a coffee there if you want it.'

'Gee, thanks.'

She headed out without another word, walked downhill to her street and unlocked her Peugeot. The cars in front and behind hadn't left much room. It took her half a dozen manoeuvres to squeeze out of the space. Though she was in a residents' zone, she noticed that the car in front was an interloper, and had already been given a parking ticket. She stopped the Peugeot and scribbled the words POLICE NOTIFIED on a page from her notebook. Then she got out and stuck it beneath the BMW's wiper-blade. Feeling better, she got back into the Peugeot and drove off.

Traffic was busy in town, and there was no clever route to the M8. She tapped her fingers on the steering wheel, humming along

40

to Jackie Leven: a birthday present from Rebus, who'd told her Leven came from the same part of the world as him.

'And that's supposed to be a recommendation?' she'd replied. She liked the album well enough, but couldn't concentrate on the lyrics. She was thinking of the skeletons in Fleshmarket Close. It annoyed her that she couldn't work out an explanation for them; annoyed her, too, that she'd placed her own coat so carefully over a fake . . .

Banehall was halfway between Livingston and Whitburn, just to the north of the motorway. The slip-road was past the village, the signpost bearing the legend 'Local Services', with drawings representing a petrol pump and a knife and fork. Siobhan doubted many travellers would bother to make a diversion, having had view of Banehall from their carriageway. The place looked bleak: rows of houses dating back to the early 1900s, a boarded-up church, and a forlorn industrial estate, which showed no sign of having been a going concern at any point in its existence. The petrol station – now no longer in operation, weeds pushing up through the forecourt – was the first thing she passed after the 'Welcome to Banehall' sign. This sign had been defaced to read 'We are the Bane'. Locals, not just teenagers, called the place 'the Bane' with no sense of irony. A sign further on had been altered from 'Children – aware!' to 'Children – a war!' She smiled at this, checking either side of the street for the hair salon. So few businesses were still active, this presented few problems. The shop was called just that – The Salon. Siobhan decided to drive past it, until she'd reached the far end of Main Street. Then she turned the car and retraced her route, this time turning into a side street which led to a housing scheme.

She found the Jardines' house easily enough, but there was no one home. No signs of life in neighbouring windows. A few parked cars, a child's trike missing one of its back wheels. Plenty of satellite dishes attached to the harled walls. She saw homemade signs in some of the living-room windows: YES TO WHITEMIRE. Whitemire, she knew, was an old prison a couple of miles outside Banehall. Two years ago, it had been turned into an immigration centre. By now it was probably Banehall's biggest employer . . . and it was marked for further development. Back on Main Street, the village's only pub boasted the name The Bane. Siobhan hadn't passed any cafés, just a solitary chip shop. The weary traveller, hoping to use a knife and fork, would be forced to try the pub, though it gave no indication that food would be available. Siobhan parked kerbside and crossed the road to the Salon. Here, too, there was a pro-Whitemire sign in the window.

Two women sat drinking coffee and smoking cigarettes. There were no customers, and neither of the staff looked thrilled at the potential arrival of one. Siobhan brought out her ID and introduced herself.

'I recognise you,' the younger of the two said. 'You're the cop from Tracy's funeral. You had your arm around Ishbel at the church. I asked her mum afterwards.'

'You've got a good memory, Susie,' Siobhan replied. No one had bothered to get up, and there was nowhere left for Siobhan to sit but one of the styling chairs. She stayed standing.

'Wouldn't mind a coffee, if there's one going,' she said, trying to sound friendly.

The older woman was slow to rise. Siobhan noticed that her fingernails had been decorated with elaborate swirls of colour. 'No milk left,' the woman warned.

'I'll take it black.'

'Sugar?'

'No thanks.'

The woman shuffled over to an alcove at the back of the shop. 'I'm Angie, by the way,' she told Siobhan. 'Owner and stylist to the stars.'

'Is it about Ishbel?' Susie asked.

Siobhan nodded, sitting down in the space that had been vacated on the cushioned bench. Susie immediately got up, as if in reaction to Siobhan's proximity, and stubbed out her cigarette in an ashtray, her last inhalation now issuing from her nostrils. She walked over to one of the other chairs and sat down in it, swinging it to and fro with her feet, checking her hair in the mirror. 'She hasn't been in touch,' she stated.

'And you've no idea where she could have gone?'

A shrug. 'Her mum and dad are up to high doh, that's all I know.'

'What about this man you saw Ishbel with?'

Another shrug. She played with her fringe. 'Short guy, stocky.'

'Hair?'

'Can't remember.'

'Maybe he was bald?'

'I don't think so.'

'Clothes?'

'Leather jacket . . . sunglasses.'

'Not from around here?'

A shake of the head. 'Driving a flash car . . . something fast.'

'A BMW? Mercedes?'

'I'm no good with cars.'

'Was it big, small . . . did it have a roof?'

'Medium . . . with a roof, but it could've been a convertible.'

Angie was returning with a mug. She handed it over and sat down in Susie's vacated space.

Siobhan nodded her thanks. 'How old was he, Susie?'

'Old . . . forties or fifties.'

Angie gave a snort. 'Old to you, maybe.' She was probably fifty herself, with hair that looked twenty years younger.

'When you asked her about him, what did she say?'

'Just told me to shut up.'

'Any idea how she could have met him?'

'No.'

'What sort of places does she go?'

'Into Livingston . . . maybe Edinburgh or Glasgow sometimes. Just pubs and clubs.'

'Anybody apart from you she might go out with?'

Susie mentioned some names, which Siobhan jotted down.

'Susie's already talked to them,' Angie warned. 'They won't be any help.'

'Thanks, anyway.' Siobhan made a show of looking around the salon. 'Is it usually this quiet?'

'We get a few customers first thing. Later in the week's busier.'

'But Ishbel not being here isn't a problem?'

'We're managing.'

'Makes me wonder . . .'

Angie narrowed her eyes. 'What?'

'Why you need two stylists.'

Angie glanced towards Susie. 'What else could I do?'

Siobhan felt she understood. Angie had taken pity on Ishbel after the suicide. 'Any reason you can think of why she'd leave home so suddenly?'

'Maybe she got a better offer . . . Plenty of people ship out of the Bane and never look back.'

'Her mystery man?'

It was Angie's turn to shrug. 'Good luck to her if that's what she wants.'

Siobhan turned to Susie. 'You told Ishbel's mum and dad he looked like a pimp.'

'Did I?' She seemed genuinely surprised. 'Well, maybe I did. The shades and the jacket . . . like something out of a film.' Her eyes widened. *'Taxi Driver!'* she said. 'The pimp in that . . . what's his name? I saw that on the telly a couple of months back.'

'And that's who this man looked like?'

'No . . . but he was wearing a hat. That's why I couldn't remember his hair!'

'What sort of hat?'

Susie's enthusiasm drained away. 'Dunno . . . just a hat.'

'Baseball cap? Beret?'

Susie shook her head. 'It had a rim.'

Siobhan looked to Angie for help. 'A fedora?' Angie suggested. 'A homburg?'

'I don't even know what those are,' Susie said.

'Something like a gangster in an old film would wear?' Angie went on.

Susie was thoughtful. 'Maybe,' she conceded.

Siobhan jotted down her mobile phone number. 'That's great, Susie. And if anything else comes back to you, maybe you could give me a call?'

Susie nodded. She was out of reach, so Siobhan handed the note to Angie. 'Same thing applies to you.' Angie nodded and folded the note in two.

The door rattled open and a stooped, elderly woman came in.

'Mrs Prentice,' Angie called out in greeting.

'Bit earlier than I told you, Angie dear. Can you fit me in?'

Angie was already on her feet. 'For you, Mrs Prentice, I'm sure I can shuffle my diary.' Susie relinquished the chair so that Mrs Prentice could sit in it, once she'd divested herself of her coat. Siobhan got up, too. 'One last thing, Susie,' she said.

'What?'

Siobhan walked over to the alcove, Susie following her. Siobhan lowered her voice when she spoke. 'The Jardines tell me Donald Cruikshank's out of prison.'

Susie's face hardened.

'Have you seen him?' Siobhan asked.

'Once or twice . . . piece of scum that he is.'

'Have you spoken to him?'

'As if I would! Council gave him a place of his own – can you credit it? His mum and dad wouldn't have anything to do with him.'

'Did Ishbel mention him at all?'

'Just that she felt the same as me. You think that's what drove her out?'

'Do you?'

'*He's* the one we should be running out of town,' Susie hissed.

Siobhan nodded her agreement. 'Well,' she said, slinging her bag on to her shoulder, 'remember to give me a call if anything else comes to you.'

'Sure,' Susie said. She studied Siobhan's hair. 'Can't do something with that for you, can I?'

Involuntarily, Siobhan's right hand went to her head. 'What's wrong with it?'

'I don't know ... It just ... it makes you look older than you probably are.'

'Maybe that's the look I'm aiming for,' Siobhan replied defensively, making her way to the door.

'Wee perm and a touch-up?' Angie was asking her client as Siobhan stepped outside. She stood for a moment, wondering what next. She'd meant to ask Susie about Ishbel's ex-boyfriend, the one she was still friends with. But she didn't want to go back in, and decided it could wait. There was a newsagent's open. She thought about chocolate, but decided to look into the pub instead. It would give her something to tell Rebus; maybe even score her some points if it turned out to be one of the few bars in Scotland not to count him as a one-time customer.

She pushed open the black wooden door and was confronted by pockmarked red linoleum and matching flock wallpaper. A design mag would call it 'kitsch' and enthuse over its revival of seventies naff ... but this was the real, unreconstructed thing. There were horse brasses on the walls, and framed cartoons showing dogs urinating, bloke-style, against a wall. Horse-racing on the TV and a haze of cigarette smoke between her and the bar. Three men stared up from their dominoes game. One of them got up and walked behind the bar.

'What can I get you, love?'

'Lime juice and soda,' she said, resting on a bar stool. There was a Glasgow Rangers scarf draped over the dartboard, a pool table alongside with ripped and patched baize. And nothing to justify the knife and fork on the motorway exit sign.

'Eighty-five pence,' the barman said, placing the drink in front of her. At this point, she knew she had only one gambit – *Does Ishbel Jardine ever come in?* – and couldn't see what she'd gain from it. For one thing, the bar would be alerted to the fact that she was a cop. For another, she doubted these men would add anything to her sum knowledge, even if they had known Ishbel. She raised the glass to her lips, and knew there was too much cordial in it. The drink was sickly sweet, and not gassy enough.

'All right?' the barman said. It was challenge more than query.

'Fine,' she replied.

Satisfied, he came back out from behind the bar and resumed his game. There was a pot of small change on the table, ten- and twenty-pence pieces. The men he was playing with looked like pensioners. They slapped each domino down with exaggerated force, tapped three times if they couldn't go. Already, they'd lost interest in her. She looked around for a ladies' loo, spotted it to the left of the dartboard and headed inside. Now they'd think she'd only come in for a pee, the soft drink conscience-money. The toilet was clean, though the mirror above the sink had gone, pen-written graffiti replacing it.

Sean's a shag
The buns on Kenny Reilly!!!
Sluts unite!
Bane Bunnies Rool

Siobhan smiled and went into the only cubicle. The lock was broken. She sat down, ready to be entertained by more of the graffiti.

Donny Cruikshank – Dead Man Walking
Donny Pervo
Fry the fucker
Cook the Cruik
Claimed in blood, sisters!!!
God bless Tracy Jardine

There was more – much more – by no means all of it in the same hand. Black marker pen, blue biro, gold felt-tip. Siobhan decided that the three exclamation marks must be by the same person as above the sink. When she'd walked in, she'd thought herself a rare example of a female customer; now she knew differently. She wondered if any of the sentiments came from Ishbel Jardine: a handwriting comparison would tell. She rummaged in her bag but realised her digital camera was in the Peugeot's glovebox. Well, she'd just go get it. To hell with what the domino-players would think.

Pulling open the door, she noticed that a new customer had arrived. He was leaning his elbows against the bar, head down low, hips wiggling. Her stool was right next to him. He heard the creak of the toilet door and turned towards her. She saw a shaved head, a jowly white face, two days' growth of beard.

Three lines on the right cheek – scar tissue.

Donny Cruikshank.

Last time she'd seen him had been in an Edinburgh courtroom. He wouldn't know her. She'd not given evidence, never had the chance to interview him. She was pleased to see him looking so dissipated. His scant time in jail had still been enough to rob him of some youth and vitality. She knew there was a pecking order in every prison, and that sex offenders were at the bottom of the tree. His mouth had opened in a slack grin, ignoring the pint which had just been placed in front of him. The barman stood stony-faced with hand held out for payment. It was clear to Siobhan that he wasn't keen on Cruikshank's presence in his pub. One of Cruikshank's eyes was bloodshot, as though he'd been punched and it had failed to heal.

'All right, darling?' he called. She walked towards him.

'Don't call me that,' she said icily.

'Ooh! "Don't call me that".' The attempted mimicry was grotesque; only Cruikshank was laughing. 'I like a doll with balls.'

'Keep talking and you'll soon be missing yours.'

Cruikshank couldn't believe his ears. After a stunned moment, he tipped back his head and howled.

'Did you ever hear the like, Malky?'

'Pack it in, Donny,' Malky the barman warned.

'Or what? You'll red-card me again?' He looked around. 'Aye, I'd certainly miss this place.' His eyes rested on Siobhan, taking in every inch of her. 'Of course, things have picked up on the totty front just lately . . .'

Incarceration had eroded him physically, but given him something in return, a kind of bravado, with attitude to spare.

Siobhan knew that if she stayed, she'd end up lashing out. She knew she was capable of hurting him; but knew also that hurting him physically would not damage him in any other way. Meaning he'd have won, by making her weak. So instead she walked, trying to shut out his words to her retreating back.

'The arse on that, eh, Malky? Come back, gorgeous, I've got a surprise package here for you!'

Outside, Siobhan headed to her car. Adrenalin had kicked in, her heartbeat racing. She sat behind the wheel and tried to control her breathing. *Bastard*, she was thinking. *Bastard, bastard, bastard* . . . She glanced at the glovebox. She would have to come back another time to take the photos. Her mobile rang and she fished it out. Rebus's number was on her screen. She took a deep breath, not wanting him to hear anything in her voice.

'What's up, John?' she asked.

'Siobhan? What's up with *you*?'

'How do you mean?'

'You sound like you've been jogging round Arthur's Seat.'

'Just dashed back to the car.' She looked out at the pale blue sky. 'It's raining here.'

'Raining? Where the hell are you?'

'Banehall.'

'And where's that when it's at home?'

'West Lothian, just off the motorway before you get to Whitburn.'

'I know it – pub called The Bane?'

Despite herself, she smiled. 'That's the place,' she said.

'What takes you out there?'

'It's a long story. What are you up to?'

'Nothing that can't be shoved to one side if a long story's on offer. Are you heading back to town?'

'Yes.'

'Then you'll practically be passing Knoxland.'

'And that's where I'll find you?'

'You can't miss me – we've got the wagons circled to keep the natives at bay.'

Siobhan saw that the door to the pub was opening from within, Donny Cruikshank throwing curses back into the place. A two-fingered salute followed by a volley of saliva. Looked like Malky had had enough of him. Siobhan turned the ignition.

'I'll see you in forty minutes or so.'

'Bring ammunition, will you? Forty Bensons Gold.'

'I draw the line at cigarettes, John.'

'The last request of a dying man, Shiv,' Rebus pleaded.

Watching the mix of anger and despair on Donny Cruikshank's face, Siobhan couldn't help breaking into a smile.

4

Rebus's 'circled wagons' actually consisted of a single-roomed Portakabin, placed in the car park next to the nearest tower block. It was dark green on the outside, with a grille protecting the only window and a reinforced door. When he'd parked his car, the ubiquitous draggle of kids had asked for money to look after it. He'd pointed a finger at them.

'A sparrow so much as farts on my windscreen, you'll be licking it off.'

He stood in the doorway of the Portakabin now, smoking a cigarette. Ellen Wylie was typing on a laptop. It had to be a laptop, so they could unplug it at day's end and take it with them. It was either that or post a night-time guard on the door. No way of hooking up a phone line, so they were using mobiles. DC Charlie Reynolds, known behind his back as 'Rat-Arse', was approaching from one of the high-rises. He was in his late forties, almost as broad as he was tall. He'd played rugby at one time, including a stint at national level with the police team. As a result, his face was a mangle of botched repairs, rips and nicks. The haircut wouldn't have looked out of place on a street urchin *circa* the 1920s. Reynolds had a reputation as a wind-up merchant, but he wasn't smiling now.

'Bloody waste of time,' he snarled.

'Nobody's talking?' Rebus guessed.

'It's the ones that *are* talking, they're the problem.'

'How so?' Rebus decided to offer Reynolds a cigarette, which the big man accepted without thanks.

'Don't speak bloody English, do they? Fifty-seven bloody varieties up there.' He gestured towards the tower block. 'And the smell . . .

Christ knows what they're cooking, but I've not noticed many cats in the vicinity.' Reynolds saw the look on Rebus's face. 'Don't get me wrong, John, I'm not a racist. But you do have to wonder . . .'

'About what?'

'The whole asylum thing. I mean, say you had to leave Scotland, right? You were being tortured or something . . . You'd make for the nearest safe country, right, 'cos you wouldn't want to be too far from the old homeland. But this lot . . .' He stared up at the tower block, then shook his head. 'You take my point though, eh?'

'I suppose I do, Charlie.'

'Half of them can't even be arsed to learn the language . . . just pick up their cash from the government, thank you very much.' Reynolds concentrated on his cigarette. He smoked with some violence, teeth clamping the filter, mouth drawing hard. 'Least you can sod off back to Gayfield whenever you like; some of us are stuck out here for the duration.'

'Wait till I go and get my violin, Charlie,' Rebus said. Another car was drawing up alongside: Shug Davidson. He'd been to a meeting to fix the budget for the inquiry, and didn't look thrilled with the result.

'No interpreters?' Rebus guessed.

'Oh, we can have all the interpreters we want,' Davidson responded. 'Thing is, we can't pay them. Our esteemed Assistant Chief Constable says we should ask around, maybe see if the council could provide one or two free of charge.'

'Along with everything else,' Reynolds muttered.

'What's that?' Davidson snapped.

'Nothing, Shug, nothing.' Reynolds stamped on the remains of his cigarette as if rucking for a ball.

'Charlie reckons the locals rely a touch too much on handouts,' Rebus explained.

'I didn't say that.'

'I can mind-read sometimes. Runs in the family, passed down from father to son. My grandad probably gave it to my dad . . .' Rebus stubbed out his own cigarette. 'He was Polish, by the way, my grandad. We're a bastard nation, Charlie – get used to it.' Rebus walked over to greet another arrival: Siobhan Clarke. She spent a few moments studying her surroundings.

'Concrete was such an attractive option in the sixties,' she commented. 'And as for the murals . . .'

Rebus had ceased to notice them: WOGS OUT . . . PAKIS ARE SHIT . . . WHITE POWER . . . Some wag had tried sneaking a 'd' into 'power' to make 'powder'. Rebus wondered how strong a hold the drug-dealers had around here. Maybe another reason for the general disaffection: immigrants probably couldn't afford drugs, even supposing they wanted them. SCOTLAND FOR THE SCOTS . . . A venerable piece of graffiti had been altered from JUNKIE SCUM to BLACK SCUM.

'This looks cosy,' Siobhan said. 'Thanks for inviting me.'

'Did you bring your invitation?'

She held out the packs of cigarettes. Rebus kissed them and slipped them into his pocket. Davidson and Reynolds had disappeared inside the cabin.

'You going to tell me that story?' he asked.

'You going to give me the tour?'

Rebus shrugged. 'Why not?' They started walking. There were four main tower blocks in Knoxland, each one eight storeys high, and sited as if at the corners of a square, looking down on to the central, devastated play area. There were open walkways on each level, and every flat had a balcony with a view of the dual carriageway.

'Plenty of satellite dishes,' Siobhan observed. Rebus nodded. He'd wondered about these dishes, about the versions of the world they transmitted into each living room and life. Daytimes, the ads would be for accident compensation; at night, they'd be for alcohol. A generation growing up in the belief that life could be controlled by a TV remote.

There were kids circling them now on their bikes. Others were congregating against a wall, sharing a cigarette and something in a lemonade bottle that didn't look like lemonade. They wore baseball caps and trainers, a fashion beamed down to them from another culture.

'He's too old for ye!' one voice barked out, followed by laughter and the usual pig-like grunting.

'I'm young but I'm hung, ya hoor!' the same voice called.

They kept walking. One uniform was stationed either end of the murder scene, showing ebbing patience as locals queried why they couldn't use the passageway.

'Jist 'cos some chinky got topped, man . . .'

'Wisnae a chinky . . . towel-head, I heard.'

The voices rising. 'Hey, man, how come they get past ye and we dinnae? Pure discrimination, by the way . . .'

Rebus had led Siobhan behind the uniform. Not that there was much to see. The ground was still stained; the place still had about it the faint whiff of urine. Scrawls covering every inch of wall space.

'Whoever he was, somebody misses him,' Rebus said quietly, noting a small bundle of flowers marking the spot. Except that they weren't really flowers, just some strands of wild grass and a few dandelions. Picked from waste ground.

'Trying to tell us something?' Siobhan guessed.

Rebus shrugged. 'Maybe they just couldn't afford flowers . . . or didn't know how to go about buying any.'

'Are there really that many immigrants in Knoxland?'

Rebus shook his head. 'Probably not more than sixty or seventy.'

'Which would be sixty or seventy more than a few years ago.'

'I hope you're not turning into Rat-Arse Reynolds.'

'Just thinking from the locals' point of view. People don't like incomers: immigrants, travellers, anyone the least bit different . . . Even an English accent like mine can get you into trouble.'

'That's different. Plenty of good historical reasons for the Scots to hate the English.'

'And vice versa, obviously.'

They had passed out of the far end of the passage. Here, there was a gathering of lower-rise blocks, four storeys high, along with a few rows of terraced houses.

'The houses were built for pensioners,' Rebus explained. 'Something to do with keeping them within the community.'

'Nice dream, as Thom Yorke would say.'

That was Knoxland, all right: a nice dream. Plenty more like it elsewhere in the city. Their architects would have been so proud of the scale drawings and cardboard models. Nobody ever set out to design a ghetto, after all.

'Why Knoxland?' Siobhan asked eventually. 'Not named after Knox the Calvinist, surely.'

'I wouldn't think so. Knox wanted Scotland to be a new Jerusalem. I doubt Knoxland qualifies.'

'All I know about him is that he didn't want statues in any of his churches, and he wasn't keen on women.'

'He also didn't want people having fun. There were ducking stools and witch trials waiting for the guilty . . .' Rebus paused. 'So he did have his good points.'

Rebus didn't know where they were walking to. Siobhan seemed all twitching energy, something needing to be grounded somehow. She'd turned back and was walking towards one of the higher tower blocks.

'Shall we?' she said, making to pull open the door. But it was locked.

'A recent addition,' Rebus explained. 'Security cameras beside the lifts, too. Trying to keep out the barbarians.'

'Cameras?' Siobhan watched Rebus punch a four-figure code into the door's keypad. He was shaking his head at her question.

'Turns out they're never switched on. Council couldn't afford the security man to keep charge of them.' He pulled the door open. There were two lifts in the lobby. Both were working, so maybe the keypad was doing its job.

'Top floor,' Siobhan said as they entered the left-hand lift. Rebus hit the button and the doors shuddered together.

'Now, about that story . . .' Rebus said. So she told him. It didn't take long. By the time she finished, they were on one of the walkways, leaning against its low wall. The wind was whistling and gusting around them. There were views to the north and east, glimpses of Corstorphine Hill and Craiglockhart.

'Look at all the space,' she said. 'Why didn't they just build houses for everybody?'

'What? And ruin the sense of community?' Rebus twisted his body towards her, so she would know he was giving her his full attention. He didn't even have a cigarette in his hand.

'You want to bring Cruikshank in for questioning?' he asked. 'I could hold him down while you give him a good kicking.'

'Old-fashioned policing, eh?'

'I've always found the notion refreshing.'

'Well, it won't be necessary: I've already given him a doing . . . in here.' She tapped her skull. 'But thanks for the thought.'

Rebus shrugged, turning to stare out at the scenery. 'You know she'll turn up if she wants to?'

'I know.'

'She doesn't qualify as a MisPer.'

'And you've never done a favour for a friend?'

'You've got a point,' Rebus conceded. 'Just don't expect a result.'

'Don't worry.' She pointed to the tower block diagonal to the one they were standing in. 'Notice anything?'

'Nothing I wouldn't see torched for the price of a pint.'

'Hardly any graffiti. I mean, compared to the other blocks.'

Rebus looked down towards ground level. It was true: the harled walls of this one block were cleaner than the others. 'That's Stevenson House. Maybe someone on the council has fond memories of *Treasure Island*. Next time one of us picks up a parking

53

ticket, they'll have the deposit on another batch of emulsion.' The lift doors behind them slid open and two uniforms emerged, unenthusiastic and carrying clipboards.

'At least this is the last floor,' one of them grumbled. He noticed Rebus and Siobhan. 'Do you live here?' he asked, readying to add them to his clipboard tally.

Rebus caught Siobhan's eye. 'We must look more desperate than I thought.' Then, to the uniform: 'We're CID, son.'

The other uniform snorted at his partner's mistake. He was already knocking on the first door. Rebus could hear rising voices heading down the hallway towards it. The door flew open from within.

The man was already furious. His wife stood behind him, fists bunched. Recognising police officers, the man rolled his eyes. 'Last bastard thing I need.'

'Sir, if you'll just calm down . . .'

Rebus could have told the young constable that this was not the way you dealt with nitroglycerine: you didn't tell it what it was.

'Calm? Easy for you to say, ya choob. It's that bastard that got himself killed, am I right? People could be screaming blue murder out here, cars burning, junkies staggering all over the place . . . Only time we plank eyes on you lot's when one of *them* starts wailing. Call that fair?'

'They deserve what's coming to them,' his wife spat. She was dressed in grey jogging pants and matching hooded top. Not that she looked the sporty type: like the officers in front of her, she was wearing a kind of uniform.

'Can I just remind you that someone's been murdered?' Blood had risen to the constable's cheeks. They'd riled him, and now they'd know it. Rebus decided to step in.

'Detective Inspector Rebus,' he said, showing his ID. 'We've got a job to do here, simple as that, and we'd appreciate your coopera-tion.'

'And what do *we* get out of it?' The woman had drawn level with her husband, the pair of them more than filling the doorway. It was as if their own argument had never happened: they were a team now, shoulder to shoulder against the world.

'A sense of civic responsibility,' Rebus answered. 'Doing your bit for the estate . . . Or maybe you're not worried by the idea that there's a murderer running around the place like he owns it.'

'Whoever he is, he's not after us, is he?'

'He can do as many of them as he likes . . . scare them off,' her husband agreed.

'I can't believe I'm hearing this,' Siobhan muttered. Maybe she hadn't meant them to hear, but they noticed her anyway.

'And who the fuck are you?' the man said.

'She's my fucking colleague,' Rebus retorted. 'Now look at me . . .' He seemed suddenly larger, and the pair did look at him. 'We do this the easy way or the hard – you choose.'

The man was sizing Rebus up. Eventually, his shoulders untensed a little. 'We don't know nothing,' he said. 'Satisfied?'

'But you're not sorry an innocent man is dead?'

The woman snorted. 'Way he carried on, it's a wonder it didn't happen sooner . . .' Her voice trailed away as her husband's glare hit home.

'Stupid bitch,' he said quietly. 'Now we're going to be here all night.' Again he looked at Rebus.

'Your choice,' Rebus said. 'Either in your living room, or down the station.'

Husband and wife decided as one. 'Living room,' they said.

Eventually the place grew crowded. The constables had been dismissed, but told to continue the door-to-doors and keep their mouths shut about what had happened.

'Which probably means the whole station will know before we get back,' Shug Davidson had conceded. He'd taken over the questioning, Wylie and Reynolds playing supporting roles. Rebus had taken Davidson to one side.

'Make sure Rat-Arse gets to talk to them.' Davidson's eyes had sought an explanation. 'Let's just say they might open up to him. I think they share certain social and political opinions. Rat-Arse makes it less "us" and "them".'

Davidson had nodded, and so far it had worked. Almost everything the pair said, Reynolds nodded his understanding.

'It's a culture-conflict sort of thing,' he would agree. Or: 'I think we all see your point.'

The room was claustrophobic. Rebus doubted the windows had ever been opened. They were double-glazed, but condensation had gathered between the panes, leaving trails like tear-stains. There was an electric fire on. The bulbs controlling its coal effect had long since blown, making the room seem even gloomier. Three pieces of furniture filled the place: a huge brown sofa flanked by vast brown

55

armchairs. These last were where husband and wife made themselves comfortable. There had been no offer of tea or coffee, and when Siobhan had mimed drinking from a cup, Rebus had shaken his head: no knowing what sort of health risks they'd be taking. For most of the interview, he had stood his ground by the wall cabinet, studying the contents of its shelves. Videotapes: romantic comedies for the lady; bawdy stand-up and football for the gentleman. Some of them were pirate copies, the sleeves not even trying to convince. There were a few paperback books, too: actors' biographies and a volume about slimming which claimed to have 'changed five million lives'. Five million: the population of Scotland, give or take. Rebus saw no sign that it had changed any lives in this room.

What it boiled down to was: the victim had lived next door. No, they'd never spoken to him, except to tell him to shut up. Why? Because he'd yell the place down some nights. All hours, he'd be stomping around. No friends or family that they knew of; never had visitors that they heard or saw.

'Mind you, he could have had a clog-dancing team in there, noise he made.'

'Noisy neighbours can be hell,' Reynolds agreed, without a hint of irony.

There wasn't much more: the flat had been vacant before he arrived, and they weren't sure exactly when that had been ... maybe five, six months back. No, they didn't know his name, or whether he worked – 'But it's odds-on he didn't . . . scavengers, the lot of them.'

At which point Rebus had stepped outside for a cigarette. It was either that or he'd have had to ask: 'And what exactly do *you* do? What do *you* add to the sum of human endeavour?' Staring out across the estate, he thought: I haven't seen any of these people, the people everyone's so angry at. He guessed they were hiding behind doors, hiding from the hate as they tried to make their own community. If they succeeded, the hate would be multiplied. But that might not matter, because if they succeeded, maybe they'd be able to move on from Knoxland altogether. And then the locals could be happy again behind their barricades and blinkers.

'It's times like this I wish I smoked,' Siobhan said, joining him.

'Never too late to start.' He reached into his pocket as if for the pack, but she shook her head.

'A drink would be nice though.'

'The one you didn't get last night?'

She nodded. 'But at home . . . in the bath . . . maybe with some candles.'

'You think you can soak away people like that?' Rebus gestured towards the flat.

'Don't worry, I know I can't.'

'All part of life's rich tapestry, Shiv.'

'Isn't that good to know?'

The lift doors opened. More uniforms, but different: stab-proof jackets and crash helmets. Four of them, trained to be mean. Drafted in from Serious Crimes. These were the Drugs Squad, and they carried the tool of their trade: the 'key', basically a length of iron pipe which acted as a battering-ram. Its job was to get them into dealers' reinforced homes as fast as possible, before evidence could be flushed away.

'A good kick would probably do the trick,' Rebus told them. The leader stared at him, unblinking.

'Which door?'

Rebus pointed to it. The man turned to his crew and nodded. They moved in, positioned the cylinder and swung it.

Wood splintered and the door opened.

'I've just remembered something,' Siobhan said. 'The victim didn't have any keys on him . . .'

Rebus checked the splintered door jamb, then turned the handle. 'Not locked,' he said, confirming her theory. The noise had brought people out on to the landing: not just neighbours, but Davidson and Wylie.

'We'll have a look-see,' Rebus offered. Davidson nodded.

'Hang on,' Wylie said. 'Shiv's not even part of this.'

'That's the team spirit we've been looking for in you, Ellen,' Rebus shot back.

Davidson twitched his head, letting Wylie know he wanted her back at the interview. They disappeared inside. Rebus turned to the team leader, who was just emerging from the victim's flat. It was dark in there, but the team carried torches.

'All clear,' the leader said.

Rebus reached into the hall and tried the light switch: nothing. 'Mind if I borrow a torch?' He could see that the leader minded very much. 'I'll bring it back, promise.' He held out a hand.

'Alan, give him your torch,' the leader snapped.

'Yes, sir.' The torch was handed over.

'Tomorrow morning,' the leader instructed.

'I'll hand it in first thing,' Rebus assured him. The leader glowered, then signalled to his men that their job was done. They marched back towards the lifts. As soon as the doors had closed behind them, Siobhan let out a snort.

'Are they for real?'

Rebus tried the torch, found it satisfactory. 'Don't forget the crap they have to deal with. Houses full of weapons and syringes: who would you rather stormed in first?'

'I take it back,' she apologised.

They went inside. The place was not only dark, it was cold. In the living room, they found old newspapers which looked as if they'd been rescued from dustbins, plus empty tins of food and milk cartons. No furniture. The kitchen was squalid, but tidy. Siobhan pointed up high on one wall. A coin meter. She produced a coin from her pocket, slotted it home and turned the dial. The lights came on.

'Better,' Rebus said, placing the torch on the worktop. 'Not that there's much to see.'

'I don't think he did much cooking.' Siobhan pulled open the cupboards, revealing a few plates and bowls, packets of rice and seasoning, two chipped tea-cups and a tea caddy half filled with loose-leaf tea. A bag of sugar sat on the worktop next to the sink, a spoon sticking out of it. Rebus peered into the sink, saw carrot shavings. Rice and veg: the deceased's final meal.

In the bathroom, it looked as if some rudimentary attempt at clothes-washing had taken place: shirts and underpants were draped over the edge of the bathtub, next to a bar of soap. A toothbrush sat by the sink, but no toothpaste.

This left only the bedroom. Rebus switched on the light. Again there was no furniture. A sleeping-bag lay unfurled on the floor. As with the living room, there was dun-coloured carpeting, which seemed unwilling to part company with the soles of Rebus's shoes as he approached the sleeping-bag. There were no curtains, but the window was overlooked only by another tower block seventy or eighty feet away.

'Not much here that would explain the noise he made,' Rebus said.

'I'm not so sure . . . If I had to live here, I think I'd probably end up having a screaming fit, too.'

'Good point.' In place of a chest of drawers, the man had used a polythene bin-liner. Rebus upended it, and saw ragged clothes, neatly folded. 'Stuff must've come from a jumble sale,' he said.

'Or a charity – plenty of those working with asylum-seekers.'

'You reckon that's what he was?'

'Well, let's just say he doesn't look exactly settled here. I'd say he arrived with a bare minimum of personal effects.'

Rebus picked up the sleeping-bag and gave it a shake. It was the old-fashioned sort: wide and thin. Half a dozen photographs tumbled from it. Rebus picked them up. Snapshots, softened at their edges by regular handling. A woman and two young children.

'Wife and kids?' Siobhan guessed.

'Where do you think they were taken?'

'Not Scotland.'

No, because of the background: the plaster-white walls of an apartment, window looking out across the roofs of a city. Rebus got the sense of a hot country, cloudless deep blue sky. The kids looked bemused; one had his fingers in his mouth. The woman and her daughter were smiling, arms around one another.

'Someone might recognise them, I suppose,' Siobhan offered.

'They might not have to,' Rebus stated. 'This is a council flat, remember?'

'Meaning the council will know who he was?'

Rebus nodded. 'First thing we need to do is fingerprint this place, make sure we're not jumping to conclusions. Then it'll be down to the council to give us a name.'

'And does any of that get us nearer to finding the killer?'

Rebus shrugged. 'Whoever did it, they went home covered in blood. No way they walked through Knoxland without being noticed.' He paused. 'Which doesn't mean anyone's going to come forward.'

'He might be a murderer, but he's *their* murderer?' Siobhan guessed.

'Either that or they could just be scared of him. Plenty of hard cases in Knoxland.'

'So we're no further forward.'

Rebus held up one of the photos. 'What do you see?' he asked.

'A family.'

Rebus shook his head. 'You see a widow, and two kids who'll never see their dad again. They're the ones we should be thinking of, not ourselves.'

Siobhan nodded her agreement. 'I suppose we could always go public with the photos.'

'I was thinking the same thing. I even think I know the man for the job.'

'Steve Holly?'

'The paper he writes for might be a rag, but plenty of people read it.' He looked around. 'Seen enough?' Siobhan nodded again. 'Then let's go tell Shug Davidson what we've found . . .'

Davidson got on the phone to the fingerprints team, and Rebus persuaded him to let him keep one of the photos, to be passed on to the media.

'Can't do any harm,' was Davidson's unenthusiastic reaction. He was lifted, however, by the realisation that Council Housing would have a name on the tenancy agreement.

'And by the way,' Rebus said, 'however much is in the budget, it just dropped by a pound.' He gestured towards Siobhan. 'Had to put money in the meter.'

Davidson smiled, reached into his pocket, and produced a couple of coins. 'There you go, Shiv. Get yourself a drink with the change.'

'What about me?' Rebus complained. 'Is this sex discrimination or what?'

'You, John, are about to hand an exclusive to Steve Holly. If he doesn't buy you a few beers on the back of that, he should be run out of the profession . . .'

As Rebus drove out of the estate, he suddenly remembered something. He called Siobhan on her mobile. She, too, was heading into town.

'I'll probably be seeing Holly at the pub,' he said, 'if you fancy tagging along.'

'Tempting as that offer sounds, I have to be elsewhere. But thanks for asking.'

'It wasn't why I called . . . You don't fancy nipping back to the victim's flat?'

'No.' She was silent for a moment, then it dawned on her. 'You promised you'd take that torch back!'

'Instead of which, it's lying on the worktop in the kitchen.'

'Phone Davidson or Wylie.'

Rebus wrinkled his nose. 'Ach, it can wait. I mean, what's going to happen to it – lying out in the open in an empty flat with a broken-down door? I'm sure they're all honest, God-fearing souls . . .'

'You're really hoping it'll go walkies, aren't you?' He could almost hear her grinning. 'Just to see what they do about it.'

'What do you reckon: dawn raid, streaming down my hall looking for something they can replace it with?'

'There's an evil streak in you, John Rebus.'

'Of course there is – no reason for me to be different from anyone else.'

He ended the call, drove to the Oxford Bar, where he slowly sank a single pint of Deuchar's, using it to wash down the last corned-beef-and-beetroot roll on the shelf. Harry the barman asked him if he knew anything about the satanic ritual.

'What satanic ritual?'

'The one in Fleshmarket Close. Some kind of coven . . .'

'Christ, Harry, do you believe every story you get told in here?' Harry tried not to look disappointed. 'But the baby's skeleton . . .'

'Fake . . . planted there.'

'Why would anybody do that?'

Rebus sought out an answer. 'Maybe you're right, Harry – could've been the barman, selling his soul to the devil.'

The corner of Harry's mouth twitched. 'Reckon mine would be worth doing a deal on?'

'Not a snowball's chance in hell,' Rebus said, lifting the pint to his mouth. He was thinking of Siobhan's *I have to be elsewhere.* Probably meant she was planning to pin down Dr Curt. Rebus took out his phone, checking that there was enough of a signal for him to make a call. He had the reporter's number in his wallet. Holly picked up straight away.

'DI Rebus, an unexpected pleasure . . .' Meaning he had caller ID, and was in company, letting whoever he was with know the sort of person who might call him out of the blue, wanting them to be impressed . . .

'Sorry to interrupt you when you're in a meeting with your editor,' Rebus said. The phone was silent for a few moments, and Rebus allowed himself a nice big smile. Holly seemed to be apologising, stepping out of whatever room he was in. His voice became a hushed hiss.

'Am I being watched, is that it?'

'Oh aye, Steve, you're right up there with those Watergate reporters.' Rebus paused. 'I just took a guess, that's all.'

'Yeah?' Holly sounded far from convinced.

'Look, I've got something for you, but it can wait till you've had that paranoia seen to.'

'Whoah, hang on . . . what is it?'

'The Knoxland victim, we found a photo belonging to him – looks like he had a wife and kids.'

'And you're giving it to the press?'

'At the moment, you're the only one it's being offered to. If you

61

want it, it's yours to print just as soon as forensics confirm it belonged to the victim.'

'Why me?'

'You want the truth? Because an exclusive means more coverage, a bigger splash, front page hopefully . . .'

'No promises,' Holly was quick to say. 'And how long afterwards does everyone else get it?'

'Twenty-four hours.'

The reporter seemed to mull this over. 'Again I have to ask: why me?'

It's not you, Rebus wanted to say – it's your paper, or more precisely, your paper's circulation figure. *That's* who's getting the photo, the story . . . Instead, he kept silent, and heard Holly exhale noisily.

'Okay, fine. I'm in Glasgow: can you bike it over to me?'

'I'll leave it behind the bar in the Ox – you can come and fetch it. By the way, there'll also be a tab for you to pay.'

'Naturally.'

'Bye, then.' Rebus flipped his phone closed and busied himself lighting a cigarette. Of course Holly would take the photo – because if he turned it down and the competition didn't, he'd have to answer to his boss.

'Another?' Harry was asking. Well, the man already had the gleaming glass in his hand, ready to commence filling it. How could Rebus refuse without causing offence?

5

'From a cursory examination of the female skeleton, I'd say it's quite old.'

'Cursory?'

Dr Curt fidgeted in his chair. They were seated in his office in the university's medical faculty, tucked away in a courtyard behind the McEwan Hall. Every now and then – usually when they were in a bar together – Rebus would remind Siobhan that many of Edinburgh's grand buildings – the Usher Hall and McEwan Hall predominantly – had been built by brewing dynasties, and that this would not have been possible without drinkers like him.

'Cursory?' she repeated into the silence. Curt made show of straightening some of the pens on his desk.

'Well, it wasn't as if I could ask for help . . . It's a teaching skeleton of some kind, Siobhan.'

'But it *is* real?'

'Very much so. In less squeamish times than our own, medical teaching had to depend on such things.'

'You don't any more?'

He shook his head. 'New technologies have replaced many of the old ways.' He sounded almost wistful.

'So that skull's not real then?' She meant the skull on the shelf behind him, resting on green felt in a wood-and-glass box.

'Oh, it's authentic enough. Once belonged to the anatomist Dr Robert Knox.'

'The one who was in cahoots with the body-snatchers?'

Curt winced. '*He* did not aid *them*; *they* destroyed *him*.'

'Okay, so real skeletons were used as teaching aids . . .' Siobhan saw that Curt's mind was now preoccupied with his predecessor. 'How long ago did that practice end?'

'Probably five or ten years back, but we held on to some of the . . . specimens for a while longer.'

'And is our mystery woman one of your specimens?'

Curt's mouth opened, but nothing came out.

'A simple yes or no will do,' Siobhan pressed.

'I can offer neither . . . I simply can't be sure.'

'Well, how were they disposed of?'

'Look, Siobhan . . .'

'What is it that's bothering you, Doctor?'

He stared at her, and seemed to come to a decision. He rested his arms on the desk in front of him, hands clasped. 'Four years ago . . . you probably won't remember . . . some body parts were found in the city.'

'Body parts?'

'A hand here, a foot there . . . When tested, it turned out they'd been preserved in formaldehyde.'

Siobhan nodded slowly. 'I remember hearing about it.'

'Turned out they'd been taken from one of the labs as a practical joke. Not that anyone was caught, but we got a lot of unnecessary press attention as well as various firm rebukes from everyone from the Vice-Chancellor down.'

'I don't see the connection.'

Curt held up a hand. 'Two years passed, and then an exhibit went missing from the hallway outside Professor Gates's office . . .'

'A female skeleton?'

It was Curt's turn to nod. 'I'm sorry to say, we hushed it up. It was at a time when we were disposing of a lot of old teaching aids . . .' He glanced up at her, before returning his gaze to his arrangement of pens. 'At that time, I think we may have thrown out some plastic skeletons.'

'Including one of an infant?'

'Yes.'

'You told me no exhibits had gone missing.' He offered only a shrug. 'You lied to me, Doctor.'

'*Mea culpa*, Siobhan.'

She thought for a moment, rubbed the bridge of her nose. 'I'm still not sure I'm getting this. Why was the female skeleton kept as an exhibit?'

Curt fidgeted again. 'Because one of Professor Gates's predecessors decided on it. Her name was Mag Lennox. You've heard of her?'

Siobhan shook her head. 'Mag Lennox was reputed to be a witch – this was two hundred and fifty years ago. She was killed by the citizens, who didn't want her buried afterwards – something about being fearful she'd climb out of the coffin. Her body was allowed to rot, and those who had an interest were free to study the remains, looking for signs of the devil, I suppose. Alexander Monro eventually came to own the skeleton and bequeathed it to the medical school.'

'And then someone stole it, and you kept it quiet?'

Curt shrugged and angled his head back, looking towards the ceiling.

'Any idea who did it?' she asked.

'Oh, we had ideas . . . Medical students are renowned for their black humour. The story was, it graced the living room of a shared flat. We arranged for someone to investigate . . .' He looked at her. 'Investigate *privately*, you understand . . .'

'A private eye? Dear me, Doctor.' She shook her head, disappointed at his choice of action.

'No such item was found. Of course, they could simply have disposed of it . . .'

'By burying it in Fleshmarket Close?'

Curt shrugged. Such a reticent man, a scrupulous man . . . Siobhan could see that this conversation was causing him almost physical pain. 'What were their names?'

'Two young men, almost inseparable . . . Alfred McAteer and Alexis Cater. I think they modelled themselves on the characters from the TV show *MASH*. Do you know it?'

Siobhan nodded. 'Are they still students here?'

'Based out at the Infirmary these days, God help us all.'

'Alexis Cater . . . any relation?'

'His son, apparently.'

Siobhan's lips formed an O. Gordon Cater was one of the few Scottish actors of his generation to have made it in Hollywood. Character parts mostly, but in profitable blockbusters. There was talk that at one time he'd been first choice to play James Bond after Roger Moore, only to be beaten by Timothy Dalton. A hellraiser in his day, and an actor most women would have watched however bad the film.

'I take it you're a fan,' Curt muttered. 'We tried to keep it quiet that Alexis was studying here. He's the son from Gordon's second or third marriage.'

'And you think he stole Mag Lennox?'

65

'He was among the suspects. You see why we didn't make the investigation official?'

'You mean other than the fact that it'd have made you and the Prof look irresponsible all over again?' Siobhan smiled at Curt's discomfort. As if irritated by them, Curt suddenly snatched up the pens and threw them into a drawer.

'Is that you channelling your aggression, Doctor?'

Curt stared at her bleakly and sighed. 'There's just one more potential fly in the ointment. Some sort of local historian . . . apparently she's been on to the papers saying she thinks there's a supernatural explanation for the Fleshmarket Close skeletons.'

'Supernatural?'

'During excavations at the Palace of Holyrood a while back, some skeletons were unearthed . . . there were theories they'd been sacrificed.'

'Who by? Mary, Queen of Scots?'

'However that may be, this "historian" is trying to link them to Fleshmarket Close . . . It may be pertinent that she has worked in the past for one of the High Street's ghost tours.'

Siobhan had been on one of these. Several companies operated walking tours of the Royal Mile and its alleyways, mixing gory storytelling with lighter moments and special effects which would not have disgraced a fairground ghost-train.

'So she has an ulterior motive?'

'I can only speculate.' Curt checked his watch. 'The evening paper may have printed some of her tripe.'

'You've had dealings with her before?'

'She wanted to know what had happened to Mag Lennox. We told her it was none of her concern. She tried to get the newspapers interested . . .' Curt waved a hand in front of him, brushing away the memory.

'What's her name?'

'Judith Lennox . . . and yes, she does claim to be a descendant.'

Siobhan wrote the name down, below those of Alfred McAteer and Alexis Cater. After a moment, she added a further name – Mag Lennox – and connected it to Judith Lennox with an arrow.

'Is my ordeal drawing to its conclusion?' Curt drawled.

'I think so,' Siobhan said. She tapped her teeth with the pen. 'So what are you going to do with Mag's skeleton?'

The pathologist shrugged. 'She seems to have come home again, doesn't she? Maybe we'll put her back in her case.'

'Have you told the Prof yet?'

'I sent him an e-mail this afternoon.'

'An e-mail? He's twenty yards down the hall . . .'

'Nevertheless, that's what I did.' Curt started to rise to his feet.

'You're scared of him, aren't you?' Siobhan teased.

Curt did not grace this remark with a reply. He held the door open for her, head bowed slightly. Maybe it was old-fashioned manners, Siobhan thought. More likely, he just didn't want to meet her eyes.

Her route home took her down George IV Bridge. She turned right at the lights, deciding on a brief detour down the High Street. There were sandwich boards outside St Giles Cathedral, advertising that evening's ghost tours. They wouldn't start for a couple of hours yet, but tourists were already perusing them. Further down, outside the old Tron Kirk, more sandwich boards, more enticements to experience 'Edinburgh's haunted past'. Siobhan was more concerned with its haunted present. She glanced down Fleshmarket Close: no sign of life. But wouldn't the tour guides love to be able to add it to their itineraries? On Broughton Street, she stopped kerbside and went into a local shop, emerging with a bag of groceries and the final printing of the evening paper. Her flat was nearby: no parking spaces left in the residents' zone, but she left her Peugeot on a yellow line, confident that she'd move it before the enforcers started their morning shift.

Her flat was in a shared four-storey tenement. She was lucky with her neighbours: no all-night parties or aspiring rock drummers. She knew a few of their faces, but none of their names. Edinburgh didn't expect you to have anything more than a passing acquaintance with your neighbours, unless there was some shared problem to be worked out, like a leaky roof or cracked guttering. She thought of Knoxland with its paper-thin dividing walls, letting everyone hear everyone else. Someone in the tenement kept cats: this was her only complaint. She could smell them on the stairwell. But once inside her flat, the world outside melted away.

She put the tub of ice cream in the freezer, the milk in the fridge. Unwrapped the ready meal and popped it in the microwave. It was low-fat, which would atone for the later possibility of an urge to gorge on chocolate mint-chip. There was a bottle of wine on the draining board. Re-corked with a couple of glasses missing. She poured some out, tasted it, decided it wasn't going to poison her. She sat down with the paper, waiting for her dinner to heat up. She almost never cooked anything from scratch, not when she was eating alone. Sitting at the table, she was aware that the few pounds she had gained recently were telling her to loosen her trousers. Her blouse, too, was tight under the arms. She got up from the table and returned a couple of minutes later, in slippers and dressing gown. The food was done, so she took it through to the living room on a tray with her glass and the paper.

Judith Lennox had made it to the inside pages. There was a photo of her at the entrance to Fleshmarket Close, probably taken that afternoon. Head and shoulders, showing voluminous dark curly hair and a bright scarf. Siobhan didn't know what look she'd been trying for, but her lips and eyes said only one thing: smug. Loving the camera's attention and ready to strike any pose asked of her. Alongside was another posed shot, this time of Ray Mangold, arms folded proprietorially as he stood outside the Warlock.

There was a smaller photo of the archaeological site in the grounds of Holyrood, where the other skeletons had been uncovered. Someone from Historic Scotland had been interviewed, and threw scorn on Lennox's suggestion that there was anything ritualistic about those deaths, or about the manner in which the bodies had been laid out. But this was in the story's final paragraph, most prominence being given to Lennox's claim that whether the Fleshmarket skeletons were real or not, it was possible that they had been placed in the same positions as those in Holyrood, and that someone had been mimicking those earlier burials. Siobhan snorted and went on eating. She flicked through the rest of the paper, spending most time on the TV page. It became clear to her that there were no programmes to keep her occupied until bed, meaning music and a book instead. She checked her telephone for nonexistent messages, started recharging her mobile, and brought book and duvet through from the bedroom. John Martyn on the CD player: Rebus had loaned her the album. She wondered how he would be spending his evening: in the pub with Steve Holly maybe; either that or in the pub by himself. Well, she'd have a quiet night in, and be the better for it in the morning. She decided she would read two chapters before laying assault to the ice cream . . .

When she woke up, her phone was ringing. She stumbled from the sofa and picked it up.

'Hello?'

'Didn't wake you, did I?' It was Rebus.

'What time is it?' She tried to focus on her watch.

'Half past eleven. Sorry if you were in bed . . .'

'I wasn't. So where's the fire?'

'Not a fire exactly; more a bit of smouldering. The couple whose daughter's walked out . . .'

'What about them?'

'They've been asking for you.'

She rubbed a hand over her face. 'I'm not sure I understand.'

'They were picked up in Leith.'

'Arrested, you mean?'

'Hassling some of the street girls. The mother was hysterical . . . Taken to Leith cop-shop to make sure she was all right.'

'And how do you know all this?'

'Leith phoned here, looking for you.'

Siobhan frowned. 'You're still at Gayfield Square?'

'It's nice when it's quiet – I can have any desk I want.'

'You've got to go home some time.'

'Actually, I was just on my way when the call came.' He chuckled. 'Know what Tibbet's up to? Nothing on his computer but train timetables.'

'So what you're actually doing is snooping on the rest of us?'

'My way of getting acquainted with new surroundings, Shiv. Do you want me to come pick you up, or will I meet you at Leith?'

'I thought you were on your way home.'

'This sounds a lot more entertaining.'

'Then I'll meet you at Leith.'

Siobhan put down the phone and went into the bathroom to get dressed. The remaining half-tub of choc mint-chip had turned liquid, but she put it back in the freezer.

Leith police station was situated on Constitution Street. It was a glum stone building, hard-faced like its surroundings. Leith, once a prosperous shipping port, with a personality distinct from that of the city, had seen hard times in the past few decades: industrial decline, the drugs culture, prostitution. Parts of it had been redeveloped, and others tidied up. Newcomers were moving in, and didn't want the old, sullied Leith. Siobhan thought it would be a pity if the area's character was lost; then again, she didn't have to live there . . .

Leith had for many years provided a 'tolerance zone' for prostitutes. It wasn't that police turned a blind eye, but they wouldn't go out of their way to interfere either. But this had come to an end, and the street-walkers had been scattered, leading to more instances of violence against them. A few had tried to move back to their old haunt, while others headed out along Salamander

Street or up Leith Walk to the city centre. Siobhan thought she knew what the Jardines had been up to; all the same, she wanted to hear it from them.

Rebus was waiting for her in the reception area. He looked tired, but then he always looked tired: dark bags under his eyes, hair unkempt. She knew he wore the same suit all week, then had it dry-cleaned each Saturday. He was chatting with the Duty Officer, but broke off when he saw her. The Duty Officer buzzed them through a locked door, which Rebus held open for her.

'They've not been arrested or anything,' he stressed. 'Just brought in for a chat. They're in here . . .' 'Here' being IR1 – Interview Room 1. It was a cramped, windowless space boasting a table and two chairs. John and Alice Jardine sat opposite one another, arms reaching out so they could hold hands. There were two drained mugs on the table. When the door opened, Alice flew to her feet, tipping one of them over.

'You can't keep us here all night!' She broke off, mouth open, when she saw Siobhan. Her face lost some of its tension, while her husband smiled sheepishly, placing the mug upright again.

'Sorry to drag you down here,' John Jardine said. 'We thought maybe if we mentioned your name, they'd just let us go.'

'As far as I'm aware, John, you're not being held. This is DI Rebus, by the way.'

There were nodded greetings. Alice Jardine had sat down again. Siobhan stood next to the table, arms folded.

'Way I hear it, you've been terrorising the honest, hard-working ladies of Leith.'

'We were just asking questions,' Alice remonstrated.

'Sadly, they don't make any money from chit-chat,' Rebus informed the couple.

'It was Glasgow last night,' John Jardine said quietly. 'That seemed to go all right . . .'

Siobhan and Rebus shared a look. 'And all this because Susie told you Ishbel had been seeing a man who looked like a pimp?' Siobhan asked. 'Look, let me fill you in on something. The girls in Leith might have a drug habit, but that's all they're supporting – no pimps like the ones you see in the Hollywood films.'

'Older men,' John Jardine said, eyes on the tabletop. 'They get hold of girls like Ishbel and exploit them. You read about it all the time.'

'Then you're reading the wrong papers,' Rebus informed them.

'It was my idea,' Alice Jardine added. 'I just thought . . .'

'What made you lose your rag?' Siobhan asked.

'Two nights of trying to get hookers to talk to us,' John Jardine explained. But Alice was shaking her head.

'This is Siobhan we're talking to,' she chided him. Then, to Siobhan: 'The last woman we spoke to . . . she said she thought Ishbel might be . . . I need to think of her exact words . . .'

John Jardine helped her out. '"Up the pubic triangle",' he said.

His wife nodded to herself. 'And when we asked her what that meant, she just started laughing . . . told us to go home. That's when I lost my temper.'

'Police car happened to be passing,' her husband added with a shrug. 'They brought us here. I'm sorry we're being a nuisance, Siobhan.'

'You're not,' Siobhan assured him, only half believing her own words.

Rebus had slipped his hands into his pockets. 'The pubic triangle's just off Lothian Road: lap-dancing bars, sex shops . . .'

Siobhan gave him a warning look, but too late.

'Maybe that's where she is then,' Alice said, voice trembling with emotion. She gripped the edge of the table as though about to stand up and be on her way.

'Wait a second.' Siobhan held up a hand. 'One woman tells you – probably jokingly – that Ishbel *might* be working as a lap-dancer . . . and you're just going to go barging in?'

'Why not?' Alice asked.

Rebus gave her the answer: 'Some of those places, Mrs Jardine, they're not always run by the most scrupulous individuals. Unlikely to be the patient types either, when someone comes nosing around . . .'

John Jardine was nodding.

'Might help,' Rebus added, 'if there was one particular establishment the young lady was thinking of . . .'

'Always supposing she wasn't just winding you up,' Siobhan warned.

'One way to find out,' Rebus said. Siobhan turned to face him. 'Your car or mine?'

They took hers, the Jardines in the back seat. They hadn't gone far when John Jardine indicated that the 'young lady' had been standing across the road, against the wall of a disused warehouse. There was no sign of her now, though one of her colleagues was pacing the pavement, shoulders hunched against the cold.

'We'll give it ten minutes,' Rebus said. 'Not many punters about tonight. With luck she'll be back soon.'

So Siobhan drove out along Seafield Road, all the way to the Portobello roundabout, turning right at Inchview Terrace and right again at Craigentinny Avenue. These were quiet residential streets. The lights in most of the bungalows were off, owners tucked up in bed.

'I like driving this time of night,' Rebus said conversationally.

Mr Jardine seemed to agree. 'Place is completely different when there's no traffic about. Bit more relaxed.'

Rebus nodded. 'Plus it's easier to spot the predators . . .'

The back seat went quiet after that, until they were back in Leith. 'There she is,' John Jardine said.

Skinny, short black hair, most of it blowing into her eyes with each gust of wind. She wore knee-length boots and a black mini-skirt with a buttoned denim jacket. No make-up, face pallid. Even from this distance, bruises were visible on her legs.

'Know her?' Siobhan asked.

Rebus shook his head. 'Looks like the new kid in town. That other one . . .' meaning the woman they'd passed earlier, 'can't be more than twenty feet away, but they're not talking.'

Siobhan nodded. Having nothing else, the city's street-walkers often showed solidarity with each other, but not here. Which meant that the older woman felt her pitch had been invaded by the incomer. Having driven past, Siobhan did a three-point turn and drew up next to the kerb. Rebus had wound his window down. The prostitute stepped forward, wary of the number of people in the car.

'No group stuff,' she said. Then she recognised the faces in the back. 'Christ, not you two again.' She turned and started to walk away. Rebus got out of the car and grabbed her arm, spinning her round. His ID was open in his other hand.

'CID,' he said. 'What's your name?'

'Cheyanne.' She raised her chin. 'Not that I *am* shy.' Trying to sound tougher than she was.

'And that's your patter, is it?' Rebus said, sounding unconvinced. 'How long've you been in town?'

'Long enough.'

'Is that a Brummie accent?'

'None of your business.'

'I could make it my business. Might need to check your real age, for one thing . . .'

'I'm eighteen!'

Rebus ploughed on as though she hadn't spoken. 'That would mean looking at your birth certificate, which would mean talking to your parents.' He paused. 'Or you could help us out. These people have lost their daughter.' He nodded towards the car and its occupants. 'She's done a runner.'

'Good luck to her.' Sounding sulky.

'But *her* parents care about her . . . maybe like you wish yours did.' He paused to let this sink in, studying her without seeming to: no apparent signs of recent drug use, but maybe that was because she hadn't made enough money yet for a hit. 'But this is your lucky night,' he continued, 'because you might be able to help them . . . always supposing you weren't spinning them a line about the pubic triangle.'

'All I know is, a few new girls have been hired.'

'Where exactly?'

'The Nook. I know 'cos I went asking . . . said I was too skinny.'

Rebus turned towards the back seat of the car. The Jardines had wound down their window. 'Did you show Cheyanne a picture of Ishbel?' Alice Jardine nodded, and Rebus turned back to the girl, whose attention was already wandering. She looked to left and right, as if for potential clients. The woman further along was pretending to ignore everything but the roadway in front of her.

'Did you recognise her?' he asked Cheyanne.

'Who?' Still not looking at him.

'The girl in the picture.'

She shook her head briskly, then had to push the hair out of her eyes.

'Not much of a career this, is it?' Rebus said.

'It'll do me for now.' She tried burrowing her hands into the tight pockets of her jacket.

'Is there anything else you can tell us? Anything that might help Ishbel?'

Cheyanne shook her head again, eyes focused on the road ahead. 'Just . . . sorry about earlier. Don't know what got me laughing . . . happens sometimes.'

'Look after yourself,' John Jardine called from the back seat. His wife was holding their photograph of Ishbel out of the window.

'If you see her . . .' she said, the words trailing off.

Cheyanne nodded, and even accepted one of Rebus's business cards. He got back into the car and closed the door. Siobhan signalled out into the road and took her foot off the brake.

'Where are you parked?' she asked the Jardines. They named a

73

street at the other end of Leith, so she did another turn, taking them past Cheyanne again. The girl ignored them. The woman further along stared at them though. She was walking towards Cheyanne, ready to ask what had just happened.

'Could be the beginning of a beautiful friendship,' Rebus mused, folding his arms. Siobhan wasn't listening. She stared into her rearview mirror.

'You're not to go there, understood?'

No one answered.

'Best if myself and DI Rebus intercede on your behalf. That is, if DI Rebus is willing.'

'Me? Go to a lap-dancing bar?' Rebus tried for a pout. 'Well, if you really think it necessary, DS Clarke . . .'

'We'll go tomorrow then,' Siobhan said. 'Some time *before* opening.' Only now did she look at him.

And smiled.

DAY THREE

Wednesday

6

Detective Constable Colin Tibbet arrived at work next morning to find that someone had placed a toy locomotive on his mouse pad. The mouse itself had been disconnected and placed in one of his desk drawers . . . a locked drawer at that – locked when he'd left work the previous evening, and needing to be unlocked this morning . . . yet somehow containing his mouse. He stared at Siobhan Clarke, and was about to speak when she silenced him with a shake of her head.

'Whatever it is,' she said, 'it can wait. I'm out of here.'

And so she was. She'd been coming out of the DI's office when Tibbet had arrived. Tibbet had heard Derek Starr's closing words: 'A day or two, Siobhan, no more than that . . .' Tibbet presumed it had something to do with Fleshmarket Close, but he couldn't guess what. One thing he did know: Siobhan knew that he'd been studying train timetables. This made her the chief suspect. But there were other possibilities: Phyllida Hawes herself was not above the odd practical joke. The same could be said of DC Paddy Connolly and DC Tommy Daniels. Might DCI Macrae have decided on a schoolboy prank? Or what about the man sipping coffee at the little foldaway table in the corner? Tibbet really only knew Rebus by reputation, but that reputation was formidable. Hawes had warned him not to be star-struck.

'Rule number one with Rebus,' she'd said: 'you don't lend him money and you don't buy him drinks.'

'Isn't that two rules?' he'd asked.

'Not necessarily . . . both are likely to happen in pubs.'

This morning, Rebus looked innocent enough: sleepy eyes and a patch of grey bristle on his throat which the razor had missed. He wore a tie the way some schoolkids did – on sufferance. Each morning, he seemed to come into work whistling some irritating hook-line from an old pop song. By mid-morning, he'd have stopped doing it, but by then it was too late: Tibbet would be whistling it for him, unable to escape the pernicious chorus.

Rebus heard Tibbet hum the opening few bars of 'Wichita Linesman' and tried not to smile. His work here was done. He got up from the table, slipping his jacket back on.

'Got to be somewhere,' he said.

'Oh?'

'Nice train,' Rebus commented, nodding towards the green locomotive. 'Hobby of yours?'

'Present from one of my nephews,' Tibbet lied.

Rebus nodded, quietly impressed. Tibbet's face gave nothing away. The lad was quick-thinking and plausible: both useful skills in a detective.

'Well, I'll see you later,' Rebus said.

'And if anyone wants you . . . ?' Angling for a bit more detail.

'Trust me, they won't.' He gave Tibbet a wink and left the office.

DCI Macrae was in the hall, clutching paperwork and on his way to a meeting.

'Where are you off to, John?'

'Knoxland case, sir. For some reason, I seem to have become useful.'

'Despite your best efforts, I'm sure.'

'Absolutely.'

'On you go then, but don't forget: you're *ours*, not theirs. Anything happens here, we can have you back in a minute.'

'Try and keep me away, sir,' Rebus said, searching in his pockets for his car keys and heading for the exit.

He was in the car park when his mobile sounded. It was Shug Davidson.

'Seen the paper today, John?'

'Anything I should know about?'

'You might want to see what your friend Steve Holly has been saying about us.'

Rebus's face tightened. 'I'll get back to you,' he said. Five minutes later, he was pulling over kerbside, lunging into a newsagent's. He pored over newsprint in the driver's seat. Holly had printed the photo, but had surrounded it with an article on the sharper practices of bogus asylum-seekers. Mention was made of suspected terrorists who'd entered Britain as refugees. There was anecdotal evidence of spongers and charlatans, along with quotes from Knoxland residents. The message given was twofold: Britain is a soft target, and we can't allow the situation to continue.

In the middle of which, the photo looked like nothing more than window-dressing.

Rebus called Holly on his mobile, but got an answering service. After a slew of judicious swear-words, he hung up.

He drove to the council housing department on Waterloo Place, where he'd arranged to meet with a Mrs Mackenzie. She was a small, bustling woman in her fifties. Shug Davidson had already faxed her his official request for information, but she still wasn't happy.

'It's a matter of privacy,' she told Rebus. 'There are all sorts of rules and restrictions these days.' She was leading him through an open-plan office.

'I don't suppose the deceased will complain, Mrs Mackenzie, especially if we catch his killer.'

'Well, all the same . . .' She had brought them into a tiny glass-walled compartment, which Rebus realised was her office.

'And I thought the walls out at Knoxland were thin.' He tapped the glass. She was shifting paperwork from a chair, gesturing for him to sit. Then she squeezed around the desk and sat in her own chair, putting on a pair of half-moon spectacles and sifting through paperwork.

Rebus didn't think charm was going to work with this woman. Maybe just as well, since he'd never scored high marks in those tests. He decided to appeal to her professionalism.

'Look, Mrs Mackenzie, we both like to see that whatever job we're doing is done properly.' She peered at him over her glasses. 'My job today happens to be a murder inquiry. We can't begin that inquiry properly until we know who the victim was. A fingerprint match came through first thing this morning: the victim was definitely your tenant . . .'

'Well, you see, Inspector, that's just my problem. The poor man who died was *not* one of my tenants.'

Rebus frowned. 'I don't understand.' She handed him a sheet of paper.

'Here are the tenant's details. I believe your victim was Asian or similar. Is he likely to have been called Robert Baird?'

Rebus's eyes were fixed to that name. The flat number was right . . . right tower block, too. Robert Baird was listed as the tenant.

'He must have moved.'

Mackenzie was shaking her head. 'These records are up-to-date. The last rent money we received was only last week. It was paid by Mr Baird.'

'You're thinking he sub-let?'

A broad smile lightened Mrs Mackenzie's face. 'Which is strictly forbidden by the tenancy agreement,' she said.

'But people do it?'

'Of course they do. The thing is, I decided to do some sleuthing myself . . .' She sounded pleased with herself. Rebus leaned forward in his chair, warming to her.

'Do tell,' he said.

'I checked with the city's other housing areas. There are several Robert Bairds on the list. Plus other forenames, all with the surname Baird.'

'Some of them could be genuine,' Rebus said, playing devil's advocate.

'And some of them not.'

'You think this guy Baird's been applying for council housing on a grand scale?'

She shrugged. 'There's only one way to be sure . . .'

The first address they tried was a tower block in Dumbiedykes, near Rebus's old police station. The woman who answered the door looked African. There were little kids scurrying around behind her.

'We're looking for Mr Baird,' Mackenzie said. The woman just shook her head. Mackenzie repeated the name.

'The man you pay rent to,' Rebus added. The woman kept shaking her head, closing the door slowly but purposefully on them.

'I think we're getting somewhere,' Mackenzie said. 'Come on.'

Out of the car, she was brisk and businesslike, but in the passenger seat she relaxed, asking Rebus about his job, where he lived, whether he was married.

'Separated,' he told her. 'Long time back. How about you?'

She held up a hand to show him her wedding ring.

'But sometimes women just wear one so they get less hassle,' he said.

She snorted. 'And I thought *I* had a suspicious mind.'

'Goes with both our jobs, I suppose.'

She gave a sigh. 'My job would be a hell of a lot easier without them.'

'Immigrants, you mean?'

She nodded. 'I look into their eyes sometimes, and I get a glimpse of what they've gone through to get here.' She paused. 'And all I can offer them are places like Knoxland . . .'

'Better than nothing,' Rebus said.

'I hope so . . .'

Their next stop was a block of flats in Leith. The lifts were out of order, so they'd to climb four storeys, Mackenzie powering ahead in her noisy shoes. Rebus took a moment to catch his breath, then nodded to let her know she could knock on the door. A male answered. He was swarthy and unshaven, wearing a white vest and jogging bottoms. He was running fingers through thick dark hair.

'Who the fuck are you?' he said, in heavily accented English.

'That's some elocution teacher you've got,' Rebus said, voice hardening to match the man's. The man stared at him, not understanding.

Mackenzie turned to Rebus. 'Slavic maybe? East European?' She turned to the man. 'Where are you from?'

'Fuck you,' the man replied. There seemed little malice in it; he was trying the words out either to note their effect or because they'd worked for him in the past.

'Robert Baird,' Rebus said. 'You know him?' The man's eyes narrowed, and Rebus repeated the name. 'You pay him money.' He rubbed his thumb and fingers together, hoping the man might understand. Instead, he grew agitated.

'Fuck off *now*!'

'We're not asking you for money,' Rebus tried to explain. 'We're looking for Robert Baird. This is his flat.' Rebus pointed to the interior.

'Landlord,' Mackenzie tried, but it was no good. The man's face was twitching; sweat was beginning to break out on his forehead.

'No problem,' Rebus told him, holding his hands up, showing the man his palms – hoping maybe this sign would get through to him. Suddenly he noticed another figure in the shadows down the hallway. 'You speak English?' he called.

The man turned his head, barked something guttural. But the figure kept coming forward, until Rebus could see that it was a teenage boy.

'Speak English?' he repeated.

'Little,' the lad admitted. He was skinny and handsome, dressed in a short-sleeved blue shirt and denims.

'You're immigrants?' Rebus asked.

'Here our country,' the boy stated defensively.

'Don't worry, son, we're not from Immigration. You pay money to live here, don't you?'

'We pay, yes.'

'The man you give the money to – he's the one we'd like to talk to.'

The boy translated some of this for his father. The father stared at Rebus and shook his head.

'Tell your dad,' Rebus told the boy, 'that a visit from the Immigration Service can be arranged, if he'd rather talk to them.'

The boy's eyes widened in fear. The translation this time took longer. The man looked at Rebus again, this time with a kind of sad resignation, as if he were used to being kicked around by authority, but had been hoping for some respite. He muttered something, and the boy padded back down the hall. He returned with a folded piece of paper.

'He comes for money. If we have problem, we this . . .'

Rebus unfolded the note. A mobile phone number and a name: Gareth. Rebus showed the note to Mackenzie.

'Gareth Baird is one of the names on the list,' she said.

'Can't be that many of them in Edinburgh. Chances are it's the same one.' Rebus took the note back, wondering what effect a phone call would have. He saw that the man was trying to offer him something: a handful of cash.

'Is he trying to bribe us?' Rebus asked the boy. The son shook his head.

'He does not understand.' He spoke to his father again. The man mumbled something, then stared at Rebus, and immediately Rebus thought of what Mackenzie had said in the car. It was true: the eyes were eloquent of pain.

'This day,' the boy told Rebus. 'Money . . . this day.'

Rebus's eyes narrowed. 'Gareth is coming here today to collect the rent?'

The son checked with his father and then nodded.

'What time?' Rebus asked.

Another discussion. 'Maybe now . . . soon,' the boy translated. Rebus turned to Mackenzie. 'I can call a car to take you back to your office.'

'You're going to wait for him?'

'That's the plan.'

'If he's abusing his tenancy, I should be here, too.'

'Could be a long wait . . . I'll keep you in the picture. The

82

alternative is hanging around with me all day.' He shrugged, telling her it was her choice.

'You'll phone me?' she asked.

He nodded. 'Meantime, you could be following up some of those other addresses.'

She saw the sense in this. 'All right,' she said.

Rebus took out his mobile. 'I'll send for a patrol car.'

'What if that scares him off?'

'Good point . . . a taxi then.' He made the call, and she headed back downstairs, leaving Rebus facing father and son.

'I'm going to wait for Gareth,' he told them. Then he peered down their hall. 'Mind if I come in?'

'You are welcome,' the boy said. Rebus walked inside.

The flat needed decorating. Towels and strips of material had been pressed to the gaps in the window frames to minimise draughts. But there was furniture, and the place was tidy. One narrow element of the living room's gas fire was lit.

'Coffee?' the boy asked.

'Please,' Rebus answered. He gestured towards the sofa, requesting permission to sit. The father nodded, and Rebus sat down. Then he got up again to study the photographs on the mantelpiece. Three or four generations of the same family. Rebus turned to the father, smiling and nodding. The man's face softened a little. There wasn't much else in the room to attract Rebus's attention: no ornaments or books, no TV or stereo. There was a small portable radio on the floor by the father's chair. It was shrouded in sellotape, presumably to stop it falling apart. Rebus couldn't see an ashtray, so kept his cigarettes in his pocket. When the boy returned from the kitchen, Rebus accepted the tiny cup from him. There was no offer of milk. The drink was thick and black, and when Rebus took his first sip, he couldn't decide whether the jolt it gave him was caffeine or sugar. He nodded to let his hosts know it was good. They were staring at him as if he were an exhibit. He decided he would ask for the boy's name, and some of the family's history. But then his mobile rang. He muttered something resembling an apology as he answered it.

It was Siobhan.

'Anything earth-shattering to report?' she asked into her phone. She was sitting in some sort of waiting room. She hadn't expected to be able to see the doctors right away, but had anticipated an office or anteroom. Here, she was in with outpatients and visitors, noisy toddlers, and staff who ignored all outsiders as they purchased snacks from the two vending machines. Siobhan had spent a lot of time examining the contents of those machines. One boasted a limited range of sandwiches – triangles of thin white bread with mixtures of lettuce, tomato, tuna, ham and cheese. The other was more popular: crisps and chocolate. There was a drinks machine, too, but it bore the legend 'Out of Order'.

Once the lure of the machines had worn off, she'd perused the reading material on the coffee table – out-of-date women's mags with the pages just about hanging together, except where photos and offers had been torn out. There were a couple of kids' comics, too, but she was saving those for later. Instead, she'd started tidying up her phone, deleting unwanted text messages and call records. Then she'd texted a couple of friends. And finally she'd crumbled altogether and called Rebus.

'Mustn't grumble,' was all he said. 'What are you up to?'

'Hanging around the Infirmary. You?'

'Hanging about in Leith.'

'Anyone would think we didn't like Gayfield.'

'But we know they're wrong, don't we?'

She smiled at this. Another kid had come in, barely old enough to push open the door. He stood on tiptoe to feed coins into the chocolate machine, but then couldn't decide. He pressed nose and hands to the glass display, mesmerised.

'We still meeting up later on?' Siobhan asked.

'If not, I'll let you know.'

'Don't tell me you're expecting a better offer.'

'You never can tell. Did you see Steve Holly's rag this morning?'

'I only read grown-up newspapers. Did he print the photograph?'

'He did . . . and then he went to town on asylum-seekers.'

'Oh, hell.'

'So if any other poor sod ends up in the deep-freeze, we'll know who to blame.'

The waiting-room door was opening again. Siobhan thought it might be the child's mum, but instead it was the woman from the reception desk. She motioned for Siobhan to follow her.

'John, we're going to have to talk later.'

'You were the one who phoned me, remember?'

'Sorry, but it looks like I'm wanted.'

'And suddenly I'm not? Cheers, Siobhan.'

'I'll see you this afternoon . . .'

But Rebus had already hung up. Siobhan followed the reception-ist down first one corridor and then another, the woman walking briskly, so that there was no possibility of conversation between them. Finally she pointed to a door. Siobhan nodded her thanks, knocked and entered.

It was some sort of office: rows of shelves, a desk and computer. One white-coated doctor sat swivelling on the only chair. The other rested against the desk, arms stretched above his head. Both were good-looking and knew it.

'I'm Detective Sergeant Clarke,' Siobhan said, shaking the first one's hand.

'Alf McAteer,' he told her, his fingers brushing over hers. He turned to his colleague, who was rising from the chair. 'Isn't it a sign that you're getting old?' he asked.

'What?'

'When the police officers start getting more ravishing.'

The other one was grinning. He squeezed Siobhan's hand. 'I'm Alexis Cater. Don't worry about him, the Viagra's almost run its course.'

'Has it?' McAteer sounded horrified. 'Time for another prescrip-tion then.'

'Look,' Cater was telling Siobhan, 'if it's about that child porn on Alf's computer . . .'

Siobhan looked stern-faced. He angled his face into hers.

'Joking,' he said.

'Well,' she replied, 'we could take the pair of you down to the station . . . impound all your computers and software . . . might take a few days, of course.' She paused. 'And by the way, the police may be getting better-looking, but we're also given a sense-of-humour bypass on the first day at work . . .'

They stared at her, standing shoulder to shoulder, both leaning back against the edge of the desk.

'That's us told,' Cater told his friend.

'Well and truly,' McAteer agreed.

They were tall and slim, widening at the shoulders. Private schools and rugby, Siobhan guessed. Winter sports, too, judging by their tans. McAteer was the swarthier of the two: thick eyebrows, almost meeting in the middle, unruly black hair, face needing a shave. Cater was fair-haired like his father, though it looked to her as if he maybe dyed it. Already a touch of male-pattern baldness was showing. Same green eyes as his father, too, but otherwise there was little resemblance. Gordon Cater's easy charm had been replaced by something much less winning: an absolute confidence that Alexis was always going to be one of life's winners, not because of what he was, any qualities he might possess, but due to that lineage.

McAteer had turned to his friend. 'Must be those tapes of our Filipino maids . . .'

Cater slapped McAteer's shoulder, kept his eyes on Siobhan.

'We *are* curious,' he told her.

'Speak for yourself, sweetie,' McAteer said, affecting campness. In that instant, Siobhan saw the way their relationship worked: McAteer working constantly at it, almost like a king's fool of old, needy for Cater's patronage. Because Cater had the power: everyone would want to be *his* friend. He was a magnet for all the things McAteer craved, the invites and the girls. As if to reinforce this, Cater gave his friend a look, and McAteer made a show of zipping his mouth shut.

'What is it we can do for you?' Cater asked with almost exaggerated politeness. 'We've really only got a few minutes between patients . . .'

It was another shrewd move: reinforcing his credentials – I'm the son of a star, but in here, my job is helping people, saving lives. I am a necessity, and there's nothing you can do to change that . . .

'Mag Lennox,' Siobhan said.

'We're in the dark,' Cater said. He broke eye contact to cross one foot over the other.

'No you're not,' Siobhan told him. 'You stole her skeleton from the medical school.'

'Did we?'

'And now she's turned up again . . . buried in Fleshmarket Close.'

'I saw that story,' Cater said with the slightest of nods. 'Grisly sort of find, isn't it? I thought the article said it had something to do with raising the devil?'

Siobhan shook her head.

'Plenty of devils in this town, eh, Lex?' McAteer said.

Cater ignored him. 'So you think we took a skeleton from the medical school and buried it in a cellar?' He paused. 'Was it reported to police at the time . . . ? Only, I don't recall seeing *that* particular story. Surely the university would have alerted the proper authorities.' McAteer was nodding his assent.

'You know that didn't happen,' Siobhan said quietly. 'They were still in the mire for letting you walk out of the pathology lab with a selection of body parts.'

'These are serious allegations.' Cater offered a smile. 'Should my solicitor be present?'

'All I need to know is what you did with the skeletons.'

He stared at her, probably the same look which had discomfited many a young woman. Siobhan didn't even blink. He sniffed and took a deep breath.

'Just how major a crime is it to bury a museum piece beneath a pub?' He tried her with another smile, head sliding over to one side. 'Aren't there any drug-pushers or rapists you should be pursuing instead?'

The memory of Donny Cruikshank came to her, his scarred face no kind of recompense for his crime . . .

'You're not in trouble,' she said at last. 'Anything you tell me will be kept between us.'

'Like pillow talk?' McAteer couldn't help saying. His chuckle died at another look from Cater.

'That means we'd be doing you a favour, Detective Clarke. A favour that might need repaying.'

McAteer grinned at his friend's comment, but kept quiet.

'That would depend,' Siobhan said.

Cater leaned towards her a little. 'Come out for a drink with me tonight, I'll tell you then.'

'Tell me now.'

He shook his head, not taking his eyes off her. 'Tonight.'

McAteer looked disappointed: presumably some prior arrangement was about to be ditched.

'I don't think so,' Siobhan said.

Cater glanced at his wristwatch. 'We need to get back to the ward . . .' He held out his hand again. 'It was interesting meeting you. I bet we'd have had a lot to talk about . . .' When she stood her ground, refusing to take his hand, he raised an eyebrow. It was a favourite move of his father's, she'd seen it in half a dozen films. Slightly puzzled and let down . . .

'Just one drink,' she said.

'And two straws,' Cater added. His sense of his own powers was returning: she hadn't managed to turn him down. Another victory to chalk up.

'Opal Lounge at eight?' he suggested.

She shook her head. 'Oxford Bar at seven thirty.'

'I don't . . . Is it new?'

'Quite the opposite. Look it up in the phone book.' She opened the door to leave, but paused as if she'd just thought of something. 'And leave your jester in his box.' Nodding towards Alf McAteer.

Alexis Cater was laughing as she made her exit.

7

The man called Gareth was laughing into his mobile phone as the door opened. There were gold rings on each of his fingers, chains dangling from his neck and wrists. He wasn't tall but he was wide. Rebus got the impression much of it was fat. A gut hung over his waistband. He was balding badly, and had allowed what hair he had to grow uncut, so that it hung down to the back of his collar and beyond. He wore a black leather trenchcoat and black T-shirt, with baggy denims and scuffed trainers. He already had his free hand out for the cash, wasn't expecting another hand to grab it and haul him inside the flat. He dropped the phone, swearing and finally taking note of Rebus.

'Who the hell are you?'

'Afternoon, Gareth. Sorry if I was a bit brusque there . . . three cups of coffee gets me that way sometimes.'

Gareth was composing himself, deciding that he wasn't about to be done over. He bent down for his phone, but Rebus stepped on it, shaking his head.

'Later,' he said, kicking the phone out of the door and slamming it shut behind them.

'Fuck's going on here?'

'We're having a chat, that's what.'

'You look like the filth to me.'

'You're a good judge of character.' Rebus gestured down the hall and encouraged Gareth into the living room with his hand pressed to the young man's back. Passing father and son in the kitchen doorway, Rebus looked towards the son and got a nod, meaning he had the right man. 'Sit down,' Rebus ordered. Gareth lowered himself on to the arm of the sofa. Rebus stood in front of him. 'This your flat?'

'What's it to you?'

'Only it's not your name on the tenancy.'

'Isn't it?' Gareth played with the chains around his left wrist. Rebus leaned over him, got right into his face.

'Is Baird your real surname?'

'Yeah.' His tone challenged Rebus to call him a liar. Then: 'What's so funny?'

'Just a wee trick, Gareth. See, I didn't actually know your surname.' Rebus paused and straightened up again. 'But I do now. Robert's what – your brother? Dad?'

'Who are we talking about?'

Rebus smiled again. 'Bit late for all that, Gareth.'

Gareth seemed to agree. He jabbed a finger in the direction of the kitchen. 'Did they grass us up? Did they?'

Rebus shook his head, waited till he had Gareth's full attention. 'No, Gareth,' he said. 'A dead man did that . . .'

After which he let the young man simmer gently for five minutes, like so much reheated cock-a-leekie. Rebus made a show of checking text messages on his mobile. Opened a new packet of cigarettes and slid one unlit between his lips.

'Can I have one of those?' Gareth asked.

'Absolutely . . . just as soon as you tell me: is Robert your brother or your dad? I'm guessing dad but I could be wrong. By the way, I can't begin to count how many criminal charges are hanging over you right now. Sub-letting's just the start of it. Does Robert declare all this illegal income? See, once the taxman gets his claws into your baws, he's worse than a Bengal tiger. Trust me on that – I've seen the results.' He paused. 'Then there's demanding money with menaces . . . that's where you come in specifically.'

'I've never done nothing!'

'No?'

'Nothing like that . . . I just collect, that's all.' A pleading tone entering his voice. Rebus guessed Gareth had been the slow, lumbering kid at school – no real friends, just people who tolerated him because of his bulk, using that bulk when occasion demanded.

'It's not you I'm interested in,' Rebus reassured him. 'Not once I've got an address for your dad – an address I'm going to get anyway. I'm just trying to save the pair of us all that hassle . . .'

Gareth looked up, wondering about that 'pair of us'. Rebus shrugged an apology.

'See, you'll be coming with me back to the station. Hold you in custody till I get the address . . . then we pay a visit . . .'

'He lives in Porty,' Gareth blurted out. Meaning Portobello: on the sea-front to the south-east of the city.

'And he's your dad?'

Gareth nodded.

'There,' said Rebus, 'that wasn't so bad. Now up you get . . .'

'What for?'

'Because you and me are going to pay him a visit.'

Gareth didn't like the sound of this, Rebus could tell, but he didn't offer any resistance either, not once Rebus had cajoled him to his feet. Rebus shook hands with his hosts, thanked them for the coffee. The father started offering banknotes to Gareth, but Rebus shook his head.

'No more rent to pay,' he told the son. 'Isn't that right, Gareth?'

Gareth gave a flick of his head, said nothing. Outside, his mobile phone had already been taken. Rebus was reminded of the torch . . .

'Somebody's pocketed it,' Gareth complained.

'You'll have to report that,' Rebus advised. 'Make sure the insurance takes care of it.' He saw the look on Gareth's face. 'Always supposing it wasn't nicked in the first place.'

At ground level, Gareth's Japanese sports car was ringed by half a dozen kids whose parents had given up on sending them to school.

'How much did he give you?' Rebus asked them.

'Two bar.' Meaning two quid.

'And how long does that get him?'

They just stared at Rebus. 'It's not a parking meter,' one of them said. 'We don't give tickets.' His pals joined in the laughter.

Rebus nodded and turned to Gareth. 'We're taking my car,' he told him. 'Just have to hope yours is still here when you get back . . .'

'And if it isn't?'

'Back to the cop-shop for a reference to help with the insurance claim . . . Always supposing you're insured.'

'Always supposing,' Gareth said resignedly.

It wasn't a long drive to Portobello. They headed out on Seafield Road, no sign of a prostitutes' day-shift. Gareth directed Rebus to a side road near the promenade. 'We need to park here and walk,' he explained. So that was what they did. The sea was the colour of slate. Dogs chased sticks across the beach. Rebus felt like he'd stepped back in time: chip shops and amusement arcades. For years when he was a kid, his parents had taken him and his brother to a caravan in St Andrews for the summer, or to a cheap bed and breakfast in Blackpool. Ever since, any seaside town could pull him back to those days.

'Did you grow up here?' he asked Gareth.

'Tenement in Gorgie, that's where I grew up.'

'You've gone up in the world,' Rebus told him.

Gareth just shrugged, pushed open a gate. 'This is it.'

A garden path led to the front door of a four-storey double-fronted terraced house. Rebus stared for a moment. Every window had uninterrupted views across the beach.

'Moved on a bit from Gorgie,' he muttered, following Gareth up the path. The young man unlocked the door and yelled that he was home. The entrance hallway was short and narrow, with doors and a staircase off. Gareth didn't bother looking in any of the rooms. He headed for the first floor instead, Rebus still close behind.

They entered the drawing room. Twenty-six feet long, with a floor-to-ceiling bay window. The place had been tastefully decorated and furnished, but too modernly: chrome and leather and abstract art. The room's shape and dimensions didn't suit any of it. The original chandelier and cornices remained, offering glimpses of what might have been. A brass telescope sat by the window, supported by a wooden tripod.

'What the hell's this you've dragged in?'

A man was sitting at the table by the telescope. He wore a pair of glasses on a string around his neck. His hair was silvery-grey, neatly barbered, the face lined by weathering rather than age.

'Mr Baird, I'm Detective Inspector Rebus . . .'

'What's he done this time?' Baird closed the newspaper he'd been reading and glared at his son. There was resignation rather than anger in his voice. Rebus guessed things weren't working out as hoped for Gareth in the family's little enterprise.

'It's not Gareth, Mr Baird . . . it's you.'

'Me?'

Rebus did a circuit of the room. 'Council's certainly doing a better class of let these days.'

'What are you on about?' The question was for Rebus, but Baird's eyes were asking his son for an explanation, too.

'He was waiting for me, Dad,' Gareth burst out. 'Made me leave my car there and everything.'

'Fraud's a serious business, Mr Baird,' Rebus was saying. 'Always mystifies me, but the courts seem to hate it more than housebreaking or mugging. I mean, who are you cheating, after all? Not a person, not exactly . . . just this big anonymous blob called "the council".' Rebus shook his head. 'But they'll still come down on you like shit from the sky.'

Baird had leaned back in his chair, arms folded across his chest.

'Mind you,' Rebus added, 'you weren't content with the small stuff . . . how many flats are you sub-letting – ten? Twenty? Got the whole family roped in, I'd say . . . maybe a few dead aunties and uncles on the paperwork, too.'

'You here to arrest me?'

Rebus shook his head. 'I'm ready to tiptoe out of your life the minute I get what I've come for.'

Baird suddenly looked interested, seeing a man he could do business with. But he wasn't altogether convinced.

'Gareth, he have anybody else with him?'

Gareth shook his head. 'Waiting for me in the flat . . .'

'Nobody outside? No driver or anything?'

Still shaking his head. 'We came here in his car . . . just me and him.'

Baird considered this. 'So, how much is this going to cost me?'

'The answers to a few questions. One of your tenants got himself killed the other day.'

'I tell them to keep themselves to themselves,' Baird started to argue, ready to defend himself against any implication that he was an uncaring landlord. Rebus was standing by the window, staring down at the beach and promenade. An old couple walked past, hand-in-hand. It annoyed him that they might be subsidising the schemes of a shark like Baird. Or maybe their grandkids were languishing on a waiting list for a council flat.

'Very public-spirited of you, I'm sure,' Rebus said. 'What I need to know is his name and where he came from.'

Baird snorted. 'I don't ask where they come from – made that mistake once and got my ear bent for my sins. Thing that concerns me is, they all need roofs over their heads. And if the council won't or can't help . . . well, I will.'

'For a price.'

'A *fair* price.'

'Yes, you're all heart. So you never knew his name?'

'Used the first name Jim.'

'Jim? Was that his idea or yours?'

'Mine.'

'How did you find him?'

93

'Customers have a way of finding *me*. Word of mouth, you could call it. Wouldn't happen if they didn't like what they were getting.'

'They're getting council flats . . . and paying *you* over the odds for the privilege.' Rebus waited in vain for Baird to say something; knew what the man's eyes were telling him – *Got that off your chest?* 'And you've no idea of his nationality? Where he was from? How he got here . . . ?' Baird was shaking his head.

'Gareth, go fetch us a beer out the fridge.' Gareth was quick to comply. Rebus wasn't fooled by the plural 'us' – he knew there'd be no drink forthcoming for him.

'So how can you communicate with all these people if you don't know their language?'

'There are ways. A few signs and bits of miming . . .' Gareth came back with a single can, which he handed to his father. 'Gareth did French at school, I reckoned that might be useful to us.' His voice dropped at the end of the sentence, and Rebus assumed that once again Gareth had fallen short of expectations.

'Jim didn't need to mime though,' the boy added, keen to contribute something to the conversation. 'He spoke a bit of English. Not as good as his pal, mind . . .' His father glared at him, but Rebus stepped between them.

'What pal?' he asked Gareth.

'Just some woman . . . about my age.'

'They were living together?'

'Jim lived on his own. I got the feeling she was just someone he knew.'

'From the estate?'

'I suppose . . .'

But now Baird was on his feet. 'Look, you've got what you came for.'

'Have I?'

'Okay, I'll put it another way – you've got all you're getting.'

'That's for me to decide, Mr Baird.' Then to the son: 'What did she look like, Gareth?'

But Gareth had taken the hint. 'Can't remember.'

'What? Not even her skin colour? You seemed to remember how old she was.'

'Lot darker-skinned than Jim . . . that's all I know.'

'She spoke English though?'

Gareth tried looking to his father for guidance, but Rebus was doing his best to block his eye-line.

'She spoke English and she was a friend of Jim's,' Rebus persisted. 'And she lived on the estate . . . Just give me a bit more.'

'That's everything.'

Baird stepped past Rebus and wrapped an arm around his son's shoulders. 'You've got the boy all confused,' he complained. 'If he remembers anything else, he'll let you know.'

'I'm sure he will,' Rebus said.

'And you meant what you said about leaving us be?'

'Every word of it, Mr Baird . . . Of course, the Housing Department may have their own feelings on the matter.'

Baird's face twisted into a sneer.

'I'll let myself out,' Rebus said.

On the promenade, there was a stiff breeze blowing. It took him four attempts to get his cigarette lit. He stood there for a while, staring up at the drawing-room window, then remembered that he'd missed lunch. There were plenty of pubs on the High Street, so he left his car where it was and took a short stroll to the nearest one. Called Mrs Mackenzie and told her about Baird, ending the call as he pushed open the pub door. Ordered a half of IPA to wash down the chicken salad roll. Earlier, they'd been serving soup and stovies, and the aroma lingered. One of the regulars asked the barman to find the horse-racing channel. Flipping the TV remote through a dozen stations, he passed on one that made Rebus stop chewing.

'Go back,' he ordered, debris flying from his mouth.

'Which one?'

'Whoah, right there.' It was a local news programme, an outside broadcast of a demo in what was recognisably Knoxland. Hastily contrived banners and placards:

NEGLECTED

WE CANNOT LIVE LIKE THIS

LOCALS NEED HELP TOO . . .

The reporter was interviewing the couple from the flat next to the victim. Rebus caught the odd word and phrase: *council has a responsibility . . . feelings ignored . . . dumping ground . . . no consultation . . .* It was almost as if they'd been briefed on which buzz-words to use. The reporter turned to a well-dressed Asian-looking man wearing silver-rimmed spectacles. His name appeared onscreen as Mohammad Dirwan. He was from something called the Glasgow New Citizens Collective.

'Load of nutters over there,' the barman commented.

'They can shove as many into Knoxland as they like,' a regular agreed. Rebus turned to him.

'As many what?'

The man shrugged. 'Call them what you like – refugees or con artists. Whatever they are, I know damned fine who ends up paying for them.'

'Right enough, Matty,' the barman said. Then, to Rebus: 'Seen enough?'

'More than enough,' Rebus said, leaving the rest of his drink untouched as he headed for the door.

8

Knoxland hadn't calmed much by the time Rebus arrived. Press photographers were busy comparing shots, huddled around the screens of their digital cameras. A radio reporter was interviewing Ellen Wylie. Rat-Arse Reynolds was shaking his head as he walked across waste ground to his car.

'What's up, Charlie?' Rebus asked.

'Might clear the air a bit if we left them to get on with it,' Reynolds growled, slamming his car door shut on the world and picking up an already open packet of crisps.

There was a scrum beside the Portakabin. Rebus recognised faces from the TV pictures: the placards were already showing signs of wear and tear. Fingers were being pointed as an argument continued between the locals and Mohammad Dirwan. Close up, Dirwan looked to Rebus like a lawyer: new-looking black woollen coat, polished shoes, silver moustache. He was gesturing with his hands, voice rising to compete against the noise. Rebus peered through the mesh grille covering the Portakabin's window. As suspected, there was no one home. He looked around, eventually took the walkway to the other side of the tower block. He remembered the little bunch of flowers at the murder scene. They'd been scattered now, trampled on. Maybe Jim's friend had left them . . .

A transit van sat on its own in a cordoned zone which normally would have provided parking for residents. There was no one in the front, but Rebus banged on the back doors. The windows were blackened, but he knew he could be seen from within. The door opened and he climbed in.

'Welcome to the toy box,' Shug Davidson said, sitting down again next to the camera operator. The back of the van had been filled with recording and monitoring equipment. Any civil disorder in the city, police liked to keep a record. Useful for identifying the troublemakers, and for compiling a case if necessary. From the video screen, it looked to Rebus as though someone had been filming from a second- or third-floor landing. Shots zoomed in and out, blurred close-ups suddenly coming into focus.

'Not that there's been any violence yet,' Davidson muttered. Then, to the operator: 'Go back a bit . . . just there . . . freeze that, will you, Chris?'

There was some flicker to the stilled image which Chris tried to rectify.

'Who is it worries you, Shug?' Rebus asked.

'Shrewd as ever, John . . .' Davidson pointed to one of the figures at the back of the demo. The man wore an olive-green parka, hood pulled over his head, so that only his chin and lips were visible. 'I think he was here a few months ago . . . We had this gang from Belfast, trying to hoover up the drugs action.'

'You put them away, didn't you?'

'Most of them are on remand. A few headed back home.'

'So why is he back?'

'Not sure.'

'Have you tried asking him?'

'Scarpered when he saw our cameras.'

'Name?'

Davidson shook his head. 'I'll have to do a bit of digging . . .' He rubbed at his forehead. 'And how's your day been so far, John?'

Rebus filled him in on Robert Baird.

Davidson nodded. 'Good stuff,' he said, not quite managing any level of enthusiasm.

'I know it doesn't get us any further . . .'

'Sorry, John, I'm just . . .' Davidson shook his head slowly. 'We need someone to come forward. The weapon's got to be out there, blood on the killer's clothes. Someone *knows*.'

'Jim's girlfriend might have some ideas. We could bring Gareth in, see if he can spot her.'

'It's an idea,' Davidson mused. 'And meantime, we watch Knoxland explode . . .'

Film was running on four different screens. On one, a crowd of youths was seen standing way to the back of the crowd. They wore scarves across their mouths, hoods up. Spotting the cameraman, they turned and gave him a view of their backsides. One of them picked up a stone and hurled it, but it fell well short.

'See,' Davidson said, 'something like that could light the fuse . . .'

'Have there been any actual attacks?'

'Just verbal stuff.' He leaned back and stretched. 'We finished the door-to-door . . . Well, we finished all the ones that would talk to us.' He paused. 'Make that *could* talk to us. This place is like the Tower of Babel . . . a posse of interpreters would be a start.' His stomach growled, and he tried to disguise it by twisting in his creaking chair.

'Time for a break?' Rebus suggested. Davidson shook his head. 'What about this guy Dirwan?'

'He's a Glasgow solicitor, been working with some of the refugees on the estates over there.'

'So what brings him here?'

'Apart from the publicity, maybe he thinks he can rake up a whole new bunch of clients. He wants the Lord Provost to come see Knoxland for herself, wants a meeting between politicians and the immigrant community. There are a lot of things he wants.'

'Right now, he's in a minority of one.'

'I know.'

'You're happy to feed him to the lions?'

Davidson stared at him. 'We've got men out there, John.'

'It was getting pretty heated.'

'You offering yourself as bodyguard?'

Rebus shrugged. 'I do whatever you tell me to, Shug. This is your show . . .'

Davidson rubbed at his forehead again. 'Sorry, John, sorry . . .'

'Take that break, Shug. A breath of air if nothing else . . .' Rebus opened the back door.

'Oh, John, message for you. The Drugs guys want their torch back. I was told to tell you it's urgent.'

Rebus nodded, got out and closed the door again. He headed up to Jim's flat. The door was flapping open. No sign of the torch in the kitchen, or anywhere else. The forensic team had been in, but he doubted they'd taken it. As he exited, Steve Holly was coming out of the flat next door, holding his tape-recorder to his ear to check it had worked.

Soft touch, that's the problem with this country . . .

'I take it you'd agree with that,' Rebus said, startling the reporter. Holly stopped the tape and pocketed the recorder.

'Objective journalism, Rebus – giving both sides of the argument.'

'You've talked to some of the poor bastards who've been thrown into this lion's den then?'

Holly nodded. He was peering over the wall, wondering if anything he should know about was happening at ground level. 'I've even managed to find Knoxers who don't mind all these new arrivals – bet you're surprised by that . . . I certainly was.' He lit a cigarette, offered one to Rebus.

'Just this minute finished one,' Rebus lied with a shake of his head.

'Any result yet from the photo we printed?'

'Maybe no one noticed it tucked away there . . . too busy reading about tax-dodgers, pay-outs and preferential housing.'

'All of it true,' Holly protested. 'I never said it applied here, but it does some places.'

'If you were any lower, I could tee a golf ball off your head.'

'Not a bad line,' Holly grinned. 'Maybe I'll use it . . .' His mobile sounded and he took the call, turning from Rebus, walking away as if the detective no longer existed.

Which, Rebus assumed, was the way someone like Holly worked. Living for the moment, attention span stretching only as far as that particular story. Once it was written out, it was yesterday's news, and something else had to fill the vacuum it left. It was hard not to compare the process with the way some of his own colleagues worked: cases erased from the mind, new ones awaited, hoping for something a bit unusual or interesting. He knew there were good journalists out there, too: they weren't all like Steve Holly. Some of them couldn't stand the man.

Rebus followed Holly downstairs and out into the lessening storm. Fewer than a dozen diehards were left to argue their grievances with the solicitor, who had been joined by a few of the immigrants themselves. This was making for a fresh photo op, and the cameras were busy again, some of the immigrants shielding their faces with their hands. Rebus heard a noise behind him, someone calling out, 'Go on, Howie!' He turned and saw a youth walking purposefully towards the crowd, his friends offering encouragement from a safe distance. The youth paid no attention to Rebus. He had his face covered, hands tucked into the pouch on the front of his jacket. His pace was increasing as he made to pass Rebus. Rebus could hear his hoarse breath, almost smell the adrenalin coming off him.

He snatched at an arm and yanked it backwards. The youth spun, hands emerging from their pouch. Something tumbled across the ground: a small rock. The youth cried out in pain as Rebus wrenched his arm higher behind his back, forcing him down on to his knees. The crowd had turned at the sound, cameras clicking, but Rebus's eyes were on the gang, checking they weren't about to attack en masse. They weren't: instead, they were walking away, no intention of rescuing their fallen comrade. A man was getting into a battered red BMW. A man in an olive-coloured parka.

The captured youth was now swearing between agonised complaints. Rebus was aware of uniformed officers standing over him, one of them handcuffing the youth. As Rebus straightened up, he came eye to eye with Ellen Wylie.

'What happened?' she asked.

'He had a rock in his pocket . . . going to attack Dirwan.'

'That's a lie,' the youth spat. 'I'm being fitted up here!' The hood had been pulled from his head, the scarf from his mouth. Rebus saw a shaved skull, a face blighted by acne. One central tooth missing, the mouth open in disbelief at the way events had turned. Rebus stooped and picked up the rock.

'Still warm,' he said.

'Take him down the station,' Wylie was telling the uniforms. Then, to the youth: 'Anything sharp on you before we search your pockets?'

'Telling you nothing.'

'Get him into a car, lads.'

The youth was led away, cameras following him as he returned to his complaints. Rebus realised that the lawyer was standing in front of him.

'You saved my life, sir!' He clasped Rebus's hands in his own.

'I wouldn't go that far . . .'

But Dirwan had turned to the crowd. 'You see? You see the way that hate drips down from father to son? It is like a slow poison, polluting the very ground that should nourish us!' He tried to embrace Rebus, but met with resistance. This didn't seem to bother him. 'You are a police officer, yes?'

'A detective inspector,' Rebus acknowledged.

'Name's Rebus!' a voice called. Rebus stared at a smirking Steve Holly.

'Mr Rebus, I am in your debt until we perish on this earth. We are *all* in your debt.' Dirwan meant the immigrant group who stood nearby, apparently unaware of what had just happened. And now Shug Davidson was coming into view, bemused by the spectacle before him and accompanied by a grinning Rat-Arse Reynolds.

'Centre of attention as usual, John,' Reynolds said.

'What's the story?' Davidson asked.

'A kid was about to clout Mr Dirwan here,' Rebus muttered. 'So I stopped him.' He offered a shrug, as if to indicate that he now wished he hadn't. A uniform, one of the ones who'd taken the youth away, was returning.

'Better take a look at this, sir,' he told Davidson. He was holding a polythene evidence bag. There was something small and angular within.

A six-inch kitchen knife.

Rebus found himself playing babysitter to his new best friend.

They were in the CID office in Torphichen Place. The youth was being questioned in one of the interview rooms by Shug Davidson and Ellen Wylie. The knife had been whisked away to the forensic lab at Howdenhall. Rebus was trying to send a text message to Siobhan, letting her know they'd have to reschedule their meeting. He suggested six o'clock.

Having given his statement, Mohammad Dirwan was sipping sugary black tea at one of the desks, his eyes fixed on Rebus.

'I never mastered the intricacies of these new technologies,' he stated.

'Me neither,' Rebus admitted.

'And yet somehow they have become imperative to our way of life.'

'I suppose so.'

'You are a man of few words, Inspector. Either that or I'm making you nervous.'

'I'm just having to re-jig a meeting, Mr Dirwan.'

'Please . . .' The lawyer held up a hand. 'I told you to call me Mo.' He grinned, showing a row of immaculate teeth. 'People tell me it's a woman's name – they associate it with the character in *EastEnders*. You know the one?' Rebus shook his head. 'I say to them, do you not remember the footballer Mo Johnston? He played for both Rangers *and* Celtic, becoming hero and villain twice over – a trick not even the best lawyer could hope to accomplish.'

Rebus managed a smile. Rangers and Celtic: the Protestant team and the Catholic. He thought of something. 'Tell me, Mr . . .' A glare from Dirwan. 'Mo . . . tell me, you've had dealings with asylum-seekers in Glasgow, right?'

'Correct.'

'One of the demonstrators today . . . we think he might be from Belfast.'

'That wouldn't surprise me. The same thing happens on the Glasgow estates. It's a spill-over from the troubles in Northern Ireland.'

'How so?'

'Immigrants have begun to move to places like Belfast – they see opportunities there. Those people involved in the religious conflict are not so keen on this. They see everything in terms of Catholic and Protestant . . . maybe these new incoming religions scare them. There have been physical attacks. I would call it a basic instinct, this need to alienate what we cannot understand.' He raised a finger. 'Which does not mean I condone it.'

'But what would bring these men from Belfast to Scotland?'

'Maybe they wish to recruit the unhappy locals to their own cause.' He shrugged. 'Unrest can seem an end in itself to some people.'

'I supppose that's true.' Rebus had seen it for himself: the need to foment trouble, to stir things up; for no other reason than a feeling of power.

The lawyer finished his drink. 'Do you think this boy is the killer?'

'Could be.'

'Everyone seems to carry a knife in this country. You know Glasgow is the most dangerous city in Europe?'

'So I hear.'

'Stabbings . . . always stabbings.' Dirwan shook his head. 'And yet people still struggle to come to Scotland.'

'Immigrants, you mean?'

'Your First Minister says he is worried about the decline in the population. He is correct in this. We need young people to fill the jobs, otherwise how can we hope to support the ageing population? We also need people with skills. Yet at the same time, the government makes immigration so difficult . . . and as for asylum-seekers . . .' He shook his head again, slowly this time, as if in disbelief. 'You know Whitemire?'

'The detention centre?'

'Such a godforsaken place, Inspector. I'm not made welcome there. You can perhaps appreciate why.'

'You've got clients in Whitemire?'

'Several, all of them appealing their cases. It used to be a prison, you know, and now it houses families, individuals scared out of their wits . . . people who know that to be sent back to their native land is a death sentence.'

'And they're kept in Whitemire because otherwise they'd ignore the judgement and do a runner.'

Dirwan looked at Rebus and gave a wry smile. 'Of course, you are part of the same apparatus of state.'

'What's that supposed to mean?' Rebus bristled.

'Forgive my cynicism . . . but you do believe, don't you, that we should just send all these black bastards home? That Scotland would be a Utopia if only it weren't for the Pakis and gypsies and sambos?'

'Christ almighty . . .'

'Maybe you have Arab or African friends, Inspector? Any Asians you go drinking with? Or are they just faces behind the till of your local newsagent's . . .?'

'I'm not getting into this,' Rebus stated, tossing an empty coffee beaker into the bin.

'It's an emotive subject, to be sure . . . and yet one I have to deal with every single day. I think Scotland was complacent for many years: we don't have room for racism, we're too busy with bigotry! But this is not the case, alas.'

'I'm not racist.'

'I was making a point merely. Don't upset yourself.'

'I'm not upset.'

'I'm sorry . . . I find it hard to switch off.' Dirwan shrugged. 'It comes with the job.' His eyes darted around the room, as if seeking a change of subject. 'You think the killer will be found?'

'We'll do our damnedest.'

'That's good. I'm sure you are all dedicated and professional people.'

Rebus thought of Reynolds, but said nothing.

'And you know that if there's anything I personally can do to assist you . . .'

Rebus nodded, then thought for a moment. 'Actually . . .'

'Yes?'

'Well, it looks like the victim had a girlfriend . . . or at any rate a young woman he knew. We could do with tracing her.'

'She lives in Knoxland?'

'Possibly. She's darker-skinned than the victim; probably speaks better English than him.'

'That's all you know?'

'It's all I know,' Rebus confirmed.

'I can ask around . . . the incomers may not be as fearful of talking to me.' He paused. 'And thank you for requesting my help.' There was a warmth to his eyes. 'You can be assured I will do what I can.'

Both men turned as Reynolds came lumbering into the room, chewing on a shortbread biscuit which had left a trail of crumbs down his shirt and tie.

'We're charging him,' he said, pausing for effect. 'But not with murder. Lab says it wasn't the same knife.'

'That was quick,' Rebus commented.

'Post-mortem says a serrated blade, this one's got a smooth edge. They're still going to test for blood, but it's not promising.' Reynolds glanced in Dirwan's direction. 'We can maybe get him for attempted assault and carrying a concealed weapon.'

'Such is justice,' the lawyer said with a sigh.

'What do you want us to do? Chop his hands off?'

'Was that remark addressed to me?' The lawyer had risen to his feet. 'It is hard to tell when you refuse to look at me.'

'I'm looking at you now,' Reynolds retorted.

'And what do you see?'

Rebus stepped in. 'What DC Reynolds sees or doesn't see is neither here nor there.'

'I'll tell him if he likes,' Reynolds said, bits of biscuit flying from his mouth. Rebus, however, was steering him to the door. 'Thank you, DC Reynolds.' Doing everything but giving him a push into the corridor. Reynolds gave one final glower towards the lawyer, then turned and left.

'Tell me,' Rebus asked Dirwan, 'do you ever make friends, or just enemies?'

'I judge people by my standards.'

'And a two-second hearing is enough for you to make up your mind?'

Dirwan thought about this. 'Actually, yes, sometimes it is.'

'Then you've made up your mind about me?' Rebus folded his arms.

'Not so, Inspector . . . you are proving difficult to pin down.'

'But all cops are racist?'

'We are *all* racist, Inspector . . . even me. It is how we deal with that ugly fact that is important.'

The phone started ringing on Wylie's desk. Rebus answered it.

'CID, DI Rebus speaking.'

105

'Oh, hello . . .' A tentative female voice. 'Are you looking into that murder? The asylum-seeker on the housing estate?'

'That's right.'

'In the paper this morning . . .'

'The photograph?' Rebus sat down hurriedly, reached for pen and paper.

'I think I know who they are . . . I mean, I *do* know who they are.' Her voice was so brittle, Rebus feared she might take fright and hang up.

'Well, we'd be very interested in any help you can give, Miss . . .?'

'What?'

'I need your name.'

'Why?'

'Because callers who won't give their name tend not to be taken so seriously.'

'But I'm . . .'

'It'll just be between us, I assure you.'

There was silence for a moment. Then: 'Eylot, Janet Eylot.'

Rebus wrote the name down in scrawled capitals.

'And can I ask how you know the people in the photo, Miss Eylot?'

'Well . . . they're here.'

Rebus was staring at the lawyer without really seeing him. 'Where's here?'

'Look . . . maybe I should have asked permission first.'

Rebus knew he was close to losing her. 'You've done absolutely the right thing, Miss Eylot. I just need a few more details. We're keen to catch whoever did this, but right now we're pretty much in the dark, and you seem to be holding the only candle.' He was trying for a light-hearted tone; couldn't risk frightening her off.

'Their names are . . .' It took Rebus an effort of will not to shout out encouragement. 'Yurgii.' He asked her to spell it, wrote it down as she did so.

'Sounds East European.'

'They're Turkish Kurds.'

'You work with refugees, do you, Miss Eylot?'

'In a manner of speaking.' She sounded a little more confident, now she'd given him the name. 'I'm calling from Whitemire – do you know it?'

Rebus's eyes focused on Dirwan. 'Funnily enough, I was just talking about it. I'm assuming you mean the detention centre?'

'We're actually an Immigration Removal Centre.'

'And the family in the photograph . . . they're there with you?'

'The mother and two children, yes.'

'And the husband?'

'He fled just before the family were picked up and brought here. It happens sometimes.'

'I'm sure it does . . .' Rebus tapped pen against notepad. 'Look, can I take a contact number for you?'

'Well . . .'

'Work or home, whichever suits.'

'I don't . . .'

'What is it, Miss Eylot? What are you scared of?'

'I should have spoken to my boss first.' She paused. 'You'll be coming here now, won't you?'

'Why didn't you talk to your boss?'

'I don't know.'

'Would your job be threatened if your boss knew?'

She seemed to consider this. 'Do they have to know it was me that called you?'

'No, not at all,' Rebus said. 'But I'd still like to be able to contact you.'

She relented and gave him her mobile number. Rebus thanked her and warned that he might need to talk to her again.

'In confidence,' he reassured her, not at all sure that this would actually be the case. Call finished, he tore the sheet from the pad.

'He has family in Whitemire,' Dirwan stated.

'I'd ask you to keep that to yourself for the time being.'

The lawyer shrugged. 'You saved my life – it's the least I can do. But would you like me to come with you?'

Rebus shook his head. Last thing he needed was Dirwan sparring with the guards. He went in search of Shug Davidson, found him in conversation with Ellen Wylie, in the corridor next to the interview room.

'Reynolds told you?' Davidson asked.

Rebus nodded. 'Not the same knife.'

'We'll sweat the little sod a while longer anyway; might be he knows something we can use. He's got a fresh tattoo on his arm – red hand and the letters UVF.' Meaning the Ulster Volunteer Force.

'Never mind that, Shug.' Rebus held up the note. 'Our victim was on the run from Whitemire. His family are still there.'

Davidson stared at him. 'Someone saw the photo?'

'Bingo. Time to pay a visit, wouldn't you say? Your car or mine?'

But Davidson was rubbing his jaw. 'John . . .'

'What?'

'The wife . . . the kids . . . they don't know he's dead, do they? You really think you're right for the job?'

'I can do tea and sympathy.'

'I'm sure you can, but Ellen's going with you. You okay with that, Ellen?'

Wylie nodded, then turned to Rebus. 'My car,' she said.

9

Her car was a Volvo S40 with only a couple of thousand miles on the clock. There were CDs on the passenger seat, which Rebus had flicked through.

'Put something on if you like,' she'd said.

'I've got to text Siobhan first,' he countered: his excuse for not having to choose between Norah Jones, the Beastie Boys and Mariah Carey. It took him several minutes to send the message *sorry cant do six might manage eight*. Afterwards, he wondered why he hadn't just called her instead, guessing it would have taken half the time. Almost immediately, she rang back.

'Are you taking the piss?'

'I'm on my way to Whitemire.'

'The detention centre?'

'Actually, I have it on good authority that it's an Immigration Removal Centre. It also happens to be home to the victim's wife and kids.'

She was silent for a moment. 'Well, I can't do eight o'clock. I'm meeting someone for a drink. I was hoping you might've been there too.'

'There's a fair chance I will be, if that's what you want. We can hit the pubic triangle afterwards.'

'When it's getting lively, you mean?'

'An accident of timing, Siobhan, that's all.'

'Well . . . go easy on them, eh?'

'What do you mean?'

'I'm assuming you're going to be the bearer of bad news at Whitemire.'

'Why is it nobody thinks I can do the sympathy thing?' Wylie

109

glanced at him and smiled. 'I can be the caring new-age cop when I want to.'

'Sure you can, John. I'll see you in the Ox around eight.'

Rebus put his phone away and concentrated on the road ahead. They were driving west out of Edinburgh. Whitemire was situated between Banehall and Bo'ness, sixteen or so miles from the city centre. It had been a prison up until the late 1970s, Rebus visiting on just the one occasion, shortly after he'd joined the force. This much he told Ellen Wylie.

'Before my time,' she commented.

'They shut it down soon after. Only thing I remember is someone showing me where they used to do the hangings.'

'Lovely.' Wylie hit the brakes. They were in the middle of the rush hour, commuters crawling home to their towns and villages. No clever route or short-cut available, every set of traffic lights seemingly against them.

'I couldn't do this every day,' Rebus said.

'Be nice to live in the country though.'

He looked at her. 'Why?'

'More space, less dog-shit.'

'Have they banned dogs from the countryside then?'

She smiled again. 'Plus, for the price of a two-bed flat in the New Town, you could have a dozen acres and a billiard room.'

'I don't play billiards.'

'Me neither, but I could learn.' She paused. 'So what's the plan for when we get there?'

Rebus had been considering this. 'We might need a translator.'

'I hadn't thought of that.'

'Maybe they've got one on the staff . . . they could break the news . . .'

'She'll have to ID her husband.'

Rebus nodded. 'The translator can tell her that too.'

'After we've gone?'

Rebus shrugged. 'We ask our questions, get out of there quick.'

She looked at him. 'And people say you can't do sympathy . . .'

They drove in silence after that, Rebus finding a news channel on the radio. There was nothing about the scuffle at Knoxland. He hoped nobody would pick up on it. Eventually, a sign pointed to the turn-off for Whitemire.

'I just thought of something,' Wylie said. 'Shouldn't we have warned them we were coming?'

'Bit late for that.' The road became a pot-holed single track. Signs warned trespassers that they would be prosecuted. The twelve-foot perimeter fence had been augmented by runs of pale-green corrugated iron.

'Means no one can see in,' Wylie commented.

'Or out,' Rebus added. He knew that there had been demonstrations against the holding centre, and guessed that these were the reason for the recently installed cladding.

'And what on earth is this?' Wylie asked. A lone figure was standing by the side of the road. It was a woman, wrapped heavily against the cold. Behind her was a tent just big enough for one person, and next to it a smouldering camp-fire with a kettle hanging over it. The woman held a candle, cupping her free hand around the spluttering flame. Rebus stared at her as they passed. She kept her eyes on the ground in front, her mouth moving slightly. Fifty yards on stood the gatehouse. Wylie stopped the car and sounded her horn, but no one appeared. Rebus got out and approached the booth. A guard sat behind the window, chewing a sandwich.

'Evening,' Rebus said. The man pressed a button, his voice issuing from a speaker.

'You got an appointment?'

'I don't need one.' Rebus showed his ID. 'Police officer.'

The man appeared unimpressed. 'Slide it through.'

Rebus placed the card in a metal drawer and watched as the guard picked it up and studied it. A phone call was made, Rebus unable to hear any of it. Afterwards, the guard jotted down Rebus's details and pressed the button again.

'Car registration.'

Rebus obliged, noting that the last three letters were WYL. Wylie had bought herself a vanity plate.

'Anyone else with you?' the guard asked.

'Detective Sergeant Ellen Wylie.'

The guard asked him to spell Wylie, then noted these details down, too. Rebus looked back towards the woman at the side of the road.

'Is she always here?' he asked.

The guard shook his head.

'She got family inside or something?'

'Just a nutter,' the guard said, sliding Rebus's ID back through. 'Park in one of the visitor bays in the car park. Someone will come to meet you.'

Rebus nodded his thanks and walked back to the Volvo. The

barrier opened automatically, but the guard had to venture outside to unlock the gates. He waved them through, Rebus pointing Wylie in the direction of their parking space.

'I see you've got a vanity plate,' he commented.

'So?'

'I thought they were boys' toys.'

'Present from my boyfriend,' she admitted. 'What else was I going to do with it?'

'So who's the boyfriend?'

'None of your business,' she said, giving him a glare which told him the subject was closed.

The car park was separated from the main compound by another fence. There was building work going on, foundations being laid.

'Nice to see at least one growth industry in West Lothian,' Rebus muttered.

A guard had emerged from the main building. He opened a gate in the fence and asked if Wylie had locked her doors.

'And set the alarm,' she confirmed. 'Lot of car crime around here?'

He failed to see the joke. 'We've some fairly desperate people in here.' Then he led them to the main entrance. A man was standing there, dressed in a suit rather than the grey uniform of a guard. The man nodded to the guard to let him know he'd take over. Rebus was studying the unadorned stone-clad building, its small windows set high into its walls. There were much newer whitewashed annexes to left and right.

'My name's Alan Traynor,' the man was saying. He shook first Rebus's hand and then Wylie's. 'How can I be of service?'

Rebus drew a copy of the morning paper from his pocket. It was folded open at the photograph.

'We think these people are being held here.'

'Really? And how did you come to that conclusion?'

Rebus didn't answer. 'The family's name is Yurgii.'

Traynor studied the photo again, then nodded slowly. 'You'd better come with me,' he said.

He led them into the prison. To Rebus's eye, that was exactly what it was, notwithstanding the tweaked job description. Traynor was explaining the security measures. If they'd been ordinary visitors they'd have been fingerprinted and photographed then frisked with metal-detectors. The staff they passed wore blue uniforms, chains of keys jangling by their sides. Just like a prison. Traynor was in his early thirties. The dark blue suit could have been tailored to fit his slim frame. His dark hair was parted from the left, long enough so that he had to push it out of his eyes occasionally. He told them he was the deputy, his boss having taken some sick leave.

'Nothing serious?'

'Stress.' Traynor shrugged to show that it was only to be expected. They followed him up some stairs and through a small open-plan office. A young woman sat hunched over a computer.

'Working late again, Janet?' Traynor asked with a smile. She didn't respond, but watched and waited. Rebus, unseen by Traynor, rewarded Janet Eylot with a wink.

Traynor's office was small and functional. Through the glass sat a bank of CCTV screens, flicking between a dozen on-site locations. 'Only one chair, I'm afraid,' he said, retreating behind his desk.

'I'm fine standing, sir,' Rebus told him, nodding for Wylie to take the seat. But she decided to stand too. Traynor, having lowered himself on to his own chair, now found himself having to look up at the detectives.

'The Yurgiis *are* here?' Rebus asked, feigning interest in the CCTV screens.

'They are, yes.'

'But not the husband?'

'Slipped away . . .' He shrugged. 'Not our problem. It was the Immigration Service that screwed up.'

'And you're not part of the Immigration Service?'

Traynor snorted. 'Whitemire is run by Cencrast Security, which in turn is a subsidiary of ForeTrust.'

'The private sector, in other words?'

'Exactly.'

'ForeTrust's American, isn't it?' Wylie added.

'That's right. They own private prisons in the United States.'

'And here in Britain?'

Traynor admitted as much with a bow of the head. 'Now, about the Yurgiis . . .' He played with his watch-strap, hinting that he had better things to do with his time.

'Well, sir,' Rebus began, 'I showed you that piece in the newspaper, and you didn't bat an eye . . . didn't seem interested in the headline or the story.' He paused. 'Which gives me the feeling you already know what happened.' Rebus pressed his knuckles to the desktop and leaned down. 'And that makes me wonder why you didn't get in touch.'

Traynor met Rebus's eyes for a second, then turned his attention to the CCTV screens. 'Know how much bad press we get, Inspector?

113

More than we deserve – a hell of a lot more. Ask the inspection teams – we're audited quarterly. They'll tell you this place is humane and efficient and we don't cut corners.' He pointed to a screen showing a group of men playing cards around a table. 'We *know* these are people, and we treat them as such.'

'Mr Traynor, if I'd wanted the brochure I could have sent away for one.' Rebus leaned down further so the young man could not escape his gaze. 'Reading between the corporate lines, I'd say you were afraid Whitemire would become part of the story. That's why you did nothing . . . and that, Mr Traynor, counts as obstruction. How long do you think Cencrast would keep you on with a criminal record?'

Traynor's face began to flush from the neck up. 'You can't prove I knew anything,' he blustered.

'But I can try, can't I?' Rebus's smile was perhaps the least pleasant the young man had ever been treated to. Rebus stood up straight and turned towards Wylie, giving her a completely different kind of smile before returning his attention to Traynor.

'Now, let's get back to the Yurgiis, shall we?'

'What do you want to know?'

'Everything.'

'I don't know everyone's life story,' Traynor said defensively.

'Then you might want to refer to their file.'

Traynor nodded and got up, heading out to ask Janet Eylot for the relevant documents.

'Nice going,' Wylie said under her breath.

'And lots of fun, to boot.'

Rebus's face hardened again as Traynor returned. The young man sat down and riffled through the sheets of paper. The story he told was simple enough on the surface. The Yurgii family were Turkish Kurds. They had arrived first in Germany, claiming to have been under threat in their own country. Family members had disappeared. The father gave his name as Stef . . . Traynor looked up at this.

'They'd no papers on them, nothing to prove he was telling the truth. Doesn't sound a very Kurdish name, does it? Then again . . . says here he was a journalist . . .'

Yes, a journalist, writing stories critical of the government. Working under various aliases in an attempt to keep his family safe. When an uncle and cousin had gone missing, it was assumed they'd been arrested and would be tortured for details about Stef.

114

'Gives his age as twenty-nine ... could be lying there too, of course.'

Wife, twenty-five, children, six and four. They'd told the authorities in Germany that they wanted to live in the UK, and the Germans had obliged – four fewer refugees for them to worry about. However, upon hearing the family's case, it had been decided by Immigration in Glasgow that they should be deported: back to Germany at first, and from there probably to Turkey.

'Any reason given?' Rebus asked.

'They hadn't proved they weren't economic migrants.'

'Tough one,' Wylie said, folding her arms. 'Like proving you're not a witch ...'

'These matters are gone into with great thoroughness,' Traynor said defensively.

'So how long have they been here?' Rebus asked.

'Seven months.'

'That's a long time.'

'Mrs Yurgii refuses to leave.'

'Can she do that?'

'She has a lawyer working for her.'

'Not Mo Dirwan?'

'How did you guess?'

Rebus cursed silently: if he'd taken up Dirwan's offer, *he* could have been the one to break the news to the widow. 'Does Mrs Yurgii speak English?'

'A little.'

'She needs to come to Edinburgh to identify the body. Will she understand that?'

'I've no idea.'

'Is there anyone who could translate?'

Traynor shook his head.

'Her kids stay with her?' Wylie asked.

'Yes.'

'All day?' She watched him nod. 'They don't go to school or anything?'

'There's a teacher comes here.'

'How many children exactly?'

'Anything from five to twenty, depending on who's being kept here.'

'All different ages, different nationalities?'

'Nigerians, Russians, Somalis ...'

'And just the one teacher?'

Traynor smiled. 'Don't swallow the media line, Detective Sergeant. I know we've been called "Scotland's Camp X-Ray" . . . protestors ringing the perimeter, hands joined . . .' He paused, suddenly looking tired. 'We're just processing them, that's all. We're not monsters and this isn't a prison camp. Those new buildings you saw as you came in – specially constructed family units. TVs and a cafeteria, table-tennis and snack machines . . .'

'And which of those don't you get in a prison?' Rebus asked.

'If they'd left the country when told, they wouldn't be here.' Traynor patted the file. 'The officials have made their decision.' He took a deep breath. 'Now, I'm assuming you'd like to see Mrs Yurgii . . .'

'In a minute,' Rebus said. 'First, what do your notes tell you about Stef doing a runner?'

'Just that when officers went to the Yurgiis' flat . . .'

'Which was where?'

'Sighthill in Glasgow.'

'A cheery spot.'

'Better than some, Inspector . . . Anyway, when they arrived, Mr Yurgii wasn't home. According to his wife, he had left the previous night.'

'He got wind you were coming?'

'It wasn't a secret. The judgement had been delivered; their lawyer had informed them of it.'

'Would he have had any means of supporting himself?'

Traynor shrugged. 'Not unless Dirwan helped him out.'

Well, that was something for Rebus to ask the lawyer. 'He didn't try to contact his family?'

'Not that I'm aware of.'

Rebus thought for a moment, turning towards Wylie to see if she had any questions. When she just twitched her mouth, Rebus nodded. 'Okay, we'll go see Mrs Yurgii now . . .'

Dinner had just finished, and the cafeteria was emptying.

'Everybody eats at the same time,' Wylie commented.

A uniformed guard was arguing with a woman whose head was covered with a shawl. She carried an infant on her shoulder. The guard was holding up a piece of fruit.

'Sometimes they smuggle food back to their rooms,' Traynor explained.

'And that's not allowed?'

He shook his head. 'I don't see them here . . . must have finished already. This way . . .' He led them down a corridor fitted with a

CCTV camera. The building might have been clean and new, but to Rebus's mind it was a compound within a compound.

'Had any suicides yet?' he asked.

Traynor glared at him. 'One or two attempts. A hunger-striker, too. Comes with the territory . . .' He had stopped at an open door, gesturing with his hand. Rebus looked in. The room was fifteen feet by twelve – not small in itself, but containing a bunk-bed, a single bed, wardrobe and desk. Two small children were working at the desk, crayonning pictures and whispering to one another. Their mother sat on her bed, staring into space, hands on her lap.

'Mrs Yurgii?' Rebus said, moving a little further into the room. The drawings were of trees and balls of yellow sunshine. The room was windowless, ventilated from a grille in the ceiling. The woman looked up at him with hollow eyes.

'Mrs Yurgii, I'm a police officer.' He had the children's interest now. 'This is my colleague. Could we maybe talk away from the children?'

Unblinking, her eyes never left his. Tears began to drip down her face, lips pursed to hold back the sobs. The children went to her, offering comfort with their arms. It had the look of something they did regularly. The boy would be six or seven. He looked up at the intruding adults with a face hardened beyond its years.

'You go now, not do this for us.'

'I need to talk to your mother,' Rebus said quietly.

'It is not allowed. Bugger off now.' He enunciated these words precisely, and with a trace of the local accent – picked up from the guards, Rebus guessed.

'I really need to talk to . . .'

'I know all,' Mrs Yurgii said suddenly. 'He . . . not . . .' Her eyes beseeched Rebus, but all he could do was nod. She hugged her children to her. 'He not,' she repeated. The girl had started crying, too, but not the boy. It was as if he knew that his world had shifted yet again, bringing another challenge.

'What is this?' The woman from the cafeteria was standing just outside the door.

'Do you know Mrs Yurgii?' Rebus asked.

'She is my friend.' The infant had gone from the woman's shoulder, leaving a patch of drying milk or saliva there. She squeezed into the room and crouched in front of the widow.

'What has happened?' she asked. Her voice was deep, imperative.

'We've brought some bad news,' Rebus told her.

'What news?'

'It's about Mrs Yurgii's husband,' Wylie interrupted.

'What has happened?' There was fear in the eyes now, realisation dawning.

'It's not good,' Rebus confirmed. 'Her husband is dead.'

'Dead?'

'He was killed. Someone needs to identify the body. Did you know the family before you came here?'

She looked at him as if he were stupid. 'None of us knew the others before this place.' She spat out the final word as though it were gristle.

'Can you tell her that she needs to identify her husband? We can send a car for her tomorrow morning . . .'

Traynor held up a hand. 'No need for that. We have transport . . .'

'Oh, yes?' Wylie said sceptically. 'With bars on the windows?'

'Mrs Yurgii has been marked down as a potential absconder. She remains *my* responsibility.'

'You'll take her to the mortuary in the back of a paddy-wagon?'

He glowered at Wylie. 'Guards will escort her.'

'I'm sure society's reassured by that.'

Rebus placed his hand on Wylie's elbow. She seemed about to add something, but turned away instead, heading off down the corridor. Rebus gave a little shrug.

'Ten in the morning?' he asked. Traynor nodded. Rebus gave him the address of the mortuary. 'Any chance Mrs Yurgii's friend here could go with her?'

'I don't see why not,' Traynor conceded.

'Thanks,' Rebus said. Then he followed Wylie out to the car park. She was pacing the ground, kicking imaginary stones, watched by a guard who was patrolling the perimeter with a torch, despite the floodlit glare. Rebus lit a cigarette.

'Feeling better now, Ellen?'

'What's there to feel better about?'

Rebus held up both hands in surrender. 'I'm not the one you're pissed off with.'

The sound which issued from her mouth started as a snarl but ended in a sigh. 'That's the problem though: who is it I *am* pissed off with?'

'The people in charge?' Rebus guessed. 'The ones we never see.' He waited to see if she'd agree. 'I've got this theory,' he went on. 'We spend most of our time chasing something called "the underworld", but it's the *overworld* we should really be keeping an eye on.'

She thought about this, nodding almost imperceptibly. The guard was walking towards them.

'No smoking,' he barked. Rebus just stared at him. 'It's not allowed.'

Rebus took another inhalation, narrowing his eyes. Wylie pointed to a faint yellow line on the ground.

'What's that for?' Trying to steer his attention away from Rebus.

'The zone of containment,' the guard answered. 'Detainees aren't allowed to cross it.'

'Why the hell not?'

He shifted his gaze to her. 'They might try to escape.'

'Have you taken a look at those gates lately? Height of the fence tell you anything? Barbed wire and corrugated iron . . . ?' She was inching towards him. He started backing away. Rebus reached out to touch her arm again.

'I think we should leave now,' he said, flicking his cigarette so that it bounced off the guard's polished toecap, sending a few momentary sparks into the night. As they drove out of the compound, the lone woman was watching them from her camp-fire.

10

'Well, this is . . . rustic.' Alexis Cater gazed at the nicotine-coloured walls of the Oxford Bar's back room.

'I'm glad you condescend to approve.'

He wagged a finger. 'There's a fire in you – I like that. I've quenched a few fires in my time, but only after inflaming them first.' He smirked as he raised his glass to his lips, sloshing the beer around in his mouth before swallowing. 'Not a bad pint, mind, and bloody cheap. I might have to remember this place. Is it your local?'

She shook her head, just as Harry the barman appeared to clear away any empty glasses. 'All right, Shiv?' he called. She nodded back.

Cater grinned. 'Your cover's blown, Shiv.'

'Siobhan,' she corrected him.

'Tell you what: I'll call you Siobhan if you'll call me Lex.'

'You're trying to cut a deal with a police officer?'

His eyes twinkled above the rim of the glass. 'Hard to picture you in uniform . . . but well worth the effort, all the same.'

She'd chosen to sit on one of the benches, reasoning that he would take the chair opposite, but he'd slid on to the bench beside her, and was creeping closer by degrees.

'Tell me,' she said, 'does this charm offensive of yours ever work?'

'Can't complain. Mind you . . .' he checked his watch, 'we've been here the best part of ten minutes and you've yet to ask me about my father – that's probably a record.'

'So what you're saying is, women humour you because of who you are?'

He winced. 'A palpable hit.'

'You remember why we're having this meeting?'

'God, you make it sound so formal.'

'If you want to see "formal", we can keep talking at Gayfield Square.'

He raised an eyebrow. 'Your flat?'

'My police station,' she corrected him.

'Bloody hell, this is hard work.'

'I was just thinking the same thing.'

'I need a ciggie,' Cater was saying. 'Do you smoke?' Siobhan shook her head, and he looked elsewhere. Another drinker had arrived, taking the table opposite them, spreading out his evening paper. Cater stared at the pack of cigarettes lying beside the newspaper. 'Excuse me,' he called. 'Have you a spare ciggie by any chance?'

'Not spare, no,' the man said. 'I need every single one I can get my hands on.' He went back to his reading. Cater turned to Siobhan.

'Nice clientele.'

Siobhan shrugged. She wasn't about to let him know there was a machine around the corner next to the toilets.

'The skeleton,' she reminded him.

'What about it?' He leaned back, as though wishing he were elsewhere.

'You took it from outside Professor Gates's office.'

'So what?'

'I'd like to know how it ended up in a concrete floor in Fleshmarket Close.'

'Me too,' he snorted. 'Maybe I could sell the idea to Dad for a mini-series.'

'After you took it . . .' Siobhan prompted.

He swirled his glass, producing a fresh head on the top of the pint. 'You mistake me for a cheap date – one drink and you think I'll spill the beans?'

'Right you are then . . .' Siobhan started to get to her feet.

'At least finish your drink,' he protested.

'No thanks.'

He rolled his head to left and right. 'All right, point made . . .' Gestured with his arm. 'Sit down again and I'll tell you.' She hesitated, then pulled out the chair opposite him. He pushed her glass towards her. 'Christ,' he said, 'you're a real drama queen when you get going.'

'I'm sure you are, too.' She lifted her tonic water. On entering the bar, Cater had ordered her a gin and tonic, but she'd managed to signal to Harry that she didn't want the gin. Straight tonic was what she'd been given – the reason the round had been so cheap . . .

'If I tell you, can we get a bite to eat after?' She glared at him. 'I'm ravenous,' he persisted.

'There's a good chippie on Broughton Street.'

'Is that anywhere near your flat? We could take the fish suppers back there . . .'

This time she had to smile. 'You never give up, do you?'

'Not unless I'm really, *really* sure.'

'Sure of what?'

'That the woman isn't interested.' He beamed a smile at her. Meantime, behind her, the man at the next table cleared his throat as he turned to a fresh page.

'We'll see,' was her response. And then: 'So tell me about the bones of Mag Lennox . . .'

He stared up at the ceiling, reminiscing. 'Dear old Mags . . .' Then he broke off. 'This is off the record, naturally?'

'Don't worry.'

'Well, you're right, of course . . . we did decide to "borrow" Mags. We were hosting a party, and decided it would be fun if Mags presided over us. Got the idea from a veterinary student's party: he'd sneaked a dead dog out of the lab, sat it in his bath, so that every time someone needed to . . .'

'I get the picture.'

He shrugged. 'Same thing with Mags. Plonked her on a chair at the head of the table during dinner. Later on, I think we even danced with her. It was just a bit of high spirits, m'lady. We planned to take her back afterwards . . .'

'But you didn't?'

'Well, when we woke up next morning, she'd left of her own volition.'

'I hardly think that likely.'

'Okay then, somebody'd walked off with her.'

'And with the baby, too – you got that when the department were chucking it out?' He nodded. 'Did you ever find out who took them?'

He shook his head. 'There were seven of us for dinner, but after that the party proper started and there must have been twenty or thirty people there. Could've been any one of them.'

'Any prime suspects?'

He considered this. 'Pippa Greenlaw brought a bit of rough with her. Turned out to be a one-nighter and he was never heard of again.'

'Did he have a name?'

122

'I should think so.' He stared at her. 'Probably not as sexy as yours, though.'

'What about Pippa? Is she a medic too?'

'Christ, no. Works in PR. Come to think of it, that's how she met her beau. He was a footballer.' He paused. 'Well, wanted to be a footballer.'

'Have you got a number for Pippa?'

'Somewhere . . . might not be up-to-date . . .' He leaned forward. 'Of course, I don't have it with me. I suppose that means we'll need another rendezvous.'

'What it means is that you'll call me and tell me it.' She handed over her card. 'You can leave a message at the station if I'm not there.'

His smile softened as he studied her, angling his face one way and then another.

'What?' she asked.

'I'm just wondering how much of this Ice Maiden routine is just that – a routine. Do you ever step out of character?' He reached across the table and snatched her wrist, placing it to his lips. She wrenched free. He sat back again, looking satisfied.

'Fire and ice,' he mused. 'It's a good combination.'

'Want to see another good combination?' the man at the next table asked, folding shut his paper. 'How about a punch in the face and a boot up the arse?'

'Bloody hell, it's Sir Galahad!' Cater laughed. 'Sorry, chum, no damsels round these parts requiring your services.'

The man was on his feet, stepping into the middle of the cramped room. Siobhan stood up, blocking his view of Cater.

'It's fine, John,' she said. Then, to Cater: 'I think you better skedaddle.'

'You know this primate?'

'One of my colleagues,' Siobhan confirmed.

Rebus was craning his neck, the better to glare at Cater. 'You better get her that phone number, pal. And no more of your fannying around.'

Cater was on his feet. He made a show of pausing long enough to finish his drink. 'It's been a delightful evening, Siobhan . . . we must do it again some time, with or without the performing monkey.'

Harry the barman was in the doorway. 'That your Aston outside, pal?'

Cater's face softened. 'Nice car, isn't it?'

'I wouldn't know about that, but some punter's just mistaken it for a urinal . . .'

Cater gasped and scrambled down the steps towards the exit. Harry gave a wink and returned to the bar. Siobhan and Rebus shared a look, then a smile.

'Smarmy little bastard,' Rebus commented.

'Maybe you'd be, too, given who his father is.'

'Silver spoon up the nose at birth, I dare say.' Rebus sat back down at his table, Siobhan turning her chair round to face him.

'Maybe it's just *his* routine.'

'Like your "Ice Maiden"?'

'And your Mr Angry.'

Rebus winked and tipped his glass to his mouth. She'd noticed before how he opened his mouth when he drank – as if attacking the liquid, showing it his teeth. 'Want another?' she asked.

'Trying to postpone the evil moment?' he teased. 'Well, why not? Got to be cheaper here than there.'

She brought the drinks through. 'How did it go at Whitemire?'

'As well as could be expected. Ellen Wylie went off on one.' He described the visit, ending with Wylie and the guard. 'Why do you think she did that?'

'Innate sense of injustice?' Siobhan suggested. 'Maybe she comes from immigrant stock.'

'Like me, you mean?'

'I seem to remember you telling me you came from Poland.'

'Not me: my grandad.'

'You probably still have family there.'

'Christ knows.'

'Well, don't forget I'm an immigrant, too. Parents both English . . . brought up south of the border.'

'You were born here, though.'

'And whisked away again before I was out of nappies.'

'Still makes you Scottish – stop trying to wriggle out of it.'

'I'm just saying . . .'

'We're a mongrel nation, always have been. Settled by the Irish, raped and pillaged by the Vikings. When I was a kid, all the chip shops seemed to be run by Italians. Classmates with Polish and Russian surnames . . .' He stared into his glass. 'I don't remember anyone getting stabbed because of it.'

'You grew up in a village, though.'

'So?'

'So maybe Knoxland's different, that's all I'm saying.'

He nodded agreement with this, finished his drink. 'Let's go,' he said.

'I've still got half a glass.'

'You losing your bottle, DS Clarke?'

A complaint sounded in her throat, but she got to her feet anyway.

'You been to one of these places before?'

'Couple of times,' he admitted. 'Stag nights.'

They'd parked the car on Bread Street, outside one of the city's more chic hotels. Rebus wondered what visitors thought, stepping out of their suite and into the pubic triangle. The area spread from the showbars of Tollcross and Lothian Road to Lady Lawson Street. Bars advertised the 'biggest jugs' in town, 'VIP table-dancing', and 'non-stop action'. There was just the one discreet sex shop as yet, and no sign that any of Leith's street-walkers had taken up residence.

'Takes me back a bit,' Rebus admitted. 'You weren't here in the seventies, were you? Go-go dancers in the pubs at lunchtime . . . a blue cinema near the university . . .'

'Glad to hear you so nostalgic,' Siobhan said coolly.

Their destination was a refurbished pub just across the road from a disused shop. Rebus could recall several of its previous names: The Laurie Tavern, The Wheaten Inn, The Snakepit. But now it was The Nook. A sign on its large blacked-out window proclaimed it 'Your First Nookie Stop In The City', and offered 'immediate gold-status membership'. There were two bouncers guarding the door from drunks and undesirables. Both were overweight and shaven-headed. They wore identical charcoal suits and black open-necked shirts, and sported earpieces to alert them to any trouble inside.

'Tweedledum and Tweedledumber,' Siobhan said under her breath. They were staring at her rather than Rebus, women not being the Nook's target demographic.

'Sorry, no couples,' one of them said.

'Hiya, Bob,' Rebus replied. 'How long you been out?'

The bouncer took a moment to place him. 'You're looking well, Mr Rebus.'

'So are you: must've been using the gym at Saughton.' Rebus turned to Siobhan. 'Let me introduce Bob Dodds. Bob was doing six for a fairly major assault.'

'Reduced on appeal,' Dodds added. 'And the bastard deserved it.'

125

'He'd dumped your sister . . . that was it, wasn't it? You went for him with a baseball bat and a Stanley knife. And here you are, large as life.' Rebus smiled broadly. 'And performing a useful function in society.'

'You're a cop?' the other bouncer finally twigged.

'Me too,' Siobhan told him. 'And that means, couples or no couples, we're going in.'

'You want to see the manager?' Dodds asked.

'That's the general idea.'

Dodds reached into his jacket and produced a walkie-talkie. 'Door to office.'

There was some static, then a crackled reply. 'What the fuck is it now?'

'Two police officers to see you.'

'They after a bung or what?'

Rebus took the walkie-talkie from Dodds. 'We just want a quiet word, sir. If you're offering to bribe us, however, that's something we'll have to discuss down the station . . .'

'It was a joke, for Christ's sake. Get Bob to bring you in.'

Rebus handed back the walkie-talkie. 'I guess that makes us gold-status members,' he said.

Through the door, there was a thin partition wall, built to stop anyone from outside being able to scope the place out before parting with the admission price. The reception desk consisted of a middle-aged woman with an old-fashioned cash register. The carpeting was crimson and purple, the walls black, with tiny lighting filaments whose purpose was either to resemble the night sky or deter drinkers from a detailed study of the bar prices and measures. The bar itself was much as Rebus remembered it from Laurie Tavern days. There was no draught beer, however, just the more profitable bottled variety. A small stage had been constructed in the centre of the room, two shiny silver poles stretching from it to the ceiling. A young, dark-skinned woman was dancing to an over-amplified instrumental, watched by maybe half a dozen men. Siobhan noticed that she kept her eyes shut throughout, concentrating on the music. Two more men were seated on a nearby sofa, while another woman danced topless between them. An arrow pointed the way to a 'Private VIP Booth', shielded by black drapes from the rest of the room. Three suited businessmen sat on stools at the bar, sharing a bottle of champagne.

'It livens up later on,' Dodds told Rebus. 'Place is mental at the weekend . . .' He led them across the floor, stopping at a door marked 'Private' and punching numbers into the keypad alongside. He pushed the door open and nodded them through.

They were in a short, narrow hallway with a door at its end. Dodds knocked and waited.

'If you must!' the voice called from the other side. Rebus motioned with his head to tell Dodds they could manage without him from here on. Then he turned the handle.

The office was not much bigger than a boxroom, and what space there was had been filled almost to capacity. Shelves groaned under paperwork and bits and pieces of discarded equipment – everything from a disconnected beer pump to a golfball typewriter. Magazines were stacked on the linoleum floor: trade mags mostly. The bottom half of a water cooler had become a support for shrink-wrapped collections of beer mats. A venerable-looking green safe stood open, to reveal boxes of drinking straws and packs of paper napkins. There was a tiny barred window behind the desk, which Rebus guessed would give a minimum of natural light in daytime. The available wall space was filled with framed cuttings from newspapers: paparazzi-style pics of men exiting the Nook. Rebus recognised a couple of footballers whose careers had stalled.

The man seated at the desk was in his thirties. He wore a tight white T-shirt, giving definition to his muscular torso and arms. The face was tanned, the cropped hair jet black. No jewellery, other than a gold watch with more dials than necessary. His blue eyes shone, even in this room's dim wattage. 'Stuart Bullen,' he said, reaching out a hand without bothering to stand.

Rebus introduced himself, then Siobhan. Handshakes completed, Bullen apologised for the lack of chairs.

'No room for them,' he shrugged.

'We're fine standing, Mr Bullen,' Rebus assured him.

'As you can see, the Nook has nothing to hide ... which makes your visit all the more intriguing.'

'That's not a local accent, Mr Bullen,' Rebus commented.

'I'm from the west coast originally.'

Rebus nodded. 'I seem to know the name ...'

Bullen's mouth twitched. 'To put your mind at rest, yes, my dad was Rab Bullen.'

'Glasgow gangster,' Rebus explained to Siobhan.

'A respected *businessman*,' Bullen corrected.

'Who died when someone fired at him from point-blank range on his own doorstep,' Rebus added. 'What was that – five, six years ago?'

'If I'd known it was my dad you wanted to talk about . . .' Bullen was staring hard at Rebus.

'It isn't,' Rebus interrupted.

'We're looking for a girl, Mr Bullen,' Siobhan said. 'A runaway called Ishbel Jardine.' She handed him the photograph. 'Maybe you've seen her?'

'And why would I have seen her?'

Siobhan shrugged. 'She might need money. We hear you've been hiring dancers.'

'Every club in town's hiring dancers.' It was his turn to shrug. 'They come and they go . . . All my dancers are legit, mind, and dancing's as far as it goes.'

'Even in the VIP booth?' Rebus asked.

'We're talking about housewives and students . . . women who need a bit of easy cash.'

'If you could just look at the photo, please,' Siobhan said. 'She's eighteen and her name's Ishbel.'

'Never seen her before in my life.' He made to hand the photo back. 'Who told you I was hiring?'

'Information received,' Rebus informed him.

'I saw you looking at my little collection.' Bullen nodded towards the photos on the wall. 'This is a classy place, we like to think we're a bit above the other clubs in the area. That means we're choosy about the girls we employ. We tend not to take the junkies.'

'Nobody said she was a junkie. And I doubt very much whether this dive could ever be described as "classy".'

Bullen sat back, the better to study him. 'You can't be too far off retiring, Inspector. I look forward to the day when I can deal with cops like your colleague.' He smiled in Siobhan's direction. 'A much pleasanter prospect.'

'How long have you had this place?' Rebus asked. He'd brought out his cigarettes.

'Don't smoke in here,' Bullen told him. 'It's a fire risk.' Rebus hesitated, then put the packet away again. Bullen gave a little nod of thanks. 'To answer your question: four years.'

'What took you away from Glasgow?'

'Well, my dad's murder might give you a clue.'

'Never caught the killer, did they?'

'Shouldn't that "they" be a "we"?'

'Glasgow and Edinburgh police – chalk and cheese.'

'You mean you'd have had more luck?'

'Luck's got nothing to do with it.'

'Well, Inspector, if that's all you came for . . . I'm sure you've got other premises to visit?'

'Mind if we talk to the girls?' Siobhan asked suddenly.

'What for?'

'Just to show them the photo. Is there a dressing room they use?'

He nodded. 'Through the black curtain. But they only go there between shifts.'

'Then we'll talk to them where we find them.'

'If you must,' Bullen snapped.

She turned to leave, but pulled up short. There was a black leather jacket hanging behind the door. She rubbed the collar between her fingers. 'What car do you drive?' she asked abruptly.

'What's it to do with you?'

'It's a simple enough question, but if you want to do it the hard way . . .' She glared at him.

Bullen let out a sigh. 'BMW X5.'

'Sounds sporty.'

Bullen snorted. 'It's an off-roader, a four-by-four. Huge big tank of a thing.'

She nodded understanding. 'Those are the cars men buy when there's something they feel the need to compensate for . . .' On which line she made her exit. Rebus offered Bullen a smile.

'How's she rating now as that "pleasanter prospect" you were talking about?'

'I know you,' Bullen replied, wagging a finger. 'You're the cop Ger Cafferty keeps in his pocket.'

'Is that right?'

'It's what everybody says.'

'I can't argue with that then, can I?'

Rebus turned to follow Siobhan out. He reckoned he'd done well not to rise to the young prick's goading. Big Ger Cafferty had for many years been king of Edinburgh's underworld. These days, he lived a quieter life: at least on the surface. But with Cafferty, you never could tell. It was true that Rebus knew him. In fact, Bullen had just given Rebus an idea, because if there was one man who might know what the hell a Glasgow low-life like Stuart Bullen was doing on the other side of the country from his natural lair, that man was Morris Gerald Cafferty.

Siobhan had taken a stool at the bar, the businessmen having moved to a table. Rebus joined her, putting the barman's mind at ease: he'd probably never had to serve a single woman before.

'Bottle of your best beer,' Rebus said. 'And whatever the lady's having.'

'Diet Coke,' she told the barman. He brought their drinks.

'Six pounds,' he said.

'Mr Bullen says they're on the house,' Rebus informed him with a wink. 'He wants to keep us sweet.'

'Ever see this girl in here?' Siobhan asked, holding up the photograph.

'Looks familiar . . . but then a lot of girls look like that.'

'What's your name, son?' Rebus asked.

The barman bristled at that use of 'son'. He was in his early twenties, short and wiry. White T-shirt, maybe trying to copy his boss's style. Hair spiked with gel. He wore the same earpiece as the bouncers. There were two stud earrings in his other ear.

'Barney Grant.'

'Worked here long, Barney?'

'Couple of years.'

'Place like this, that probably qualifies you as a lifer.'

'Nobody's been here as long as me,' Grant agreed.

'Bet you've seen a few things.'

Grant nodded. 'But one thing I haven't seen in all that time is Stuart offering free drinks.' He held his hand out. 'Six pounds, please.'

'I admire your persistence, son.' Rebus handed over the money. 'What's your accent?'

'Aussie. And I'll tell you something else – I've got a memory for faces, and I seem to know yours.'

'I was in here a few months back . . . stag party. Didn't stay long.'

'So to get back to Ishbel Jardine,' Siobhan cajoled, 'you think maybe you've seen her?'

Grant took another look at the photo. 'Might not have been here, though. Plenty of clubs and pubs . . . could've been anywhere.' He took the money to the till. Siobhan turned round to study the room and almost wished she hadn't. One of the dancers was leading a suit towards the VIP booth. Another, the one she'd seen earlier, concentrating on the music, was now sliding up and down the silver pole, minus her thong.

'Christ, this is sleazy,' she commented to Rebus. 'What the hell do you get out of it?'

'A lightening of the wallet,' he replied.

Siobhan turned to Grant again. 'How much do they charge?'

'Tenner a dance. Lasts a couple of minutes, no touching allowed.'

'And in the VIP booth?'

'Couldn't tell you.'

'Why not?'

'Never been in. Want another drink?' He motioned to her glass, which was as full of ice as when it had arrived, but otherwise empty.

'Trick of the trade,' Rebus told her. 'More ice you put in, less room there is for the actual drink.'

'I'm fine, thanks,' she told Grant. 'Do you think any of the girls would talk to us?'

'Why should they?'

'What if I leave the photo with you . . . would you show it around?'

'Could do.'

'And my card.' She handed it over with the photograph. 'You can phone me if there's any news.'

'Okay.' He placed both items under the bar. Then, to Rebus: 'What about you? Fancy another?'

'Not at those prices, Barney, thanks all the same.'

'Remember,' Siobhan said, 'call me.' She slid from the stool and headed for the exit. Rebus had stopped to study another row of framed photos – copies of the newspaper cuttings in Bullen's office. He tapped one of them. Siobhan looked closer: Lex Cater and his film-star father, their faces turned ghostly white by the photographer's flash gun. Gordon Cater had raised his hand to his face, but too late. His eyes looked haunted, but his son was grinning, happy to be captured for posterity.

'Look at the by-line,' Rebus told her. Each story was accompanied by an 'exclusive' tag, and beneath the headlines sat the same bold-print name: Steve Holly.

'Funny how he's always in the right place at the right time,' Siobhan said.

'Yes, isn't it?' Rebus agreed.

Outside, he paused to light a cigarette. Siobhan kept walking, unlocking the car and getting in, sitting there with hands gripped around the steering wheel. Rebus walked slowly, inhaling deeply. There was still half a cigarette left by the time he reached the Peugeot, but he flicked it on to the road and climbed into the passenger side.

'I know what you're thinking,' he said.

'Do you?' She signalled to move away from the kerb.

He turned to her. 'More than one kind of flesh market,' he stated. 'Why did you ask about his car?'

131

Siobhan considered her reply. 'Because he looked like a pimp,' she said, Rebus's words turning over in her mind:

More than one kind of flesh market . . .

DAY FOUR

Thursday

11

Next morning, Rebus was back in Knoxland. Some of the previous day's banners and placards were strewn around, their slogans blurred by footprints. Rebus was in the Portakabin, drinking a coffee he'd brought with him and finishing the newspaper. Stef Yurgii's name had been revealed to the media at a press conference yesterday evening. It merited just the one mention in Steve Holly's tabloid, while Mo Dirwan got a couple of paragraphs. There was also a series of pictures of Rebus: wrestling the youth to the ground, being proclaimed a hero by an arms-aloft Dirwan, and watched by Dirwan's followers. The headline – almost certainly the work of Holly himself – was the single word STONED!

Rebus tossed the paper into the bin, aware that someone would in all probability just fish it out again. He found a cup half full of cold slops and poured it over the newsprint, feeling better for it. His watch said it was nine fifteen. Earlier, he'd made the request for a patrol car to head out to Portobello. By his reckoning, it would be here any minute. The Portakabin was quiet. Wise counsel had decided that it would be foolish to bring a computer into Knoxland, so instead all the door-to-door reports were being collated back at Torphichen. Walking over to the window, Rebus scraped some shards of glass into a pile. Despite its grille, the window had been broken: a stick of some kind or a thin metal pole. Something sticky had then been sprayed through the window, marking the floor and the nearest desk. To add a final touch, the word FILTH had been spray-painted on every available surface of the exterior. By close of play today, Rebus knew that the window would be boarded up. In fact, the Portakabin might even have been declared surplus to requirements. They'd gleaned what they could, taken what evidence was available. Rebus knew that Shug Davidson had one main strategy: shame the estate into pointing the finger. So maybe Holly's stories were no bad thing.

Well, it would be nice to think so, but Rebus doubted many people in Knoxland would read of racism and feel anything but complete justification. However, Davidson was counting on just one person seeing the light – one witness was all he needed.

One name.

There would have been blood; a weapon to dispose of; clothes to be burned or thrown out. Someone knew. Hidden away in one of those blocks, hopefully with guilt gnawing away at them.

Someone knew.

Rebus had called Steve Holly first thing, asked him how come he always seemed to be outside the Nook when a celeb came stumbling out.

'Just good investigative journalism. But you're talking ancient history.'

'How so?'

'When the place opened, it was hot for a few months. That's when those pics got taken. Go there often, do you?'

Rebus had hung up without replying.

Now he heard a car approaching, peered through the cracked glass and saw it. Allowed himself a little smile as he drained his coffee.

He walked out to meet Gareth Baird, nodding a greeting at the two uniforms who'd brought him here.

'Morning, Gareth.'

'What's the game then?' Gareth dug his fists into his pockets. 'Harassment, is that it?'

'Not at all. It's just that you're a valuable witness. Remember, *you're* the one who knows what Stef Yurgii's girlfriend looks like.'

'Christ, I barely noticed her!'

'But she did the talking,' Rebus said calmly. 'And I've an inkling you'd know her if you saw her again.'

'You want me to do a photofit for you, is that it?'

'That comes later. Right now, you're going to go on a recce with these two officers.'

'A recce?'

'Door-to-door. Give you a taste of police work.'

'How many doors?' Gareth was scanning the tower blocks.

'All of them.'

He stared at Rebus, wide-eyed, like a kid given detention on the flimsiest of evidence.

'Sooner you start...' Rebus patted the young man on the shoulder. Then, to the uniforms: 'Take him away, lads.'

Watching Gareth trudge, head down, towards the first of the blocks, sandwiched by the two constables, Rebus felt a buzz of satisfaction. It was good to know the job could still offer the odd perk...

Two more cars were arriving: Davidson and Wylie in one, Reynolds in another. They'd probably travelled in convoy from Torphichen. Davidson carried the morning paper with him, folded open at STONED!

'Seen this?' he asked.

'I wouldn't lower myself, Shug.'

'Why not?' Reynolds grinned. 'You're the towel-heads' new hero.'

Davidson's cheeks reddened. 'One more crack like that, Charlie, and I'll have you on report – is that clear?'

Reynolds stiffened his back. 'Slip of the tongue, sir.'

'You've collected more slips than a bookie's dustbin. Don't let it happen again.'

'Sir.'

Davidson let the silence lie for a moment, then decided he'd made his point. 'Is there anything useful you can be doing?'

Reynolds relaxed a little. 'Inside gen – there's a woman in one of the flats does a pot of tea and some biscuits.'

'Oh yes?'

'Met her yesterday, sir. She said she wouldn't mind making us a brew as and when.'

Davidson nodded. 'Then go fetch.' Reynolds made to move off. 'Oh, and Charlie? The clock's running – don't get too comfy in there...'

'I'll remain professional, sir, don't worry.' Giving Rebus a leer as he passed him.

Davidson turned to Rebus. 'Who was that with the uniforms?'

Rebus lit a cigarette. 'Gareth Baird. He's going to see if the victim's lady friend is hiding behind one of those doors.'

'Needle-in-a-haystack stuff?' Davidson commented.

Rebus just shrugged. Ellen Wylie had disappeared inside the Portakabin. Davidson was only now registering the fresh daubs. 'Filth, eh? I've always thought that the people who call us that *are* that.' He pushed his hair back from his forehead, scratching at his scalp. 'Anything else on today?'

'Victim's wife's ID-ing the body. Thought I'd maybe attend.' He paused. 'Unless you want to do it.'

'It's all yours. Nothing waiting for you back at Gayfield then?'

'Not even a proper desk.'

'They're hoping you'll take the hint?'

Rebus nodded. 'Think I should?'

Davidson looked sceptical. 'What's waiting for you when you retire?'

'Liver disease, probably. I've already made the down-payment . . .'

Davidson smiled. 'Well, I'd say we're still short-handed, which means I'm happy for you to stick around.' Rebus was about to say something – thanks, perhaps – but Davidson raised a finger. 'So long as you don't go off on any wild tangents, understood?'

'Crystal clear, Shug.'

Both men turned at a sudden bellow from two storeys up: 'Good morning to you, Inspector!' It was Mo Dirwan, waving down to Rebus from the walkway. Rebus gave a half-hearted wave back, but then remembered that he had a few questions for the lawyer.

'Stay there, I'm coming up!' he called.

'I'm in flat two-o-two.'

'Dirwan's been working for the Yurgii family,' Rebus reminded Davidson. 'Few things I need to clear up with him.'

'Don't let me stop you.' Davidson placed a hand on Rebus's shoulder. 'But no more photo-calls, eh?'

'Don't worry, Shug, there won't be.'

Rebus took the lift to the second floor, and walked to the door marked 202. Looking down, he saw that Davidson was studying the damage to the outside of the Portakabin. There was no sign of Reynolds with the promised tea.

The door was ajar, so Rebus walked in. The place was carpeted with what looked like off-cuts. A broom rested against the lobby wall. A plumbing problem had left a large brown stain on the cream ceiling.

'In here,' Dirwan called. He was seated on a sofa in the living room. Again, the windows were frosted with condensation. Both bars of the electric fire were glowing. Ethnic music was playing softly from a tape machine. An elderly couple were standing in front of the sofa.

'Join me,' Dirwan said, slapping the cushion beside him with one hand, cup and saucer gripped in the other. Rebus sat down, the couple bowing slightly at his smiled greeting. It was only when he was seated that he realised there were no other chairs, nothing for the couple to do but stand there. Not that this seemed to bother the lawyer.

'Mr and Mrs Singh have been here eleven years,' he was saying. 'But not for much longer.'

'I'm sorry to hear that,' Rebus replied.

Dirwan chuckled. 'They're not being deported, Inspector: their son has done very well for himself in business. Big house in Barnton . . .'

'Cramond,' Mr Singh corrected, naming one of the city's better areas.

'Big house in Cramond,' the lawyer ploughed on. 'They're moving in with him.'

'Into the granny flat,' Mrs Singh said, seeming to take pleasure in the phrase. 'Would you like tea or coffee?'

'I'm fine actually,' Rebus apologised. 'But I do need a word with Mr Dirwan.'

'You would like us to leave?'

'No, no . . . we'll talk outside.' Rebus gave Dirwan a meaningful look. The lawyer handed his cup to Mrs Singh.

'Tell your son I wish him everything he could wish himself,' he barked, his voice seeming out of all proportion to what was necessary. The room echoed as he stopped.

The Singhs bowed again, and Rebus got to his feet. Hands had to be shaken before Rebus could lead Dirwan out on to the walkway.

'A lovely family, you must agree,' Dirwan said after the door had closed. 'Immigrants, you see, can make a vital contribution to the community at large.'

'I've never doubted it. You know we have a name for the victim? Stef Yurgii.'

Dirwan sighed. 'I just found out this morning.'

'You didn't see the photos we placed in the tabloids?'

'I do not read the gutter press.'

'But you were going to come and talk to us, to let us know you knew him?'

'I didn't know him: I know his wife and children.'

'And you hadn't had any contact with him? He didn't try getting a message to his family?'

Dirwan shook his head. 'Not through me. I would not hesitate to tell you.' He fixed his eyes on Rebus. 'You must trust me on that, John.'

'Only my best friends call me John,' Rebus warned, 'and trust has

139

to be earned, Mr Dirwan.' He paused to let this sink in. 'You didn't know he was in Edinburgh?'

'I did not.'

'But you've been working on the wife's case?'

The lawyer nodded. 'It's not right, you know: we call ourselves civilised, but are happy to let her rot with her children in Whitemire. You've seen them?' Rebus nodded. 'Then you will know – no trees, no freedom, the bare minimum of education and nourishment . . .'

'But nothing to do with this inquiry,' Rebus felt the need to say.

'My God, I don't believe I just heard that! You've seen first-hand the problems with racism in this country.'

'Doesn't seem to be harming the Singhs.'

'Just because they smile doesn't mean anything.' He broke off suddenly, started rubbing the back of his neck. 'I should not drink so much tea. It heats the blood, you know.'

'Look, I appreciate what you're doing, talking to all these people . . .'

'Regarding which, would you like to know what I've gleaned?'

'Sure.'

'I was knocking on doors all of last evening, and from first thing this morning . . . Of course, not everyone was relevant or would speak with me.'

'Thanks for trying anyway.'

Dirwan received the praise with a motion of his head. 'You know that Stef Yurgii was a journalist in his own country?'

'Yes.'

'Well, people here – the ones who knew him – did not know that. However, he was good at getting to know people; at getting them to talk – it is in a journalist's nature, yes?'

Rebus nodded.

'So,' the lawyer continued, 'Stef spoke to people about their lives, asking many questions without revealing much of his own past.'

'You think he was going to write about it?'

'That is a possibility.'

'What about the girlfriend?'

Dirwan shook his head. 'No one seems to know about her. Of course, with a family in Whitemire, it is entirely possible that he would want her existence to remain a secret.'

Rebus nodded again. 'Anything else?' he asked.

'Not as yet. You wish me to continue knocking on doors?'

'I know it's a chore . . .'

'But that's exactly what it isn't! I am gaining a feel for this place, and I'm meeting people who may wish to form their own collective.'

'Like the one in Glasgow?'

'Exactly. People are stronger when they act together.'

Rebus considered this. 'Well, good luck to you – and thanks again.' He shook the proffered hand, unsure how far he trusted Dirwan. The man was a lawyer, after all; added to which, he had his own agenda.

Someone was walking towards them. They had to move to let him past. Rebus recognised the youth from yesterday, the one with the rock. The youth just stared at the two men, unsure as to who deserved his scorn more. He stopped at the lifts and jabbed the button.

'I hear you like tattoos,' Rebus called out. He nodded to Dirwan to let the lawyer know they were finished. Then he walked over to join the youth, who backed away as if fearing contamination. Like the youth, Rebus kept his eyes on the lift doors. Dirwan meantime was getting no answer at 203; moved further away to try 204.

'What do you want?' the youth muttered.

'Just passing the time of day. It's what humans do, you know: communicate with each other.'

'Fuck that.'

'Something else we do: accept the opinions of others. We're all different, after all.' There was a dull ping as the doors on the left-hand lift shuddered open. Rebus made to step in, then saw that the youth was going to stay behind. Rebus grabbed him by his jacket and hauled him inside, held him till the doors had closed again. The youth pushed him away, tried the 'Door Open' button, but too late. The lift was starting its creeping descent.

'You like the paramilitaries?' Rebus went on. 'UVF, all that lot?'

The youth clamped his mouth shut, lips sucked in behind his teeth.

'Gives you something to hide behind, I suppose,' Rebus said, as if to himself. 'Every coward needs some sort of shield . . . They'll look lovely later on, too, those tattoos, when you're married with kids . . . Catholic neighbours and a Muslim boss . . .'

'Aye, right, like I'd let that happen.'

'A lot of things are going to happen to you that you can't control, son. Take it from a veteran.'

The lift came to a stop, its doors not opening fast enough for the youth, who started trying to pull them apart, squeezing out and loping off. Rebus watched him cross the stretch of playground. Shug Davidson, too, was watching from the Portakabin's doorway.

'Been fraternising with the locals?' he asked.

'A bit of lifestyle advice,' Rebus acknowledged. 'What's his name, by the way?'

Davidson had to think. 'Howard Slowther ... calls himself Howie.'

'Age?'

'Nearly fifteen. Education are after him for truancy. Young Howie's heading down the pan big-time.' Davidson shrugged. 'And there's bugger-all we can do about it until he does something really stupid.'

'Which could be any day now,' Rebus said, eyes still on the rapidly retreating figure, following it as it descended the slope towards the underpass.

'Any day,' Davidson agreed. 'What time's your meeting at the mortuary?'

'Ten.' Rebus checked his watch. 'Time I was going.'

'Remember: keep in touch.'

'I'll send you a postcard, Shug: "Wish you were here".'

12

Siobhan had no reason to think that Ishbel's 'pimp' was Stuart Bullen: Bullen seemed too young. He had the leather jacket, but not a sports car. She'd looked at an X5 on the internet, and it was anything but sporty.

Then again, she'd asked him a specific question: what car did he drive? Maybe he had more than one: the X5 for day-to-day stuff, and something else garaged for nights and weekends. Was it worth checking? Worth another visit to the Nook? Right now, she didn't think so.

Having squeezed into a space on Cockburn Street, she was walking up Fleshmarket Close. A couple of middle-aged tourists were gazing at the cellar door. The man held a videocam, the woman a guidebook.

'Excuse me,' the woman asked. Her accent was English Midlands, maybe Yorkshire. 'Do you know if this is where the skeletons were found?'

'That's right,' Siobhan told her.

'The tour guide told us about it,' the woman explained. 'Last night.'

'One of the ghost tours?' Siobhan guessed.

'That's it, pet. She told us it were witchcraft.'

'Is that right?'

The husband had already started filming the studded wooden door. Siobhan found herself apologising as she brushed past. The pub wasn't open yet, but she reckoned someone would be there, so she rattled the door with her foot. The lower half was solid, but the top half comprised green glass circles, like the bottoms of wine

143

bottles. She watched a shadow move behind the glass, the click of a key being turned.

'We open at eleven.'

'Mr Mangold? DS Clarke . . . remember me?'

'Christ, what is it now?'

'Any chance I can come in?'

'I'm in a meeting.'

'It won't take long . . .'

Mangold hesitated, then pulled open the door.

'Thanks,' Siobhan said, stepping in. 'What happened to your face?'

He touched the bruising on his left cheek. The eye above was swollen. 'Bit of a disagreement with a punter,' he said. 'One of the perils of the job.'

Siobhan looked towards the barman. He was transferring ice from one bucket to another, gave her a nod of greeting. There was a smell of disinfectant and wood polish. A cigarette smouldered in an ashtray on the bar, a mug of coffee next to it. There was paperwork, too: the morning post by the look of things.

'Looks like you got off lightly,' she said. The barman shrugged. 'Wasn't my shift.'

She noticed two more mugs of coffee on a corner table, a woman cupping one of them in both hands. There was a small pile of books in front of her. Siobhan could make out a couple of the titles: *Edinburgh Haunts* and *The City Above and Below*.

'Make it quick, will you? I'm up to my eyes today.' Mangold seemed in no hurry to introduce his other visitor, but Siobhan offered her a smile anyway, which the woman returned. She was in her forties, with frizzy dark hair tied back with a black velvet bow. She'd kept on her Afghan coat. Siobhan could see bare ankles and leather sandals beneath. Mangold stood with arms folded, legs apart, in the centre of the room.

'You were going to look out the paperwork,' Siobhan reminded him.

'Paperwork?'

'For the laying of the floor in the cellar.'

'There aren't enough hours in the day,' Mangold complained.

'Even so, sir . . .'

'Two fake skeletons – where's the fire?' He held his arms out in supplication.

Siobhan realised that the woman was coming towards them. 'You're interested in the burials?' she asked in a soft, sibilant voice.

'That's right,' Siobhan said. 'I'm Detective Sergeant Clarke, and you're Judith Lennox.' Lennox went wide-eyed. 'I recognise you from your picture in the paper,' Siobhan explained.

Lennox took Siobhan's hand, gripping rather than shaking it. 'You're so full of energy, Miss Clarke. It's like electricity.'

'And you're giving Mr Mangold here a history lesson.'

'Quite right.' The woman's eyes had widened again.

'The titles on the spines,' Siobhan explained, nodding towards the books. 'Bit of a giveaway.'

Lennox looked at Mangold. 'I'm helping Ray develop his new theme bar . . . it's very exciting.'

'The cellar?' Siobhan guessed.

'He wants some idea of historical context.'

Mangold coughed an interruption. 'I'm sure Detective Sergeant Clarke has better things to do with her time . . .' Hinting that he, too, was a man with things to do. Then, to Siobhan: 'I did have a quick look for anything to do with the job, but came up blank. Could have been cash-in-hand. Plenty cowboys out there who'll lay a floor, no questions asked, nothing in writing . . .'

'Nothing in writing?' Siobhan repeated.

'You were here when the skeletons were found?' Judith Lennox asked.

Siobhan tried to ignore her, focused on Mangold instead. 'You're trying to tell me . . .'

'It was Mag Lennox, wasn't it? It was her skeleton you found.'

Siobhan stared at the woman. 'What makes you say that?'

Judith Lennox squeezed shut her eyes. 'I had a premonition. I'd been trying to arrange tours of the medical faculty . . . they wouldn't let me. Wouldn't even let me see the skeleton . . .' Her eyes burned with zeal. 'I'm her descendant, you know.'

'Are you?'

'She laid a curse on this country, and on anyone who would do her harm or mischief.' Lennox nodded to herself.

Siobhan thought of Cater and McAteer: not much sign of any curse befalling them. She thought of saying as much, but remembered her promise to Curt.

'All I know is, the skeletons were fake,' Siobhan stressed.

'My point exactly,' Mangold broke in. 'So why are you so bloody interested?'

'It would be nice to have an explanation,' Siobhan said quietly. She thought back to the scene in the cellar, the way her whole body

145

had contracted at the sight of the infant . . . placing her coat gently over the bones.

'They found skeletons in the grounds of Holyrood,' Lennox was saying. '*Those* were real enough. And a coven in Gilmerton.'

Siobhan knew of the 'coven': a series of chambers buried beneath a bookmaker's shop. But last she'd heard, it had been proven to belong to a blacksmith. Not a view she guessed would be shared by the historian.

'And that's as much as you can tell me?' she asked Mangold instead.

He opened his arms again, gold bracelets sliding over his wrists.

'In which case,' said Siobhan, 'I'll let you get back to work. It was nice to meet you, Miss Lennox.'

'And you,' the historian said. She pushed a palm forwards. Siobhan took a step back. Lennox had her eyes closed again, lashes fluttering. 'Make use of that energy. It is replenishable.'

'That's good to hear.'

Lennox opened her eyes, focusing on Siobhan. 'We give some of our life force to our children. *They* are the true replenishment . . .'

The look Mangold gave Siobhan was mostly apologetic, partly self-pitying: his time with Judith Lennox, after all, still had a ways to run . . .

Rebus had never seen children in a mortuary before, and the sight offended him. This was a place for professionals, for adults, for the widowed. It was a place for unwelcome truths about the human body. It was the antithesis of childhood.

Then again, what was childhood to the Yurgii children but confusion and desperation?

Which didn't stop Rebus pinning one of the guards to the wall. Not physically, of course, not using his hands. But by dint of placing himself at an intimidating proximity to the man and then inching forward, until the guard had his back to the wall of the waiting area.

'You brought kids *here*?' Rebus spat.

The guard was young; his ill-fitting uniform offered no protection against someone like Rebus. 'They wouldn't stay,' he stammered. 'Bawling and grabbing on to her . . .' Rebus had turned his head to look at where the seated mother was folding the children in towards her, showing no interest in this scene, and in turn being embraced by her friend in the headscarf, the one from Whitemire.

146

The boy, however, was watching intently. 'Mr Traynor thought it best to let them come.'

'They could have stayed in the van.' Rebus had seen it outside: custodial blue with bars on its windows, a toughened grille between the front seats and the benches in the back.

'Not without their mum . . .'

The door was opening, a second guard entering. This man was the elder. He held a clipboard. Behind him came the white-coated figure of Bill Ness, who ran the mortuary. Ness was in his fifties, with Buddy Holly glasses. As ever, he was chewing a piece of gum. He went over to the family and offered the rest of the packet to the children, who reacted by moving even closer to their mother. Left standing in the doorway was Ellen Wylie. She was there to witness the ID procedure. She hadn't known Rebus was coming, and he'd since told her that she was welcome to the job.

'Everything all right here?' the elder guard was asking Rebus now.

'Hunky dory,' Rebus said, taking a couple of paces back.

'Mrs Yurgii,' Ness was coaxing, 'we're ready when you are.'

She nodded and tried rising to her feet, had to be helped up by her friend. She placed a hand on either child's head.

'I'll stay here with them, if you like,' Rebus said. She looked at him, then whispered something to the children, who gripped her all the harder.

'Your mum'll just be through that door,' Ness told them, pointing. 'We'll only be a minute . . .'

Mrs Yurgii crouched in front of son and daughter, whispered more words to them. Her eyes were glazed with tears. Then she lifted either child on to a chair, smiled at them, and backed away towards the door. Ness held it open for her. Both guards followed her, the elder glaring a warning towards Rebus: *Keep an eye on them*. Rebus didn't even blink.

When the door closed, the girl ran towards it, placing her hands against its surface. She said nothing, and wasn't crying. Her brother went to her, put his arm around her and led her back to where they'd been sitting. Rebus crouched down, resting his back against the wall opposite. It was a desolate spot: no posters or notices, no magazines. Nothing to pass the time because no one passed time here. Usually you waited only a minute, enough time for the body to be moved from its refrigerated shelf to the viewing room. And afterwards, you left swiftly, not wishing to spend another minute in this place. There wasn't even a clock, for, as Ness

147

had said once to Rebus, 'Our clients are out of time.' One of countless puns which helped him and his colleagues do the job they did.

'My name's John, by the way,' Rebus told the children. The girl was transfixed by the door, but the boy seemed to understand.

'Police bad,' he stated with passion.

'Not here,' Rebus told him. 'Not in this country.'

'In Turkey, very bad.'

Rebus nodded acceptance of this. 'But not here,' he repeated. 'Here, police good.' The boy looked sceptical, and Rebus didn't blame him. After all, what did he know of the police? They had accompanied the Immigration officials, taking the family into custody. The Whitemire guards probably looked like police officers, too: anyone in a uniform was suspect. Anyone in authority.

They were the people who had made his mother cry, his father disappear.

'You want to stay here? In this country?' Rebus asked. This concept was beyond the lad. He blinked a few times, until it was clear he wasn't about to answer.

'What toys do you like?'

'Toys?'

'Things you play with.'

'I play with my sister.'

'You play games, read books?'

Again, the question seemed unanswerable. It was as if Rebus were quizzing him on local history or the rules of rugby.

The door opened. Mrs Yurgii was sobbing quietly, supported by her friend, the officials behind them sombre, as befitted the moment. Ellen Wylie nodded at Rebus to let him know identity had been confirmed.

'That's us then,' the elder guard stated. The children were clinging to their mother again. The guards started manoeuvring all four figures towards the opposite door, the one leading back to the outside world, the land of the living.

The boy turned just the once, as if to gauge Rebus's reaction. Rebus tried a smile which was not returned.

Ness headed back into the heart of the building, which left only Rebus and Wylie in the waiting area.

'Do we need to talk to her?' she asked.

'Why?'

'To establish when she last heard from her husband . . .'

Rebus shrugged. 'That's up to you, Ellen.'

148

She looked at him. 'What's wrong?'

Rebus shook his head slowly.

'It's tough on the kids,' she said.

'Tell me,' he asked, 'when do you reckon was the last time life *wasn't* tough on those kids?'

She shrugged. 'Nobody asked them to come here.'

'I suppose that's true.'

She was still looking at him. 'But it's not the point you were making?' she guessed.

'I just think they deserve a childhood,' he responded. 'That's all.'

He went outside to smoke a cigarette, watched Wylie drive off in her Volvo. He paced the small car park, three of the mortuary's unmarked vans standing there, awaiting their next call. Inside, the attendants would be playing cards and drinking tea. There was a nursery school across the street, and Rebus considered the short journey between the two, then squashed the remains of the cigarette underfoot and got into his own car. Drove towards Gayfield Square, but continued past the police station. There was a toy shop he knew: Harburn Hobbies on Elm Row. He parked outside and headed in. Didn't bother looking at the prices, just picked out a few things: a simple train-set, a couple of model kits, and a doll's house and doll. The assistant helped him load the car. Back behind the steering wheel, he had another idea, this time driving to his flat in Arden Street. In the hall cupboard, he found a box full of old annuals and story books from when his daughter was twenty years younger. Why were they still there? Maybe awaiting the grandchildren who'd not yet come. Rebus put them on the back seat beside the other toys, and drove west out of town. Traffic was light, and within half an hour he was at the Whitemire turn-off. There were wisps of smoke from the camp-fire, but the woman was rolling up her tent, paying him no heed. A different guard was on duty at the gatehouse. Rebus had to show his ID, drive to the car park, and be met by another guard, who was reluctant to help with the haul.

There was no sign of Traynor, but that didn't matter. Rebus and the guard took the toys inside.

'They'll have to be checked,' the guard said.

'Checked?'

'We can't have people just bring anything in here . . .'

'You think there are drugs hidden inside the doll?'

'It's standard procedure, Inspector.' The guard lowered his voice.

149

'You and I know it's completely bloody stupid, but it still has to be done.'

The two men shared a look. Rebus nodded eventually. 'But they *will* get to the kids?' he asked.

'By the end of the day, if I've got anything to do with it.'

'Thanks.' Rebus shook the guard's hand, then looked around. 'How do you stand it here?'

'Would you rather have the place staffed by people different from me? God knows there are enough of them . . .'

Rebus managed a smile. 'You've got a point.' He thanked the man again. The guard just shrugged.

Driving out, Rebus noticed that the tent had gone. Its owner was now trudging down the side of the road, a rucksack on her back. He stopped, winding down his window.

'Need a lift?' he asked. 'I'm headed for Edinburgh.'

'You were here yesterday,' she stated. He nodded. 'Who are you?'

'I'm a police officer.'

'The murder in Knoxland?' she guessed. Rebus nodded again. She peered into the back of the car.

'Plenty room for your rucksack,' he told her.

'That's not why I was looking.'

'Oh?'

'Just wondering what happened to the doll's house. I saw a doll's house on the back seat when you drove in.'

'Then your eyes obviously deceived you.'

'Obviously,' she said. 'After all, why would a policeman bring toys to a detention centre?'

'Why indeed?' Rebus agreed, getting out to help her stash her things.

They drove the first half-mile in silence, then Rebus asked her if she smoked.

'No, but you go ahead if you like.'

'I'm all right,' Rebus lied. 'How often do you do that vigil thing?'

'As often as I can.'

'All by yourself?'

'There were more of us to start with.'

'I remember seeing it on the telly.'

'Others join me when they can: weekends, usually.'

'They have jobs to go to?' Rebus guessed.

'I work too, you know,' she snapped. 'It's just that I can juggle my time.'

'You're an acrobat?'

150

She smiled at this. 'I'm an artist.' She paused, awaiting a response. 'And thank you for not snorting.'

'Why would I snort?'

'Most people like you would.'

'People like me?'

'People who see anyone who's different to them as a threat.'

Rebus made a show of taking this in. 'So that's what I'm like. I'd always wondered . . .'

She smiled again. 'All right, I'm jumping to conclusions, but not without some grounds. You'll have to trust me on that.' She leaned forward to operate the seat mechanism, sliding it back as far as it would go, giving her room to put her feet on the dashboard in front of her. Rebus thought she was probably in her mid-forties, long mousy-brown hair woven into braids. Three hooped golden earrings in either lobe. Her face was pale and freckled, and her front two teeth overlapped, giving her the look of an impish schoolgirl.

'I trust you,' he said. 'I also take it you're not a big fan of our asylum laws?'

'That's because they stink.'

'And what do they stink of?'

She turned from the windscreen to look at him. 'Hypocrisy, for starters,' she said. 'This is a country where you can buy your way to a passport if you know the right politician. If you don't, and we don't like your skin colour or your politics, then forget it.'

'You don't think we're a soft touch then?'

'Give me a break,' she said dismissively, turning her attention back to the scenery.

'I'm just asking.'

'A question to which you think you already know the answer?'

'I know we've got better welfare than some countries.'

'Yeah, right. That's why people pay their life savings to gangs who smuggle them over borders? That's why they suffocate in the backs of lorries, or squashed into cargo containers?'

'Don't forget the Eurostar: don't they cling to its undercarriage?'

'Don't you *dare* patronise me!'

'Just making conversation.' Rebus concentrated on driving for a few moments. 'So what kind of art do you do?'

It took her a few moments to answer him. 'Portraits mostly . . . the occasional landscape . . .'

'Would I have heard of you?'

'You don't look like a collector.'

'I used to have an H.R. Giger on my wall.'

'An original?'

Rebus shook his head. 'LP cover – *Brain Salad Surgery*.'

'At least you remember the artist's name.' She sniffed, running a hand across her nose. 'Mine's Caro Quinn.'

'Caro short for Caroline?' She nodded. Rebus reached out awkwardly with his right hand. 'I'm John Rebus.'

Quinn slipped off a grey woollen glove and they shook, the car creeping over the carriageway's central dividing line. Rebus quickly corrected the steering.

'Promise to get us back to Edinburgh in one piece?' the artist pleaded.

'Where do you want dropped?'

'Are you going anywhere near Leith Walk?'

'I'm based at Gayfield.'

'Perfect . . . I'm just off Pilrig Street, if it's not too much trouble.'

'Fine by me.' They were quiet for a few minutes until Quinn spoke.

'You couldn't move sheep around Europe the way some of these families have been moved . . . nearly two thousand of them in detention in Britain.'

'But a lot of them get to stay, right?'

'Not nearly enough. Holland's getting ready to deport twenty-six *thousand*.'

'Seems a lot. How many are there in Scotland?'

'Eleven thousand in Glasgow alone.'

Rebus whistled.

'Go back a couple of years, we took more asylum-seekers than any country in the world.'

'I thought we still did.'

'Numbers are dropping fast.'

'Because the world's a safer place?'

She looked at him, decided he was being ironic. 'Controls are tightening all the time.'

'Only so many jobs to go round,' Rebus said with a shrug.

'And that's supposed to make us less compassionate?'

'Never found much room for compassion in my job.'

'That's why you went to Whitemire with a car full of toys?'

'My friends call me Santa . . .'

Rebus double-parked, as directed, outside her tenement flat. 'Come up for a minute,' she said.

'What for?'

'Something I'd like you to see.'

He locked his car, hoping the owner of the boxed-in Mini wouldn't mind. Quinn lived on the top floor – in Rebus's experience the usual haunt of student renters. Quinn had another explanation.

'I get two storeys,' she said. 'There's a stair into the roof-space.' She unlocked the door, Rebus lagging half a flight behind her. He thought he heard her call out something – a name maybe – but when he entered the hallway there was no one there. Quinn had rested her rucksack against the wall and was beckoning him up the steep, narrow stairway into the eaves of the building. Rebus took a few deep breaths and started climbing again.

There was just the one room, illuminated by natural light from four large Velux windows. Canvases were stacked against the walls, black and white photographs pinned to every available inch of the eaves.

'I tend to work from photos,' Quinn told him. 'These are what I wanted you to see.' They were close-ups of faces, the camera seeming to focus on the eyes specifically. Rebus saw mistrust, fear, curiosity, indulgence, good humour. Surrounded by so many stares, he felt like an exhibit himself, and said as much to the artist, who seemed gratified.

'My next exhibition, I don't want any wall-space showing, just ranks of painted faces demanding we pay them some attention.'

'Staring us down.' Rebus nodded slowly. Quinn was nodding too. 'So where did you take them?'

'All over: Dundee, Glasgow, Knoxland.'

'They're all immigrants?'

She nodded, studying her work.

'When were you in Knoxland?'

'Three or four months back. I was kicked out after a couple of days . . .'

'Kicked out?'

She turned to him. 'Well, let's say made to feel unwelcome.'

'Who by?'

'Locals . . . bigots . . . people with a grudge.'

Rebus was looking more closely at the photos. He didn't see anyone he recognised.

'Some don't want to be photographed, of course, and I have to respect that.'

'Do you ask their names?' He watched her nod. 'No one called Stef Yurgii?'

She started to shake her head, then went rigid, her eyes widening. 'You're interrogating me!'

'Just asking a question,' he countered.

'Seeming friendly, giving me a lift . . .' She shook her head at her own stupidity. 'Christ, and to think I invited you in.'

'I'm trying to solve a case here, Caro. And for what it's worth, I gave you a lift out of natural curiosity . . . no other agenda.'

She stared at him. 'Natural curiosity about what?' Folding her arms defensively.

'I don't know . . . Maybe about why you'd hold a vigil like that. You didn't look the type.'

Her eyes narrowed. 'The type?'

He shrugged. 'No matted hair or combat jacket, no ratty-looking dog on a length of clothes-line . . . and not too many body piercings either, by the look of it.' He was trying to lighten the mood, and was relieved to see her shoulders relax. She gave a half-twitch of a smile and unfolded her arms, sliding her hands into her pockets instead.

There was a noise from downstairs: a baby crying. 'Yours?' Rebus asked.

'I'm not even married these days . . .' She turned and started down the narrow stairs again, Rebus lingering a moment before following, feeling all those eyes on him as he went.

One of the doors off the hallway was open. It led to a small bedroom. There was a single bed inside, on which sat a dark-skinned, sleepy-eyed woman, a baby suckling at her breast.

'Is she okay?' Quinn was asking the young woman.

'Okay,' came the reply.

'I'll leave you in peace then.' Quinn started closing the door.

'Peace,' came the quiet voice from within.

'Guess where I found her?' the artist asked Rebus.

'On the street?'

She shook her head. 'At Whitemire. She's a trained nurse, only she's not allowed to work here. Others in Whitemire are doctors, teachers . . .' She smiled at the look on his face. 'Don't worry, I didn't sneak her out or anything. If you offer an address and bail money, you can free any number of them.'

'Really? I didn't know. How much does it cost?'

Her smiled widened. 'Someone you're thinking of helping out, Inspector?'

'No . . . I was just wondering.'

'Plenty have been bailed already by people like me . . . Even the odd MSP has done it.' She paused. 'It's Mrs Yurgii, isn't it? I saw them bringing her back with her kids. Then, not much more than an hour later, you turn up with the doll's house.' She paused again. 'They won't give her bail.'

'Why not?'

'She's listed as an "abscond risk" – probably because her husband did the same thing.'

'Only now he's dead.'

'I'm not sure that'll change their minds.' She angled her head, as though seeking his potential as a future portrait. 'You know something? Maybe I *was* too quick to judge you. Have you got time for some coffee?'

Rebus made a show of studying his watch. 'Things to do,' he said. The sound of a car horn blared from below. 'Plus I've a Mini driver downstairs to mollify.'

'Another time maybe.'

'Sure.' He handed her his card. 'My mobile's on the back.'

She held the card in the palm of her hand, as though weighing it. 'Thanks for the lift,' she said.

'Let me know when the exhibition opens.'

'Just two things you'll need to bring – your chequebook, for one . . .'

'And?'

'Your conscience,' she said, opening the door for him.

13

Siobhan was fed up waiting. She'd called ahead to the hospital, and they'd tried paging Dr Cater – to no effect. So she'd driven out there anyway and asked for him at reception. Again he'd been paged – again, to no effect.

'I'm sure he's here,' a passing nurse had said. 'I saw him half an hour back.'

'Where?' Siobhan had demanded.

But the nurse hadn't been sure, offering half a dozen suggestions, so now Siobhan was prowling the wards and corridors, listening at doors, peering through the gaps in partitions, waiting outside rooms until consultations were finished and the doctor proved not to be Alexis Cater.

'Can I help?' She'd been asked this question a dozen times or more. Each time, she would ask for the whereabouts of Cater, receiving conflicting answers for her efforts.

'You can run, but you can't hide,' she muttered to herself as she entered a corridor she recognised from not ten minutes before. Stopping at a vending machine, she selected a can of Irn-Bru, sipping from it as she continued her quest. When her mobile sounded, she didn't recognise the number on the screen: another mobile.

'Hello?' she said, turning another corner.

'Shiv? Is that you?'

She stopped dead in her tracks. 'Of course it's me – you're calling *my* phone, aren't you?'

'Well, if that's your attitude . . .'

'Hang on, hang on.' She gave a noisy sigh. 'I've been trying to catch you.'

Alexis Cater chuckled. 'I'd heard rumours. Nice to know I'm so popular . . .'

'But sliding down the charts as we speak. I thought you were going to get back to me.'

'Was I?'

'With your friend Pippa's details,' Siobhan replied, not bothering to hide her exasperation. She lifted the can to her lips.

'It'll rot your teeth,' Cater warned.

'What will . . . ?' Siobhan broke off suddenly, did a one-hundred-and-eighty-degree turn. He was watching her through the glass panel of a swing door halfway down the corridor. She started stalking towards him.

'Nice hips,' his voice said.

'How long have you been following me?' she asked into her own phone.

'Not long.' He pushed open the door, closing his phone just as she closed hers. He was wearing his white coat unbuttoned, revealing a grey shirt and narrow pea-green tie.

'Maybe you've got time for games, but I haven't.'

'Then why drive all the way out here? A simple call would have sufficed.'

'You weren't answering.'

He formed his substantial lips into a pout. 'You're sure you weren't dying to see me?'

She narrowed her eyes. 'Your friend Pippa,' she reminded him.

He nodded. 'What about a drink after work? I'll tell you then.'

'You'll tell me *now*.'

'Good idea – we can have the drink without business intruding.' He slipped his hands into his pockets. 'Pippa works for Bill Lindquist: do you know him?'

'No.'

'Hotshot PR guy. Based in London for a time, but got to like golf and fell in love with Edinburgh. He's played a few rounds with my father . . .' He saw that Siobhan was impressed by none of this.

'Work address?'

'It'll be in the phone book under "Lindquist PR". Down in the New Town somewhere . . . maybe India Street. I'd call first if I were you: PR isn't PR if you're sitting on your jacksy in the office . . .'

'Thanks for the advice.'

'Well, then . . . about that drink . . . ?'

Siobhan nodded. 'Opal Lounge, nine o'clock?'

'Sounds good to me.'

'Great.' Siobhan smiled at him and started walking away. He called out to her, and she stopped.

'You've no intention of turning up, have you?'

'You'll have to be there at nine to find out,' she said, waving as she headed down the corridor. Her mobile sounded and she took the call. Cater's voice.

'You've still got great hips, Shiv. Shame not to give them some fresh air and exercise . . .'

She drove straight to India Street, calling ahead to make sure Pippa Greenlaw was there. She wasn't: she was meeting some clients on Lothian Road, but was expected back by the top of the hour. As Siobhan had estimated, traffic on the way back into town meant that she, too, arrived at the offices of Lindquist PR almost exactly on the hour. The office was in the basement of a traditional Georgian block, reached by a winding set of stone steps. Siobhan knew that a lot of properties in the New Town had been turned into office accommodation, but many were now reverting to their origins as private homes. There were plenty of For Sale signs on this and surrounding streets. The buildings in the New Town were proving unable to adapt to the needs of the new century: most had listed interiors. You couldn't just rip walls out to put in new cabling systems or reconfigure the available space, and you couldn't build new extensions. Local council red tape was there to ensure that the New Town's famed 'elegance' was retained, and when the local council failed, there were still plenty of local pressure groups to contend with . . .

Some of which became the topic of discussion between Siobhan and the receptionist, who was apologetic that Pippa had obviously been delayed. She poured coffee from the machine for Siobhan, offered her one of her own biscuits from the desk drawer, and chatted between answering phone calls.

'Ceiling's gorgeous, isn't it?' she said. Siobhan agreed, staring up at the ornate cornicing. 'You should see the fireplace in Mr Lindquist's office.' The receptionist screwed shut her eyes in rapture. 'It's absolutely . . .'

'Gorgeous?' Siobhan offered. The receptionist nodded.

'More coffee?'

Siobhan declined, having yet to start the first cup. A door opened and a male head appeared. 'Pippa back?'

'She must have been delayed, Bill,' the receptionist apologised breathily. Lindquist looked at Siobhan but said nothing, then disappeared back into his room.

The receptionist smiled at Siobhan and raised her eyebrows slightly, the gesture telling Siobhan that she thought Mr Lindquist, too, was gorgeous. Maybe everyone was gorgeous in PR, Siobhan decided – everyone and everything.

The outer door opened with some violence. 'Fuckwits . . . bunch of brain-dead fuckwits.' A young woman strode in. She was slim, wearing a skirt and jacket which showed off her figure. Long red hair and glossy red lipstick. Black high heels and black stockings: something told Siobhan they were definitely stockings rather than tights. 'How the hell are we supposed to help them when they've got gold medals in fuckwittery – answer that, Sherlock!' She slammed her briefcase down on the reception desk. 'As God is my witness, Zara, if Bill sends me down there again, I'm taking an Uzi and as much bloody ammo as I can stuff into this case.' She slapped her briefcase, noticing only now that Zara's eyes were on the line of chairs by the window.

'Pippa,' Zara said tremulously, 'this lady's been waiting to see you . . .'

'Name's Siobhan Clarke,' Siobhan said, taking a step forward. 'I'm a potential new client . . .' Seeing the look of horror on Greenlaw's face, she held up a hand. 'Only joking.'

Greenlaw rolled her eyes with relief. 'Thank the sweet baby Jesus for that.'

'I'm actually a police officer.'

'I wasn't serious about the Uzi . . .'

'Quite right – I believe they're notorious for jamming. Much better with a Heckler and Koch . . .'

Pippa Greenlaw smiled. 'Come into my office while I write that down.'

Her office was probably the maid's room of the original multi-storey house, narrow and not especially long, with a barred window looking on to a cramped car park where Siobhan recognised a Maserati and a Porsche.

'I'm guessing yours is the Porsche,' she said.

'Of course it is – isn't that why you're here?'

'What makes you think that?'

'Because that bloody speed camera near the zoo caught me again last week.'

'Nothing to do with me. Do you mind if I sit?'

Greenlaw frowned, nodding at the same time. Siobhan shifted some paperwork from a chair. 'I want to ask you about one of Lex Cater's parties,' she said.

'Which one?'

'About a year ago. It was the one with the skeletons.'

'Well ... I was just about to say that no one ever remembers *anything* about Lex's little gatherings – not with the amount of booze we get through – but I do remember that one. At least, I remember the skeleton.' She winced. 'Bastard didn't tell me it was real till after I'd kissed it.'

'You kissed it?'

'For a dare.' She paused. 'After about ten glasses of champagne ... There was a baby, too.' She winced again. 'I remember now.'

'You remember who else was there?'

'Usual crowd probably. What's this all about?'

'The skeletons went missing after the party.'

'Did they?'

'Lex never said?'

Pippa shook her head. Close up, her face was covered in freckles, which her tan only partially concealed. 'I thought he'd just got rid of them.'

'You had a partner with you that night.'

'I'm never short of partners, darling.'

The door opened and Lindquist's head appeared. 'Pippa?' he said. 'My office in five?'

'No problem, Bill.'

'And the meeting this afternoon ... ?'

Greenlaw shrugged. 'Absolutely fine, Bill, just as you said.'

He smiled and retreated again. Siobhan wondered if there was actually a body attached to the head and neck; maybe the rest of him was wires and metal. She waited a moment before speaking. 'He must've heard you when you came in, or is his room sound-proofed?'

'Bill only hears good news, that's his golden rule ... Why are you asking about Lex's party?'

'The skeletons have turned up again – in a cellar in Fleshmarket Close.'

Greenlaw's eyes widened. 'I heard about that on the radio!'

'What did you think?'

'Had to be a publicity stunt – that was my first reaction.'

'They were hidden under a concrete floor.'

'But dug up again.'

'They lay there the best part of a year ...'

'Evidence of forward planning ...' But Greenlaw sounded less sure. 'I still don't see what this has to do with me.' She leaned forward, elbows on her desk. There was nothing else there but a slim silver laptop: no printer or trailing wires.

'You were with someone. Lex reckons he might have taken the skeletons.'

Greenlaw's whole face creased. 'Who was I with?'

'That's what I was hoping you might tell me. Lex seems to remember he was a footballer.'

'A footballer?'

'That's how you met him . . .'

Greenlaw was thoughtful. 'I don't think I've ever . . . no, wait, there was one guy.' She angled her head towards heaven, revealing a slender neck. 'He wasn't a *real* footballer . . . played for some amateur side. Christ, what was his name?' Triumphantly, her eyes met Siobhan's. 'Barry.'

'Barry?'

'Or Gary . . . something like that.'

'You must know a lot of men.'

'Not that many at all, really. But plenty of forgettables like Barry-or-Gary.'

'Does he have a surname?'

'I probably never knew it.'

'Where did you meet him?'

Greenlaw tried to think back. 'Almost certainly in a bar . . . maybe at a party or some launch for a client.' She smiled in apology. 'It was a one-nighter; he was good-looking enough to be my date. Actually, I think I do remember him. I reckoned he might shock Lex.'

'Shock him how?'

'You know . . . a bit of rough.'

'And how rough was he?'

'Christ, I don't mean he was a biker or anything. He was just a bit more . . .' She sought the right word. 'More of a *prole* than I'd normally have hooked up with.'

She gave another shrug of apology and leaned back in her chair, rocking it slightly, fingertips pressed together.

'Any idea where he came from? Where he lived? How he earned a living?'

'I seem to remember he had a flat in Corstorphine . . . not that I saw it. He was . . .' She screwed shut her eyes for a moment. 'No, I can't remember what he did. Flashed the cash around though.'

'What did he look like?'

'Bleached hair with dark highlights. Wiry, willing to show off his six-pack ... Plenty of energy in bed, but no finesse. Not over-endowed either.'

'That's probably enough to be going on with.'

The two women shared a smile.

'Seems like a lifetime ago,' Greenlaw commented.

'You haven't seen him since?'

'No.'

'And you don't happen to've kept his phone number?'

'Every New Year, I make a little funeral pyre of all those scraps of paper ... you know the ones – the numbers and initials, people you'll never call again; some you're not sure you ever knew in the first place. All those ghastly, garish fucking hypocrites who grab your bum on the dance floor or slip a hand around your tit at a party and assume that PR means Patently Rogerable ...' Greenlaw let out a groan.

'This meeting you've just come from, Pippa ... anything to drink, perchance?'

'Just champagne.'

'And you drove back here in the Porsche?'

'Oh, Christ, are you planning to breathalyse me, officer?'

'Actually, I'm quietly impressed: it's taken me till now to notice.'

'Thing about champagne is, it always makes me so bloody thirsty.' She examined her watch. 'Fancy joining me?'

'Zara's got some coffee going spare,' Siobhan countered.

Greenlaw made a face. 'I've got to talk to Bill, but that's me finished for the day.'

'Lucky you.'

Greenlaw stuck out her bottom lip. 'What about later?'

'I'll let you into a secret: Lex is going to be at the Opal Lounge at nine.'

'Is he?'

'I'm sure he'd buy you a drink.'

'But that's *hours* away,' Greenlaw protested.

'Tough it out,' Siobhan advised, rising to her feet. 'And thanks for talking to me.'

She was ready to leave, but Greenlaw gestured for her to sit down again. She started rummaging in the desk drawers, finally producing a pad of paper and a biro.

'That gun you were talking about,' she said, 'what was it called again ... ?'

At Knoxland, the Portakabin was being lifted by crane on to the back of a lorry. Heads were at windows, the tower-block residents watching the manoeuvre. More graffiti had been added to the Portakabin since Rebus's last visit, its window had been smashed further, and someone had tried setting fire to its door.

'And the roof,' Shug Davidson added for Rebus's benefit. 'Lighter fluid, newspapers and an old car tyre.'

'That amazes me.'

'What does?'

'Newspapers – you mean someone in Knoxland actually *reads*?'

Davidson's smile was short-lived. He folded his arms. 'I wonder sometimes why we bother.'

As he spoke, Gareth Baird was being led from the nearest tower block by the same two uniforms. All three looked numb with exhaustion.

'Nothing?' Davidson asked. One of the uniforms shook his head.

'Forty or fifty flats, we got no answer.'

'No way I'm coming back!' Gareth complained.

'You will if we want you to,' Rebus warned him.

'Should we drop him home?' the uniform asked.

As Rebus shook his head, his eyes were on Gareth. 'Nothing wrong with the bus. There's one every half-hour.'

Gareth's eyebrows dipped in disbelief. 'After everything I've done.'

'No, son,' Rebus corrected him, '*because* of everything you've done. You've only just started paying for that. Bus stop's over that way, I think.' Rebus pointed towards the dual carriageway. 'Through the subway, if you're brave enough.'

Gareth looked around him, seeing not one sympathetic face. 'Thanks a bunch,' he muttered, stomping off.

'Back to the station, lads,' Davidson told the uniforms. 'Sorry you drew today's short straw . . .'

The uniforms nodded and headed for their patrol car.

'Nice little surprise for them,' Davidson told Rebus. 'Someone's smashed a whole carton of eggs on their windscreen.'

Rebus shook his head in mock disbelief. 'You mean someone in Knoxland buys fresh food?' he said.

Davidson didn't smile this time. He was reaching for his mobile. Rebus recognised the ring-tone: 'Scots Wha Hae'. Davidson shrugged. 'One of my kids was mucking around last night . . . I forgot to change it back.' He answered the call, Rebus listening.

'Speaking . . . Oh yes, Mr Allan.' Davidson rolled his eyes. 'Yes, that's right . . . He did?' Davidson locked eyes with Rebus. 'That's interesting. Any chance I could speak to you in person?' He glanced at his watch. 'Some time today ideally . . . happens I'm free right now if you can spare . . . No, I'm sure it won't take long . . . we could be there in twenty minutes . . . Yes, I'm sure of that. Thanks then. Cheers.' Davidson ended the call and stared at his handset.

'Mr Allan?' Rebus prompted.

'Rory Allan,' Davidson said, still distracted.

'The *Scotsman* editor?'

'One of his news team's just told him they took a phone call a week or so back from a foreign-sounding guy calling himself Stef.'

'As in Stef Yurgii?'

'Sounds likely . . . said he was a reporter and had a story he wanted to write.'

'What about?'

Davidson shrugged. 'That's why I'm meeting Rory Allan.'

'Need some company, big boy?' Rebus gave his most winning smile.

Davidson thought for a moment. 'It should be Ellen, really . . .'

'Except she's not here.'

'But I could call her.'

Rebus tried for a look of outrage. 'Are you spurning me, Shug?'

Davidson hesitated a few more moments, then put the mobile back into his pocket. 'Only if you're on your best behaviour,' he said.

'Scout's honour.' Rebus gave a salute.

'God help me,' Davidson said, as if he already regretted his momentary weakness.

Edinburgh's daily broadsheet was housed in a new building opposite the BBC on Holyrood Road. There was a good view of the cranes which still dominated the sky above the emerging Scottish Parliament complex.

'Wonder if they'll finish it before the cost finishes *us*,' Davidson mused, walking into the *Scotsman* building. The security guard let them through a turnstile and told them to take the lift to the first floor, from where they could look down on to the journalists in their open-plan environment below. To the rear was a glass wall, offering views of Salisbury Crags. Smokers were puffing away on a balcony outside, letting Rebus know that he wouldn't be able to indulge in this place. Rory Allan came towards them.

'DI Davidson,' he said, instinctively homing in on Rebus.

'I'm actually DI Rebus. Just because I look like his dad doesn't mean he's not the boss.'

'Guilty of ageism as charged,' Allan said, shaking first Rebus's hand and then Davidson's. 'There's a meeting room free . . . follow me.'

They entered a long, narrow room with an elongated oval table at its centre.

'Smells brand new,' Rebus commented of the furnishings.

'Place doesn't get used much,' the editor explained. Rory Allan was in his thirties, with rapidly receding hair, prematurely silver, and John Lennon-style glasses. He'd left his jacket back in his own office, and wore a pale blue shirt with red silk tie, sleeves rolled up in workmanlike fashion. 'Sit down, won't you? Can I get either of you a coffee?'

'We're fine, thanks, Mr Allan.'

Allan nodded his satisfaction with this. 'To business then . . . You'll appreciate that we could have gone to print with this and let you find out for yourselves?'

Davidson bowed his head slightly in acknowledgement. There was a knock at the door.

'Come!' Allan barked.

A smaller version of the editor seemed to appear: same hairstyle, similar glasses, sleeves rolled up.

'This is Danny Watling. Danny's one of our news staff. I asked him to join us so he could tell you himself.' Allan gestured for the journalist to sit.

'Not much to tell,' Danny Watling said, in a voice so quiet Rebus, seated across the table from him, strained to catch it. 'I was working the desk . . . picked up a phone call . . . guy said he was a reporter, had a story he wanted to write.'

Shug Davidson sat with his fingers pressed together on the table. 'Did he say what it was about?'

Watling shook his head 'He was cagey . . . and his English wasn't great. It was like the words had come from a dictionary.'

'Or he was reading them out?' Rebus interrupted.

Watling considered this. 'Maybe reading them out, yes.'

Davidson asked for an explanation. 'Girlfriend might have written them,' Rebus replied. 'Her English is supposed to be better than Stef's.'

'He told you his name?' Davidson asked the reporter.

'Stef, yes.'

'No surname?'

'I don't think he wanted me to know.' Watling looked to his editor. 'Thing is, we get dozens of crank calls . . .'

'Danny perhaps didn't take him as seriously as he might have,' Allan commented, picking at an invisible thread on his trousers.

'No, well . . .' Watling blushed at the throat. 'I said we didn't normally use freelancers, but if he wanted to talk to someone, we might give him a share of the by-line.'

'What did he say to that?' Rebus asked.

'Didn't seem to understand. That made me a bit more suspicious.'

'He didn't know what "freelance" meant?' Davidson guessed.

'Or maybe he just didn't have an equivalent in his own language,' Rebus argued.

Watling blinked a few times. 'With benefit of hindsight,' he told Rebus, 'I think that may be right . . .'

'And he gave you no inkling what this story of his might be?'

'No. I think he wanted a face-to-face with me first.'

'An offer you turned down?'

Watling's back stiffened. 'Oh no, I agreed to see him. Ten o'clock that night outside Jenner's.'

'Jenner's department store?' Davidson asked.

Watling nodded. 'It was about the only place he knew . . . I tried a few pubs, even the really well-known ones that only tourists would be seen dead in. But he hardly seemed to know the city at all.'

'Did you ask *him* to name a meeting place?'

'I said I'd go anywhere he wanted, but he couldn't think of a single place. Then I mentioned Princes Street, and he knew that, so I decided on the biggest landmark there.'

'But he didn't show up?' Rebus guessed.

The reporter shook his head slowly. 'That was probably the night before he died.'

The room was quiet for a moment. 'Could be something or nothing,' Davidson felt compelled to spell out.

'It might give you a motive, though,' Rory Allan added.

'*Another* motive, you mean,' Davidson corrected him. 'The papers – including your own, I think, Mr Allan – have been happy till now to focus on it as a race crime.'

The editor shrugged. 'I'm just speculating . . .'

Rebus was staring at the reporter. 'Have you got any notes?' he asked. Watling nodded, then looked to his boss, who granted permission with a nod. Watling handed Davidson a single folded sheet of notepaper, torn from a lined pad. Davidson took only a few seconds to digest the contents and slide the sheet across the table to Rebus.

Steph . . . East European???

'Doesn't add what I'd call a new dimension,' Rebus stated blandly. 'He didn't call again?'

'No.'

'Not even to one of the other staffers?' A shake of the head. 'And when he spoke to you, that was the first call he'd made?' A nod. 'I don't suppose you thought to get a phone number from him, or trace where he was calling from?'

'Sounded like a callbox. Traffic was close by.'

Rebus thought of the bus stop on the edge of Knoxland . . . there was a phone box about fifteen yards from it, next to the roadway. 'Do we know where the 999 call came from?' he asked Davidson.

'Phone box near the underpass,' Davidson confirmed.

'Maybe the same one?' Watling guessed.

'Almost a news story in itself,' his editor joked. '"Working phone box found in Knoxland".'

Shug Davidson was looking at Rebus, who offered a twitch of one shoulder, indicating that he'd run out of questions. Both men started to rise.

'Well, thanks for getting in touch, Mr Allan, we do appreciate it.'

'I know it's not much . . .'

'Still, it's another piece of the jigsaw.'

'And how's that jigsaw progressing, Inspector?'

'I'd say we've finished the border, just got to fill in the middle.'

'The most difficult part,' Allan offered, his voice sympathetic. There were handshakes all round. Watling bustled back to his desk. Allan waved to the two detectives as the lift doors closed. Out on the street, Davidson pointed to a café across the road.

'My treat,' he said.

Rebus was lighting a cigarette. 'Fine, but give me a minute to smoke this . . .' He took in a lungful and exhaled through his nostrils, picked a loose shred of tobacco from his tongue. 'So it's a jigsaw, eh?'

'Man like Allan works with clichés . . . thought I'd give him one to chew over.'

'Thing about jigsaws,' Rebus commented, 'is that they all depend on the number of pieces.'

'That's true, John.'

'And how many pieces have we got?'

'To be honest, half are lying on the floor, maybe even a few under

167

the sofa and the edge of the carpet. Now will you hurry up and smoke that bastard? I need an espresso pronto.'

'It's a terrible thing to see someone so addicted to their fix,' Rebus said, before drawing more deeply on his cigarette.

Five minutes later, they were sitting stirring their coffees, Davidson chewing on sticky gobbets of cherry cake.

'By the way,' he said between mouthfuls, 'I've got something for you.' He patted his jacket pockets, and produced a cassette tape. 'It's a recording of the emergency call.'

'Thanks.'

'I let Gareth Baird hear it.'

'And was it Yurgii's girlfriend?'

'He wasn't sure. Like he said, it's not exactly Dolby Pro Logic.'

'Thanks anyway.' Rebus pocketed the tape.

14

He played it in his car on the way home. Fiddled with the controls for bass and treble, but wasn't able to improve much on the quality. The voice of a frantic woman, counterpointed by the professional calm of the emergency operator.

Dying . . . he's dying . . . oh my God . . .

Can you give us an address, madam?

Knoxland . . . between the buildings . . . the tall buildings . . . he is pavement . . .

You need an ambulance?

Dead . . . dead . . . Collapsing into shrieks and sobs.

The police have been alerted. Can you stay there till they arrive, please? Madam? Hello, madam . . . ?

What? What?

Can I take your name, please?

They've killed him . . . he said . . . oh my God . . .

We'll send an ambulance. Is that the only address you can give? Madam? Hello, are you still there . . . ?

But she wasn't. The line was dead. Rebus wondered again if she'd used the same phone box as Stef, when he'd called Danny Watling. He wondered, too, what the story might be, the one which had necessitated a face-to-face . . . Stef Yurgii with his own journalistic instincts, talking to Knoxland's immigrants . . . reluctant to see his story stolen by others. Rebus wound the tape back.

They've killed him . . . he said . . .

Said what? Warned her this would happen? Told her his life was in danger?

Because of a story?

Rebus signalled and pulled over to the side of the road. He played the tape one more time, all the way through and with the volume up. The background hiss seemed still to be there once the tape had been stopped. He felt like he was at altitude, needing his ears to pop.

It was a race crime, a hate crime. Ugly but simple, the killer bitter and twisted, his act earthing all that anger.

Well, wasn't it?

Kids without a father . . . guards brainwashed into a fear of toys . . . tyres burning on a roof . . .

'What in Christ's name is happening here?' he found himself asking. The world passed by, determined not to notice: cars grinding homewards; pedestrians making eye contact only with the pavement ahead of them, because what you didn't see couldn't hurt you. A fine, brave world awaiting the new parliament. An ageing country dispatching its talents to the four corners of the globe . . . unwelcoming to visitor and migrant alike.

'What in Christ's name?' he whispered, hands strangling the steering wheel. He noticed there was a pub just a few yards further on. His car might get a ticket, but he could always risk it.

But no . . . if he'd wanted a drink, he'd have headed to the Ox. Instead he was going home, same as the other workers. A long hot bath and maybe one or two nips from a bottle of malt. There was a new batch of CDs he hadn't listened to yet, picked up the weekend before: Jackie Leven, Lou Reed, John Mayall's Bluesbreakers . . . Plus the ones Siobhan had loaned him: Snow Patrol and Grant-Lee Phillips . . . he'd promised them back by last week.

Maybe he could give her a call, see if she was busy. They didn't have to go drinking: curry and beer at his place or hers, some music and chat. Things had been a bit awkward since the time he'd wrapped her in his arms and kissed her. Not that they'd talked about it; he reckoned she just wanted to put it behind them. But it didn't mean they couldn't sit in a room together, sharing curry.

Did it?

But then she'd probably have other plans. She had friends, after all. And what did he have? All his years in this city, doing the job he did, and what was waiting for him back home?

Ghosts.

Vigils at his window, staring past his reflection.

He thought of Caro Quinn, surrounded by pairs of eyes . . . her own ghosts. She interested him in part because she represented a challenge: he had his own prejudices, and she had hers. He was wondering how much common ground they might turn out to share.

She had his number, but he doubted she would call. And if he *did* go drinking, he would drink alone, turning into what his dad had called a 'barley king' – the soured hardmen who drank at the bar, facing the row of optics, supping the cheapest brand of whisky. Speaking to no one, because they'd stepped away from society, away from dialogue and laughter. The kingdoms they ruled had populations of one.

Finally, he ejected the tape. Shug could have it back. It wasn't going to reveal any sudden secrets. All it told him was that a woman had cared about Stef Yurgii.

A woman who might know why he'd died.

A woman who'd gone to ground.

So why worry? Leave the job at the office, John. That's all it should be to you: a job. The bastards who'd found him a lowly corner at Gayfield Square merited nothing more. He shook his head, scrubbed at his scalp with his hands, trying to clear everything out of there. Then he signalled back into the stream of traffic.

He was going home, and the world could go shaft itself.

'John Rebus?'

The man was black. And tall, built from muscle. As he stepped forward from the shadows, what Rebus saw first were the whites of his eyes.

The man had been waiting in the stairwell of Rebus's tenement, standing by the rear door, the one leading to the overgrown drying-green. It was a mugger's spot, which was why Rebus tensed, even when his name was mentioned.

'You're Detective Inspector John Rebus?'

The black man had closely cropped hair and wore a smart-looking suit with an open-necked purple shirt. His ears were tiny triangles, with almost no lobes. He was standing in front of Rebus, and neither man had blinked in the best part of twenty seconds.

Rebus had a carrier bag in his right hand. There was a bottle of twenty-quid malt inside, and he was loath to take a swing with it unless absolutely necessary. For some reason his mind flashed on an old Chic Murray sketch: a man falling over with a half-bottle in his pocket, feeling a damp patch and touching it: *Thank Christ for that . . . it's only blood.*

'Who the hell are you?'

'Sorry if I startled you . . .'

'Who says you did?'

'Tell me you're not thinking of going for me with whatever's in that bag?'

'I'd be lying. Who are you and what do you want?'

'Okay to show you ID?' The man hesitated with his hand halfway to the inside pocket of his jacket.

'Fire away.'

A wallet came out. The man flipped it open. His name was Felix Storey. He was an Immigration official.

'Felix?' Rebus said, one eyebrow rising.

'It means happy, so they tell me.'

'And a cartoon cat . . .'

'That too, of course.' Storey started tucking the wallet away again. 'Anything drinkable in that bag?'

'Might be.'

'I notice it's from an off-licence.'

'You're very observant.'

Storey almost smiled. 'That's why I'm here.'

'How's that?'

'Because you, Inspector, were observed last night, coming out of a place called the Nook.'

'Was I?'

'I've got a nice set of ten-by-eights to prove it.'

'And what the hell has any of that got to do with Immigration?'

'For the price of a drink, maybe I can tell you . . .'

Rebus wrestled with a dozen questions, but the carrier bag was growing heavy. He gave the slightest of nods and headed up the stairs, Storey following. Unlocked his door and pushed it open, sweeping the day's mail aside with his foot, so that it came to rest on top of the previous day's. Rebus went into the kitchen long enough to grab two clean glasses, then led Storey into the living room.

'Nice,' Storey said, nodding as he surveyed the room. 'High ceilings, bay window. Are all the flats round here this size?'

'Some are bigger.' Rebus had removed the malt from its box and was wrestling with the stopper. 'Sit yourself down.'

'I like a nice drop of Scotch.'

'Up here we don't call it that.'

'What do you call it then?'

'Whisky, or malt.'

'Why not Scotch?'

'I think it goes back to when "Scotch" was a put-down.'

'A pejorative term?'

'If that's the fancy word for it . . .'

Storey grinned, showing gleaming teeth. 'In my job, you have to know the jargon.' He rose slightly from the sofa to accept a glass from Rebus. 'Cheers, then.'

'*Slainte.*'

'That's Gaelic, is it?' Rebus nodded. 'You speak Gaelic then?'

'No.'

Storey seemed to ponder this as he savoured a mouthful of Lagavulin. Finally he nodded his appreciation. 'Bloody hell, it's strong though.'

'You want some water?'

The Englishman shook his head.

'Your accent,' Rebus said, 'London, is it?'

'That's right: Tottenham.'

'I was in Tottenham once.'

'Football game?'

'Murder case . . . Body found by the canal . . .'

'I think I remember. I was a kid at the time.'

'Thanks for that.' Rebus poured a little more into his glass, then offered the bottle to Storey, who took it and refilled his own. 'So you're from London and you work for Immigration. And you've got the Nook under surveillance for some reason.'

'That's right.'

'Explains how you clocked me, but not how you knew who I was.'

'We've got local CID assistance. I can't name names, but the officer recognised yourself and DS Clarke straight off.'

'That's interesting.'

'Like I say, I can't name names . . .'

'So what's your interest in the Nook?'

'What's yours?'

'I asked first . . . But let me take a guess: some of the girls at the club are from overseas?'

'I'm sure they are.'

Rebus's eyes narrowed slightly over the rim of his tumbler. 'But they're not why you're here?'

'Before I can talk about it, I really need to know what you were doing there.'

'I was partnering DS Clarke, that's all. She had a few questions for the owner.'

'What sort of questions?'

'A teenager's gone missing. Her parents are worried she'll end up in a place like the Nook.' Rebus shrugged. 'That's all there is to it. DS Clarke knows the family, so she's going an extra yard.'

'She didn't fancy going to the Nook on her own?'

'No.'

Storey was thoughtful, making a show of studying his glass as he swirled its contents. 'Mind if I verify that with her?'

'You think I'm lying?'

'Not necessarily.'

Rebus glared at him, then produced his mobile phone and called her. 'Siobhan? You up to anything?' He listened to her response, eyes still fixed on Storey. 'Listen, I've got someone here. He's from Immigration and he wants to know what we were doing at the Nook. I'm passing you over . . .'

Storey took the handset. 'DS Clarke? My name's Felix Storey. I'm sure DI Rebus will fill you in later, but for now, could you just confirm why you were at the Nook?' He paused, listening. Then: 'Yes, that's pretty much what DI Rebus said. I appreciate you telling me. Sorry to've troubled you . . .' He handed the phone back to Rebus.

'Cheers, Shiv . . . we'll talk later. Right now, it's Mr Storey's turn.' Rebus snapped the phone closed.

'You didn't have to do that,' the Immigration official said.

'Best to clear things up . . .'

'What I meant was, you didn't have to use your mobile – house phone's just over there.' He nodded towards the dining table. 'It'd have been a lot cheaper.'

Rebus eventually conceded a smile. Felix Storey placed his tumbler on the carpet and straightened up, hands clasped.

'The case I'm working, I can't take chances.'

'Why not?'

'Because a bent cop or two might sidle into the picture . . .' Storey let this sink in. 'Not that I've any evidence to back that up. It's just the sort of thing that can happen. The sort of people I deal with, they wouldn't think twice about buying off a whole division.'

'Maybe there are more bent cops in London.'

'Maybe there are.'

'If the dancers aren't illegal, it must be Stuart Bullen,' Rebus stated. The Immigration official nodded slowly. 'And for someone to make the trip from London . . . go to the expense of setting up a surveillance . . .'

Storey was still nodding. 'It's big,' he said. 'Could be very big.' He shifted position on the sofa. 'My own parents arrived here in the fifties: Jamaica to Brixton, just two among many. A proper migration that was, but dwarfed by the situation we've got now. Tens of thousands a year, coming ashore illegally . . . often paying handsomely for the privilege. Illegals have become big business, Inspector. Thing is, you never see them until something goes wrong.' He paused, allowing Rebus room for a question.

'How's Bullen involved?'

'We think he might run the whole Scottish operation.'

Rebus snorted. 'That wee nyaff?'

'He's his father's son, Inspector.'

'Chicory Tip,' Rebus muttered. Then, to answer Storey's quizzical look: 'They had a big hit with "Son of My Father" . . . before your time, though. How long have you been watching the Nook?'

'Just the past week.'

'The closed-down newsagent's?' Rebus guessed. He was remembering the shop across the road from the club, with its whited-out windows. Storey nodded. 'Well, having been inside the Nook, I can tell you it doesn't look to me like there are rooms heaped high with illegal immigrants.'

'I'm not suggesting he stashes them there . . .'

'And I didn't see any hoards of fake passports.'

'You went into his office?'

'He didn't look like he was hiding anything: the safe was wide open.'

'Throwing you off the scent?' Storey speculated. 'When he found out why you were there, did you notice a change in him? Maybe he relaxed a little?'

'Nothing that told me he might have other worries. So what is it exactly that you think he does?'

'He's a link in a chain. That's one of the problems: we don't know how many links there are, or what part each one plays.'

'Sounds to me like you know the square root of bugger-all.'

Storey decided not to argue. 'Had you met Bullen before?'

'Didn't even know he was in Edinburgh.'

'So you knew who he was?'

'I know of the family, yes. Doesn't mean I tuck them in at night.'

'I'm not accusing you of anything, Inspector.'

'You're sounding me out, which amounts to the same thing – and none too subtly, I might add.'

'Sorry if it seems that way . . .'

'It *is* that way. And here I am, sharing my whisky with you . . .' Rebus shook his head.

'I know your reputation, Inspector. Nothing I've heard leads me to believe you'd cosy up to Stuart Bullen.'

'Maybe you've just not been talking to the right people.' Rebus poured himself a little more whisky, offering none to Storey. 'So what is it you hope to find by spying on the Nook? Apart from cops on the take, naturally . . .'

'Associates . . . hints and a few fresh leads.'

'Meaning the old ones have gone cold? How much hard evidence do you have?'

'His name's been mentioned . . .'

Rebus waited for more, but there wasn't any. He gave a snort. 'Anonymous tip-off? Could be any one of his competitors in the pubic triangle, looking to dump on him.'

'The club would make for good cover.'

'Ever been inside?'

'Not yet.'

'Because you think you'd stick out?'

'You mean my skin colour?' Storey shrugged. 'Maybe that's got something to do with it. Not many black faces on your streets, but that'll change. Whether you choose to see them or not is another matter.' He looked around the room again. 'Nice place . . .'

'So you said.'

'Been here long?'

'Just the twenty-odd years.'

'That's a long time . . . Am I the first black person you've invited in?'

Rebus considered this. 'Probably,' he admitted.

'Any Chinese or Asians?' Rebus chose not to answer. 'All I'm saying is . . .'

'Look,' Rebus interrupted, 'I've had enough of this. Finish your drink and vamoose . . . and that's not me being racist, just bloody annoyed.' He rose to his feet. Storey did the same, handing the glass back.

'It was good whisky,' he said. 'See? You've taught me not to say "Scotch".' He reached into his breast pocket and produced his business card. 'In case you feel the need to get in touch.'

Rebus took the card without looking at it. 'Which hotel are you in?'

'It's near Haymarket, on Grosvenor Street.'

'I know the one.'

'Drop in some night, I'll buy you a drink.'

Rebus said nothing to this, just: 'I'll see you out.'

Which he did, switching off the lights on his way back to the living room, standing by the uncurtained window, peering down towards pavement level. Sure enough, Storey emerged. As he did so, a car cruised to a stop and he got in the back. Rebus could make out neither driver nor number plate. It was a big car, maybe a Vauxhall. It turned right at the bottom of the street. Rebus walked over to the table and picked up the house phone, called for a taxi. Then he headed downstairs himself, waiting for it outside. As it drew up, his mobile chirped: Siobhan.

'You finished with our mystery guest?' she asked.

'For now.'

'What the hell was that all about?'

He explained it to her as best he could.

'And this arrogant prick thinks we're in Bullen's pocket?' was her first question. Rebus guessed it was rhetorical.

'He might want to talk to you.'

'Don't worry, I'll be ready for him.' An ambulance pulled out from a side street, siren wailing. 'You're in the car,' she commented.

'Taxi,' he corrected her. 'Last thing I need right now is a conviction for drunk-driving.'

'Where are you off to?'

'Just out on the town.' The cab had passed the Tollcross intersection. 'I'll talk to you tomorrow.'

'Have fun.'

'I'll try.'

He ended the call. The cabbie was taking them around the back of Earl Grey Street, making best use of the one-way system. They would cross Lothian Road at Morrison Street . . . next stop: Bread Street. Rebus handed over a tip, and decided to take a receipt. He could try adding it to his expenses on the Yurgii case.

'Not sure lap-dancing's tax-deductible, pal,' the cabbie warned him.

'Do I really look the type?'

'How honest an answer do you want?' the man called, crunching gears as he moved off.

'Last time you get a tip,' Rebus muttered, pocketing the receipt. It wasn't quite ten o'clock. Packs of men prowled the streets, looking for their next watering-hole. Bouncers protecting most of the harshly lit doorways: some wore three-quarter-length coats, others bomber jackets. Rebus saw them as clones beneath the clothing: it wasn't so much that they looked identical, more in the way they saw the world – divided into two groups: threat and prey.

177

Rebus knew he couldn't linger outside the closed-down shop – if one of the Nook's doormen became suspicious, it could mean the end of Storey's operation. Instead, he crossed the road, on the same side now as the Nook, but ten yards shy of the entrance. He stopped and lifted his phone to his ear, conducting one side of an inebriated conversation.

'Aye, it's me . . . where are you? You were supposed to be at the Shakespeare . . . no, I'm on Bread Street . . .'

It didn't matter what he was saying. To anyone who saw or overheard, he was just another night person, uttering the low gutturals of the local drunk. But he was also making study of the shop. There was no light inside, no movement or shadowplay. If the surveillance was twenty-four/seven, then it was bloody good. He reckoned they'd be filming, but couldn't work out how. If they removed a small square of white from the window, anyone outside would be able to see in, eventually spotting the reflection from the lens. There were no gaps in the window anyway. The door was covered in a wire grille, a roller-blind blocking any view. Again, no obvious spy-hole. But hang on . . . above the door there was another, smaller window, maybe three feet by two, whited out except for a small square in one corner. It was ingenious: no passing eyes would stray there. Of course, it meant one of the surveillance team would have to be placed atop a step-ladder or similar, armed with the camera. Awkward and uncomfortable, but perfect nonetheless.

Rebus finished his imaginary call and turned away from the Nook, walking back in the direction of Lothian Road. On Saturday nights, the place was best avoided. Even now, on a week-night, there were songs and chants and people kicking bottles along the pavement, scampering across the lanes of traffic. The high-pitched laughter of hen parties, girls in short skirts with flashing head-bands. A man was selling these headbands, plus pulsing plastic wands. He carried a fistful of each as he paced up and down. Rebus looked at him, remembering Storey's words: *Whether you choose to see them or not* . . . The man was wiry and young and tan-skinned. Rebus stopped in front of him.

'How much are they?'

'Two pounds.'

Rebus made a show of searching his pockets for change. 'Where you from?' The man didn't respond, eyes everywhere but on Rebus. 'How long have you been in Scotland?' But the man was moving off. 'You not going to sell me one, then?' Obviously not: the man kept walking. Rebus headed in the opposite direction, towards Princes Street's west end. A flower-seller was emerging from the Shakespeare pub, one arm cradled around tight bunches of roses.

'How much?' Rebus asked.

'Five pounds.' The seller was barely into his teens. His face was tan, maybe Middle Eastern. Again, Rebus fumbled in his pockets.

'Where you from?'

The youth pretended not to understand. 'Five,' he repeated.

'Is your boss anywhere around?' Rebus persisted.

The youth's eyes darted to left and right, seeking help.

'How old are you, son? Which school are you at?'

'Not understand.'

'Don't give me that . . .'

'You want roses?'

'I just need to find my money . . . Bit late for you to be out working, isn't it? Mum and Dad know what you're up to?'

The rose-seller had had enough. He ran, dropping one of his bunches, not looking back, not stopping. Rebus picked it up, handed it to a group of passing girls.

'That doesn't get you in my knickers,' one of them said, 'but it does get you this.' She pecked him on the cheek. As they staggered away, screeching and clattering in their noisy heels, another of the group yelped that he was old enough to be their grandad.

So I am, Rebus thought, and feel it, too . . .

He scrutinised the faces all along Princes Street. More Chinese than he'd expected. The beggars all had Scottish and English accents. Rebus stopped in at a hotel. The head barman there had known him fifteen years; didn't matter if Rebus needed a shave or wasn't wearing his best suit, his crispest shirt.

'What'll it be, Mr Rebus?' Placing a coaster in front of him. 'Maybe a wee malt?'

'Lagavulin,' Rebus said, knowing a single measure here would cost him the price of a quarter-bottle . . . The drink was placed in front of him, the barman knowing better than to suggest ice or water.

'Ted,' Rebus said, 'does this place ever use foreign staff?'

No question ever seemed to faze Ted: sign of a good barman. He moved his jaws as he considered a response. Rebus meantime was helping himself from the bowl of nuts which had appeared beside his drink.

'Had a few Australians behind the bar,' Ted said, starting to polish glasses with a towel. 'Doing the world tour . . . stopping off here for a few weeks. We never take them without experience.'

'What about elsewhere? The restaurant maybe.'

'Oh aye, there's all sorts waiting tables. Even more in housekeeping.'

'Housekeeping?'

'Chambermaids.'

Rebus nodded at this clarification. 'Look, this is strictly between us . . .' Ted leaned in a little closer at these words. 'Any chance illegals could work here?'

Ted looked askance at the suggestion. 'All above board, Mr Rebus, management wouldn't . . . couldn't . . .'

'Fair enough, Ted. Didn't mean to suggest otherwise.'

Ted seemed consoled by this. 'Mind you,' he said, 'I'm not saying other establishments are quite as choosy . . . Here, I'll tell you a story. My local, I usually have a drink there on a Friday night. This group's started coming in, dunno where they're from. Two guys playing guitars . . . "Save All Your Kisses For Me", songs like that. And an older guy toting a tambourine, using it to collect money round the tables.' He shook his head slowly. 'Pound to a penny they're refugees.'

Rebus lifted his glass. 'It's a whole other world,' he said. 'I never really thought about it before.'

'Looks like you could use a refill.' Ted gave a wink which creased his whole face. 'On the house, if you'll permit . . .'

The cold air hit Rebus when he left the bar. A turn to the right would send him in the direction of home, but instead he crossed the road and walked towards Leith Street, ending up on Leith Walk, passing Asian supermarkets, tattoo parlours, takeaways. He didn't really know where he was headed. At the foot of the Walk, Cheyanne might be plying her trade. John and Alice Jardine might be cruising in their car, seeking a sighting of their daughter. All kinds of hunger out there in the dark. He had his hands in his pockets, jacket buttoned against the chill. Half a dozen motorbikes rumbled past, only to find their progress thwarted by a red light. Rebus decided to cross the road, but the lights were already changing. He stepped back as the leading bike roared away.

'Minicab, sir?'

Rebus turned towards the voice. There was a man standing in the doorway of a shop. The shop was illuminated from within and had obviously become a minicab office. The man looked Asian. Rebus shook his head but then changed his mind. The driver led him to a parked Ford Escort well past its sell-by date. Rebus told him the address, and the man reached for an A to Z.

'I'll give you directions,' Rebus said. The driver nodded and started the engine.

'Been enjoying a few drinks, sir?' The accent was local.

'A few.'

'Day off work tomorrow, is it?'

'Not if I can help it.'

The man laughed at this, though Rebus couldn't think why. They headed back along Princes Street and up Lothian Road, heading for Morningside. Rebus told the driver to pull over, said he'd only be a minute. He went into an all-night shop and emerged with a litre bottle of water, swigging from it as he got back into the passenger seat, using it to wash down a four-pack of aspirin.

'Good idea, sir,' the driver agreed. 'Get your retaliation in first, eh? No hangover in the morning; no excuse for a sickie.'

Half a mile further on, Rebus told the driver they were taking a detour. Headed for Marchmont and stopped outside Rebus's flat. He went inside, unlocked the door. Extracted a bulging folder from a drawer in the living room. Opened it, decided he'd take a few of the cuttings with him. Back downstairs and into the cab.

When they got to Bruntsfield, Rebus said to take a right, then another. They were in a dimly lit suburban street of large, detached houses, most of them hidden behind shrubbery and fencing. The windows were darkened or shuttered, the occupants safely asleep. But lights burned in one of them, and that was where Rebus told the driver to drop him. The gate opened noisily. Rebus found the doorbell and rang it. There was no response. He took a few steps back and peered at the upstairs windows. They were lit but curtained. There were larger windows at ground level, either side of the porch, but both had their wooden shutters firmly closed. Rebus thought he could hear music coming from somewhere. He peered through the letter-box, but saw no movement, and realised that the music was coming from behind the house. There was a gravel driveway to one side and he headed up it, security lights tripping as he passed them. The music was coming from the garden. It was dark, except for a strange reddish glow. Rebus saw a structure in the middle of the lawn, wooden decking leading to it from the glass conservatory. Steam was rising from the structure. And music, too, something classical. Rebus walked forward towards the jacuzzi.

That was what it was: a jacuzzi, open to the Scottish elements. And in it sat Morris Gerald Cafferty, known as 'Big Ger'. He was wedged into one corner, arms stretched along the rim of the moulded tub. Jets of water streamed out from either side of him. Rebus looked around, but Cafferty was alone. There was some sort of light in the water, a coloured filter casting a red glow over everything. Cafferty's head was tipped back, eyes closed, a look on his face of concentration rather than relaxation.

And then he opened his eyes, and was staring directly at Rebus. The pupils were small and dark, the face overfed. Cafferty's short grey hair stuck damply to his skull. The upper half of his chest, visible above the surface of the water, was covered in a mat of darker, curled hair. He didn't seem surprised to see someone standing in front of him, even at this time of night.

'Have you brought your trunks?' he asked. 'Not that I'm wearing any . . .' He glanced down at himself.

'I heard you'd moved house,' Rebus said.

Cafferty turned to a control panel by his left hand and pressed a button. The music faded. 'CD player,' he explained. 'The speakers are inside.' He rapped the tub with his knuckles. Pressing another button, the motor ceased, and the water became still.

'Light show, too,' Rebus commented.

'Any colour you like.' Cafferty jabbed a further button, changing the water from red to green, and from green to blue, then ice-white and back to red.

'Red suits you,' Rebus stated.

'The Mephistopheles look?' Cafferty chuckled. 'I love it out here, this time of night. Hear the wind in the trees, Rebus? They've been here longer than any of us, those trees. Same with these houses. And they'll still be here when we've gone.'

'I think you've been in there too long, Cafferty. Your brain's getting all wrinkled.'

'I'm getting old, Rebus, that's all . . . And so are you.'

'Too old to bother with a bodyguard? Reckon you've buried all your enemies?'

'Joe knocks off at nine, but he's never too far away.' A two-beat pause. 'Are you, Joe?'

'No, Mr Cafferty.'

Rebus turned to where the bodyguard was standing. He was bare-footed, dressed hurriedly in underpants and a T-shirt.

'Joe sleeps in the room above the garage,' Cafferty explained. 'Off you go now, Joe. I'm sure I'm safe with the Inspector.'

Joe glowered at Rebus, then padded back across the lawn.

'It's a nice area this,' Cafferty was saying conversationally. 'Not much in the way of crime . . .'

'I'm sure you're doing your best to change that.'

'I'm out of the game, Rebus, same as you'll be pretty soon.'

'Oh aye?' Rebus held up the clippings he'd brought from home. Photos of Cafferty from the tabloids. They'd all been taken in the past year; all showed him with known villains from as far afield as Manchester, Birmingham, London.

'Are you stalking me or something?' Cafferty said.

'Maybe I am.'

'I don't know whether to be flattered . . .' Cafferty stood up. 'Hand me that robe, will you?'

Rebus was glad to. Cafferty climbed over the edge of the tub on to a wooden step, wrapping himself in the white cotton gown and sliding his feet into a pair of flip-flops. 'Help me put the cover on,' Cafferty said. 'Then we'll go indoors and you'll tell me whatever the hell it is you want from me.'

Again, Rebus obliged.

At one time, Big Ger Cafferty had run practically every criminal aspect of Edinburgh, from drugs and saunas to business scams. Since his last stretch of jail-time, however, he'd kept his head down. Not that Rebus believed the crap about retirement: people like Cafferty didn't ever jack it in. To Rebus's mind, Cafferty had just grown wilier with age – and wiser to the ways police might go about investigating him.

He was around sixty now, and had known most of the well-known gangsters from the 1960s on. There were stories that he'd worked with the Krays and Richardson in London, as well as some of the better-known Glasgow villains. Past inquiries had tried linking him to drug gangs in Holland and the sex-slavers of Eastern Europe. Very little had ever stuck. Sometimes it was down to a lack of either resources or evidence compelling enough to persuade the Procurator Fiscal into a prosecution. Sometimes it was because witnesses vanished from the face of the earth.

Following Cafferty into the conservatory, and from there to the limestone-floored kitchen, Rebus stared at the broad back and shoulders, wondering not for the first time how many executions the man had ordered, how many lives he'd wrecked.

'Tea or something stronger?' Cafferty said, shuffling across the floor in his flip-flops.

'Tea's fine.'

'Christ, it must be serious . . .' Cafferty smiled a little smile to himself as he switched the kettle on and dropped three tea bags into the pot. 'I suppose I better put some clothes on,' he said. 'Come on, I'll show you the drawing room.'

It was one of the rooms at the front, with a large bay window and a dominating marble fireplace. An assortment of canvases hung from the picture rails. Rebus didn't know much about art, but the frames looked expensive. Cafferty had headed upstairs, giving Rebus the opportunity to browse, but there was precious little to attract his attention: no books or hi-fi, no desk . . . not even any ornaments on the mantelpiece. Just a sofa and chairs, a huge Oriental rug, and the exhibits. It wasn't a room for living in. Maybe Cafferty held meetings there, impressing with his collection. Rebus placed his fingers against the marble, hoping against hope that it would prove fake.

'Here you go,' Cafferty said, carrying two mugs into the room. Rebus took one from him.

'Milk, no sugar,' Cafferty informed him. Rebus nodded. 'What are you smiling at?'

Rebus nodded towards the corner of the ceiling above the door, where a small white box was emitting a blinking red light. 'You've got a burglar alarm,' he explained.

'So?'

'So . . . that's funny.'

'You think nobody'd break in here? It's not like there's a big sign on the wall saying who I am . . .'

'I suppose not,' Rebus said, trying to be agreeable.

Cafferty was dressed in grey jogging bottoms and a V-neck sweater. He seemed tanned and relaxed; Rebus wondered if there was a sunbed somewhere on the premises. 'Sit down,' Cafferty said.

Rebus sat. 'I'm interested in someone,' he began. 'And I think you might know him: Stuart Bullen.'

Cafferty's top lip curled. 'Wee Stu,' he said. 'I knew his old man better.'

'I don't doubt it. But what do you know about the son's recent activities?'

'He been a naughty boy then?'

'I'm not sure.' Rebus took a sip of tea. 'You know he's in Edinburgh?'

Cafferty nodded slowly. 'Runs a strip club, doesn't he?'

'That's right.'

'And as if that wasn't hard enough work, now he's got you digging at his scrotum.'

Rebus shook his head. 'All it is, a girl's run off from home and her mum and dad got the idea she might be working for Bullen.'

'And is she?'

'Not that I know of.'

'But you went to see Wee Stu and he got up your nose?'

'I just came away with a few questions . . .'

'Such as?'

'Such as what's he doing in Edinburgh?'

Cafferty smiled. 'You telling me you don't know any west-coast hard men who've made the move east?'

'I know a few.'

'They come here because in Glasgow they can't walk ten yards without someone having a go at them. It's the culture, Rebus.' Cafferty gave a theatrical shrug.

'You're saying he wants a clean break?'

'Through there, he's Rab Bullen's son, always will be.'

'Which means someone somewhere just might have put a price on his head?'

'He's not running scared, if that's what you're thinking.'

'How do you know?'

'Because Stu's not the type. He wants to prove himself . . . stepping out from his old man's shadow . . . you know what it's like.'

'And running a lap bar's going to do that?'

'Maybe.' Cafferty studied the surface of his drink. 'Then again, maybe he's got other plans.'

'Such as.'

'I don't know him well enough to answer that. I'm an old man, Rebus: people don't tell me as much as they used to. And even if I did know something . . . why the hell would I bother to tell you?'

'Because you nurse a grudge.' Rebus placed his half-empty mug on the varnished wooden floor. 'Didn't Rab Bullen rip you off on one occasion?'

'Mists of time, Rebus, mists of time.'

'So as far as you know, the son's clean?'

'Don't be stupid – nobody's *clean*. Have you looked around you recently? Not that there's much to see from Gayfield Square. Can you still smell the drains in the corridors?' Cafferty smiled at Rebus's silence. '*Some* people still tell me stuff . . . just now and again.'

'Which people?'

Cafferty's smile widened. '"Know thine enemy", that's what they say, isn't it? I dare say it's why you keep all my press cuttings.'

'It's not for your pop-star looks, that's for sure.'

Cafferty's mouth gaped in a huge yawn. 'Hot tub always does that to me,' he said by way of apology, fixing Rebus with a stare. 'Something else I hear is that you're working the Knoxland stabbing. Poor sod had . . . what? Twelve? Fifteen wounds? What do Messrs Curt and Gates think of that?'

'How do you mean?'

'Looks to me like a frenzy . . . someone out of control.'

'Or just very, very angry,' Rebus countered.

'Same thing in the end. All I'm saying is, it might have given them a taste.'

Rebus's eyes narrowed. 'You know something, don't you?'

'Not me, Rebus . . . I'm happy just sitting here and growing old.'

'Or heading down to England to meet your scumbag friends.'

'Sticks and stones . . . sticks and stones.'

'The Knoxland victim, Cafferty . . . what is it you're not telling me?'

'Think I'm going to sit here and do your job for you?' Cafferty shook his head slowly, then grasped the arms of the chair and started to rise to his feet. 'But now it's time for bed. Next time you come, bring that nice DS Clarke with you, and tell her to pack her bikini. In fact, if you're sending her, *you* can stay at home.' Cafferty laughed longer and louder than was merited as he led Rebus towards the front door.

'Knoxland,' Rebus said.

'What about it?'

'Well, since you brought it up . . . remember a few months back, we had the Irish trying to muscle in on the drugs scene there?' Cafferty made a noncommittal gesture. 'Seems they could be back . . . Would you happen to know anything about that?'

'Drugs are for losers, Rebus.'

'That's an original line.'

'Maybe I don't think you merit any of my better ones.' Cafferty held the front door open. 'Tell me, Rebus . . . all those stories about me, do you keep them in a scrapbook with little hearts doodled on the front?'

'Daggers, actually.'

'And when they make you retire, that's what you'll have waiting for you . . . a few final years alone with your scrapbook. Not much of a legacy, is it?'

'And what exactly are *you* leaving behind, Cafferty? Any hospitals out there named after you?'

186

'Amount I give to charity, there might well be.'

'All that guilt money, it doesn't change who you are.'

'It doesn't need to. Thing you have to realise is, I'm happy with my lot.' He paused. 'Unlike some I could name.'

Cafferty was chuckling softly as he closed the door on Rebus.

DAY FIVE

Friday

15

The first Siobhan heard of it was on the morning news.

Muesli with skimmed milk; coffee; multivitamin juice. She always ate at the kitchen table, wrapped in her dressing gown – that way, if she spilled anything, she didn't have to worry. A shower afterwards, and then her clothes. Her hair took only a few minutes to dry, which was why she was keeping it short. Radio Scotland was usually just background noise, a babble of voices to fill the silence. But then she picked up the word 'Banehall', and turned the volume up. She'd missed the gist, but the studio was handing over to an outside broadcast:

'Well, Catriona, police from Livingston are at the scene as I speak. We're being kept behind a cordon, of course, but a forensic team, dressed in regulation white overalls with hoods and masks, is entering the terraced house. It's a council-owned property, maybe two or three bedrooms, with grey harled walls and all its windows curtained. The front garden's overgrown, and a small crowd of onlookers has gathered. I've managed to talk to some of the neighbours and it appears the victim was known to police, though whether this will have any bearing on the case remains to be seen . . .'

'Colin, have they revealed his identity yet?'

'Nothing official, Catriona. I can tell you that he was a local man of twenty-two years, and that his demise appears to have been pretty brutal. Again, though, we'll have to await the press conference for a more detailed account. Officers here say that'll happen in the next two to three hours.'

'Thank you, Colin . . . and there'll be more on that story in our

191

lunchtime programme. Meantime, a Central Scotland list MSP is calling for the closure of the Whitemire detention centre sited just outside Banehall . . .'

Siobhan unhooked her phone from its charger, but then couldn't remember the number for Livingston police station. And who did she know there anyway? Only DC Davie Hynds, and he'd been there less than a fortnight: another casualty of the changes at St Leonard's. She headed to the bathroom, checked her face and hair in the mirror. A splash and a wet comb might do for once. She didn't have time for anything else. Decided, she dashed into the bedroom and yanked open the wardrobe doors.

Less than an hour later, she was in Banehall. Drove past the Jardines' old house. They'd moved so they wouldn't be so close to Tracy's rapist. Donny Cruikshank, whose age Siobhan calculated as twenty-two . . .

There were a couple of police vans parked in the next street. The milling crowd had grown. A guy with a microphone was doing a vox pop – she guessed he was the same radio reporter she'd been listening to. The house at the centre of all the attention was flanked by two others. All three doors stood open. She saw Steve Holly disappear into the right-hand one. Doubtless money had changed hands and Holly was being given access to the rear garden, where he might have a better view of things. Siobhan double-parked and approached the uniform standing guard at the blue-and-white tape. She showed her warrant card and he raised the tape for her so she could duck beneath.

'Body been ID-d?' she asked.

'Probably the guy who lived there,' he said.

'Pathologist been?'

'Not yet.'

She nodded and moved on, pushing open the gate, walking up the path towards the shadowy interior. She took a few deep breaths, releasing them slowly; needed to look casual when she stepped indoors, needed to be professional. The lobby was narrow. Downstairs there appeared to be only a cramped living room and an equally small kitchen. A door led from the kitchen to the back garden. The stairs were steep to the only other floor: four doors here, all of them open. One was a hall cupboard, filled with cardboard boxes, spare duvets and sheets. Through another she could see part of a pale pink bath. Two bedrooms then: one a single, unused. Which left the larger, facing the front of the house. This was where all the activity was: scene-of-crime officers; photographers; a local GP consulting with a detective. The detective noticed her.

'Can I help you?'

'DS Clarke,' she said, showing him her ID. So far, she hadn't as much as glanced at the body, but it was there all right: no mistaking it. Blood soaking into the biscuit-coloured carpet beneath it. Face twisted, mouth sagging as though in an effort to suck in a final lungful of life. The shaven head crusted with blood. The SOCOs were running detectors over the walls, seeking spatters which would give them a pattern, the pattern in turn giving clues to the ferocity and nature of the attack.

The detective handed back her ID. 'You're a ways from home, DS Clarke. I'm DI Young, officer in charge of this inquiry . . . and I don't remember asking for any help from the big city.'

She tried a winning smile. DI Young was just that – young; younger than her anyway, and already above her in rank. A sturdy face above a sturdier body. Probably played rugby, maybe came from farming stock. He had red hair and fairer eyelashes, a few burst blood-veins either side of his nose. If someone had told her he wasn't long out of school, she'd probably have believed them.

'I just thought . . .' She hesitated, trying to find the right combination of words. Looking around, she noticed the pictures stuck to the walls – soft porn, blondes with their mouths and legs open.

'Thought what, DS Clarke?'

'That I might be able to help.'

'Well, that's a very kind thought, but I think we can manage, if that's all right with you.'

'But the thing is . . .' And now she stared down at the corpse. Her stomach felt as though it had been replaced by a punchbag, but her face showed only professional interest. 'I know who he is. I know quite a bit about him.'

'Well, we know who he is too, so thanks again . . .'

Of course they knew him. With his reputation and his scarred face. Donny Cruikshank, lifeless on the floor of his bedroom.

'But I know things you don't,' she persisted.

Young's eyes narrowed, and she knew she was in.

'Plenty more porn in here,' one of the SOCOs was saying. He meant the living room: the floor beside the TV stacked with pirate DVDs and videos. There was a computer, too, another officer sitting in

193

front of it, busy with the mouse. He had a lot of floppies and CD-ROMs to get through.

'Remember: this is work,' Young reminded them. He decided the room was still too busy, so led Siobhan into the kitchen.

'I'm Les, by the way,' he said, softening now that she had something to offer him.

'Siobhan,' she replied.

'So . . .' He leaned against a worktop, arms folded. 'How did you come to know Donald Cruikshank?'

'He was a convicted rapist – I worked that case. His victim committed suicide. She lived locally . . . parents still do. They came to me a few days back because their other daughter's run off.'

'Oh?'

'They said they talked to someone at Livingston about it . . .' Siobhan tried to sound anything but judgemental.

'Any reason to think . . . ?'

'What?'

Young shrugged. 'That this might have something to do with . . . I mean, connect in some way?'

'That's what I'm wondering. It's why I decided to come here.'

'If you could write this up as a report . . . ?'

Siobhan nodded. 'I'll do it today.'

'Thanks,' Young eased himself away from the worktop, readying to head back upstairs. But he paused in the doorway. 'You busy in Edinburgh?'

'Not really.'

'Who's your boss?'

'DCI Macrae.'

'Maybe I could have a word with him . . . see if he can spare you for a few days.' He paused. 'Always supposing you're agreeable?'

'I'm all yours,' Siobhan said. She could have sworn he was blushing as he left the room.

She was walking back through to the living room when she almost collided with a new arrival: Dr Curt.

'You do get around, DS Clarke,' he said. He looked to left and right to make sure no one was eavesdropping. 'Any progress on Fleshmarket Close?'

'A little. I bumped into Judith Lennox.'

Curt winced at the name. 'You didn't tell her anything?'

'Of course not . . . your secret's safe with me. Any plans to put Mag Lennox back on display?'

'I should think so.' He moved aside to let a SOCO past. 'Well, I suppose I'd better . . .' He motioned to the stairs.

'Don't worry – he's not going anywhere.'

Curt stared at her. 'If you don't mind me saying, Siobhan,' he drawled, 'that remark says much about you.'

'Such as?'

'You've been around John Rebus for far too long . . .' The pathologist started climbing the stairs, taking his black leather medical case with him. Siobhan could hear his knees clicking with each step.

'What's the interest, DS Clarke?' someone outside was shouting. She looked towards the cordon, saw Steve Holly there, waving his notebook at her. 'Bit off the beaten track, aren't you?'

She muttered something under her breath and walked down the path, opening the gate again, ducking under the cordon. Holly was at her shoulder as she made for her car.

'You worked on the case, didn't you?' he was saying. 'The rape case, I mean. I remember trying to ask you . . .'

'Buzz off, Holly.'

'Look, I'm not going to quote you or anything . . .' He was in front of her now, walking backwards so he could make eye contact. 'But you must be thinking the same as me . . . same as lots of us . . .'

'And what's that?' she couldn't help asking.

'Good riddance to bad rubbish. I mean, whoever did this, they deserve a medal.'

'I know limbo-dancers that couldn't go as low as you.'

'Your mate Rebus said much the same thing.'

'Great minds think alike.'

'But, come on, you must . . .' He broke off as he backed into her car, losing his balance and falling into the road. Siobhan got in and started the engine before he could climb to his feet again. He was brushing himself down as she reversed down the street. He made to pick up his biro, but noticed that she'd crushed it under her wheels.

She didn't drive far, just to the junction with Main Street and across it. Found the Jardines' house easily enough. Both were at home, and ushered her inside.

'You've heard?' she said.

They nodded, looking neither pleased nor displeased.

'Who could have done it?' Mrs Jardine asked.

'Just about anyone,' her husband replied. His eyes were on Siobhan. 'Nobody in Banehall wanted him back, not even his own family.'

Which explained why Cruikshank had lived alone.

'Is there any news?' Alice Jardine asked, trying to press Siobhan's hands between her own. It was as if she'd already dismissed the murder from her mind.

'We went to the club,' Siobhan admitted. 'Nobody seemed to know Ishbel. Still no word from her?'

'You're the first person we'd tell,' John Jardine assured her. 'But we're forgetting our manners — you'll take a cup of tea?'

'I really don't have time.' Siobhan paused. 'Something I did want, though . . .'

'Yes?'

'A sample of Ishbel's handwriting.'

Alice Jardine's eyes widened. 'What for?'

'It's nothing really . . . might just come in handy later on.'

'I'll see what I can find,' John Jardine said. He went upstairs, leaving the two women alone. Siobhan had pushed her hands into her pockets, safe from Alice.

'You don't think we'll find her, do you?'

'She'll let herself be found . . . when she's ready,' Siobhan said.

'You don't think anything's happened to her?'

'Do you?'

'I'm guilty of thinking the worst,' Alice Jardine said, rubbing her hands together as though washing them clean of something.

'You know we'll want to interview you?' Siobhan spoke softly. 'There'll be questions about Cruikshank . . . about how he died.'

'I suppose so.'

'You'll be asked about Ishbel, too.'

'Gracious me, they can't think . . . ?' The woman's voice had risen.

'It's just something that has to be done.'

'And will it be you asking the questions, Siobhan?'

Siobhan shook her head. 'I'm too close. It might be a man called Young. He seems okay.'

'Well, if you say so . . .'

Her husband was returning. 'There's not much, to be honest,' he said, handing over an address book. It listed names and phone numbers, most of them in green felt-tip. Inside the cover, Ishbel had written her own name and address.

'Might do it,' Siobhan said. 'I'll bring it back when I'm finished.'

Alice Jardine had grabbed her husband's elbow. 'Siobhan says the police will want to talk to us about . . .' She couldn't bring herself to use his name. 'About *him*.'

'Will they?' Mr Jardine turned to Siobhan.

'It's routine,' she said. 'Turning the victim's life into a pattern . . .'

'Yes, I see.' Though he sounded unsure. 'But they can't . . . they *won't* think Ishbel had anything to do with it?'

'Don't be so stupid, John!' his wife hissed. 'Ishbel wouldn't do something like that!'

Maybe not, Siobhan thought, but then Ishbel was by no means the only member of the family who'd be regarded as a suspect . . .

Tea was offered again, and politely refused. She managed to get out of the door, escaping to her car. As she drove off, she looked in her rearview mirror and saw Steve Holly striding along the pavement, checking house numbers. For a moment, she considered stopping – heading back and warning him off. But that sort of thing would only pique his curiosity. However he acted, whatever he asked, the Jardines would have to survive without her help.

She turned along Main Street and stopped outside the Salon. Inside, the place smelled of perms and hairspray. Two customers sat beneath driers. They had magazines open on their laps, but were busy talking, voices raised above the machines.

'. . . and the best of British luck to them, I say.'

'No great loss, that's for sure . . .'

'It's Sergeant Clarke, isn't it?' This last came from Angie. She spoke even more loudly than her clients, and they heeded her warning, falling silent, eyes on Siobhan.

'What can we do for you?' Angie said.

'It's Susie I want to see.' Siobhan smiled at the young assistant.

'Why? What've I done?' Susie protested. She was taking a cup of instant cappuccino to one of the women beneath the driers.

'Nothing,' Siobhan reassured her. 'Unless, of course, you murdered Donny Cruikshank.'

The four women looked horrified. Siobhan held up her hands. 'Bad joke,' she said.

'No shortage of suspects,' Angie admitted, lighting a cigarette for herself. Her nails were painted blue today, with tiny spots of yellow, like stars in the sky.

'Care to name your favourites?' Siobhan asked, trying to make light of the question.

'Look around you, sweetheart.' Angie blew smoke ceilingwards. Susie was taking another drink over to the driers – a glass of water this time.

'It's one thing to think about doing someone in,' she said.

Angie nodded. 'It's like an angel heard us and decided for once to do the right thing.'

197

'An avenging angel?' Siobhan ventured.

'Read your Bible, sweetheart: they weren't all just feathers and haloes.' The women under the driers shared a smile at this. 'You expect us to help you put whoever did that behind bars? It's the patience of Job you'll be needing.'

'Sounds like you know your Bible, which means you also know murder's a sin against God.'

'Depends on your God, I suppose.' Angie took a step closer. 'You're a friend of the Jardines – I know, they've told me. So come on now, you tell me straight out . . .'

'Tell you what?'

'Tell me you're not glad the bastard's dead.'

'I'm not.' She held the hairdresser's gaze.

'Then you're not an angel, you're a saint.' Angie went to check how the women's hair was progressing. Siobhan seized the chance to talk to Susie.

'It's really just that I could do with your details.'

'My details?'

'Your vital statistics, Susie,' Angie said, the two customers laughing with her.

Siobhan managed to smile. 'Just your full name and address, maybe your phone number. In case I need to write up a report.'

'Oh, right . . .' Susie looked flustered. She went to the till, found a notepad next to it, started writing. She tore off the sheet and handed it to Siobhan. The writing was in capitals, but that didn't worry Siobhan: so was most of the graffiti in the Bane's ladies' lavatory.

'Thanks, Susie,' she said, slipping the note into her pocket, next to Ishbel's address book.

There were a few more drinkers in the Bane than on her previous visit. They moved aside to give her some room at the bar. The barman recognised her, nodded something that could have been either a greeting or an apology for Cruikshank's behaviour last time round.

She ordered a soft drink.

'On the house,' he said.

'Aye, aye,' said one of the drinkers, 'Malky's trying some foreplay for a change.'

Siobhan ignored this. 'I don't usually get free drinks until after I've identified myself as a detective.' She held up her warrant card as proof.

'Good choice, Malky,' a man said. 'I suppose it's about young Donny?' Siobhan turned to the speaker. He was in his sixties, a flat cap perched above a shiny dome of a head. He held a pipe in one hand. There was a dog lying at his feet, fast asleep.

'That's right,' she admitted.

'The lad was a bloody idiot, we all know that . . . Didn't deserve to die for it, though.'

'No?'

The man shook his head. 'Lassies cry rape too quick these days.' He held up a hand to stifle the barman's protest. 'No, Malky, I'm just saying, though . . . put a bit of drink in a girl, she'll walk into trouble. Look at the way they dress when they parade up and down Main Street. Go back fifty years, women covered themselves up a bit . . . and you didn't read about indecent assaults every day in your paper.'

'Here it comes,' someone called out.

'Things have changed . . .' The drinker almost relished the groans all around him. Siobhan realised that this was a regular performance, unscripted but dependable. She glanced at Malky, but he shook his head, telling her it wasn't worth fighting her corner. The drinker would relish such a prospect. Instead she excused herself and headed to the loo. Inside the cubicle, she sat down, placing Ishbel's address book and Susie's note on her lap, comparing the writing to the messages on the wall. Nothing new had been added since her last visit. She was pretty sure that 'Donny Pervo' had been done by Susie, 'Cook the Cruik' by Ishbel. But there were other hands at work. She thought of Angie, and even the women under the driers.

Claimed in blood . . .

Dead Man Walking . . .

Neither Ishbel nor Susie had written those, but someone had.

The solidarity of the hair salon.

A town full of suspects . . .

Flicking through the address book, she noticed that under the letter C there was an address that looked familiar – HMP Barlinnie. E Wing, which was where they kept the sex offenders. Written there in Ishbel's hand, filed under C for Cruikshank. Siobhan went through the rest of the book but found nothing else of note.

All the same, did this mean Ishbel had written to Cruikshank? Were there ties between them Siobhan didn't yet know of? She doubted the parents would know – they'd be horrified at the

199

thought. She walked back into the bar, lifted her drink, fixed her eyes on those of Malky the barman.

'Do Donny Cruikshank's parents still live locally?'

'His dad comes in here,' one of the drinkers said. 'He's a good man, Eck Cruikshank. Near did for him when Donny was put away . . .'

'Donny didn't live at home, though,' Siobhan added.

'Not once he came out of jail,' the drinker said.

'Mum wouldn't have him in the house,' Malky chipped in. Soon, the whole bar was talking about the Cruikshanks, forgetting they had a detective in their midst.

'Donny was aye a terror . . .'

'Dated my lassie for a couple of months, never said boo to a goose . . .'

'Dad works at a machine-tool place in Falkirk . . .'

'Didn't deserve an end like that . . .'

'No one does . . .'

Siobhan stood there taking sips of her drink, adding the occasional comment or question. When her glass was empty, two of the drinkers offered to buy her another, but she shook her head.

'My shout,' she said, reaching into her bag for money.

'I won't have a lass buying me drinks,' one of the men tried to protest. But he allowed the fresh pint to be placed in front of him anyway. Siobhan started putting her change away.

'What about since he got out?' she asked casually. 'Been catching up with any old mates?'

The men fell silent, and she realised she hadn't been casual enough. She offered a smile. 'Someone else will come round, you know . . . asking the self-same questions.'

'Doesn't mean we have to answer,' Malky said sternly. 'Careless talk and all that . . .'

The drinkers nodded their agreement.

'It's a murder inquiry,' Siobhan reminded him. There was a chill in the pub now, all goodwill frozen.

'Maybe so, but we're not grasses.'

'I'm not asking you to be.'

One of the men slid his pint back towards Malky. 'I'll buy my own,' he said. The man beside him did the same.

The door opened and two uniforms walked in. One of them carried a clipboard.

'You'll have heard about the fatality?' he asked. Fatality: a nice euphemism, but also accurate. It wouldn't be murder until the pathologist gave his verdict. Siobhan decided to leave. The uniform with the clipboard said he'd need to take down her details. She showed him her warrant card instead.

Outside, a car horn sounded. It was Les Young. He came to a stop and waved her over, winding down his window as she approached.

'Has the sleuth from the big city broken the case?' he asked.

She ignored this, instead filling him in on her visits to the Jardines, the Salon, and the Bane.

'So it's not that you've got a drink problem then?' he asked, gazing past her to the door of the bar. When she said nothing, he seemed to decide the time for teasing was past. 'Good work,' he said. 'We'll maybe get someone to study the handwriting, see who else Donny Cruikshank might have considered an enemy.'

'He's got a few champions, too,' Siobhan countered. 'Men who think he shouldn't have gone to jail in the first place.'

'Maybe they're right . . .' Young saw the look on her face. 'I don't mean he was innocent. It's just . . . when a rapist goes to jail, they end up segregated for their own safety.'

'And the only people they mix with are other rapists?' Siobhan guessed. 'You think one of them might've killed Cruikshank?'

Young shrugged. 'You saw the amount of porn he had – pirate stuff, CD-ROMs . . .'

'So?'

'So his computer wasn't up to making them. Not the right software or processor. He must have got them from somewhere.'

'Mail order? Sex shops?'

'Possibly . . .' Young gnawed at his bottom lip.

Siobhan hesitated before speaking. 'There's something else.'

'What?'

'Ishbel Jardine's address book – looks like she was writing to Cruikshank when he was in prison.'

'I know.'

'You do?'

'Found her letters in a drawer in Cruikshank's bedroom.'

'What did they say?'

Young reached over to the passenger seat. 'Take a look, if you like.' Two sheets of paper, with an envelope for each, encased in polythene evidence bags. Ishbel wrote in angry capitals.

WHEN YOU RAPED MY SISTER, YOU MIGHT AS WELL HAVE KILLED ME, TOO . . .

MY LIFE'S GONE, AND YOU'RE TO BLAME . . .

201

'You can see why we're suddenly keen to speak to her,' Young said.

Siobhan just nodded. She thought she could understand why Ishbel had written the letters – the need for Cruikshank to feel guilt. But why had he kept them? To gloat over? Did her anger fuel something within him? 'How come the prison censor let them through?' she asked.

'I wondered the same thing . . .'

She looked at him. 'You called Barlinnie?'

'Spoke to the censor,' Young confirmed. 'He let them through because he thought they might make Cruikshank face up to his guilt.'

'And did they?'

Young shrugged.

'Did Cruikshank ever write back to her?'

'Censor says not.'

'And yet he kept her letters . . .'

'Maybe he planned to tease her about them.' Young paused. 'Maybe she took the teasing to heart . . .'

'I don't see her as a killer,' Siobhan stated.

'Problem is, we don't *see* her at all. Finding her is going to be your priority, Siobhan.'

'Yes, sir.'

'Meantime, we're setting up a murder room.'

'Where?'

'Apparently there's a space we can use at the library.' He nodded down the road. 'Next to the primary school. You can help us set up if you like.'

'We need to let my boss know where I am first.'

'Hop in then.' Young reached for his mobile. 'I'll let him know you've been poached.'

16

Rebus and Ellen Wylie were back at Whitemire.

An interpreter had been brought in from Glasgow's Kurdish community. She was a small, bustling woman who spoke with a broad west-coast accent and wore a lot of gold and layers of bright clothing. To Rebus's eyes, she looked as if she should be reading palms in a fairground caravan. Instead, she was sitting at a table in the cafeteria with Mrs Yurgii, the two detectives, and Alan Traynor. Rebus had told Traynor that they'd be fine on their own, but he'd insisted on being present, sitting a little apart from the group, arms folded. There were staff in the cafeteria – cleaners and cooks. Pots occasionally clanked on to metal surfaces, causing Mrs Yurgii to jump every time. Her children were being looked after in their room. She carried a handkerchief with her, rolled around the fingers of her right hand.

It was Ellen Wylie who had found the interpreter; and it was Wylie who asked the questions.

'Did she never hear from her husband? Never try contacting him?'

The translated question would follow, and then the answer, translated back into English again.

'How could she? She didn't know where he was.'

'Inmates are allowed to make phone calls out,' Traynor clarified. 'There's a pay-phone . . . they're welcome to use it.'

'If they have the money,' the interpreter snapped.

'He never tried contacting her?' Wylie persisted.

'It's always possible he heard things from those on the outside,' the interpreter answered, without posing the question to the widow.

'How do you mean?'

'I'm assuming people do actually *leave* this place?' Again she glared at Traynor.

'Most are sent home,' he retorted.

'To be disappeared,' she spat back.

'Actually,' Rebus interrupted, 'it's true that some people are bailed out of here, aren't they, Mr Traynor?'

'That's right. If someone stands as a referee . . .'

'And that's how Stef Yurgii might have heard news of his family – from people he met who'd been in here.'

Traynor looked sceptical.

'Do you have a list?' Rebus asked.

'A list?'

'Of people who've been bailed.'

'Of course we do.'

'And the addresses they're staying at?' Traynor nodded. 'So it would be easy to say how many of them are in Edinburgh, maybe even in Knoxland itself?'

'I don't think you understand the system, Inspector. How many people in Knoxland do you think would give shelter to an asylum-seeker? I admit I don't know the place, but from what I've seen in the newspapers . . .'

'You've got a point,' Rebus agreed. 'But all the same, maybe you could pull those records for me?'

'They're confidential.'

'I don't need to see all of them. Just the ones living in Edinburgh.'

'And just the Kurds?' Traynor added.

'I suppose so, yes.'

'Well, that's feasible, I suppose.' Traynor still sounded less than enthusiastic.

'Maybe you could do it now, while we're talking to Mrs Yurgii?'

'I'll do it later.'

'Or one of your staff . . . ?'

'Later, Inspector.' Traynor had firmed up his voice. Mrs Yurgii was talking. The interpreter nodded when she'd finished.

'Stef could not go home. They would kill him. He was a human rights journalist.' She frowned. 'I think that's correct.' She checked with the widow, nodded again. 'Yes, he worked on stories of state corruption, of campaigns against the Kurdish people. She tells me he was a hero, and I believe her . . .'

The interpreter sat back, as if daring them to doubt her.

Ellen Wylie leaned forward. 'Was there anyone on the outside . . . anyone he knew? Someone he might have gone to?'

The question was asked and answered.

'He did not know anyone in Scotland. The family did not want to leave Sighthill. They were beginning to be happy there. The children made friends . . . they found places in a school. And then they were thrown into a van – a police van – and brought to this place in the middle of the night. They were terrified.'

Wylie touched the interpreter on the forearm. 'I don't know how best to phrase this . . . maybe you can help me.' She paused. 'We're pretty sure Stef had at least one "friend" on the outside.'

It took the interpreter a moment to realise. 'You mean a woman?'

Wylie nodded slowly. 'We need to find her.'

'How can his widow help?'

'I'm not sure . . .'

'Ask her,' Rebus said, 'what languages her husband spoke.'

The interpreter looked at him as she asked the question. Then: 'He spoke a little English, and some French. His French better than his English.'

Wylie was looking at him too. 'The girlfriend speaks French?'

'It's a possibility. Got any French-speakers in here, Mr Traynor?'

'From time to time.'

'What countries are they from?'

'Africa, mostly.'

'Do you think any of them might have been given bail?'

'Can I assume you'd like me to check?'

'If it's not too much trouble.' Rebus's lips formed a smile of sorts. Traynor just sighed. The translator was talking again. Mrs Yurgii answered by bursting into tears, burying her face in her handkerchief.

'What did you say to her?' Wylie asked.

'I asked if her husband was faithful.'

Mrs Yurgii wailed something. The translator wrapped an arm around her.

'And now we have her answer,' she said.

'Which is . . . ?'

'"Until death",' the translator quoted.

The silence was broken by a blast from Traynor's walkie-talkie. He placed it to his ear. 'Go ahead,' he said. Then, having listened: 'Oh Christ . . . I'll be right there.'

He left without a word. Rebus and Wylie exchanged a look, and Rebus rose to his feet, readying to follow.

It wasn't hard to keep his distance: Traynor was in a hurry, not quite running exactly but doing everything but. Down one corridor, and then left into another, until, at the far end, he pulled open a door. This led to a shorter corridor dead-ended by a fire exit. There were three small rooms – isolation cells. From inside one, someone was thumping the locked door. Thumping and kicking and yelling in a language Rebus didn't recognise. But this wasn't what interested Traynor. He'd entered another room, its door held open by a guard. There were further guards inside, crouched around the prone figure of a near-skeletal man, dressed only in underpants. The rest of his clothing had been removed to form a makeshift noose. It was still tied tight around his throat, his head purple and swollen, tongue bursting from its mouth.

'Every ten bloody minutes,' Traynor was saying angrily.

'We *checked* every ten minutes,' a guard was stressing.

'I'll bet you did . . .' Traynor looked up, saw Rebus standing in the doorway. 'Get him out of here!' he roared. The nearest guard started pushing Rebus back into the corridor. Rebus held up both hands.

'Easy, pal, I'm going.' He was backing away, the guard following. 'Suicide watch, eh? Sounds like his neighbour's going to be next, judging by the uproar he's making . . .'

The guard said nothing. He just closed the door on Rebus and stood there, watching through its glass panel. Rebus held his hands up again, then turned and walked away. Something told him that his requests to Traynor would have slipped a little down the man's list of priorities . . .

The session at the cafeteria was ending, Wylie shaking hands with the interpreter, who then guided the widow in the direction of the family unit.

'So,' Wylie asked Rebus, 'where was the fire?'

'No fire, but some poor sod topped himself.'

'Bloody hell . . .'

'Let's get out of here.' He started walking ahead of her towards the exit.

'How did he do it?'

'Turned his clothes into a kind of tourniquet. He couldn't hang himself: there was nothing up high for him to swing from . . .'

'Bloody hell,' she repeated. When they were out in the fresh air, Rebus lit a cigarette. Wylie unlocked her Volvo. 'We're getting nowhere with this, are we?'

'It was never going to be easy, Ellen. The girlfriend's the key.'

'Unless she did it,' Wylie offered.

Rebus shook his head. 'Listen to her phone call . . . she *knows* why it happened, and that "why" leads to the "who".'

'That's a bit metaphysical, coming from you.'

He shrugged again, flicked the remains of his cigarette on to the ground. 'I'm a renaissance man, Ellen.'

'Oh aye? Spell it for me then, Mr Renaissance Man.'

As they drove out of the compound, he looked towards the site of Caro Quinn's camp. When they'd arrived, she hadn't been there, but she was there now, standing by the roadside, drinking from a thermos. Rebus asked Wylie to stop the car.

'I'll only be a minute,' he said, getting out.

'What are you . . . ?' He closed his door on her question. Quinn smiled when she recognised him.

'Hello, there.'

'Listen,' he said, 'do you know any friendly media people? I mean, friendly to what you're trying to accomplish here?'

Her eyes narrowed. 'One or two.'

'Well, you could slip them an exclusive: one of the inmates has just committed suicide.' As soon as the words were out, he knew he'd made a mistake. Could have phrased that better, John, he told himself as tears welled in Caro Quinn's eyes.

'I'm sorry,' he said. He could see Wylie watching in the wing mirror. 'I just thought you could do something with it . . . There'll be an inquiry . . . the more press interest there is, the worse it is for Whitemire . . .'

She was nodding. 'Yes, I can see that. Thanks for telling me.' The tears were pouring down her face. Wylie sounded the horn. 'Your friend's waiting,' Quinn said.

'Are you going to be all right?'

'I'll be fine.' She rubbed her face with the back of her free hand. The other hand still held a cup, though most of the tea inside was dribbling on to the ground unnoticed.

'Sure?'

She nodded. 'It's just . . . so . . . *barbaric*.'

'I know,' he said quietly. 'Look . . . have you got a phone with you?' She nodded. 'You've got my number, right? Can I take yours?' She reeled it off, and he jotted it down in his notebook.

'You better go,' she said.

Rebus nodded, backing away towards the car. He waved before getting into the passenger seat.

'I hit the horn by accident,' Wylie lied. 'So you know her then?'

'A little,' he admitted. 'She's an artist – paints portraits.'

'So it's true then . . .' Wylie put the car into first gear. 'You really *are* a renaissance man.'

'One "n", two "s"s, right?'

'Right,' she said. Rebus angled the rearview mirror so he could watch Caro Quinn recede as the car gathered pace.

'So how do you know her?'

'I just do, all right?'

'Sorry I asked. Do your friends always burst into tears when you talk to them?'

He gave her a look, and they drove in silence for a few moments.

'Want to drop into Banehall?' Wylie eventually asked.

'Why?'

'I don't know,' she said. 'Just to take a look.' They'd talked about the murder on the outward journey.

'What'll we see?'

'We'll see F Troop at work.'

F Troop because Livingston was 'F Division' of the Lothian and Borders Police, and few in Edinburgh really rated them. Rebus was forced to concede a smile.

'Why not?' he said.

'That's decided then.'

Rebus's mobile sounded. He wondered if it might be Caro Quinn, thought maybe he should have stayed a bit longer, kept her company. But it was Siobhan.

'I've just been on the phone to Gayfield,' she said.

'Oh aye?'

'DCI Macrae's got the pair of us marked down as AWOL.'

'What's your excuse?'

'I'm in Banehall.'

'Funny, we'll be there in two minutes . . .'

'We?'

'Me and Ellen. We've been out to Whitemire. You still looking for that girl?'

'There's been a bit of lateral movement . . . you heard they found a body?'

'I thought it was a bloke.'

'It's the guy who raped her sister.'

'I can see that would change things. So now you're helping F Troop with their inquiries?'

'In a manner of speaking.'

208

Rebus snorted. 'Jim Macrae must think there's something about Gayfield we don't like.'

'He's not too thrilled ... And he told me to give you another message.'

'Oh aye?'

'Someone else who's fallen out of love with you ...'

Rebus thought for a moment. 'Is that sad bastard still after me for the torch?'

'He's talking about an official complaint.'

'Christ's sake ... I'm buying him a new one.'

'Apparently it's specialist kit – over a hundred quid's worth.'

'You could buy a chandelier for that!'

'Don't shoot the messenger, John.'

The car was passing the sign into town: BANEHALL had become BANEHELL.

'That's inventive,' Wylie muttered. Then: 'Ask her where she is.'

'Ellen wants to know where you are,' Rebus said into the phone.

'There's a room at the library ... we're using it as a base.'

'Good idea: F Troop can see if there are any reference books to help them. *My Big Book of Murders*, maybe ...'

Wylie smiled at this, but Siobhan sounded anything but amused. 'John, don't bring that attitude here ...'

'Only a bit of fun, Shiv. See you in a few minutes.'

Rebus told Wylie where they were headed. The library's narrow car park was already full. Uniformed officers were carrying computers into the single-storey pre-fabricated building. Rebus held the door open for one, then followed, Wylie waiting outside while she checked her phone for messages. The room set aside for the investigation was only about fifteen feet by twelve. Two folding tables had been appropriated from somewhere, along with a couple of chairs.

'We don't have space for all these,' Siobhan was telling one of the uniforms, as he crouched to deposit an oversized computer screen at her feet.

'Orders,' he said, breathing hard.

'Can I help you?' This question was directed at Rebus from a young man in a suit.

'DI Rebus,' Rebus said.

Siobhan stepped forward. 'John, this is DI Young. He's in charge.'

The two men shook hands. 'Call me Les,' the young man said. He was already losing interest in this new visitor: he had a murder room to get ready.

'Lester Young?' Rebus mused. 'Like the jazz musician?'

'Leslie, actually – like the town in Fife.'

'Well, good luck, Leslie,' Rebus offered. He walked back into the body of the library, Siobhan following. A few retired people were peering at newspapers and magazines, seated at a large circular table. In the kids' corner, a mother lay on a bean-bag, apparently dozing, while her toddler, dummy in mouth, pulled books off the shelves and piled them on the carpet. Rebus found himself in the history aisle.

'Les, eh?' he said in an undertone.

'He's a good guy,' Siobhan whispered back.

'You're a quick judge of character.' Rebus picked a book off the shelf. It seemed to be saying that the Scots had invented the modern world. He looked around to make sure they weren't in the fiction section. 'So what happens about Ishbel Jardine?' he asked.

'I don't know. That's one reason I'm sticking around.'

'Do the parents know about the murder?'

'Yes.'

'Party time tonight then . . .'

'I went to see them . . . they weren't celebrating.'

'And was either of them caked in blood?'

'No.'

Rebus placed the title back on its shelf. The toddler sent up a squeal as the tower of books toppled over. 'And the skeletons?'

'A dead end, as you might say. Alexis Cater says the chief suspect was a guy who came to a party with a friend of Cater's. Only the friend barely knew him, wasn't even sure of his name. Barry or Gary, I think she said.'

'So that's it then? The bones can lie in peace?'

Siobhan shrugged. 'What about you? Any luck with the stabbing?'

'Inquiries are continuing . . .'

'. . . a police spokesman said today. I take it you're floundering?'

'I wouldn't go that far. A break would be nice though.'

'Isn't that what you're doing here – having a break?'

'Not the kind I meant . . .' He looked around. 'You reckon F Troop are up to this?'

'No shortage of suspects.'

'I suppose not. How was he killed?'

'Whacked with something not unlike a hammer.'

'Where?'

'On the head.'

'I meant where in the house.'

'His bedroom.'

'So it was probably someone he knew?'

'I'd say so.'

'Reckon Ishbel could swing a hammer hard enough to kill someone?'

'I don't think she did it.'

'Maybe you'll get the chance to ask her.' Rebus patted her on the arm. 'But with F Troop on the case, you may have to work that wee bit harder . . .'

Outside, Wylie was finishing a call. 'Anything worth looking at indoors?' she asked. Rebus shook his head. 'Back to base then,' she guessed.

'With just one more detour along the way,' Rebus informed her.

'Where's that then?'

'The university.'

17

They parked in a pay-bay on George Square and walked through the gardens, emerging in front of the university library. Most of the buildings here had gone up in the 1960s, and Rebus hated them: blocks of sand-coloured concrete replacing the square's original eighteenth-century town houses. Rows of treacherous steps, and a notorious wind-tunnel effect which could blow over the unwary on the wrong day. Students walked between the buildings, hugging books and folders in front of them. Some stood and chatted in groups.

'Bloody students,' was Wylie's concise summing-up of the situation.

'Didn't you used to go to college yourself, Ellen?' Rebus asked.

'That's why I'm entitled to say it.'

A *Big Issue* vendor stood beside the George Square Theatre. Rebus approached him.

'All right, Jimmy?'

'Not so bad, Mr Rebus.'

'Are you going to survive another winter?'

'It's that or die in the trying.'

Rebus handed over a couple of coins, but refused to take one of the magazines. 'Anything I should know?' he asked, dropping his voice a little.

Jimmy looked thoughtful. He wore a frayed baseball cap over long grey matted hair. A green cardigan hung down almost to his knees. There was a Border collie – or a version thereof – asleep at his feet. 'Nothing much,' he eventually said, voice coarsened by the usual vices.

'Sure?'

'You know I keep my eyes and ears open . . .' Jimmy paused. 'Price of blaw is falling, if that's any use.'

Blaw: cannabis. Rebus smiled. 'Sadly, I'm not in the market. My drugs of choice, prices only ever seem to rise.'

Jimmy laughed loudly, causing the dog to open one eye. 'Aye, the fags and the booze, Mr Rebus, the most pernicious drugs known to man!'

'Take care of yourself,' Rebus said, moving away again. Then, to Wylie: 'This is the building we want.' He pulled open the door for her.

'You've been here before then?'

'There's a linguistics department – we've used them in the past for voice tests.' A grey-uniformed servitor sat in a glass reception booth.

'Dr Maybury,' Rebus said.

'Room two-twelve.'

'Thanks.'

Rebus led Wylie to the lifts. 'Do you know everyone in Edinburgh?' she asked.

He looked at her. 'This is the way it used to be done, Ellen.' He ushered her into the lift and punched the button for the second floor. Knocked on the door of 212 but there was no one home. A frosted-glass window to the side of the door showed no movement within. Rebus tried the next office along, and was told he might find Maybury in the basement language lab.

The language lab was at the end of a corridor, through a set of double doors. Four students sat in a row of booths, unable to see each other. They wore headphones, and spoke into microphones, repeating a set of random-seeming words:

Bread
Mother
Think
Properly
Lake
Allegory
Entertainment
Interesting
Impressive

They looked up as Rebus and Wylie entered. A woman was facing them, seated at a large desk with what looked like a switchboard attached to it, and a large cassette recorder hooked up to that. She made an impatient sound and switched off the recorder.

'What is it?' she snapped.

'Dr Maybury, we've met before. I'm Detective Inspector John Rebus.'

'Yes, I think I remember: threatening phone calls . . . you were trying to identify the accent.'

Rebus nodded and introduced Wylie. 'Sorry to interrupt. Just wondered if you might spare a few minutes.'

'I'll be finished here at the top of the hour.' Maybury checked her watch. 'Why don't you go up to my office and wait for me? There's a kettle and stuff.'

'A kettle and stuff sounds great.'

She fished in her pocket for the key. By the time they'd turned to leave, she was already telling the students to prepare for the next set of words.

'What do you think she was up to?' Wylie asked as the lift took them back to the second floor.

'Christ knows.'

'Well, I suppose it keeps them off the streets . . .'

Dr Maybury's room was a clutter of books and papers, videos and audio cassettes. The computer on her desk was well camouflaged by more paperwork. A table meant to accommodate tutorial groups was laden with books borrowed from the library. Wylie found the kettle and plugged it in. Rebus stepped outside and headed to the toilets, where he took out his mobile and called Caro Quinn.

'You okay?' he asked.

'I'm fine,' she assured him. 'I called a reporter on the *Evening News*. The story might make the final edition this evening.'

'What's been happening?'

'A lot of comings and goings . . .' She broke off. 'Is this another interrogation?'

'Sorry if it looks that way.'

She paused. 'Do you want to come round later on? To the flat, I mean.'

'What for?'

'So my team of highly trained anarcho-syndicalists can start the indoctrination process.'

'They like a challenge then?'

She managed a short laugh. 'I'm still wondering what makes you tick.'

'Apart from my wristwatch, you mean? Best be careful, Caro. I'm the enemy, after all.'

'Don't they say it's best to know your enemy?'

214

'Funny, someone told me that just recently . . .' He paused. 'I could buy you dinner.'

'Thus propping up the masculine hegemony?'

'I've no idea what that means, but I'm probably guilty as charged.'

'It means we split the bill,' she told him. 'Come to the flat at eight o'clock.'

'See you then.' Rebus ended the call, and almost at once wondered how she would get home from Whitemire. He hadn't thought to ask. Did she hitch? He was halfway through calling her number again when he stopped himself. She wasn't a kid. She'd been holding her vigil for months. She could get home without his help. Besides, she would only accuse him of propping up the masculine hegemony.

Rebus went back into Maybury's office and took a cup of coffee from Wylie. They sat at opposite ends of the table.

'Weren't you ever a student, John?' she asked.

'Could never be bothered,' he answered. 'Plus I was a lazy sod at school.'

'I hated it,' Wylie said. 'Never seeemed to know what to say. I sat in rooms much like this one, year after year, keeping my mouth shut so nobody'd notice I was thick.'

'How thick were you exactly?'

Wylie smiled. 'Turned out the other students thought I never spoke because I already knew it all.'

The door opened and Dr Maybury shuffled in, squeezing behind Wylie's chair. She muttered an apology and reached the safety of her own desk. She was tall and thin and seemed self-conscious. Her hair was a mass of thick dark waves, pulled back into something resembling a ponytail. She wore old-fashioned glasses, as if these could disguise the classical beauty of her face.

'Can I get you a coffee, Dr Maybury?' Wylie asked.

'I'm awash with the stuff,' Maybury said briskly. Then she uttered another apology, thanking Wylie for the offer.

Rebus remembered this about her: that she was easily flustered, and she always apologised more than was necessary.

'Sorry,' she said again, for no apparent reason, as she shuffled together some of the papers in front of her.

'What was happening downstairs?' Wylie asked.

'You mean reeling off those lists?' Maybury's mouth twitched. 'I'm doing some research into elision . . .'

Wylie held up a hand, like a pupil in class. 'While you and I know what that means, Doctor, maybe you could explain it for DI Rebus?'

'I think, when you came in, the word I was interested in was "properly". People have started pronouncing it with part of its middle missing – that's what elision is.'

Rebus had to stop himself from asking what the point of such research was. Instead, he tapped the table in front of him with his fingertips. 'We've got a tape we'd like you to listen to,' he said.

'Another anonymous caller?'

'In a manner of speaking . . . It was a 999 call. We need to establish nationality.'

Maybury slid her glasses back up the steep slope of her nose and held out a hand, palm upwards. Rebus rose from his seat and gave her the tape. She slid it into a cassette deck on the floor beside her and pressed 'play'.

'You might find it a bit distressing,' Rebus warned her. She gave a nod, listened to the message all the way through.

'Regional accents are my field, Inspector,' she said after a few moments' silence. 'Regions of the United Kingdom. This woman is non-native.'

'Well, she's a native of somewhere.'

'But not these shores.'

'So you can't help? Not even a guess?'

Maybury tapped her finger against her chin. 'African, maybe Afro-Caribbean.'

'She probably speaks some French,' Rebus added. 'Might even be her first language.'

'One of my colleagues in the French department might be able to say with more certainty . . . Hang on a minute.' When she smiled, the whole room seemed to light up. 'There's a postgraduate student . . . she's done a bit of work on French influences in Africa . . . I wonder . . .'

'We'll settle for anything you can give us,' Rebus said.

'Can I keep the tape?'

Rebus nodded. 'There *is* a certain amount of urgency . . .'

'I'm not sure where she is.'

'Maybe you could try calling her at home?' Wylie asked.

Maybury peered at her. 'I think she's somewhere in south-west France.'

'That could be a problem,' Rebus offered.

'Not necessarily. If I can contact her by phone, I could play the tape down the line to her.'

It was Rebus's turn to smile.

'Elision,' Rebus said, leaving the word to hang there.

They were back at Torphichen Place. The police station was quiet, the Knoxland squad wondering what the hell to do next. When a case wasn't solved within the first seventy-two hours, it started to feel as if everything slowed down. The initial adrenalin rush was long gone; the doorstepping and interviews had come and gone; everything conspiring to wear down appetite and application both. Rebus had cases that still weren't closed twenty years after the fact. They gnawed away at him because he couldn't shrug off the man-hours spent labouring on them to no effect whatsoever, knowing throughout that you were one phone call – one name – away from a solution. The culprits might have been interviewed and dismissed, or ignored altogether. Some clue might be loitering amidst the mouldering pages of each case file . . . And you were never going to find it.

'Elision,' Wylie agreed, nodding. 'Good to know research is being done into it.'

'And done "proply".' Rebus snorted to himself. 'You ever study geography, Ellen?'

'I did it at school. You reckon it's more important than linguistics?'

'I was just thinking of Whitemire . . . some of the nationalities there – Angola, Namibia, Albania – I couldn't point to them on a map.'

'Me neither.'

'Yet half of them are probably better educated than the people guarding them.'

'What's your point?'

He stared at her. 'Since when does a conversation need a point?'

She gave a long sigh and shook her head.

'Seen this?' Shug Davidson asked. He was standing in front of them, holding up a copy of the city's daily evening newspaper. The front-cover headline was WHITEMIRE HANGING.

'Nothing if not direct,' Rebus said, taking the paper from Davidson and starting to read.

'I've had Rory Allan on the blower, asking for a quote for tomorrow's *Scotsman*. He's planning a spread about the whole problem – Whitemire to Knoxland and all points between.'

'That should stir the pot,' Rebus said. The story itself was thin. Caro Quinn was quoted on the inhumanity of the detention centre.

217

There was a paragraph about Knoxland, and a few old photos of the original Whitemire protests. Caro's face had been circled. She was one among many, toting placards and shouting at the staff as they arrived for the centre's opening day.

'Your friend again,' Wylie commented, reading over his shoulder.

'What friend?' Davidson asked, suspicious.

'Nothing, sir,' Wylie said quickly. 'Just the woman who's holding vigil at the gates.'

Rebus had reached the end of the story, which directed him towards a 'comment' piece elsewhere in the paper. He flicked pages and perused the editorial: *inquiry needed . . . time for politicians to stop turning a blind eye . . . intolerable situation for all concerned . . . backlogs . . . appeals . . . future of Whitemire itself left hanging by this latest tragedy . . .*

'Mind if I keep this?' he asked, knowing Caro might be heartened by it.

'Thirty-five pence,' Davidson said, hand outstretched.

'I can get a new one for that!'

'But this one's been cherished, John, and only one careful owner.' The hand was still outstretched; Rebus paid up, reasoning that it was still cheaper than a box of chocolates. Not that he reckoned Caro Quinn had much of a sweet tooth . . . But there he was, pre-judging her again. His job had taught him prejudice at the most basic 'us and them' level. Now, he wanted to see what lay beyond.

So far, all it had cost him was thirty-five pence.

Siobhan was back at the Bane. This time, she'd brought a police photographer with her, plus Les Young.

'Could do with a drink anyway,' he'd sighed, having found that three out of the four computers in the murder room had software problems, and none of them would connect successfully to the library's telephone system. He ordered a half of Eighty-Shilling.

'Lime and soda for the lady?' Malky guessed. Siobhan nodded. The photographer was sitting at a table next to the toilets, attaching a lens to his camera. One of the drinkers approached and asked him how much he wanted for it.

'Settle down, Arthur,' Malky called. 'They're cops.'

Siobhan sipped her drink while Young handed over the money. She stared at Malky as he placed Young's change on the bar. 'It's not what I'd call a typical reaction,' she said.

'What?' Les Young asked, wiping the thin line of foam from his top lip.

'Well, Malky here knows we're CID. And we've got a man over there setting up a camera . . . And Malky hasn't asked why.'

The barman offered a shrug. 'Doesn't bother me what you do,' he muttered, turning away to wipe one of the beer taps.

The photographer seemed almost ready. 'DS Clarke,' he said, 'maybe you should go first, check no one's in there.'

Siobhan smiled. 'How many women do you think come in here?'

'All the same . . .'

Siobhan turned to Malky. 'Anyone in the ladies'?'

Malky gave another shrug. Siobhan turned to Young. 'See? He's not even surprised we're taking photos in the loo . . .' Then she walked to the door and pushed it open. 'All clear,' she told the photographer. But then, peering into the cubicle, she saw that changes had been made. The various pieces of graffiti had been gone over with a thick black marker-pen, rendering them almost illegible. Siobhan let out a hiss of air and told the photographer to do his best. She strode back to the bar. 'Nice work, Malky,' she said coldly.

'What?' Les Young asked.

'Malky here's as sharp as a tack. Saw me using the toilet both times I was here, and it dawned on him why I was so interested. So he decided to cover over the messages as best he could.'

Malky said nothing, but raised his jaw-line a little, as if to show that he felt no guilt.

'You don't want to give us any leads, is that it, Malky? You're thinking: Banehall's well shot of Donny Cruikshank, good luck to whoever did it. Am I right?'

'I'm saying nothing.'

'You don't need to . . . there's still ink on your fingers.'

Malky looked down at the black smudges.

'Thing is,' Siobhan went on, 'first time I came in here, you and Cruikshank were having a falling-out.'

'I was sticking up for you,' Malky retorted.

Siobhan nodded. 'But after I left, you slung him out. Bit of bad blood between the two of you?' She leaned her elbows on the bar and stood on tiptoe, stretching towards him. 'Maybe we need to take you in for a proper interview . . . What do you say, DI Young?'

'Sounds good to me.' He put down his empty glass. 'You can be our first official suspect, Malky.'

'Get stuffed.'

'Or . . .' Siobhan paused, 'you can tell us whose work the graffiti is. I know some belongs to Ishbel and Susie, but who else?'

'Sorry, I don't frequent the ladies' lavs.'

'Maybe not, but you knew about the graffiti.' Siobhan smiled again. 'So you must go in there sometimes . . . maybe when the bar's shut?'

'Got a bit of a perv thing going, Malky?' Young prodded. 'That why you didn't get on with Cruikshank . . . too much alike?'

Malky pushed a finger towards Young's face. 'You're talking pish!'

'Seems to me,' Young said, ignoring the proximity of Malky's forefinger to his left eye, 'we're talking straight common sense. Case like this, one connection's sometimes all you need to make . . .' He straightened up. 'Would you be okay to come with us just now, or do you need a minute to close up the bar?'

'You're having a laugh.'

'That's right, Malky,' Siobhan said. 'You can see it in our faces, can't you?'

Malky looked from one to the other. Their faces were stern, serious.

'I'm guessing you only work here,' Young pressed on. 'Best phone the owner and tell him you're being taken in for questioning.'

Malky had allowed the finger to retreat back into his fist, the fist to fall to his side. 'Come on . . .' he said, hoping to make them see sense.

'Can I just remind you,' Siobhan told him, 'that interfering with the course of a murder inquiry is a big no-no . . . judges tend to pounce on it.'

'Christ, all I . . .' But he clamped shut his mouth. Young sighed and pulled out his mobile, called a number.

'Can I get a couple of uniforms to the Bane? Suspect to be detained . . .'

'All right, all right,' Malky said, holding up his hands in a pacifying gesture. 'Let's sit down and have a talk. Nothing we can't do here, eh?' Young snapped shut his phone.

'We'll let you know once we've heard what you've got to say,' Siobhan informed the barman. He looked around, making sure none of the regulars needed a refill, then helped himself to a whisky from the optic. Opened the serving hatch and came out, nodding towards the table with the camera bag on it.

The photographer was just emerging from the toilets. 'Did what I could,' he said.

'Thanks, Billy,' Les Young said. 'Let me have them by close of play.'

'I'll see what I can do.'

'Digital camera, Billy . . . take you five minutes to do me some prints.'

'Depends.' Billy had packed his bag, slipped it on to his shoulder. He gave a general nod of farewell and headed for the door. Young sat with arms folded, businesslike. Malky had drained his drink in one go.

'Tracy was well-liked,' he began.

'Tracy Jardine,' Siobhan said, for Young's benefit. 'The girl Cruikshank raped.'

Malky nodded slowly. 'She was never the same afterwards . . . when she topped herself, it didn't surprise me.'

'And then Cruikshank came back home?' Siobhan prompted.

'Bold as brass, like he owned the place. Figured we should all be scared of him because he'd done prison time. Fuck that . . .' Malky examined his empty glass. 'Anyone for another?'

They shook their heads, so he headed back behind the bar and fetched himself a refill. 'This is my last today,' he told himself.

'Bit of a drink problem in the past?' Young asked, sounding sympathetic.

'I used to put a bit away,' Malky admitted. 'I'm fine now.'

'Good to hear it.'

'Malky,' Siobhan said, 'I know Ishbel and Susie wrote some of those things in the toilet, but who else?'

Malky took a deep breath. 'I'd guess a pal of theirs called Janine Harrison. She was more a pal of Tracy's, to be honest, but after Tracy died, she started going around with Ishbel and Susie.' He leaned back, staring at the glass as if willing himself to eke it out. 'She works at Whitemire.'

'Doing what?'

'She's one of the guards.' He paused. 'Did you hear what happened? Someone hanged himself. Christ, if they shut that place . . .'

'What?'

'Banehall was built on coalfields. Only there's no coal left. Whitemire's the only employer round here. Half the folk you see – the ones with new cars and satellite dishes – they've got something to do with Whitemire.'

'Okay, so that's Janine Harrison. Anyone else?'

'There's another friend of Susie's. Right quiet, she is, until the drink hits her . . .'

'Name?'

'Janet Eylot.'

'And does she work at Whitemire too?'

He nodded. 'I think she's one of the secretaries.'

'They live locally, Janine and Janet?'

He nodded again.

'Well,' Siobhan said, having jotted the names down, 'I don't know, DI Young . . .' She looked at Les Young. 'What do you think? Do we still need to take Malky in for questioning?'

'Not right this moment, DS Clarke. But we need his surname and a contact address.'

Malky was happy to provide both.

18

They took Siobhan's car to Whitemire. Young admired the interior.

'This is a bit sporty.'

'Is that good or bad?'

'Good, probably . . .'

A tent had been pitched next to the access road, and its owner was being interviewed by a TV crew, more reporters listening in, hoping for a few useable quotes. The guard at the gate told them it was 'an even bigger bloody circus' inside.

'Don't worry,' Siobhan assured him, 'we've brought our leotards.'

Another uniformed guard was there to meet them at the car park. He greeted them coolly.

'I know this isn't the best of days,' Young said consolingly, 'but we're working a murder inquiry, so you can appreciate that it couldn't wait.'

'Who is it you need to see?'

'Two members of staff – Janine Harrison and Janet Eylot.'

'Janet's gone home,' the guard said. 'She was a bit upset at the news . . .' He saw Siobhan raise an eyebrow. 'News of the suicide,' he clarified.

'And Janine Harrison?' she asked.

'Janine works the family wing . . . I think she's on duty till seven.'

'We'll talk to her then,' Siobhan said. 'And if you could give us Janet's home address . . .'

Inside, the corridors and public areas were empty. Siobhan guessed that the inmates were being kept corralled until the fuss had died down. She caught glimpses of meetings behind doors left only slightly ajar: men in suits with grim looks on their faces;

223

women in white blouses and half-moon glasses, pearls around their necks.

Officialdom.

The guard led them to an open-plan office and put in a call to Officer Harrison. While they were waiting, a man walked past, back-tracking so he could ask the guard what was going on.

'Police, Mr Traynor. About a murder in Banehall.'

'Have you told them all our clients are accounted for?' He sounded profoundly irritated by this latest news.

'It's just background, sir,' Siobhan piped up. 'We're talking to anyone who knew the victim . . .'

This seemed to satisfy him. He made a grunting noise and moved off.

'Brass?' Siobhan guessed.

'Second-in-command,' the guard confirmed. 'Not having a good day.'

The guard left the room when Janine Harrison appeared. She was in her mid-twenties with short dark hair. Not tall, but with some muscle beneath the uniform. Siobhan would guess she worked out, maybe did martial arts or the like.

'Sit down, will you?' Young offered, having introduced himself and Siobhan.

She stayed standing, hands behind her back. 'What's this about?'

'It's about the suspicious death of Donny Cruikshank,' Siobhan said.

'Somebody nailed him – what's suspicious about that?'

'You weren't a fan of his?'

'A man who rapes a drunk teenager? No, you couldn't call me a fan.'

'The local pub,' Siobhan prompted, 'graffiti in the ladies' loo . . .'

'What about it?'

'You contributed a little something of your own.'

'Did I?' She looked thoughtful. 'Might've done, I suppose . . . female solidarity and all that.' She gave Siobhan a look. 'He raped a young girl, beat her up. And now you're going to knock yourself out trying to pin someone down for getting rid of him?' She gave a slow shake of her head.

'No one deserves to be murdered, Janine.'

'No?' Harrison sounded doubtful.

'So which one did you write? "Dead Man Walking" maybe? Or how about "Claimed in blood"?'

'I honestly don't remember.'

'We might ask for a specimen of your writing,' Les Young interrupted.

She shrugged. 'I've got nothing to hide.'

'When did you last see Cruikshank?'

'About a week ago in the Bane. Playing pool by himself, because no one would give him a game.'

'I'm surprised he drank there, if he was such a hate figure.'

'He liked it.'

'The pub?'

Harrison shook her head. 'All the attention. Didn't seem to bother him what kind it was, as long as he was at the centre ...'

From the little Siobhan had seen of Cruikshank, she could accept this. 'You were a friend of Tracy's, weren't you?'

Harrison wagged a finger. 'I know who you are now. You hung around with Tracy's mum and dad, went to her funeral.'

'I didn't really know her.'

'But you saw what she'd been through.' Again the tone was accusatory.

'Yes, I saw,' Siobhan said quietly.

'We're police officers, Janine,' Young interrupted. 'It's our *job*.'

'Fine ... so go and do your job. Just don't expect too much help.' She brought her arms out from behind her back and folded them across her chest, creating a picture of hardened resolve.

'If there's anything you can tell us,' Young persisted, 'best we should hear it from your own lips.'

'Then hear this – I didn't kill him, but I'm glad he's dead all the same.' She paused. 'And if I *had* killed him, I'd be shouting it from the rooftops.'

A few seconds of silence followed, then Siobhan asked: 'How well do you know Janet Eylot?'

'I know Janet. She works here ... That's her chair you're sitting in.' She nodded towards Young.

'What about socially?'

Harrison nodded.

'You go out drinking?' Siobhan prompted.

'Occasionally.'

'Was she with you in the Bane the last time you saw Cruikshank?'

'Probably.'

'You don't remember?'

'No, I don't.'

'I hear she gets a bit daft with a drink in her.'

'Have you seen her? She's five-foot-nothing in high heels.'

'You're saying she wouldn't have attacked Cruikshank?'

'I'm saying she wouldn't have succeeded.'

'On the other hand, *you* look pretty fit, Janine.'

Harrison gave a glacial smile. 'You're not my type.'

Siobhan paused. 'Have you any idea what might have happened to Ishbel Jardine?'

Harrison was thrown momentarily by the change of subject. 'No,' she said at last.

'She never talked about running away?'

'Never.'

'She must have spoken about Cruikshank, though.'

'Must have.'

'Care to elaborate?'

Harrison shook her head. 'Is that what you do when you're stuck? Pin the blame on someone who's not around to stick up for herself?' She fixed her eyes on Siobhan. 'Some friend you are.' Young started to say something, but she cut him off. 'It's your job, I know . . . Just a job . . . like working in this place . . . Someone dies in our care, we all feel it.'

'I'm sure you do,' Young said.

'Speaking of which, I've got checks I need to make before I clock off . . . Are we finished here?'

Young looked to Siobhan, who had one final question. 'Did you know Ishbel had written to Cruikshank while he was in prison?'

'No.'

'Does it surprise you?'

'Yes, I suppose so.'

'Maybe you didn't know her as well as you think you did.' Siobhan paused. 'Thanks for talking to us.'

'Yes, thank you very much,' Young added. Then, as she started to leave: 'We'll be in touch about that sample of your handwriting . . .'

After she'd gone, Young leaned back in his chair, hands clasped behind his head. 'If it wasn't so politically incorrect, I'd call her a ball-breaker.'

'Probably comes with the job she does.'

The guard who'd brought them in appeared suddenly in the doorway, as though he'd been waiting within earshot.

'She's fine once you get to know her,' he said. 'Here's Janet Eylot's address.' As Siobhan took the note from him, she saw that he was studying her. 'And by the way . . . for what it's worth, you're *exactly* Janine's type . . .'

*

226

Janet Eylot lived in a new-build bungalow on the edge of Banehall. For now, the view from her kitchen window was of fields.

'Won't last,' she said. 'Developer's got his eye on it.'

'Enjoy it while you can, eh?' Young said, accepting the mug of tea. The three of them sat down around the small square table. There were two young kids in the house, struck dumb by a noisy video game.

'I limit them to an hour,' Eylot explained. 'And only once the homework's done.' Something about the way she said it told Siobhan that Eylot was a single mum. A cat jumped on to the table, Eylot sweeping it off with her arm. 'I've bloody told you!' she shouted, as the cat retreated into the hall. Then she put a hand to her face. 'Sorry about that . . .'

'We realise you're upset, Janet,' Siobhan said softly. 'Did you know the man who hanged himself?'

Eylot shook her head. 'But he did it fifty yards from where I was sitting. It just makes you think about all the horrible things that could be happening around you, and you don't know about it.'

'I see what you mean,' Young said.

She looked at him. 'Well, in your job . . . you see things all the time.'

'Like Donny Cruikshank's body,' Siobhan said. She'd noticed the neck of an empty wine bottle jutting out from beneath the lid of the kitchen bin; a single wine-glass drying on the draining board. Wondered how much Janet Eylot put away of an evening.

'He's the reason we're here,' Young was telling Eylot. 'We're looking at his lifestyle, people who might have known him, maybe even harboured a grudge.'

'What's that got to do with me?'

'Didn't you know him?'

'Who'd want to?'

'We just thought . . . after what you wrote about him on the wall of the Bane . . .'

'I wasn't the only one!' Eylot snapped.

'We know that.' Siobhan's voice had grown even quieter. 'We're not accusing anyone, Janet. We're just filling in the background.'

'This is all the thanks I get,' Eylot said, shaking her head. 'Bloody typical . . .'

'How do you mean?'

'That asylum-seeker . . . the one who got himself stabbed. It was me phoned you lot. You'd never have known who he was otherwise. And this is how I'm paid back.'

'You gave us Stef Yurgii's name?'

'That's right – and if my boss ever hears that, I'll be for the high jump. Two of your lot came to Whitemire: big hefty bloke and a younger woman . . .'

'DI Rebus and DS Wylie?'

'Couldn't tell you their names. I was keeping my head down.' She paused. 'But instead of solving that poor sod's murder, you'd rather focus on a sleazebag like Cruikshank.'

'Everyone's equal under the law,' Young said. She stared at him so hard, he started to blush, disguising the fact by lifting the mug to his lips.

'See?' she said accusingly. 'You say the words, but you know it's all crap.'

'All DI Young means,' Siobhan interrupted, 'is that we have to be objective.'

'But that's not true either, is it?' Eylot rose to her feet, the chair legs scraping across the floor. She opened the fridge door, realised what she'd done and slammed it shut again. Three bottles of wine chilling on the middle shelf.

'Janet,' Siobhan said, 'is Whitemire the problem? You don't like working there?'

'I hate it.'

'Then leave.'

Eylot laughed harshly. 'And where's the other job coming from? I've two kids, I need to provide for them . . .' She sat down again, staring out at the view. 'Whitemire's what I've got.'

Whitemire, two kids, and a fridge . . .

'What was it you wrote on the toilet wall, Janet?' Siobhan asked quietly.

There were sudden tears in Eylot's eyes. She tried blinking them back. 'Something about him being claimed,' she said, voice cracking.

'Claimed in blood?' Siobhan corrected her. The woman nodded, tears trickling down either cheek.

They didn't stay much longer. Both found themselves taking lungfuls of fresh air when they emerged.

'You got kids, Les?' Siobhan asked.

He shook his head. 'I've been married, though. Lasted a year; we split up eleven months ago. How about you?'

'Never even come close.'

'She's coping, though, isn't she?' He risked a glance back at the house.

'I don't think we need to phone social services just yet.' She paused. 'Where to now?'

'Back to base.' He checked his watch. 'Nearly time to knock off. I'm buying, if you're interested.'

'As long as you're not suggesting the Bane.'

He gave a smile. 'I'm heading into Edinburgh, actually.'

'I thought you lived in Livingston.'

'I do, but I'm in this bridge club . . .'

'Bridge?' She couldn't completely suppress a smile.

He shrugged. 'I started playing years ago in college.'

'Bridge,' she repeated.

'What's wrong with that?' He tried a laugh, but sounded defensive all the same.

'Nothing's wrong with it. I'm just trying to picture you in a dinner jacket and bow tie . . .'

'It's not like that.'

'Then we'll meet for a drink in town and you can tell me all about it. The Dome on George Street . . . six thirty?'

'Six thirty it is,' he said.

Maybury was as good as gold: called Rebus back at five fifteen. He jotted the time down so it could be added to the case notes . . . One of the truly great Who songs, he thought to himself. *Out of my brain on the five-fifteen . . .*

'I've played her the tape,' Maybury was saying.

'You didn't waste any time.'

'I found her mobile number. Extraordinary how they seem to work anywhere these days.'

'She's in France then?'

'Bergerac, yes.'

'So what did she say?'

'Well, the sound quality wasn't brilliant . . .'

'I appreciate that.'

'And the connection kept breaking up.'

'Yes?'

'But after I'd played it back to her a few times, she came up with Senegal. She's not a hundred per cent sure, but that's her best guess.'

'Senegal?'

'It's in Africa, French-speaking.'

'Okay, well . . . thanks for that.'

'Good luck, Inspector.'

Rebus put the phone down, found Wylie working at her computer. She was typing a report of the day's activities, to be added to the Murder Book.

'Senegal,' he told her.

'Where's that?'

Rebus sighed. 'In Africa, of course. French-speaking.'

She narrowed her eyes. 'Maybury just told you that, didn't she?'

'Oh ye of little faith.'

'Little faith, but big resources.' She closed down her document and logged on to the Web, typed Senegal into a search engine. Rebus pulled a chair up next to her.

'Just there,' she said, pointing to an onscreen map of Africa. Senegal was on the continent's north-west coast, dwarfed by Mauritania to the north and Mali to the east.

'It's tiny,' Rebus commented.

Wylie clicked on an icon and a reference page opened up. 'Just the seventy-six thousand square miles,' she said. 'I think that's three-quarters the size of Britain. Capital: Dakar.'

'As in the Dakar rally?'

'Presumably. Population: six and a half million.'

'Minus one . . .'

'She's sure the caller was from Senegal?'

'I think we're talking best guess.'

Wylie's finger ran down the list of statistics. 'No sign here that the country's in turmoil or anything.'

'Meaning what?'

Wylie shrugged. 'She might not be an asylum-seeker . . . maybe not even an illegal.'

Rebus nodded, said he might know someone who'd know, and called Caro Quinn.

'You're crying off?' she guessed.

'Far from it – I've even bought you a present.' For Wylie's information, he patted his jacket pocket, from which jutted the folded newspaper. 'Just wondering if you can shed any light on Senegal?'

'The country in Africa?'

'That's the one.' He peered at the screen. 'Mostly Muslim and an exporter of ground nuts.'

He heard her laugh. 'What about it?'

'Do you know of any refugees from there? Maybe in Whitemire?'

'Can't say I do . . . Refugee Council might help.'

'That's a thought.' But as he said it, Rebus was having another thought entirely. If anyone would know, Immigration would.

'See you later,' he said, ending the call.

Wylie had her arms folded, a smile on her face. 'Your friend from outside Whitemire?' she guessed.

'Her name's Caro Quinn.'

'And you're meeting her later.'

'So?' Rebus twitched his shoulders.

'So what was she able to tell you about Senegal?'

'Just that she doesn't think there are any Senegalese in Whitemire. She says we should talk to the Refugee Council.'

'What about Mo Dirwan? He seems the sort who might know.'

Rebus nodded. 'Why don't you give him a call?'

Wylie pointed at herself. 'Me? You're the one he seems to worship.'

Rebus's face creased. 'Give me a break, Ellen.'

'But then I forgot ... you've got a date tonight. You probably want to nip home for a facial.'

'If I hear that you've been blabbing about this ...'

She raised both hands in a show of surrender. 'Your secret's safe with me, Don Juan. Now skedaddle ... I'll see you after the weekend.'

Rebus stared at her, but she fluttered her hands, shooing him off. He'd gone three steps towards the door when she called out his name. He turned his head towards her.

'Take a tip from one who knows.' She gestured towards the newspaper in his pocket. 'A bit of gift-wrapping goes a long way ...'

19

That evening, fresh from a bath and a shave, Rebus arrived at Caro Quinn's flat. He looked around, but there seemed no sign of mother and child.

'Ayisha's gone to visit friends,' Quinn explained.

'Friends?'

'She's allowed to have friends, John.' Quinn was bending over to hook a low-heeled black shoe on to her left foot.

'I didn't mean anything,' he said defensively.

She straightened up. 'Yes you did, but don't worry about it. Did I tell you Ayisha was a nurse back in her homeland?'

'Yes.'

'She wanted work here, doing the same thing ... but asylum-seekers aren't allowed to work. Still, she made friends with some nurses. One of them's having a get-together.'

'I brought something for the baby,' Rebus said, sliding a rattle from his pocket. Quinn came towards him, took the rattle and tried it out. She looked at him and smiled.

'I'll put it in her room.'

Left on his own, Rebus realised he was sweating, his shirt clinging to his back. He thought of removing his jacket, but feared the stain would be visible. It was the jacket's fault: hundred per cent wool, too warm for indoors. He visualised himself at dinner, beads of perspiration falling into his soup ...

'You haven't told me how nicely I scrub up,' Quinn said, coming back into the room. She still had only the one shoe on. Her feet were covered in black tights, which disappeared beneath a knee-length black skirt. Her top was mustard-coloured, with a wide neckline stretching almost to both shoulders.

'You look great,' he said.

'Thanks.' She slipped the other shoe on.

'I've got you a present, too.' He handed over the newspaper.

'And here I was, thinking you'd brought it along in case you got bored of my company.' Then she saw that he'd tied a narrow red bow around it. 'Nice touch,' she added, removing it.

'Reckon the suicide will make any difference?'

She seemed to consider this, patting the newspaper against the palm of her left hand. 'Probably not,' she finally conceded. 'As far as the government's concerned, they have to be kept somewhere. Might as well be Whitemire.'

'The newspaper talks about a "crisis".'

'That's because the word "crisis" sounds like news.' She'd opened the paper to the page with her photograph. 'That circle around my head makes me look like a target.'

Rebus narrowed his eyes. 'Why do you say that?'

'John, I've been a radical all my life. Nuclear subs at Faslane, the Torness power station, Greenham Common . . . You name it, I've been there. Is my phone tapped right this second? I couldn't tell you. Has it been tapped in the past? Almost certainly.'

Rebus stared at the telephone apparatus. 'Do you mind if I . . . ?' Without waiting for an answer, he picked up the receiver, pressed the green button and listened. Then he closed the connection, opened it and closed it again. Looked at her and shook his head, replacing the handset.

'You reckon you could tell?' she asked him.

He shrugged. 'Maybe.'

'You think I'm exaggerating, don't you?'

'Wouldn't mean you don't have a reason.'

'I'm betting you've bugged phones in the past – during the miners' strike maybe?'

'Now who's the one doing the interrogating?'

'That's because we're enemies, remember?'

'Are we?'

'Most of your lot would see me that way, with or without the combat jacket.'

'I'm not like most of my lot.'

'I'd say that's true. Otherwise I'd never have let you over the threshold.'

'Why did you? It was to show me those photos, right?'

She eventually nodded. 'I wanted you to see them as human beings rather than problems.' She brushed down the front of her

233

skirt, took a deep breath to indicate a change of subject. 'So where are we gracing with our custom tonight?'

'There's a good Italian on Leith Walk.' He paused. 'You're probably vegetarian, right?'

'God, you're just full of assumptions, aren't you? But as it happens, this time you're right. Italian's good, though: plenty of pasta and pizza.'

'Italian it is then.'

She took a step towards him. 'You know, you'd probably put your foot in your mouth less often if you could try and relax.'

'This is about as relaxed as I get without the demon alcohol.'

She slipped her arm into his. 'Then let's go find your demons, John . . .'

'. . . and then there were those three Kurds, you must have seen it on the news, they sewed their mouths shut in protest, and another asylum-seeker sewed his eyes shut . . . his *eyes*, John . . . most of these people are desperate by anyone's standards, most don't speak English, and they're fleeing the most dangerous places on earth – Iraq, Somalia, Afghanistan . . . a few years back, they had a good chance of being allowed to stay, but the restrictions now are crippling . . . some of them resort to desperate measures, tearing up any ID, thinking it means they can't be sent home, but instead they're sent to prison or end up on the streets . . . and now we've got politicians arguing that the country's already too diverse . . . and I . . . well, I just feel there must be *something* we can do about it.'

Finally she stopped for a breath, picking up the wine-glass which Rebus had just refilled. Though flesh and fowl were off Caro Quinn's menu, alcohol, it appeared, was not. She'd eaten only half her mushroom pizza. Rebus, having demolished his own calzone, was restraining himself from reaching over for one of her remaining slices.

'I was under the impression,' he said, 'that Britain takes more refugees than anywhere else.'

'That's true,' she conceded.

'Even more than the United States?'

She nodded with the wine-glass at her lips. 'But what's important is the number who are allowed to stay. The world's number of refugees is doubling every five years, John. Glasgow has more asylum-seekers than any other council in Britain – more than Wales and Northern Ireland combined – and do you know what's happened?'

'More racism?' Rebus guessed.

'More racism. Racial harassment is up; race attacks are growing by half each year.' She shook her head, sending her long silver earrings flying.

Rebus checked the bottle. It was three-quarters empty. Their first bottle had been Valpolicella; this one was Chianti.

'Am I talking too much?' she asked suddenly.

'Not at all.'

Her elbows were on the table. She rested her chin on her hands. 'Tell me a bit about *you*, John. What made you join the police?'

'A sense of duty,' he offered. 'Wanting to help my fellow human beings.' She stared at him and he smiled. 'Only joking,' he said. 'I just wanted a job. I'd been in the Army for a few years ... maybe I still had a thing for uniforms.'

She narrowed her eyes. 'I can't see you as the bobby-on-the-beat type ... So what is it exactly that you get out of the job?'

Rebus was saved from answering by the appearance of the waiter. Being Friday night, the restaurant was busy. Their table was the smallest in the place, and situated in a dark corner between the bar and the door to the kitchen.

'You enjoy?' the waiter asked.

'It was fine, Marco, but I think we're finished.'

'Dessert for the lady?' Marco suggested. He was small and round and had not lost his Italian accent, despite having lived in Scotland for the best part of forty years. Caro Quinn had quizzed him on his roots when they'd first entered the restaurant, realising later that Rebus knew Marco of old.

'Sorry if I sounded like I was interrograting him,' she'd said by way of apology.

Rebus had just shrugged and told her she'd make a good detective.

She was shaking her head now, as Marco reeled off a list of desserts, each of which, apparently, was a particular speciality of the house.

'Just coffee,' she said. 'A double espresso.'

'Same for me, thanks, Marco.'

'And a *digestif*, Mr Rebus?'

'Just coffee, thanks.'

'Not even for the lady?'

Caro Quinn leaned forward. 'Marco,' she said, 'no matter how drunk I get, there's no way I'm sleeping with Mr Rebus, so don't put yourself out trying to aid and abet, okay?'

Marco just shrugged and held up his hands, then turned sharply towards the bar and barked out the order for coffees.

'Was I a bit hard on him?' Quinn asked Rebus.

'A bit.'

She leaned back again. 'Does he often help you in your seductions?'

'You might find this hard to fathom, Caro, but seduction had never entered my mind.'

She looked at him. 'Why not? What's wrong with me?'

He laughed. 'There's nothing wrong with you. I was just trying to be . . .' He sought the right word. 'Gentlemanly,' was the one he came up with.

She seemed to think about this, then shrugged and pushed her glass away. 'I shouldn't drink so much.'

'We haven't even finished the bottle yet.'

'Thanks, but I think I've had enough. I get the feeling I've been guilty of speechifying . . . probably not what you had in mind for a Friday night.'

'You've filled in a few gaps for me . . . I didn't mind listening.'

'Really?'

'Really.' He could have added that this was partly down to the fact that he would rather listen to her than talk about himself any day.

'So how's the work going?' he asked.

'It's fine . . . when I get time to do any.' She studied him. 'Maybe I should do a portrait of you.'

'You want to scare small children?'

'No . . . but there's something about you.' She angled her head. 'It's hard to see what's going on behind your eyes. Most people try to hide the fact that they're calculating and cynical . . . with you, that's what seems to be on the surface.'

'But I've got a soft, romantic centre?'

'I'm not sure I'd go that far.'

They leaned back in their chairs as the coffees arrived. Rebus started to unwrap his amaretto biscuit.

'Have mine, too, if you want,' Quinn said, getting to her feet. 'I need to pay a visit . . .' Rebus rose an inch from his chair, the way he'd seen actors do in old films. She seemed to realise that this was new to his repertoire and gave another smile. 'Quite the gentleman . . .'

Once she'd gone, he searched his pockets for his mobile, switched

236

it on to check for messages. There were two: both from Siobhan. He called her number, heard background noise.

'It's me,' he said.

'Hang on a sec . . .' Her voice was breaking up. He heard a door swinging open and then shut again, muting the background voices.

'You at the Ox?' he guessed.

'That's right. I was at the Dome with Les Young, but he had a prior engagement, so I drifted along here. What about you?'

'Dining out.'

'Alone?'

'No.'

'Anyone I know?'

'Her name's Caro Quinn. She's an artist.'

'The Whitemire one-woman crusade?'

Rebus's eyes narrowed. 'That's right.'

'I read the papers, too, you know. What's she like?'

'She's fine.' His eyes looked up to where Quinn was returning to the table. 'Look, I'd better ring off . . .'

'Wait a second. The reason I was calling . . . well, two reasons actually . . .' Her voice was drowned out by a vehicle as it rumbled past her. '. . . and I wondered if you'd heard.'

'Sorry, I missed that. Heard what?'

'Mo Dirwan.'

'What about him?'

'He's been beaten up. Happened around six.'

'In Knoxland?'

'Where else?'

'How is he?' Rebus's eyes were on Quinn. She was playing with her coffee spoon, making a show of not listening.

'He's okay, I think. Cuts and bruises.'

'Is he in hospital?'

'Recuperating at home.'

'Do we know who did it?'

'I'm guessing racists.'

'I mean anyone in particular.'

'It's Friday night, John.'

'Meaning?'

'Meaning it'll wait till Monday.'

'Fair enough.' He thought for a second. 'So what was your other reason for calling? You said there were two.'

'Janet Eylot.'

'I know the name.'

'She works at Whitemire. Says she gave you Stef Yurgii's name.'

'She did. What about it?'

'Just wanted to check she was on the level.'

'I told her she wouldn't get into trouble.'

'She's not.' Siobhan paused. 'Not yet, at any rate. Any chance we'll be seeing you at the Ox?'

'I might manage along later.'

Quinn's eyebrows rose at this. Rebus ended the call and slipped the phone back into his pocket.

'A girlfriend?' she teased.

'Colleague.'

'And where is it you might "manage along" to?'

'Just a place we sometimes drink.'

'The bar with no name?'

'It's called the Oxford.' He picked up his cup. 'Someone got a doing tonight, a lawyer called Mo Dirwan.'

'I know him.'

Rebus nodded. 'Thought you might.'

'He often visits Whitemire. Likes to stop and talk to me afterwards, letting off steam.' She seemed lost in thought for a moment. 'Is he all right?'

'Seems to be.'

'He calls me his "Lady of the Vigils" . . .' She broke off. 'What's wrong?'

'Nothing.' Rebus lowered the cup on to its saucer.

'You can't be his white knight every time.'

'It's not that . . .'

'What then?'

'He was attacked in Knoxland.'

'So?'

'It was me who asked him to stick around, knock on doors.'

'And that makes it your fault? If I know Mo Dirwan, he'll bounce back stronger and more bolshy than ever.'

'You're probably right.'

She drained her coffee. 'You should go to your pub. Might be the only place you can relax.'

Rebus signalled to Marco for the bill. 'I'll see you home first,' he told Quinn. 'Got to keep up the pretence of being a gentleman.'

'I don't think you understand, John . . . I'm coming with you.' He stared at her. 'Unless you don't want me to.'

'It's not that.'

'What then?'

238

'I'm just not sure it's your kind of place.'

'But it's yours, and that's what I'm curious about.'

'You think my choice of watering-hole will tell you something about me?'

'It might.' She narrowed her eyes. 'Is that what you're afraid of?'

'Who said I'm afraid?'

'I can see it in your eyes.'

'Maybe I'm just worried about Mo Dirwan.' He paused. 'Remember when you said you'd been run out of Knoxland?' The nod she gave was exaggerated, affected by the wine. 'Could be the same guys.'

'Meaning I was lucky to get away with a warning?'

'No chance of you remembering what they looked like . . . ?'

'Baseball caps and hooded tops.' The shrug she gave was exaggerated too. 'That's just about all I saw of them.'

'And their accents?'

She slapped a hand down on the tablecloth. 'Switch off for the night, will you? Just for the rest of tonight.'

Rebus raised his hands in surrender. 'How can I refuse?'

'You can't,' she told him, as Marco arrived with the bill.

Rebus tried to hide his annoyance. It wasn't just that Siobhan was in the front bar – standing where he usually stood. But she seemed to've taken the place over, a crowd of men around her, listening to her stories. As Rebus pushed the door open, there was a blast of laughter to accompany the end of another anecdote.

Caro Quinn followed hesitantly. There were probably only a dozen or so bodies in the front bar, but this made for a crowd in the cramped space. She fanned her face with her hand, commenting either on the heat or the fug of cigarette smoke. Rebus realised he hadn't lit up now for the best part of two hours; reckoned he could manage another thirty or forty minutes . . .

Tops.

'The prodigal returns!' one of the regulars barked, slapping Rebus's shoulder. 'What're you having, John?'

'No, ta, Sandy,' Rebus said. 'I'm getting these.' Then, to Quinn: 'What'll it be?'

'Just an orange juice.' During the short taxi ride, she'd seemed to doze off for a moment, her head leaning against Rebus's shoulder. He'd kept his body rigid, not wanting to disturb her, but a pothole had brought her upright again.

'Orange juice and a pint of IPA,' Rebus told Harry the barman.

Siobhan's circle of admirers had broken up just enough to make room for the new arrivals. Introductions were made, hands shaken. Rebus paid for the drinks, noting that Siobhan appeared to be on the gin and tonics.

Harry was channel-hopping with the TV remote, dismissing the various sports channels and ending up with the Scottish news. There was a photo of Mo Dirwan behind the announcer, a head-and-shoulders shot, showing him with a huge grin. The announcer became just a voice, as the picture changed to some video footage of Dirwan outside what appeared to be his house. He sported a black eye and some grazes, a pink plaster sitting awkwardly on his chin. He held up a hand to show that it was bandaged.

'That's Knoxland for you,' one of the drinkers commented.

'You're saying it's a no-go zone?' Quinn asked lightly.

'I'm saying you don't go there if your face doesn't fit.'

Rebus could see Quinn begin to bristle. He touched her elbow. 'How's your drink?'

'It's fine.' She looked at him and seemed to see what he was doing. Nodded just enough to let him know she wouldn't rise . . . not this time.

Twenty minutes later, Rebus had given in and was smoking. He looked towards where Siobhan and Quinn were in conversation, heard Caro's question:

'So what's he like to work with?'

Excused himself from a three-way argument about the parliament and squeezed between two drinkers to get to the women.

'Did anyone remember to put a pair of ear-muffs in the fridge?' he asked.

'What?' Quinn looked genuinely perplexed.

'He means his ears are burning,' Siobhan explained.

Quinn laughed. 'I was just trying to find out a little bit more about you.' She turned to Siobhan. 'He won't tell me anything.'

'Don't worry: I know all John's dirty little secrets . . .'

As happened on a good night in the Ox, conversations ebbed and flowed, people joining in two discussions at once, bringing them together only for them to splinter again after a few minutes. There were bad jokes and worse puns, Caro Quinn becoming upset because 'nobody seems to take anything seriously any more'. Someone else agreed that it was a dumbed-down culture, but Rebus whispered what he felt to be the truth into her ear:

'We're never more serious than when we seem to be joking . . .'

And later still, the back room now filled with noisy tables of drinkers, Rebus queued at the bar for more drinks and noticed that both Siobhan and Caro were missing. He frowned at one of the regulars, who angled his head towards the women's toilet. Rebus nodded and paid for the drinks. He was having one tot of whisky before calling it a night. One tot of Laphroaig and a third . . . no, fourth cigarette . . . and that would be him. Soon as Caro came back, he'd ask if she wanted to share a taxi. Voices were rising from the top of the steps which led to the toilets. Not a full-blown fight as yet, but getting there. People were stopping their own conversations the better to appreciate the argument.

'All I'm saying is, those people need jobs, same as anyone else!'

'You don't think the guards in the concentration camps said the same thing?'

'Christ's sake, you can't compare the two!'

'Why not? They're both morally abhorrent . . .'

Rebus left the drinks where they were and started pushing through the throng. Because he'd recognised the voices now: Caro and Siobhan.

'I'm just trying to say that there's an economic argument,' Siobhan was telling the whole bar. 'Because whether you like it or not, Whitemire's the only game in town if you happen to live in Banehall!'

Caro Quinn raised her eyes to heaven. 'I can't believe I'm hearing this.'

'You had to hear it some time – not everyone out here in the real world can *afford* the moral high ground. There are single mums working in Whitemire. How easy is it going to be for *them* if you get your way?'

Rebus was at the top of the steps. The two women were inches apart, Siobhan slightly taller, Caro Quinn standing on tiptoe the better to lock eyes with her opponent.

'Whoah there,' Rebus said, trying for a placatory smile. 'I think I can hear the drink talking.'

'Don't patronise me!' Quinn growled. Then, to Siobhan: 'What about Guantanamo Bay? I don't suppose you see anything wrong with locking people up without the barest human rights?'

'Listen to yourself, Caro – you're all over the place! The point I was making was specific to Whitemire . . .'

Rebus looked at Siobhan and saw the whole working week raging within her; saw the need to let all that pressure out. He guessed the same could be said for Caro. The argument could have come at any time, involved any topic.

He should have seen it sooner; decided to try again.

'Ladies . . .'

Now both of them glowered at him.

'Caro,' he said, 'your taxi's outside.'

The glower became a frown. She was trying to remember making the arrangement. He locked eyes with Siobhan, knew she could see he was lying. He watched as her shoulders relaxed.

'We can pick this up again another time,' he continued to cajole Caro. 'But for tonight, I think we should call it a day . . .'

Somehow, he managed to manoeuvre Caro down the steps and through the crowd, miming the making of a phone call to Harry, who nodded back: a taxi would be ordered.

'We'll see you later, Caro,' one of the regulars called.

'Watch out for him,' another warned her, jabbing Rebus in the chest.

'Thanks, Gordon,' Rebus said, slapping the hand away.

Outside, she sank to the pavement, feet by the roadside, head in her hands.

'You okay?' Rebus asked.

'I think I lost it a bit in there.' She took her hands away from her face, breathed the night air. 'It's not that I'm drunk or anything. I just can't believe anyone could stick up for that place!' She turned to stare at the door of the pub, as if considering rejoining the fray. 'I mean . . . tell me you don't feel that way.' Now her eyes were on his. He shook his head.

'Siobhan likes to play devil's advocate,' he explained, crouching down beside her.

It was Caro's turn to shake her head. 'That's not it at all . . . she really believed what she was saying. She can see Whitemire's *good points*.' She looked at him to fathom his reaction to those words, words he guessed were quoted verbatim from Siobhan's argument.

'It's just that she's been spending some time in Banehall,' Rebus continued to explain. 'Not a lot of jobs going begging out that way . . .'

'And that justifies the whole ugly enterprise?'

Rebus shook his head. 'I'm not sure anything justifies Whitemire,' he said quietly.

She took his hands in hers and squeezed them. He thought he could see the beginnings of tears in her eyes. They sat in silence like that for a few minutes, groups of revellers passing them on each side of the road, some of them staring, saying nothing. Rebus thought back to a time when he, too, had harboured ideals. They'd

242

been knocked out of him early on: he'd joined the Army at sixteen. Well, not knocked out of him exactly, but replaced with other values, mostly less concrete, less passionate. By now, he was almost inured to the idea. Faced with someone like Mo Dirwan, his first instinct was to look for the con, the hypocrite, the money-making ego. And faced with someone like Caro Quinn . . . ?

Initially, he'd thought her the typical spoilt middle-class conscience. All that affordable liberal suffering − so much more palatable than the real thing. But it took more than that to drive someone out to Whitemire day after day, sneered at by the workforce, unthanked by the inmates. It took a large measure of guts.

He could see, right now, the toll it was taking. She'd leaned her head against his shoulder again. Her eyes were still open, staring at the building across the narrow lane. It was a barber's shop, complete with red-and-white striped pole. Red and white meaning blood and bandages, Rebus seemed to think, though he couldn't remember why. And now there was the sound of a diesel engine chugging towards them, the taxi bathing them in its headlights.

'Here's the cab,' Rebus said, helping Caro to her feet.

'I still don't remember asking for one,' she confessed.

'That's because you didn't,' he said with a smile, holding open the door for her.

She told him 'coffee' meant just that: no euphemisms. He nodded, wanting to see her safely indoors. Then he reckoned he would walk all the way home, burn some of the alcohol out of his system.

Ayisha's bedroom door was closed. They tiptoed past it and into the living room. The kitchen was through another doorway. While Caro filled the kettle, he took a look at her record collection − all vinyl, no CDs. There were albums he hadn't seen in years: Steppenwolf, Santana, Mahavishnu Orchestra . . . Caro came back through holding a card.

'This was on the table,' she said, handing it to him. It was a thank-you for the rattle. 'Decaf all right? It's either that or mint tea . . .'

'Decaf's fine.'

She made tea for herself, its aroma filling the small square room. 'I like it at night,' she said, staring out of the window. 'Sometimes I work for a few hours . . .'

'Me too.'

She gave a sleepy smile and sat down on the chair opposite him, blowing across the surface of her cup. 'I can't decide about you, John. Most people, we know within half a minute of meeting them whether they're on the same wavelength.'

'So am I FM or medium wave?'

'I don't know.' They were keeping their voices low so as not to wake mother and child. Caro tried stifling a yawn.

'You should get some sleep,' Rebus told her.

She nodded. 'Finish your coffee first.'

But he shook his head, placing the mug on the bare floorboards and rising to his feet. 'It's late.'

'I'm sorry if I . . .'

'What?'

She shrugged. 'Siobhan's your friend . . . the Oxford's your pub . . .'

'Both are pretty thick-skinned,' he assured her.

'I should have left you to it. I was in the wrong mood.'

'Will you be going to Whitemire this weekend?'

She gave a shrug. 'That depends on my mood, too.'

'Well, if you get bored, give me a call.'

She was on her feet now too. Walked over to him and pushed up with her toes so she could plant a kiss on his left cheek. When she stepped back, her eyes widened suddenly and a hand flew to her mouth.

'What's wrong?' Rebus asked.

'I've just remembered . . . I let you pay for dinner!'

He smiled and headed for the door.

He walked back up Leith Walk, checking his mobile to see if Siobhan had left a message. She hadn't. Midnight was chiming. He reckoned it would take him half an hour to get home. There'd be plenty of drunks on South Bridge and Clerk Street, stoking up on whatever was left under the chip shops' heat lamps, then maybe heading down the Cowgate to the two a.m. bars. There were some railings on South Bridge, and you could stop there and peer down on to the Cowgate, like watching exhibits in a zoo. This time of night, traffic was banned from the street – too many drinkers falling into the road and being side-swiped by cars. He knew he could probably still get a drink at the Royal Oak, but the place would be heaving. No, he was headed straight home, and at as brisk a pace as he could manage: sweating off tomorrow's hangover. He wondered if Siobhan was back in her flat. He could call her, try to clear the air. Then again, if she was drunk . . . Better to wait till morning.

Everything would look better in the morning: streets hosed down, bins emptied, broken glass swept away. All the ugly energy of the night earthed for a few hours. Crossing Princes Street, Rebus saw that a fight was taking place in the middle of North Bridge, taxis slowing and veering around the two young men. They held one another by the backs of their shirt collars, so that only the tops of their heads were showing. Swinging with their free hands and their feet. No sign of weapons. It was a dance to which Rebus knew all the steps. He kept walking, passing the girl for whose affections they were vying.

'Marty!' she was yelling. 'Paul! Dinnae be sae fuckn daft!'

Of course, she didn't really mean what she was saying. Her eyes were alight at the spectacle – and all of it for *her*! Friends were trying to comfort her, arms embracing her, wanting to be close to the drama's core.

Further along, someone was singing to the effect that they were too sexy for their shirt, which went some way towards explaining why they'd ditched it somewhere along the route. A patrol car cruised by to jeers and V-signs. Someone kicked a bottle into the road, eliciting cheers when it exploded under a wheel. The patrol car didn't seem to mind.

A young woman appeared suddenly in Rebus's path, hair falling in dirty ringlets, eyes hungry as she asked him first for money, then for a cigarette, and finally whether he wanted to do 'a bit of business'. The phrase sounded curiously old-fashioned. He wondered if she'd learned it from a book or film.

'Bugger off home before I arrest you,' he told her.

'Home?' she mouthed, as though this were some new and alien concept. She sounded English. Rebus just shook his head and moved on. He cut through to Buccleuch Street. Things were quieter here, and quieter still as he crossed the expanse of the Meadows, its name reminding him that at one time much of this had been farmland. As he entered Arden Street, he looked up at the tenement windows. There were no signs of student parties, nothing to keep him awake. He heard car doors open behind him, spun round expecting to confront Felix Storey. But these two men were white, dressed in black from their polonecks to their shoes. It took him a moment to place them.

'You've got to be kidding,' he said.

'You owe us a torch,' the leader said. His colleague was younger and scowling. Rebus recognised him as Alan, the man whose torch he had borrowed in the first place.

'It got stolen,' Rebus told them with a shrug.

'It was an expensive piece of kit,' the leader said. 'And you promised to return it.'

'Don't tell me you've never lost stuff before.' But the man's face told Rebus that he was unlikely to be won over by any argument, any appeal to a spirit of camaraderie. The Drugs Squad saw itself as a force of nature, independent from other cops. Rebus held his hands up in surrender. 'I can write you a cheque.'

'We don't want a cheque. We want a torch identical to the one we gave you.' The leader held out a slip of paper, which Rebus took. 'That's the make and model number.'

'I'll nip down Argos tomorrow . . .'

The leader was shaking his head. 'Think you're a good detective? Tracking that down will be the proof.'

'Argos or Dixon's – I'll let you have what I find.'

The leader took a step closer, chin jutting. 'You want us off your back, you'll find *that* torch.' He stabbed a finger at the piece of paper. Then, satisfied he'd made his point, he pivoted and headed for the car, followed by his young colleague.

'Look after him, Alan,' Rebus called. 'Bit of TLC and he'll be right as rain.'

He waved the car off, then climbed the steps to his flat and unlocked the door. The floorboards creaked underfoot, as though in complaint. Rebus switched on the hi-fi: a Dick Gaughan CD, just audible. Then he collapsed on to his favoured chair, searching his pockets for a cigarette. He inhaled and closed his eyes. The world seemed to be tilting, taking him with it. His free hand gripped the arm of the chair, feet pressed solidly to the floor. When the phone rang, he knew it would be Siobhan. He reached down and picked up the receiver.

'You're home then,' her voice said.

'Where did you expect me to be?'

'Do I need to answer that?'

'You've got a dirty little mind.' Then: 'I'm not the one you should be apologising to.'

'Apologise?' Her voice had risen. 'What in God's name is there to apologise about?'

'You'd had a bit too much to drink.'

'That's got nothing to do with it.' She sounded grimly sober.

'If you say so.'

'I admit I don't quite see the attraction . . .'

'You sure you want us to have this conversation?'

'Will it be taken down and used in evidence?'

'Hard to take things back once they're said out loud.'

'Unlike you, John, I've never been good at bottling things up.'

Rebus had spotted a mug on the carpet. Cold coffee, half full. He took a mouthful, swallowed. 'So you don't approve of my choice of companion . . .'

'It's not up to me who you go out with.'

'That's generous of you.'

'But the two of you just seem so . . . *different.*'

'And that's a bad thing?'

She gave a loud sigh, which rumbled like static down the line. 'Look, all I'm trying to say . . . We don't just work together, do we? There's more to us than that – we're . . . pals.'

Rebus smiled to himself, smiled at the pause before 'pals'. Had she considered 'mates', discarding it because of its other, more awkward meaning?

'And as a pal,' he said, 'you don't want to see me make a bad decision?'

Siobhan was silent for a moment, long enough for Rebus to drain the mug. 'Why *are* you so interested in her anyway?' she asked.

'Maybe because she *is* different.'

'You mean because she holds to a set of woolly ideals?'

'You don't know her well enough to be able to say that.'

'I think I know the type.'

Rebus closed his eyes, rubbed the bridge of his nose, thinking: that's pretty much what I'd have said before this case came along. 'We're back on thin ice, Shiv. Why don't you get some sleep? I'll call you in the morning.'

'You think I'm going to change my mind, don't you?'

'That's up to you.'

'I can assure you I'm not.'

'Your prerogative. We'll talk tomorrow.'

She paused so long, Rebus feared she'd already drifted off. But then: 'What's that you're listening to?'

'Dick Gaughan.'

'He sounds angry about something.'

'That's just his style.' Rebus had taken out the slip of paper with the torch's details.

'A Scottish trait maybe?'

'Maybe.'

'Good night, then, John.'

'Before you go . . . if you didn't phone to apologise, then why exactly did you phone?'

'I didn't want us falling out.'

'And are we falling out?'

'I hope not.'

'So you weren't just checking that I was safely tucked up on my lonesome?'

'I'm going to ignore that.'

'Night, Shiv. Sleep tight.'

He put down the receiver, rested his head against the back of the chair and closed his eyes again.

Not mates . . . just pals.

DAYS SIX AND SEVEN

Saturday/Sunday

20

Saturday morning the first thing he did was call Siobhan's number. When her machine picked up, he left a brief message – 'This is John, keeping that promise from last night . . . talk to you soon' – then tried her mobile, and was forced to leave one there, too.

After breakfast, he dug in the hall cupboard, and in the boxes beneath his bed, and emerged with dust and cobwebs clinging to him, clasping packets of photographs to his chest. He knew he didn't have many family snaps – his ex-wife had taken most of them with her. But he did retain a few photos she hadn't felt able to claim right to – members of his family, his mother and father, uncles and aunts. Again, there weren't many of these. He reckoned either his brother had the majority, or they'd been lost over time. Years back, his daughter Sammy would want to play with them, staring at them for long periods, running fingers over their ribbed edges, touching sepia faces, studio poses. She would ask who people were, and Rebus would turn the photo over, hoping to find clues pencilled on the back, then offering a shrug.

His grandfather – his father's father – had arrived in Scotland from Poland. Rebus didn't know why he'd emigrated. It had been before the rise of fascism, so he could only guess that it had been for economic reasons. He'd been a young man, and single, marrying a woman from Fife a year later or thereabouts. Rebus was sketchy on that whole period of his family's history. He didn't think he'd ever really asked his father. If he had, then his father either hadn't wanted to answer or simply didn't know. There could have been things his grandfather hadn't wanted to remember, far less share and discuss.

Rebus held a photo now. He thought it was his grandfather: a middle-aged man, thinning black hair combed close to the skull, a wry smile on his face. He was dressed in Sunday best. It was a studio shot, showing a painted background of hayfield and bright sky. On the back was printed the photographer's address in Dunfermline. Rebus turned the photo over again. He was searching for something of himself in his grandfather – the way the facial muscles worked, or the posture when at rest. But the man was a stranger to him. His whole family history was a collection of questions asked too late: photos with no names attached, no hint of year or provenance. Blurry, smiling mouths, the pinched faces of workers and their families. Rebus considered his own remaining family: daughter Sammy; brother Michael. He phoned them infrequently, usually after one drink too many. Maybe he'd call both of them later on, making sure he hadn't been drinking first.

'I don't know anything about you,' he said to the man in the photograph. 'I can't even be a hundred per cent sure that you *are* who I think you are . . .' He wondered if he had any relatives in Poland. There could be whole villages of them, a clan of cousins who would speak no English but be pleased to see him all the same. Maybe Rebus's grandfather hadn't been the only one to leave. The family might well have spread to America and Canada, or east to Australia. Some could have ended up assassinated by the Nazis, or aiding that self-same cause. Untold histories, criss-crossing with Rebus's own life . . .

He thought again of the refugees and asylum-seekers, the economic migrants. The mistrust and resentment they brought with them, the way tribes feared anything new, anything from outside the camp's tight confines. Maybe that explained Siobhan's reaction to Caro Quinn, Caro not part of the gang. Multiply that mistrust and you got a situation like Knoxland.

Rebus didn't blame Knoxland itself: the estate was a symptom rather than anything else. He realised he wasn't going to glean anything from these old photographs, representing as they did his own lack of roots. Besides, he had a trip to take.

Glasgow had never been his favourite place. It seemed all teeming concrete and high-rise. He got lost there, and always had trouble finding landmarks to navigate by. There were areas of the city which felt as if they could swallow up Edinburgh wholesale. The people were different, too; he couldn't say what it was exactly – accent or mind-set. But the place made him uncomfortable.

Even with an A to Z, he managed to take an apparent wrong

turning almost as soon as he left the motorway. He'd come off too soon, and found himself not far from Barlinnie prison, working his way slowly towards the centre of the city, through a sludge of Saturday shopping traffic. It didn't help that the fine mist had developed into rain, blurring street names and road signs. Mo Dirwan had said that Glasgow was the murder capital of Europe; Rebus wondered if the traffic system might have something to do with it.

Dirwan lived in Calton, between the Necropolis and Glasgow Green. It was a pleasant enough area, with plenty of green spaces and mature trees. Rebus found the house, but there was nowhere to park nearby. He did a circuit, and eventually ended up jogging the hundred yards from the car to the front door. It was a solidly built red-stone semi, with a small front garden. The door was new: glazed with leaded diamonds of frosted glass. Rebus rang the bell and waited, only to find that Mo wasn't home. His wife, however, knew who Rebus was and tried to pull him inside.

'I really just wanted to check he's okay,' Rebus argued.

'You must wait for him. If he finds out I pushed you away . . .'

Rebus glanced down at the grip she had on his arm. 'Doesn't look like you're doing much pushing.'

She relented, smiling in embarrassment. She was probably ten or fifteen years younger than her husband, with lustrous waves of black hair framing her face and neck. Her make-up had been applied liberally, but with great care, turning her eyes dark and her mouth crimson. 'I am sorry,' she told Rebus.

'Don't be, it's nice to feel wanted. Will Mo be back soon?'

'I'm not sure. He had to go to Rutherglen. There has been some trouble recently.'

'Oh?'

'Nothing serious, we hope, just gangs of young men fighting each other.' She shrugged. 'I'm sure the Asians are just as much to blame as the others.'

'So what's Mo doing there?'

'Attending a residents' meeting.'

'You know where it's being held?'

'I have the address.' She motioned indoors, Rebus nodding to let her know she should retrieve it. She left no hint of perfume in her wake. He stood just inside the doorway, sheltering from the rain. It was still a fine, persistent drizzle. There was a word in Scots for it – 'smirr'. He wondered if other cultures had similar vocabularies.

When she returned and handed him the slip of paper, their fingers brushed and Rebus felt a momentary spark.

'Static,' she explained, nodding towards the hall carpet. 'I keep telling Mo we need to change it to all-wool.'

Rebus nodded and thanked her, jogging back to his car. He checked in his A to Z for the address she'd given him. It looked like a fifteen-minute drive, most of it south on the Dalmarnock Road. Parkhead wasn't far away, but Celtic weren't at home today, meaning less chance of finding his route closed or diverted. The rain, however, had forced shoppers and travellers into their vehicles. Ignoring his map for a few minutes, he found that he'd managed to take yet another wrong turn and was heading for Cambuslang. Pulling over, prepared to wait until he could execute a U-turn, he was startled when the back doors were yanked open and two men fell in.

'Good on ye,' one of them said. He smelled of beer and cigarettes. His hair was a mess of soaked curls, which he shook free of raindrops much as a dog would.

'What the hell is this?' Rebus asked, voice rising. He'd turned in his seat, the better to let both men examine the expression on his face.

'You no' our minicab?' the other man said. His nose was like a strawberry, breath soured and teeth blackened by dark rum.

'Bloody right I'm not!' Rebus shouted.

'Sorry, pal, sorry . . . genuine misunderstanding.'

'Aye, no offence meant,' his companion added. Rebus looked out of the passenger-side window, saw the pub they'd just raced from. Breeze blocks and a solid door – no windows. They were preparing to exit the car.

'Not headed to Wardlawhill by any chance, gents?' Rebus asked, voice suddenly calmer.

'We'd usually hike it, but wi' the rain an' that . . .'

Rebus nodded. 'Tell you what, then . . . how about I drop you at the community centre there?'

The men looked at one another, then at him. 'And how much do you plan to charge?'

Rebus waved the mistrust aside. 'Just playing the Good Samaritan.'

'You going to try and convert us or something?' The first man's eyes had narrowed to slits.

Rebus laughed. 'Don't worry, I don't want to "show you the way" or anything.' He paused. 'In fact, quite the opposite.'

'Eh?'

'I want *you* to show *me*.'

By the end of the short twisty drive through the housing scheme, the three were on first-name terms, Rebus asking if neither of his passengers had thought to attend the residents' meeting.

'Best keep your head down, that's always been my philosophy,' he was told.

The rain had eased by the time they arrived outside the single-storey building. Like the pub, it, too, seemed to have no windows on first appraisal. However, it was just that they were tucked away high on the front elevation, almost at the eaves. Rebus shook hands with his guides.

'Getting you in here's one thing . . .' they offered with a laugh. Rebus nodded and smiled. He, too, had been wondering if he'd ever find the motorway back to Edinburgh. Neither passenger had asked why a visitor might be interested in the residents' meeting. Rebus put this down to that philosophy of life again: keeping your head down. If you didn't ask questions, no one could accuse you of sticking your nose in where it wasn't wanted. In some ways it was sound advice, but he'd never lived like that and never would.

There were figures huddled around the building's main entrance doors. Having waved goodbye to his passengers, Rebus parked as close to those doors as he could, worrying that the meeting had already broken up, meaning he'd missed Mo Dirwan. But as he approached, he saw he'd been wrong. A middle-aged white man in a suit, tie and black coat was holding a leaflet out to him. The man's head was shaven, gleaming with droplets of rainwater. His face looked pale and doughy, the neck composed of rolls of fat.

'BNP,' he said in what sounded to Rebus like a London accent. 'Let's make Britain's streets safe again.' The front of the leaflet showed a photo of an elderly woman, looking terrified as a blur of coloured youths charged towards her.

'All pictures posed by models?' Rebus guessed, mashing the dampened leaflet in his fist. The other men on the scene, keeping in the background but flanking the man in the suit, were considerably younger and scruffier, wearing what had almost become rabble chic: trainers, jogging bottoms and windcheaters, baseball caps low on their foreheads. Their jackets were zipped tight, so that the bottom half of each face disappeared into the collar. It meant they were harder to identify from photographs.

'All we want is fair rights for British people.' The word 'British' almost came out as a bark. 'Britain for the British – you tell me what's wrong with that.'

Rebus dropped the leaflet and kicked it aside. 'I get the feeling your definition might be a bit narrower than most.'

'You won't know unless you give us a try.' The man's lower jaw jutted forward. Christ, Rebus thought, and this is him trying to be nice ... It was like watching a gorilla's first attempt at flower-arranging. From inside, he could hear a mixture of handclaps and boos.

'Sounds lively,' Rebus said, pulling open the doors.

There was a reception area, with another set of double doors leading to the main hall. There was no stage as such, but someone had provided a PA system, meaning that whoever held the microphone should have the advantage. But some in the audience had other ideas. Men were standing up, trying to shout down opponents, fingers stabbing the air. Women were on their feet, too, screaming with equal gusto. There were rows of chairs, most of them full. Rebus saw that these chairs faced a trestle table at which sat five glum-looking figures. He guessed this table comprised a mix of local worthies. Mo Dirwan was not among them, but Rebus saw him nevertheless. He was standing up in the front row, flapping his arms as if trying to emulate flight, but actually gesturing for the audience to settle. His hand was still bandaged, the pink sticking plaster still covering his chin.

One of the worthies, however, had had enough. He flung some paperwork into a satchel, slung it over his shoulder, and marched towards the exit. More booing erupted. Rebus couldn't tell if this was because he was chickening out, or because he'd been forced to withdraw.

'You're a wanker, McCluskey,' someone called out. This failed to clarify things for Rebus. But now others were following their leader. A small, plump woman at the table held the mike, but her innate good manners and reasonable tone of voice were never going to restore order. Rebus saw that the audience comprised a melting-pot: it wasn't white faces on one side of the room, coloureds on the other. The age range was mixed, too. One woman had brought her baby-stroller with her. Another was waving her walking-cane wildly in the air, causing those in the vicinity to duck. Half a dozen uniformed police officers had been trying to melt into the back-ground, but now one of them was on his walkie-talkie, almost certainly summoning reinforcements. Some kids had decided that the uniforms should be the focus of their own complaints. The two groups stood only eight or ten feet apart, and that gap was closing with each moment that passed.

Rebus could see that Mo Dirwan didn't know what to do next. There was a look of consternation on his face, as if he were realising that he was a human rather than a superman. This situation was beyond even his control, because his powers depended on the willingness of others to listen to his arguments, and no one here was going to listen to anything. Rebus reckoned Martin Luther King could have been standing there with a bullhorn and gone unheeded. One young man seemed bewildered by it all. His eyes rested on Rebus's for a moment. He was Asian, but wore the same clothes as the white kids. There was a single hooped earring through one of his lobes. His bottom lip was puffy and crusted with old blood, and Rebus saw that he stood awkwardly, as though trying to keep the weight off his left leg. That leg was hurting. Was this the reason for his bewilderment? Was he the latest victim, the one who'd led to the meeting being called? If he looked anything, it was scared . . . scared that a single act could escalate so ceaselessly.

Rebus would have tried for reassurance if he'd known how, but the doors were bursting open, more uniforms crowding in. There was a senior face there: more silver on his lapels and cap than any of the others. Silver, too, in the hair that emerged from below his cap.

'Let's have some order!' he yelled, marching confidently towards the front of the hall and the microphone, which he snatched without ceremony from the now mumbling woman.

'A bit of order, please, people!' The voice booming through the loudspeakers. 'Let's try and calm things down.' He looked down at one of the figures seated at the table. 'I think this meeting's probably best adjourned for now.' The man he'd been looking towards nodded just perceptibly. Maybe the local councillor, Rebus guessed; certainly someone the policeman had to pretend to defer to.

But there was only one man in charge now.

When a hand slapped Rebus's shoulder, he flinched, but it was a grinning Mo Dirwan, who'd somehow spotted him and made his approach unseen.

'My very good friend, what in God's name brings you here at this time?'

Close up, Rebus saw that Dirwan's injuries were no more serious than would be sustained during a weekend brawl between drunks:

just a minimum of scrapes and nicks. He was suddenly dubious of the plaster and the bandage, wondering if they were for show.

'Wanted to see how you were.'

'Ha!' Dirwan pounded his shoulder again. The fact that he was using his bandaged hand reinforced Rebus's suspicions. 'You were feeling perhaps a little bit of guilt?'

'I also want to know how it happened.'

'Bloody hell, that's easily told – I was jumped. Didn't you read your newspaper this morning? Whichever one you chose, I was in them all.'

And Rebus didn't doubt those papers would be spread across the floor of Dirwan's living room . . .

But now the lawyer's attention was diverted by the fact that everyone was being ushered from the hall. He squeezed through the crowd until he met the senior uniform, whose hand he shook, sharing a few words. Then it was on to the councillor, whose expression told Rebus that one more wasted, thankless Saturday like this and he'd be tapping out that letter of resignation. Dirwan had strong words for this man, but when he attempted to grip his arm, it was shrugged off with a force which had probably been building for the whole length of the meeting. Dirwan wagged a finger instead, then patted the man's shoulder and headed back towards Rebus.

'Bloody hell, isn't this an absolute mêlée?'

'I've seen worse.'

Dirwan stared at him. 'Why do I get the feeling you'd say that whatever the circumstances in front of you?'

'Happens to be true,' Rebus told him. 'So . . . can I have that word now?'

'What word?'

But Rebus said nothing. Instead, it was his turn to slap a hand down on Dirwan's shoulder, holding it there as he steered the lawyer out of the building. A scuffle was taking place, one of the BNP man's minions having come to blows with a young Asian. Dirwan looked ready to step in, but Rebus held him back, and the uniforms waded in. The BNP man was standing on a grassy bank across the road, hand held high in what looked like a Nazi salute. To Rebus's mind, he seemed ridiculous, which didn't mean he wasn't dangerous.

'Shall we go to my house?' Dirwan was suggesting.

'My car,' Rebus said, shaking his head. They got in, but there was too much still happening all around. Rebus started the ignition, figuring he'd drive into one of the side streets, the better to talk without distractions. As they made to pass the BNP man, he pushed his foot a little harder on the accelerator, and steered the car close to the kerb, sending up a spray which doused the man, much to Mo Dirwan's delight.

Rebus reversed into a tight kerbside space, switched off the ignition, and turned to face the lawyer.

'So what happened?' he asked.

Dirwan shrugged. 'It is quickly told . . . I was doing as you asked, questioning as many of Knoxland's incomers as would speak with me . . .'

'Some refused?'

'Not everyone trusts a stranger, John, not even when he boasts the same colour of skin.'

Rebus nodded his acceptance of this. 'So where were you when they jumped you?'

'Waiting for one of the lifts in Stevenson House. They came from behind, maybe four or five of them, faces hidden.'

'Did they say anything?'

'One of them did . . . right at the end.' Dirwan looked uncomfortable, and Rebus was reminded that he was dealing with the victim of an assault. No matter how minor the injuries, it was unlikely to be the sort of memory the lawyer would cherish.

'Look,' Rebus said, 'I should have said right at the start – I'm sorry this had to happen.'

'It wasn't your fault, John. I should have been better prepared.'

'I'm assuming you were targeted?'

Dirwan nodded slowly. 'The one who spoke, he told me to get out of Knoxland. He said I'd be dead otherwise. He held a knife to my cheek as he spoke.'

'What sort of knife?'

'I can't be sure . . . You're thinking of the murder weapon?'

'I suppose so.' And, he could have added, the knife found on Howie Slowther. 'You didn't recognise any of them?'

'I spent most of my time on the ground. Fists and shoes were about the only things I saw.'

'What about the one who spoke. Did he sound local?'

'As opposed to what?'

'I don't know . . . Irish maybe.'

'I find Irish and Scots hard to tell apart sometimes.' Dirwan shrugged an apology. 'Shocking, I know, in someone who has spent some years here . . .'

Rebus's mobile sounded from deep within one of his pockets. He dug it out and studied the screen. It was Caro Quinn. 'I have to take this,' he told Dirwan, opening the car door. He walked a few paces along the pavement and held the phone to his ear.

'Hello?' he said.

'How could you do that to me?'

'What?'

'Let me drink like that,' she groaned.

'Nursing a sore head, are we?'

'I'm never touching alcohol again.'

'An excellent proposition . . . maybe we could discuss it over dinner?'

'I can't tonight, John. I'm off to the Filmhouse with a mate.'

'Tomorrow then?'

She seemed to consider this. 'I'm supposed to be doing some work this weekend . . . and thanks to last night I'm already losing today.'

'You can't work with a hangover?'

'Can you?'

'I've turned it into an art form, Caro.'

'Look, let's see how tomorrow pans out . . . I'll try to give you a call.'

'Is that the best I can hope for?'

'Take it or leave it, chum.'

'Then I'll take it.' Rebus had turned and was heading back towards the car. 'Bye, Caro.'

'Bye, John.'

Off to the Filmhouse with a mate . . . A mate, not a 'pal'. Rebus got in behind the steering wheel. 'Sorry about that.'

'Business or pleasure?' Mo Dirwan asked.

Rebus didn't answer; he had a question of his own. 'You know Caro Quinn, don't you?'

Dirwan frowned, trying to place the name. 'Our Lady of the Vigils?' he guessed. Rebus nodded. 'Yes, she is quite a character.'

'A woman of principles.'

'My goodness, yes. She has given a room in her home to an asylum-seeker – did you know that?'

'I did, as it happens.'

The lawyer's eyes widened. 'She was the one you were speaking to just now?'

'Yes.'

'You know that she, too, was chased out of Knoxland?'

'She told me.'

'We share a common thread, she and I . . .' Dirwan studied him. 'Perhaps you are part of that thread too, John.'

'Me?' Rebus started the engine. 'More likely I'm one of those knots you come across from time to time.'

Dirwan chuckled. 'I'm quite sure you think of yourself that way.'

'Can I give you a lift home?'

'If it's not any trouble.'

Rebus shook his head. 'It might actually help me get back to the motorway.'

'So the offer masked an ulterior motive?'

'I suppose you could put it like that.'

'And if I accept, will you allow me to offer some hospitality?'

'I really need to be getting back . . .'

'I am being snubbed.'

'It's not that . . .'

'Well, that is exactly how it looks.'

'Bloody hell, Mo . . .' Rebus gave a loud sigh. 'All right then, a quick cup of coffee.'

'My wife will insist that you eat something.'

'A biscuit then.'

'And some cake perhaps.'

'Just a biscuit.'

'She will prepare a little bit more . . . you will see.'

'All right, cake then. Coffee and cake.'

The lawyer's face broke open in a grin. 'You are new to the bartering method, John. Had I been selling carpets, your credit card would now be maxing out.'

'What makes you think it's not there already?'

Besides, Rebus could have added, he really *was* hungry . . .

261

21

On a bright, blustery Sunday morning, Rebus walked to the bottom of Marchmont Road and headed across the Meadows. Teams were already gathering for pre-arranged football games. Some of the sides wore uniform strips in emulation of professional sides. Others were more ragged affairs, denims and trainers in place of shorts and boots. Traffic cones were the favoured replacements for proper goalposts, and the lines marking the boundary of each pitch were invisible to all but the players.

Further on, a game of frisbee saw a panting dog playing piggy-in-the-middle, while a couple on one of the benches made hard work of trying to turn the pages of their Sunday newspapers, each gust of wind threatening to turn the many supplements into airborne kites.

Rebus had spent a quiet evening at home, but only after a saunter down Lothian Road had established that the movies showing at the Filmhouse were not his kind of thing. He now had a little bet with himself about which of the offerings had received Caro's custom. He also wondered what excuse he'd have used if she'd happened to bump into him in the foyer ...

Nothing I like better than a good Hungarian family saga ...

Home had seen him demolish an Indian takeaway (his fingers still redolent, even after a morning shower) and a double helping of videos he'd watched before: *Rock 'n' Roll Circus* and *Midnight Run*. While he'd smiled throughout the De Niro, it was Yoko Ono's performance on the former which had sent him into hoots of laughter.

Just the four bottles of IPA to wash it all down, which meant he'd awakened early and clear-headed, breakfast consisting of half a leftover nan and a mug of tea. Now it was approaching lunchtime and Rebus was walking. The old Infirmary was surrounded by hoardings, doing nothing to mask the building work within. Last he'd heard, the compound would become a mix of retail and housing. He wondered who would pay to move into a reconfigured cancer ward. Would the place be haunted by a century of distress? Maybe they'd end up running ghost tours, same as they did with places like Mary King's Close, said to be home to the spirits of plague victims, or Greyfriars Kirkyard, where covenanters had perished.

He'd often thought of moving from Marchmont; had gone as far as quizzing a solicitor on a likely asking price. Two hundred K, he'd been told . . . probably not enough to buy even half a cancer ward, but with money like that in his pocket he could jack the job in on full pension and do some travelling.

Problem was, nowhere appealed. He'd be far more likely to piss it all away. Was this the fear that kept him working? The job was his whole life; over the years, he'd let it push aside everything else: family, friends, pastimes.

Which was why he was working now.

He walked up Chalmers Street, passing the new school, and crossed the road at the art college, heading down Lady Lawson Street. He didn't know who Lady Lawson had been, but doubted she'd be impressed by the road named in her honour – and probably less so by the huddle of pubs and clubs adjoining it. Rebus was back in the pubic triangle. Not that much was happening. It was probably only seven or eight hours since some of the premises had closed for the night. People would be sleeping off Saturday's excesses: dancers with the best pay packet of the week; owners like Stuart Bullen dreaming of their next expensive car; businessmen wondering how to explain that forthcoming credit card statement to their spouses . . .

The street had been cleaned, the neon turned off. Church bells in the distance. Just another Sunday.

A metal bar held the Nook's doors closed, fixed by a heavy-duty padlock. Rebus came to a stop, hands in pockets, staring at the empty shop opposite. If there was no answer, he was prepared to walk the extra mile to Haymarket, drop in on Felix Storey at his hotel. He doubted they'd be at work this early. Wherever Stuart Bullen was, he wasn't in the Nook. Despite which, Rebus crossed the road and rapped his knuckles against the shop window. He waited, looking to left and right. There was no one in the vicinity, no passing traffic, no heads at any of the windows above street level. He knocked again, then noticed a dark green van. It was parked kerbside, fifty feet further along. Rebus strolled towards it. Whoever had owned it originally, their name had been painted out, the shapes of the letters just about discernible beneath the paint-job. There was no one visible inside. Around the back, the windows had been painted over. Rebus remembered the surveillance van at Knoxland, Shug Davidson ensconced within. He took another look up and down the street, then pounded his fist on the van's back doors, placing his face to one of the windows before walking away. He didn't look back, but did pause as if to examine the small ads in a newsagent's window.

'You trying to endanger our operation?' Felix Storey asked. Rebus turned. Storey stood with hands in pockets. He wore green combat trousers and an olive T-shirt.

'Nice disguise,' Rebus commented. 'You must be keen.'

'What do you mean?'

'Working a Sunday shift – the Nook doesn't open till two.'

'Doesn't mean there's nobody there.'

'No, but the bolts on the door give a pretty big clue . . .'

Storey slid his hands from his pockets and folded his arms. 'What do you want?'

'I'm after a favour actually.'

'And you couldn't just leave a message at my hotel?'

Rebus shrugged. 'Not my style, Felix.' He studied the Immigration man's clothing again. 'So what are you supposed to be? Urban guerrilla or something?'

'A clubber at repose,' Storey admitted.

Rebus snorted. 'Still . . . the van's not a bad idea. I dare say the shop's too risky of a daytime – people might spot someone sitting atop a stepladder.' Rebus looked to left and right. 'Shame the street's so quiet: you stick out like a sore thumb.'

Storey just glowered. 'And you thumping the van doors . . . that was supposed to look natural, was it?'

Rebus shrugged again. 'It got your attention.'

'That it did. So go ahead and ask your favour.'

'Let's do it over coffee.' Rebus gestured with his head. 'There's a place not two minutes' walk away.' Storey thought for a moment, glancing towards the van. 'I'm assuming you've got someone covering for you,' Rebus said.

'I just need to tell them . . .'

'On you go then.'

264

Storey pointed down the street. 'You walk on ahead, I'll catch you up.'

Rebus nodded. He turned and started to leave, turned back to see that Storey was watching over his shoulder as he made his way to the van.

'What do you want me to order?' Rebus called.

'Americano,' the Immigration man called back. Then, when Rebus had turned to face the other way, he quickly opened the van doors and jumped in, closing them after him.

'He wants a favour,' he said to the person within.

'I wonder what it is.'

'I'm going with him to find out. Will you be all right here?'

'Bored to tears, but I'll manage somehow.'

'I'll be ten minutes at most . . .' Storey broke off as the door was yanked open from outside. Rebus's head appeared.

'Hiya, Phyl,' he said with a smile. 'Want us to fetch you anything?'

Rebus felt better for knowing. Ever since he'd been clocked going into the Nook, he'd wondered who Storey's source was. Had to be someone who knew him; knew Siobhan, too.

'So Phyllida Hawes is working with you,' he said as the two men sat down with their coffees. The café was on the corner of Lothian Road. They got the table only because a couple were leaving as they arrived. People were immersed in reading: newspapers and books. A woman nursed a small baby as she sipped from her mug. Storey busied himself peeling open the sandwich he'd bought.

'It's none of your business,' he growled, working hard at keeping his voice low, not wanting to be overheard. Rebus was trying to place the background music: sixties-style, California-style. He doubted very much it was original; plenty of bands out there trying to sound like the past.

'None of my business,' Rebus agreed.

Storey slurped from his mug, wincing at the near-molten temperature. He bit into the refrigerated sandwich to ease the shock.

'Making any headway?' Rebus was asking.

'Some,' Storey said through a mouthful of lettuce.

'But nothing you'd care to share?' Rebus blew across the surface of his own mug: he'd been here before, knew the contents would be super-heated.

'What do you think?'

'I'm thinking this whole operation of yours must be costing a fortune. If I was blowing money like that on a surveillance, I'd be sweating a result.'

'Do I look like I'm sweating?'

'That's what interests me. Someone somewhere is either desperate for a conviction, or else scarily confident of getting one.' Storey was ready with a comeback, but Rebus held up a hand. 'I know, I know ... it's none of my business.'

'And that's the way it's going to stay.'

'Scout's honour.' Rebus raised three fingers in mock-salute. 'Which brings me to my favour ...'

'A favour I'm not inclined to help with.'

'Not even in a spirit of cross-border cooperation?'

Storey pretended to be interested only in his sandwich, flecks of which he was brushing from his trousers.

'You suit those combats, by the way,' Rebus flattered him. Finally, this produced the ghost of a smile.

'Ask your favour,' the Immigration man said.

'The murder I'm working on ... the one in Knoxland.'

'What of it?'

'Looks like there was a girlfriend, and I've got word she's from Senegal.'

'So?'

'So I'd like to find her.'

'Do you have a name?'

Rebus shook his head. 'I don't even know if she's here legally.' He paused. 'That's where I thought you could help.'

'Help how?'

'The Immigration Service must know how many Senegalese there are in the UK. If they're here legally, you'll know how many of them live in Scotland ...'

'I think, Inspector, you may be mistaking us for a fascist state.'

'You're telling me you don't keep records?'

'Oh, there are records all right, but only of registered migrants. They wouldn't show up an illegal, or even a refugee.'

'The thing is, if she's here illegally, she'd probably try to find other people from her home country. They'd be most likely to help her, and those are the ones you'd have records of.'

'Yes, I can see that, but all the same ...'

'You've got better things to occupy your time?'

Storey took a tentative sip of his drink, brushed the foam from his top lip with the back of his hand. 'I'm not even sure the information exists, not in a form you'd find useful.'

'Right now I'd settle for anything.'

'You think this girlfriend is involved in the murder?'

'I think she's running scared.'

'Because she knows something?'

'I won't know that until I ask her.'

The Immigration man went quiet, making milky circles on the tabletop with the bottom of his mug. Rebus bided his time, watched the world outside the window. People were heading down to Princes Street; maybe with shopping in mind. There was a queue now at the counter, people looking around for a table they could share. There was a spare chair between Rebus and Storey, which he hoped no one would ask to use: refusal could often offend . . .

'I can authorise an initial search of the database,' Storey said at last.

'That would be great.'

'I'm not promising anything, mind.'

Rebus nodded his understanding.

'Have you tried students?' Storey added.

'Students?'

'Overseas students. There may be some around town from Senegal.'

'That's a thought,' Rebus said.

'Glad to be of service.' The two men sat in silence until their drinks were finished. Afterwards, Rebus said he'd walk back to the van with Storey. He asked how Stuart Bullen had first appeared on Immigration's radar.

'I thought I already told you.'

'My memory's not what it was,' Rebus apologised.

'It was a tip-off – anonymous. That's how it often starts: they want to stay anonymous until we get a result. After that, they want paying.'

'So what was the tip-off?'

'Just that Bullen's dirty. People-smuggling.'

'And you set this whole thing in motion on the evidence of one phone call?'

'This same tipster, he's come good before – a cargo of illegals coming into Dover in the back of a lorry.'

'I thought you had all this high-tech stuff at the ports these days.'

Storey nodded. 'We do. Sensors that can pick up body-heat . . . electronic sniffer dogs . . .'

267

'So you'd have picked these illegals up anyway?'

'Maybe, maybe not.' Storey stopped and faced Rebus. 'What exactly is it you're implying, Inspector?'

'Nothing at all. What is it you *think* I'm implying?'

'Nothing at all,' Storey echoed. But his eyes gave the lie to his words.

That evening, Rebus sat by his window with the telephone in his hand, telling himself there was still time for Caro to call. He'd gone through his record collection, pulling out albums he hadn't played in years: Montrose, Blue Oyster Cult, Rush, Alex Harvey . . . None of them lasted more than a couple of tracks until he reached *Goat's Head Soup*. It was a stew of sounds, ideas stirred into the pot with only half the ingredients improving the flavour. Still, it was better – more melancholy – than he remembered. Ian Stewart played on a couple of tracks. Poor Stu, who'd grown up not far from Rebus in Fife and been a fully fledged member of the Stones until the manager decided he didn't have the right image, the band keeping him around for sessions and touring.

Stu hanging in there, even though his face didn't fit.

Rebus could sympathise.

Day Eight

Monday

22

Monday morning, Banehall Library. Beakers of instant coffee, sugar doughnuts from a bakery. Les Young was wearing a three-button grey suit, white shirt, dark blue tie. There was a faint aroma of shoe polish. His team sat at desks and on desks, some scratching at bleary faces; others sucking on the bitter coffee as though it were elixir. There were posters on the walls advertising children's authors: Michael Morpurgo; Francesca Simon; Eoin Colfer. Another poster depicted a cartoon hero called Captain Underpants, and for some reason this had become Young's nickname, Siobhan overhearing an exchange to that effect. She didn't think he would be flattered.

Having somehow run out of sensible trousers, Siobhan was wearing a skirt and tights – a rare outfit for her. The skirt came to her knees, but she kept tugging at it in the hope that it might magically transform into something a few inches longer. She'd no idea whether her legs were 'good' or 'bad' – she just didn't like the idea that people were studying them, maybe even judging her by them. Moreover, she knew that before the end of the day the tights would have contrived to ladder themselves. As a precaution, she'd stuffed a second pair into her bag.

Laundry had failed to be part of her weekend. She'd driven to Dundee on Saturday, spending the day with Liz Hetherington, the two of them swapping work stories as they sat in a wine bar, then hitting a restaurant, the flicks, and a couple of clubs, Siobhan sleeping on Liz's sofa, then driving home again in the afternoon, still groggy.

She was now on her third cup of coffee.

One reason she'd gone to Dundee was to escape Edinburgh and

271

the possibility that she might bump into or be cornered by Rebus. She hadn't been so drunk on Friday night; didn't regret the stance she'd taken or the ensuing shouting-match. It was bar-room politics, that was all. But even so, she doubted Rebus would have forgotten, and she knew whose side he'd be on. She was conscious, too, that Whitemire was less than two miles away, and that Caro Quinn was probably back on sentry duty there, struggling to become the conscience of the place.

Sunday night she'd drifted into the city centre, climbing Cockburn Street, passing through Fleshmarket Close. On the High Street, a group of tourists had huddled around their guide, Siobhan recognising her by her hair and voice – Judith Lennox.

'. . . in Knox's day, of course, rules were much stricter. You could be punished for plucking a chicken on the Sabbath. No dancing, no theatre or gambling. Adultery carried a death sentence, while lesser crimes could be punished by the likes of the branks. This was a padlocked helmet which forced a metal bar into the mouth of liars and blasphemers . . . At the end of the tour, there'll be a chance for you to enjoy a drink in the Warlock, a traditional inn celebrating the grisly end of Major Weir . . .'

Siobhan had wondered whether Lennox was being paid for her endorsement.

'. . . and in conclusion,' Les Young was saying now, 'blunt trauma's what we're looking at. A couple of good whacks, fracturing the skull and causing bleeding in the brain-pan. Death almost certainly instantaneous . . .' He was reading from the autopsy notes. 'And according to the pathologist, circular indentations would indicate that something like an everyday hammer was used . . . sort of thing you'd find in DIY stores, diameter of two-point-nine centimetres.'

'What about the force of the blow, sir?' one of the team asked.

Young gave a wry smile. 'The notes are a bit coy, but reading between the lines I think we can safely say we're dealing with a male attacker . . . and more likely to be right- than left-handed. The pattern of the indents makes it look as though the victim was struck from behind.' Young walked over to where a room-divider had become a makeshift noticeboard, crime-scene photos pinned to it. 'We'll be getting close-ups from the autopsy later today.' He was pointing to a photo from Cruikshank's bedroom, the head helmeted in blood. 'It was the back of the skull that took most damage . . . that's hard to do if you're standing in front of the person you're attacking.'

'It definitely happened in the bedroom?' someone else asked. 'He wasn't moved afterwards?'

'He died where he fell, best as we can tell.' Young looked around the room. 'Any more questions?' There were none. 'Right then . . .' He turned to a roster of the day's workload, started assigning tasks. The focus seemed to be on Cruikshank's porn collection, its provenance and who might have been party to it. Officers were being sent to Barlinnie to ask the warders about any friends Cruikshank had made while serving his sentence. Siobhan knew that sex offenders were kept in a separate wing from other prisoners. This stopped them being attacked on a daily basis, but also meant that they tended to form friendships with each other, which only made matters worse on release: a lone offender might be introduced to a whole network of similar-minded individuals, completing a circle which led to further offending and future brushes with the law.

'Siobhan?' She focused her eyes on Young, realising he'd been speaking to her.

'Yes?' She looked down, saw her cup was once again empty, craved another refill.

'Did you get round to interviewing Ishbel Jardine's boyfriend?'

'You mean her ex?' Siobhan cleared her throat. 'No, not yet.'

'You didn't think he might know something?'

'They'd split amicably.'

'Yes, but all the same . . .'

Siobhan could feel her face reddening. Yes, she'd been too preoccupied elsewhere, concentrating her efforts on Donny Cruikshank.

'He was on my list,' was all she could think to say.

'Well, would you like to see him now?' Young checked his watch. 'I'm due to talk to him as soon as we're finished here.'

Siobhan nodded her agreement. She could feel eyes on her, knew there were some ill-disguised grins around the room, too. In the team's collective mind, she and Young were already linked, the DI smitten with this interloper.

Captain Underpants now had a sidekick.

'Roy Brinkley's his name,' Young told her. 'All I know is, he dated Ishbel for seven or eight months, then a couple of months back they split up.' They were alone in the murder room, the others having set out with their assignments.

'You see him as a suspect?'

'There's a link there we need to ask him about. Cruikshank does time for attacking Tracy Jardine . . . Tracy tops herself and her sister does a runner . . .' Young gave a shrug, arms folded.

'But he was Ishbel's boyfriend, not Tracy's . . . surely if anyone was going to have a go at Cruikshank, it's more likely to've been one of Tracy's boyfriends than one of Ishbel's . . .' Siobhan broke off, fixing her eyes on Young's. 'But then Roy Brinkley's not the suspect, is he? You're wondering what he knows about Ishbel's disappearance . . . You think *she* did it!'

'I don't recall saying that.'

'But it's what you're thinking. Didn't I just hear you say the blows came from a man?'

'And you'll keep hearing me saying that.'

Siobhan nodded slowly. 'Because you don't want her to know. You're scared she'd become even more invisible.' Siobhan paused. 'You think she's close, don't you?'

'I've no proof of it.'

'Is this what you've been doing all weekend, mulling it over?'

'Actually, it came to me on Friday night.' He unfolded his arms, started walking towards the door, Siobhan following.

'While you were playing bridge?'

Young nodded. 'Unfair on my partner – we hardly won a hand.'

They'd left the murder room now and were in the main library. Siobhan reminded him that he hadn't locked the door.

'Not necessary,' he said, giving a half-smile.

'I thought we were going to talk to Roy Brinkley.'

Young just nodded, making to pass the reception desk, where the morning's first batch of returns were being run through a scanner by the male librarian. Siobhan had taken a few more steps before she realised Young had stopped. He was standing directly in front of the librarian.

'Roy Brinkley?' he said. The young man looked up.

'That's right.'

'Any chance we could have a word?' Young gestured towards the murder room.

'Why? What's wrong?'

'Nothing to worry about, Roy. We just need a little bit of background . . .'

As Brinkley emerged from behind his desk, Siobhan stepped up next to Les Young and poked him in the side with her finger.

*

'Sorry,' Young apologised to the librarian, 'there's nowhere else we can do this . . .'

He'd pulled out a chair for Brinkley. It gave a direct line of sight to the murder-scene photos. Siobhan knew he was lying; knew the interview was being conducted here because of those very photos. Try as he might to ignore them, the young man's eyes were drawn towards them anyway. The look of horror on his face would have been defence enough in most juries' minds.

Roy Brinkley was in his early twenties. He wore an open-necked denim shirt, his wavy mop of brown hair reaching the collar. There were thin threaded bracelets on his wrists, but no watch. Siobhan would have called him pretty rather than handsome. He could pass for seventeen or eighteen. She could see the attraction for Ishbel, but wondered how he had coped with her noisy ladette friends . . .

'Did you know him?' Young was asking. Neither detective was seated. Young leaned against a table, arms folded, legs crossed at the ankles. Siobhan stood at a distance to Brinkley's left, so that he would be aware of her from the corner of his eye.

'Didn't so much know him as knew *of* him.'

'Two of you at school together?'

'But different years. He was never really a bully . . . more the class joker. I got the feeling he never found a way to fit in.'

Siobhan was reminded for a moment of Alf McAteer, playing jester for Alexis Cater.

'But this is a small town, Roy,' Young was protesting. 'You must have known him to speak to, at the very least?'

'If we happened to meet, I suppose we'd say hello.'

'Maybe you always had your head in a book, eh?'

'I like books . . .'

'So what about you and Ishbel Jardine? How did that start?'

'First time we met was at a club . . .'

'You didn't know her at school?'

Brinkley shrugged. 'She was three years below me.'

'So you met at this club and started going out?'

'Not straight away . . . we had a few dances, but then I danced with her mates, too.'

'And who were her mates, Roy?' Siobhan asked. Brinkley looked from Young to Siobhan and back again.

'I thought this was about Donny Cruikshank?'

Young made a noncommittal gesture. 'Background, Roy,' was all he said.

275

Brinkley turned to Siobhan. 'There were two of them – Janet and Susie.'

'Janet from Whitemire, Susie from the Salon?' Siobhan clarified. The young man just nodded. 'And which club was this?'

'Somewhere in Falkirk . . . I think it closed down . . .' He wrinkled his brow in concentration.

'The Albatross?' Siobhan guessed.

'That's the one, yes.' Brinkley was nodding enthusiastically.

'You know it?' Les Young asked Siobhan.

'It came up in connection with a recent case,' she said.

'Oh?'

'Afterwards,' she said in warning, nodding towards Brinkley, letting Young know this wasn't the time. He twitched his head in agreement.

'Ishbel and her friends were pretty close, weren't they, Roy?' Siobhan asked.

'Sure.'

'So why would she run off without so much as a word to them?'

He shrugged. 'Have you asked them that?'

'I'm asking you.'

'I don't have an answer.'

'Well, what about this then: why did the two of you split up?'

'Just drifted apart, I suppose.'

'Had to be a reason, though,' Les Young added, taking a step towards Brinkley. 'I mean, did she dump you or was it the other way round?'

'It was more a mutual thing.'

'Which is why you stayed friends?' Siobhan guessed. 'So what was your first thought when you heard she'd run off?'

He twisted in his chair, making it creak. 'Her mum and dad turned up at my place, wanted to know if I'd seen her. To be honest . . .'

'Yes?'

'I thought it might be *their* fault. They never really got over Tracy's suicide. Always talking about her, telling stories from the past.'

'And Ishbel? Are you telling me she *did* get over it?'

'She seemed to.'

'So why did she dye her hair, style it so she looked more like Tracy?'

'Look, I'm not saying they're bad people . . .' He squeezed his hands together.

'Who? John and Alice?'

He nodded. 'It's just that Ishbel got the idea . . . the notion they really wanted Tracy back. I mean, Tracy rather than her.'

'And that's why she tried to look like Tracy?'

He nodded again. 'I mean, it's a lot to take on, isn't it? Maybe that's why she left . . .' His head dropped disconsolately. Siobhan looked across to Les Young, whose lips formed a thoughtful pout. The silence lasted the best part of a minute, until broken by Siobhan.

'Do you know where Ishbel is, Roy?'

'No.'

'Did you kill Donny Cruikshank?'

'Part of me wishes I had.'

'Who do you think did it? Has Ishbel's dad crossed your mind?'

Brinkley raised his head. 'Crossed my mind . . . yes. But only for a moment.'

She nodded as if in agreement.

Les Young had a question of his own. 'Did you see Cruikshank after his release, Roy?'

'I saw him.'

'To speak to?'

He shook his head. 'Saw him with a guy a couple of times, though.'

'What guy?'

'Must've been a mate of his.'

'But you didn't know him?'

'No.'

'Probably not local then.'

'Might've been . . . I don't know every single person in Banehall. Like you said yourself, too often I've got my head stuck in a book.'

'Can you describe the man?'

'You'll know him if you see him,' Brinkley said, half his mouth forming the beginnings of a smile.

'How's that then?'

'Tattoo all across his neck.' He touched his own throat to indicate the area. 'A spider's web . . .'

Not wanting to be overheard by Roy Brinkley, they sat in Siobhan's car.

'Spider's-web tattoo,' she commented.

'Not the first time it's come up,' Les Young informed her. 'One of

277

the drinkers at the Bane mentioned it. Barman admitted he'd served the guy once, didn't like the look of him.'

'No name?'

Young shook his head. 'Not yet, but we'll get one.'

'Someone he met in jail?'

Young didn't answer; he had a question for her. 'So what's this about the Albatross?'

'Don't tell me you know the place too?'

'When I was a teenager in Livingston, if you didn't go to Lothian Road for your kicks, you might get lucky at the Albatross.'

'It had a reputation then?'

'A bad sound system, watered beer and sticky dance floor.'

'But people still went?'

'For a while it was the only game in town . . . some nights, there were more women there than men – women old enough to've known better.'

'So it was a knocking-shop?'

He shrugged. 'I never got the chance to find out.'

'Too busy playing bridge,' she teased.

He ignored this. 'But I'm intrigued that you know about it.'

'Did you read in the paper about those skeletons?'

He smiled. 'I didn't need to: plenty of gossip flying around the station. It's not often Dr Curt screws up.'

'He didn't screw up.' She paused. 'And even if he did, they fooled me too.'

'How so?'

'I covered the baby with my jacket.'

'The plastic baby?'

'Half covered in earth and cement . . .'

He held up his hands in surrender. 'I still don't see the connection.'

'It's thin,' she agreed. 'The man who runs the pub, he used to own the Albatross.'

'Coincidence?'

'I suppose so.'

'But you'll talk to him again, in case he knew Ishbel?'

'Might do.'

Young sighed. 'Leaving us with the tattooed man and not much else.'

'It's more than we had an hour ago.'

'I suppose so.' He stared out across the car park. 'How come Banehall doesn't have a decent café?'

'We could nip up the M8 to Harthill.'

'Why? What's at Harthill?'

'Motorway services.'

'I did say decent, didn't I?'

'Just a suggestion . . .' Siobhan decided to stare out through the windscreen too.

'All right then,' Young eventually conceded. 'You drive, and the drinks are on me.'

'Deal,' she said, starting the car.

23

Rebus was back at George Square, standing outside Dr Maybury's office. He could hear voices within, which didn't stop him knocking.

'Enter!'

He opened the door and peered in. It was a tutorial, eight sleepy-looking faces arranged around the table. He smiled at Maybury. 'Mind if I speak to you for a minute?'

She let her spectacles slip from her nose, to dangle from a cord just above her chest. Stood up without saying anything, managed to squeeze through what gaps there were between chairs and wall. She closed the door behind her and exhaled loudly.

'I'm really sorry to bother you again,' Rebus began to apologise.

'No, it's not that.' She pinched the bridge of her nose.

'Bit of a dippy group?'

'I'll never know why we bother to hold tutorials this early on a Monday.' She stretched her neck to left and right. 'Sorry – not your problem. Any luck tracing the woman from Senegal?'

'Well, that's why I'm here . . .'

'Yes?'

'Our latest theory is that she might know some of the students.' Rebus paused. 'Actually, she could even *be* a student.'

'Oh?'

'Well, what I was wondering was . . . how do I go about finding out for sure? I know it's not your territory, but if you could point me in the right direction . . .'

Maybury thought for a moment. 'Registry office would be your best bet.'

'And where's that?'

'Old College.'

'Opposite Thin's Bookshop?'

She smiled. 'Been a while since you bought any books, Inspector? Thin's went bust; it's run by Blackwell's now.'

'But that's where Old College is?'

She nodded. 'Sorry for the pedantry.'

'Will they talk to me, do you think?'

'The only people they ever see down there are students who've lost their matric cards. You'll be like some exotic new species to them. Walk across Bristo Square and take the underpass. You can get into Old College from West College Street.'

'I think I knew that, but thanks anyway.'

'You know what I'm doing?' she seemed to realise. 'I'm yacking away to postpone the inevitable.' She glanced at her wristwatch. 'Forty minutes still to go . . .'

Rebus made a show of listening at the door. 'Sounds like they've dropped off anyway. Be a shame to wake them.'

'Linguistics waits for no man, Inspector,' Maybury said, stiffening her spine. 'Once more unto the fray.' She took a deep breath and opened the door.

Disappeared inside.

As he walked, Rebus called Whitemire and asked to be put through to Traynor.

'I'm sorry, Mr Traynor's not available.'

'Is that you, Janet?' There was silence for a moment.

'Speaking,' Janet Eylot said.

'Janet, it's DI Rebus here. Look, I'm sorry you've had my colleagues bothering you. If I can help at all, just let me know.'

'Thank you, Inspector.'

'So what's up with your boss? Don't tell me he's off with stress.'

'He just doesn't want any interruptions this morning.'

'Fine, but can you try him for me? Tell him I wouldn't take no for an answer.'

She took her time replying. 'Very well,' she said at last. A few moments later, Traynor picked up.

'Look, I'm up to my eyes . . .'

'Aren't we all?' Rebus sympathised. 'I was just wondering if you'd run those checks for me.'

'What checks?'

'Kurds and French-speaking Africans, bailed from Whitemire.'

Traynor sighed. 'There aren't any.'

'You're sure?'

'Positive. Now, was that all you were wanting?'

'For now,' Rebus said. The call was disconnected before the final word had died away. Rebus stared at his mobile, decided it wasn't worth making a nuisance of himself. He had his answer after all.

He just wasn't sure he believed it.

'Highly unusual,' the woman at the registry said, not for the first time. She had led Rebus across the quadrangle to another set of offices in Old College. Rebus seemed to remember that this had once been the medical faculty, a place where grave-robbers brought their wares to sell to inquisitive surgeons. And hadn't the serial killer William Burke been dissected here after his hanging? He made the mistake of asking his guide. She peered at him over her half-moon glasses. If she thought him exotic, she was hiding it well.

'I wouldn't know anything about that,' she trilled. Her walk was brisk, feet kept close together. Rebus reckoned she was around the same age as him, but it was hard to imagine her ever having been younger. 'Highly irregular,' she said now, as if to herself, stretching her vocabulary.

'Any help you can give would be appreciated.' It was the same line he'd used during their initial conversation. She'd listened closely, then made a call to someone higher up the admin ladder. Assent had been given, but with a caution – personal data was a confidential matter. There would need to be a written request, a discussion, a good reason for the handing over of any information.

Rebus had agreed to all of this, adding that it would be irrelevant should there turn out to be no Senegalese students registered at the university.

As a result of which, Mrs Scrimgour was going to make a search of the database.

'You could have waited in the office, you know,' she said now. Rebus just nodded as they turned into an open doorway. A younger woman was working at a computer. 'I'll need to relieve you, Nancy,' Mrs Scrimgour said, managing to make it sound like admonishment rather than request. Nancy almost tipped over the chair in her rush to comply. Mrs Scrimgour nodded to the other side of the desk, meaning for Rebus to stand there, where he couldn't see the screen. He complied up to a point, leaning forward so his elbows rested against the edge of the desk, eyes at a level with Mrs Scrimgour's own. She frowned at this, but Rebus just smiled.

'Anything?' he asked.

She was tapping keys. 'Africa's divided into five zones,' she informed him.

'Senegal's in the north-west.'

She peered at him. 'North or west?'

'One or the other,' he said with a shrug. She gave a little sniff and kept typing, eventually pausing with her hand on the mouse.

'Well,' she said, 'we do have one student from Senegal . . . so that's that.'

'But I'm not allowed to know name and whereabouts?'

'Not without the procedures we discussed.'

'Which just end up taking more time.'

'Proper procedures,' she intoned, 'as laid down by *law*, if you need reminding.'

Rebus nodded slowly. His face had inched closer to hers. She pulled back in her seat.

'Well,' she said, 'I think that's as much as we can do today.'

'And it's unlikely that you'd absent-mindedly leave the screen showing when you walked away . . . ?'

'I think we both know the answer to that, Inspector.' Saying which, she clicked twice with the mouse. Rebus knew that the information had disappeared, but that was all right. He'd seen just about enough from the reflection in her lenses. A smiling photo of a young woman with dark curly hair. He was pretty sure her name was Kawake, with an address at the university's halls of residence on Dalkeith Road.

'You've been very helpful,' he told Mrs Scrimgour.

She tried not to look too disappointed at this news.

Pollock Halls was sited at the foot of Arthur's Seat, on the edge of Holyrood Park. A sprawling, maze-like compound which mixed old architecture with new, crow-stepped gables and turrets with boxy modernity. Rebus stopped his car at the gatehouse, getting out to meet the uniformed guard.

'Hiya, John,' the man said.

'You're looking well, Andy,' Rebus offered, shaking the proffered hand.

Andy Edmunds had been a police constable from the age of eighteen, meaning he'd been able to retire on a full pension while still well shy of his fiftieth birthday. The guard's job was part-time, a way of filling some of the hours in the day. The two men had been useful to one another in the past: Andy feeding Rebus info on any dealers attempting to sell to the students at Pollock; Andy feeling still part of the force as a result.

'What brings you here?' he asked now.

'A bit of a favour. I've got a name – could be her first or last – and I know this is her most recent address.'

'What's she done?'

Rebus looked around, as if to emphasise the importance of what he was about to say. Edmunds took the bait, moved a step closer.

'That murder at Knoxland,' Rebus said under his breath. 'There may be a tie-in.' He placed his finger to his mouth, Edmunds nodding his understanding.

'What's said to me stays with me, John, you know that.'

'I know, Andy. So . . . is there any way we can track her down?'

The 'we' seemed to galvanise Edmunds. He retreated to his glass box and made a call, then returned to Rebus. 'We'll go talk to Maureen,' he said. Then he winked. 'Wee thing going on between the two of us, but she's married . . .' It was his turn to place a finger to his mouth.

Rebus just nodded. He had shared a confidence with Edmunds, so a confidence had to be traded in return. Together, they walked the ten yards or so to the main admin building. This was the oldest structure on the site, built in the Scots baronial style, the interior dominated by a vast wooden staircase, the walls panelled with more slabs of dark-stained wood. Maureen's office was on the ground floor, boasting an ornate green marble fireplace and a panelled ceiling. She wasn't quite what Rebus had been expecting – small and plump, almost mousy. Hard to imagine her carrying on an illicit affair with a man in uniform. Edmunds was staring at Rebus, as though seeking some sort of appraisal. Rebus raised an eyebrow and gave a little nod, which seemed to satisfy the ex-cop.

Having shaken Maureen's hand, Rebus spelt the name for her. 'I might have the odd letter in the wrong place,' he cautioned.

'Kawame Mana,' Maureen corrected him. 'I've got her here.' Her screen was showing the identical information to Mrs Scrimgour's. 'She's got a room in Fergusson Hall . . . studying psychology.'

Rebus had flipped open his notebook. 'Date of birth?'

Maureen tapped the screen and Rebus jotted down what was printed there. Kawame was a second-year student, aged twenty.

'Calls herself Kate,' Maureen added. 'Room two-ten.'

Rebus turned to Andy Edmunds, who was already nodding. 'I'll show you,' he said.

*

284

The narrow, cream-coloured corridor was quieter than Rebus had expected.

'Nobody playing hip-hop full blast?' he queried. Edmunds snorted.

'They've all got earphones these days, John, shuts them right away from the world.'

'So even if we knock, she won't hear us?'

'Time to find out.' They paused at the door marked 210. It boasted stickers of flowers and smiley faces, plus the name *Kate* picked out in tiny silver stars. Rebus made a fist and gave three hard thumps. The door across the corridor opened a fraction, male eyes gazing at them. The door closed again quickly and Edmunds made a show of sniffing the air.

'One hundred per cent herbal,' he said. Rebus's mouth twitched.

When there was still no answer at the second attempt, he kicked the other door, causing it to rattle in its frame. By the time it opened, he already had his warrant card out. He reached forward and plucked at the tiny earphones, dislodging them. The student was in his late teens, dressed in baggy green combats and a shrunken grey T-shirt. A breeze was coming from a just-opened window.

'What's up?' the boy asked in a lazy drawl.

'You are, by the look of things.' Rebus walked to the window and angled his head out. A thin wisp of smoke was coming from the bush immediately below. 'Hope there wasn't too much of it left.'

'Too much of what?' The voice was educated, Home Counties.

'Whatever it is you call it – draw, blaw, wacky baccy, weed . . .' Rebus smiled. 'But the last thing I want to do is go back downstairs, retrieve the spliff, check the saliva on the cigarette papers for DNA, and come all the way back up here to arrest you.'

'Didn't you hear? Grass has been decriminalised.'

Rebus shook his head. 'Downgraded – there's a difference. Still, you'll be allowed a phone call to your parents – that's one law they've yet to tinker with.' He looked around the room: single bed, with a rumpled duvet on the floor beside it; shelves of books; a laptop computer on a desk. Posters advertising drama productions.

'You like the theatre?' Rebus asked.

'I've done a bit of acting – student productions.'

Rebus nodded. 'You know Kate?'

'Yeah.' The student was switching off the machine attached to the earphones. Siobhan, Rebus guessed, would know what it was. All *he* could tell was that it was too small to play CDs.

285

'Know where we could find her?'

'What's she done?'

'She hasn't done anything; we just need a word.'

'She's not here much . . . probably in the library.'

'John . . .' This from Edmunds, who was holding open the door, allowing a view of the corridor. A dark-skinned young woman, her tightly curled hair held back in a band, was unlocking the door, glancing over her shoulder as she did so, curious about the scene in her neighbour's room.

'Kate?' Rebus guessed.

'Yes. What is the matter?' Her accent gave each syllable equal stress.

'I'm a police officer, Kate.' Rebus had stepped into the corridor. Edmunds let the door swing shut on the male student, dismissing him. 'Mind if we have a word?'

'My God, is it my family?' Her already wide eyes grew wider still. 'Has something happened to them?' The satchel slid from her shoulder to the ground.

'It's nothing to do with your family,' Rebus assured her.

'Then what . . . ? I do not understand.'

Rebus reached into his pocket, produced the tape in its little clear box. He gave it a rattle. 'Got a cassette player?' he asked.

When the tape had finished playing, she raised her eyes towards his.

'Why do you make me listen to this?' she asked, voice trembling.

Rebus was standing against the wardrobe, hands behind his back. He'd asked Andy Edmunds to wait outside, which hadn't pleased the security man. Partly, Rebus hadn't wanted him to hear – this was a police inquiry, and Edmunds was no longer a cop, whatever he might like to think. Partly also – and this was the argument Rebus would use to Edmunds's face – there simply wasn't room for the three of them. Rebus didn't want to make things any less comfortable for Kate. The cassette radio sat on her desk. Rebus leaned towards it, hitting 'stop' and then 'rewind'.

'Want to hear it again?'

'I do not see what it is you want me to do.'

'We think she's from Senegal, the woman on the tape.'

'From Senegal?' Kate pursed her lips. 'I suppose it is possible . . . Who told you such a thing?'

'Someone in the linguistics department.' Rebus ejected the tape. 'Are there many Senegalese in Edinburgh?'

286

'I'm the only one I know of.' Kate stared at the cassette. 'What has this woman done?'

Rebus was making a show of perusing her collection of CDs. There was a whole rack of them, plus further teetering piles on the windowledge. 'You like your music, Kate.'

'I like to dance.'

Rebus nodded. 'I can see that.' In fact, what he could see were the names of bands and performers completely unknown to him. He straightened up. 'You don't know anyone else from Senegal?'

'I know there are some in Glasgow . . . What has she done?'

'Just what you heard on the tape – made an emergency call. Someone she knew was murdered, and now we need to talk to her.'

'Because you think she did it?'

'You're the psychologist here – what do *you* think?'

'If she had killed him, why would she then make the call to police?'

Rebus nodded. 'That's pretty well what we think. All the same, she may have information.' Rebus had taken note of everything, from Kate's array of jewellery to the new-smelling leather satchel. He looked around for photos of the parents he presumed were paying for it all. 'Family back in Senegal, Kate?'

'Yes, in Dakar.'

'That's where the rally finishes, right?'

'That is correct.'

'And your family . . . you keep in touch with them?'

'No.'

'Oh? So you're supporting yourself?' She glared at him.

'Sorry . . . nosiness is a hazard of the job. How are you liking Scotland?'

'It's a much colder place than Senegal.'

'I'd imagine it is.'

'I am not talking about the climate merely.'

Rebus nodded his understanding. 'So you can't help me then, Kate?'

'I am truly sorry.'

'Not your fault.' He placed a business card on the desk. 'But if a stranger from home should suddenly cross your path . . .'

'I will be sure to tell you.' She'd risen from the bed, apparently eager to see him on his way.

'Well, thanks again.' Rebus stretched a hand towards her. When she took it, her own was cold and clammy. And as the door closed behind him, Rebus wondered about the look in her eyes, a look very much of relief.

Edmunds was sitting on the topmost stair, arms wrapped around his knees. Rebus apologised, giving his explanation. Edmunds didn't say anything till they were back outside, making for the barrier and Rebus's car. Eventually, he turned to Rebus.

'Is that right, about DNA from cigarette papers?'

'How the hell should I know, Andy? But it put the fear of God into that wee toerag, and that's all that matters.'

The porn had gone to Divisional HQ in Livingston. There were three other women officers in the viewing room, and Siobhan saw that this made it an uncomfortable experience for the dozen or so men. The only available TV had an eighteen-inch screen, meaning they'd to cluster round it. The men stayed tight-lipped for the most part, or chewed on their pens, keeping jokes to a minimum. Les Young spent most of his time pacing the floor behind them, arms folded, peering down at his shoes, as if wanting to dissociate himself from the whole enterprise.

Some of the films were commercially made, bought in from America and the Continent. One was in German, another Japanese, the latter featuring school uniforms and girls who looked no more than fifteen or sixteen.

'Kiddie porn,' was one officer's comment. He would ask for an occasional freeze-frame, using a digital camera to take a photo of the relevant face.

One of the DVDs was badly filmed and edited. It showed a suburban living room. One couple on the green leather sofa, another on the shag-pile carpet. Another woman, darker-skinned, crouched topless by the electric fire, appearing to masturbate as she watched. The camera was all over the place. At one point, the cameraman's hand came into shot so he could squeeze one woman's breast. The soundtrack, which until then had been a series of mumbles, grunts and wheezings, picked up his question.

'All right there, big man?'

'Sounds local,' one of the officers commented.

'Digital camera and some computer software,' someone else added. 'Anyone can direct their own porn film these days.'

'Happily, not everyone would want to,' a woman officer qualified.

'Wait a second,' Siobhan interrupted. 'Go back a bit, will you?'

The officer holding the remote obliged, freezing the frame and backtracking moment by moment.

'Is this you looking for tips, Siobhan?' one of the men asked, to a few snorts.

'That's enough, Rod,' Les Young called out.

An officer near Siobhan leaned in towards his neighbour. 'That's exactly what the woman on the rug just said,' he whispered.

This produced another snort, but Siobhan's mind was on the TV screen. 'Freeze it there,' she said. 'What's that on the back of the cameraman's hand?'

'Birthmark?' someone guessed, angling their head for a better view.

'Tattoo,' one of the women offered. Siobhan nodded agreement. She slid from her chair, getting even closer to the screen. 'I'd say if it's anything, it's a spider.' She looked up at Les Young.

'A spider tattoo,' he said softly.

'With maybe the web on his neck?'

'Meaning the victim's friend makes porn films.'

'We need to know who he is.'

Les Young looked around the room. 'Who's in charge of finding us names for Cruikshank's known associates?'

The team shared looks and shrugs, until one of the women cleared her throat and offered an answer.

'DC Maxton, sir.'

'And where is he?'

'I think he said he was headed back to Barlinnie.' Meaning he was checking for prisoners who'd been close to Cruikshank.

'Call him and tell him about the tattoos,' Young ordered. The officer walked over to a desk and picked up a phone. Siobhan meantime was on her mobile. She'd moved away from the TV, was standing next to the curtained window.

'Can I speak to Roy Brinkley, please?' She caught Young's eye and he nodded, realising what she was doing. 'Roy? DS Clarke here . . . Listen, this friend of Donny Cruikshank's, the one with the spider's web . . . you didn't happen to notice any other tattoos on him?' She listened, broke into a grin. 'On the back of his hand? Okay, thanks for that. I'll let you get back to your books.'

She ended the call. 'Spider tattoo on the back of his hand.'

'Nice work, Siobhan.'

There were a few resentful glances at this. Siobhan ignored them. 'Doesn't get us any further until we know who he is.'

Young seemed to agree. The officer in charge of the remote was running the film again.

'Maybe we'll get lucky,' he said. 'If this guy's as hands-on as he looks, he might pass the camera to somebody else.'

They sat down again to watch. Something was niggling Siobhan, but she couldn't say what. Then the camera panned round from the sofa to the crouching woman, only she was no longer crouching. She'd risen to her feet. There was some music in the background. It wasn't a soundtrack, but actually playing in the living room as the filming happened. The woman was dancing to this music, seeming lost in it, oblivious to the other choreographies around her.

'I've seen her before,' Siobhan said quietly. From the corner of her eye she could see one of the team rolling his eyes in disbelief.

Here she was again: Captain Underpants's sidekick, showing them all up.

Live with it, she wanted to tell them. But instead, she turned to Young, who looked as though he couldn't quite believe it himself. 'I think I saw her dancing once.'

'Where?'

Siobhan looked at the team, then back towards Young. 'A place called the Nook.'

'The lap-dancing bar?' one of the men said, eliciting laughter and jabbed fingers. 'It was a stag,' he tried explaining.

'So did you pass the audition?' one of the others was asking Siobhan, to even more laughter.

'You're behaving like schoolkids,' Les Young snapped. 'Either grow up or ship out.' He hooked a thumb towards the door. Then, to Siobhan: 'When was this?'

'A few days back. In connection with Ishbel Jardine.' She had the full attention of the room now. 'We had information she might've ended up working there.'

'And?'

Siobhan shook her head. 'No sign of her. But . . .' pointing towards the TV, 'I'm fairly sure *she* was there, doing much the same dance she's doing right now.' On the screen, one of the men, naked apart from his socks, was approaching the dancer. He pressed his hands to her shoulders, trying to push her to her knees, but she twisted free and kept on dancing, eyes closed. The man looked to the camera and shrugged. Now the camera was jerked downwards, the focus blurring. When it came up again, someone new had entered the frame.

Shaven-headed, his facial scars more prominent on film than in real life.

Donny Cruikshank.

He was fully dressed, a grin spreading across his face, can of lager in one hand.

'Gie's the camera,' he said, holding out his free hand.

'Know how to use it?'

'Get away, Mark. If you can do it, I can do it.'

'Cheers, Donny,' said one of the officers, scribbling the name 'Mark' into his notebook.

The discussion continued, the camera eventually changing hands. And now Donny Cruikshank swung the camera up to capture his friend. The hand went up too slowly to cover the face from identification. Without needing to be told, the officer with the remote tracked back and froze the frame. His colleague with the digital camera raised it to his face.

On the screen: a huge shaved head, the dome shiny with sweat. Studs in both ears and through the nose, a nick in one of the thick black eyebrows, one central tooth missing from the protesting mouth.

And the spider's-web tattoo, of course, covering the whole of the neck . . .

24

From Pollock Halls, it was a short drive to Gayfield Square. There was only one other body in the CID office, and it belonged to Phyllida Hawes, whose face started to redden the moment Rebus walked in.

'Grassed up any good colleagues lately, DC Hawes?'

'Look, John . . .'

Rebus laughed. 'Don't worry about it, Phyl. You did what you felt you had to.' Rebus rested against the edge of her desk. 'When Storey came to see me, he said he thought I was on the level because he knew my reputation – I'm guessing I've got you to thank for that.'

'All the same, I should have warned you.' She sounded relieved, and Rebus realised she'd been dreading this encounter.

'I'm not going to hold it against you.' Rebus stood up and made for the kettle. 'Can I make you one?'

'Please . . . thanks.'

Rebus spooned coffee into the only two clean mugs left. 'So,' he asked casually, 'who introduced you to Storey?'

'It came down the line: Fettes HQ to DCI Macrae.'

'And Macrae decided you were the woman for the job?' Rebus nodded, as if in agreement with the choice.

'I wasn't to tell anyone,' Hawes added.

Rebus waved the spoon at her. 'I can't remember . . . do you take milk and sugar?'

She tried a thin smile. 'It's not that you've forgotten.'

'What then?'

'This is the first time you've offered.'

Rebus raised an eyebrow. 'You're probably right. First time for everything, eh?'

She'd risen from her chair and come part of the way towards him. 'I just take milk, by the way.'

'Duly noted.' Rebus was sniffing the contents of a half-litre carton. 'I'd make one for young Colin, but I'm guessing he's down at Waverley, on the lookout for travelling sneak-thieves.'

'Actually, he got called away.' Hawes nodded towards the window. Rebus peered out at the car park. Uniforms were packing themselves into the available patrol cars, four or five to each vehicle.

'What's going on?' he asked.

'Reinforcements needed at Cramond.'

'Cramond?' Rebus's eyes widened. Sandwiched between a golf course and the River Almond, it was one of the city's more douce neighbourhoods, with some of the most expensive homes. 'Are the peasants revolting?'

Hawes had joined him at the window. 'Something to do with illegal immigrants,' she said. Rebus stared at her.

'What exactly?'

She shrugged. Rebus took her arm and guided her back to her desk, lifted the telephone receiver and handed it to her. 'Give your friend Felix a call,' he said, making it sound like an order.

'What for?'

Rebus just shook away the question and watched her punch the numbers.

'His mobile?' he guessed. She nodded, and he took the receiver from her. The call was picked up on the seventh ring.

'Yes?' The voice impatient.

'Felix?' Rebus said, his eyes on Phyllida Hawes. 'It's Rebus here.'

'I'm a bit pushed right now.' He sounded as if he was in a car, either driving or being driven at speed.

'Just wondering how my search is coming along?'

'Your search . . . ?'

'Senegalese living in Scotland. Don't tell me you've forgotten?' Trying to sound hurt.

'I've had other things on my mind, John. I'll get to it eventually.'

'So what's been keeping you so busy? Is that you on your way to Cramond, Felix?'

There was silence on the line, Rebus's face breaking into a grin.

'Okay,' Storey said slowly. 'As far as I'm aware, I never got round to giving you this number . . . meaning you probably got it from DC

293

Hawes, which in turn means you're probably calling from Gayfield Square . . .'

'And watching the cavalry ride out as we speak. So what's the big deal at Cramond, Felix?'

More silence on the line, and then the words Rebus had been waiting for.

'Maybe you'd best come along and find out . . .'

The car park wasn't in Cramond itself, but a little way along the coast. People would stop there and take a winding path through grass and nettles towards the beach. It was a barren, windswept spot, probably never before as crowded as now. There were a dozen patrol cars and four marked vans, plus the powerful saloons favoured by Customs and Immigration. Felix Storey was gesticulating as he gave orders to the troops.

'It's only about fifty yards to the shore, but be warned – soon as they see us, they'll start running. The saving grace is, there's nowhere for them to run *to*, unless they plan to swim to Fife.' There were smiles at this, but Storey held up a hand. 'I'm serious. It's happened before. That's why the coastguard's on stand-by.' A walkie-talkie crackled into life. He held it to his ear. 'Go ahead.' Listened to what seemed to Rebus like a wash of static. 'Over and out.' He lowered the handset again. 'That's the two flanking teams in position. They'll start moving in about thirty seconds, so let's get going.'

He set off, making to pass Rebus, who had just given up trying to get a cigarette lit.

'Another tip-off?' Rebus guessed.

'Same source.' Storey kept walking, his men – DC Colin Tibbet included – behind him. Rebus started walking too, right by Storey's shoulder.

'So what's happening then? Boats bringing illegals ashore?'

Storey glanced at him. 'Cockling.'

'Say again?'

'Picking cockles. The gangs behind it use immigrants and asylum-seekers, pay them a pittance. The two Land Rovers back there . . .' Rebus turned his head, saw the vehicles in question, parked in a corner of the car park. They both had small trailers attached to their tow-bars. A couple of uniforms stood guard beside each. 'That's how they bring them in. They sell the cockles to restaurants; some of them probably go overseas . . .' At that moment they passed a sign warning them that any crustaceans

294

found on the seashore were likely to be contaminated and unfit for human consumption. Storey gave Rebus another glance. 'The restaurants aren't to know what they're buying.'

'I'll never look at paella the same way.' Rebus was about to ask about the trailers, but he could hear the high whine of small engines, and as they crested the rise he saw two quad bikes, laden with bulging sacks, and dotted all around the shore stooped figures with shovels, reflected in the shimmer of the wet sand.

'Now!' Storey called, breaking into a run. The others followed as best they could down the incline, across its powder-dry surface. Rebus held back to watch. He saw the cockle-pickers look up, saw sacks and shovels dropped. Some stood where they were, others started to flee. Uniforms were approaching from both directions. With Storey's men descending on them from the dunes, the only possible escape route was provided by the Firth of Forth. One or two waded further out, but seemed to come to their senses by the time the icy water started numbing legs and waists.

Some of the invaders were yelling and whooping; others lost their footing and went down on all fours, spattered with sand. Rebus had finally found shelter enough to get his lighter to work. He inhaled deeply, holding the smoke in as he enjoyed the spectacle. The quad bikes were circling, the two drivers shouting at one another. One of them took the initiative and headed up the slope, perhaps imagining that if he made it to the car park he might manage to escape. But he was going too fast for the cargo still strapped to the bike's rear. The machine's front tyres flew upwards, the bike somersaulting, throwing its driver to the ground, where he was pounced on by four uniforms. The other rider saw no reason to follow suit. Instead, he held up his hands, the bike idling until its ignition was switched off by a besuited Immigration officer. It reminded Rebus of something . . . yes, that was it – the end of the Beatles film *Help*. All they needed now was Eleanor Bron.

As he walked on to the beach, he saw that some of the workers were young women. A few were sobbing. They all looked Chinese, including the two men on the bikes. One of Storey's men seemed to know the relevant language. He had his hands cupped to his mouth and was rattling off instructions. Nothing he said seemed to appease the women, who wailed all the harder.

'What are they saying?' Rebus asked him.

'They don't want to be sent home.'

Rebus looked around. 'Can't be any worse than this, can it?'

The officer's mouth twitched. 'Forty-kilo sacks . . . they get paid maybe three quid for each one, and it's not as if they can go to an employment tribunal, is it?'

'I suppose not.'

'Slavery's what it boils down to . . . turning human beings into something you can buy and sell. In the north-east, it's fish-gutting. Other places, it's picking fruit and veg. The gangmasters have a supply for every possible demand.' He started barking out more advice to the workers, most of whom looked exhausted and glad of any excuse to down tools. The flanking officers had arrived, having picked up a few strays.

'One call!' one of the bike-riders was screeching. 'Get to make one call!'

'When we get to the station,' an officer corrected him. '*If* we're feeling generous.'

Storey had stopped in front of the rider. 'Who is it you want to call? Got a mobile on you?' The rider made to move his hands towards his trouser pocket, hampered by the handcuffs. Storey took the phone out for him, held it in front of his face. 'Give me the number, I'll dial it for you.'

The man stared at him, then gave a grin and shook his head, letting Storey know he wasn't falling for it.

'You want to stay in this country?' Storey persisted. 'You better start cooperating.'

'I am legal . . . work permit and everything.'

'Good for you . . . we'll be sure to check it's not a forgery or expired.'

The grin melted, like a sandcastle hit by the incoming tide.

'I'm always open to negotiation,' Storey informed the man. 'Soon as you feel like talking, let me know.' He nodded for the prisoner to be marched uphill with the others. Then he noticed Rebus standing beside him. 'Bugger is,' he said, 'if his paperwork's in order, he doesn't have to tell us a thing. It's not illegal to pick cockles.'

'And what about them?' Rebus gestured in the direction of the stragglers. These were the oldest of the workers, seeming to move with a permanent stoop.

'If they're illegals, they'll be locked up till we can ship them home.' Storey straightened up, sliding his hands into the pockets of his knee-length camel-hair coat. 'Plenty more like them to take their place.'

Rebus saw that the Immigration man was staring out at the unceasing grey swell. 'Canute and the tide?' he offered by way of comparison.

Storey took out a huge white handkerchief and blew his nose noisily, then started climbing the dune, leaving Rebus to finish his cigarette.

By the time he reached the car park, the vans had moved off. However, a new, handcuffed figure had entered the picture. One of the uniforms was explaining to Storey what had happened.

'He was heading along the road . . . saw the patrol cars and did a three-point turn. We managed to head him off . . .'

'I told you,' the man barked, 'it was nothing to do with youse!' He sounded Irish. A few days' growth on his square chin, lower jaw pushed out belligerently. His car had been brought into the car park. It was an old-model BMW 7-series, its red paint fading, sills turning to rust. Rebus had seen it before. He walked around it. There was a notebook visible on the passenger seat, folded open at a list of what looked like Chinese names. Storey caught Rebus's eye and nodded: he already knew about it.

'Name, please?' he asked the driver.

'Let's have your ID first,' the man snapped back. He was wearing an olive-green parka, maybe the same coat he'd been wearing when Rebus had first set eyes on him the previous week. 'Fuck are you staring at?' he asked Rebus, looking him up and down. Rebus just smiled and took out his own mobile, made a call.

'Shug?' he said when it was answered. 'Rebus here . . . Remember at the demo? You were going to come up with a name for that Irishman . . .' Rebus listened, eyes on the man in front of him. 'Peter Hill?' He nodded to himself. 'Well, guess what: if I'm not mistaken, he's standing right in front of me . . .'

The man just scowled, making no attempt to deny it.

It was Rebus's suggestion that they take Peter Hill to Torphichen police station, where Shug Davidson was already waiting in the Stef Yurgii murder room. Rebus introduced Davidson to Felix Storey, and the two men shook hands. A few of the detectives couldn't help staring. It wasn't the first time they'd seen a black man, but it was the first time they'd welcomed one to this particular corner of the city.

Rebus contented himself with listening, while Davidson explained the connection between Peter Hill and Knoxland.

'You have evidence he was dealing drugs?' Storey asked at the end.

'Not enough to convict him . . . but we did put away four of his friends.'

'Meaning either he was too small a fish, or . . .'

'Too clever to get caught,' Davidson conceded with a nod.

'And the connection to the paramilitaries?'

'Again, hard to pin down, but the drugs had to come from somewhere, and intelligence in Northern Ireland pointed to that particular source. Terrorists need to raise money any way they can . . .'

'Even by acting as gangmasters to illegal immigrants?'

Davidson shrugged. 'First time for everything,' he speculated.

Storey rubbed his chin thoughtfully. 'That car he was driving . . .'

'BMW seven-series,' Rebus offered.

Storey nodded. 'Those weren't Irish number plates, were they? Northern Ireland, they're usually three letters and four numbers.'

Rebus looked at him. 'You're well informed.'

'I worked Customs for a while. When you're checking passenger ferries, you get to know number plates . . .'

'I'm not sure I see what you're getting at,' Shug Davidson was forced to admit. Storey turned to him.

'Just wondering how he came by the car, that's all. If he didn't bring it over here with him, then he either bought it here, or . . .'

'Or it belongs to someone else.' Davidson nodded slowly.

'Unlikely he's working alone, not a set-up of that size.'

'Something else we can ask him,' Davidson said. Storey offered a smile, and turned his gaze to Rebus, as if seeking further agreement. But Rebus's eyes had narrowed slightly. He was still wondering about that car . . .

The Irishman was in Interview Room 2. He took no notice of the three men when they came in, relieving the uniform who'd been standing guard. Storey and Davidson sat down opposite him at the table, Rebus finding a section of wall to rest his weight against. There was the sound of pneumatic drilling from the roadworks outside. It would punctuate any discussion, ending up on the cassette tapes Davidson was unwrapping. He slotted both into the recording machine and made sure the timer was correct. Then he did the same with a couple of blank videotapes. The camera was above the door, pointing straight at the table. If any suspect wanted to claim intimidation, the tapes would give the lie to the accusation.

The three officers identified themselves for the benefit of the tapes, then Davidson asked the Irishman to give his full name. He seemed content to let the silence lie, flicking threads from his trousers and then clasping his hands in front of him on the edge of the desk.

Hill continued to stare at a patch of wall between Davidson and Storey. Finally, he spoke.

'I could do with a cup of tea. Milk, three sugars.' He was missing some teeth from the back of his mouth, giving his cheeks a sunken look, emphasising the skull beneath the sallow skin. His hair was cropped and silver-grey, eyes pale blue, neck scrawny. Probably not much more than five feet nine tall and ten stone in weight.

Most of it attitude.

'In due course,' Davidson said quietly.

'And a lawyer . . . a phone call . . .'

'Same applies. Meantime . . .' Davidson opened a manila folder and extracted a large black-and-white photograph. 'This is you, isn't it?'

Only half the face was showing, the rest hidden by the parka's hood. It had been taken the day of the Knoxland demo, the day Howie Slowther had gone for Mo Dirwan with a rock.

'Don't think so.'

'How about this?' The photographer this time had caught a full-face shot. 'Taken a few months back, also in Knoxland.'

'And your point is . . . ?'

'My point is, I've been waiting a good long time to get you for *some*thing.' Davidson smiled and turned to Felix Storey.

'Mr Hill,' Storey began, crossing one knee over the other, 'I'm an Immigration officer. We'll be checking the credentials of all those workers to see how many of them are here illegally.'

'No idea what you're talking about. I was out for a drive down the coast – not against the law, is it?'

'No, but a jury might just wonder at the coincidence of that list of names on the passenger seat, if it turns out they match the names of the people we've detained.'

'What list?' Finally, Hill's eyes met those of his questioner. 'If there's any list been found, it's been planted.'

'So we won't expect to find your fingerprints on it then?'

'And none of the workers will be able to identify you?' Davidson added, twisting the knife.

'Not against the law, is it?'

'Actually,' Storey confided, 'I think slavery may have come off the statute book a few centuries back.'

'That why they let a nigger like you wear a suit?' the Irishman spat.

Storey gave a wry smile, as if satisfied that things had come to this so readily. 'I've heard the Irish referred to as the blacks of Europe – does that make us brothers beneath the skin?'

'It means you can go arse yourself.'

Storey tipped his head back and laughed from deep within his chest. Davidson had closed the file again – leaving the two photographs out, facing Peter Hill. He was tapping a finger against the file, as if drawing to Hill's attention the thickness of it, the sheer quantity of information within.

'So how long have you been in the slave trade?' Rebus asked the Irishman.

'I'm saying nothing till I get a mug of tea.' Hill leaned back and folded his arms. 'And I want it brought in by my lawyer.'

'You've got a lawyer then? Seems to suggest you thought you'd be needing one.'

Hill turned his gaze towards Rebus, but his question was aimed across the table. 'How long do youse think you can keep me here?'

'That depends,' Davidson told him. 'You see, these links of yours to the paramilitaries . . .' He was still tapping the file. 'Thanks to the legislation on terrorism, we can hold you a bit longer than you might think.'

'So now I'm a terrorist?' Hill sneered.

'You were always a terrorist, Peter. The only thing that's changed is how you go about funding it. Last month you were a dealer; today you're a slaver . . .'

There was a knock at the door. The head of a detective constable appeared.

'Have you got it?' Davidson asked. The head nodded. 'Then you can come in here and keep the suspect company.' Davidson started rising to his feet, intoning for the benefit of the various recording devices that the interview was being suspended, checking his watch to give the exact time. The machines were switched off. Davidson offered the DC his chair, and accepted a scrap of paper in return. Outside in the corridor, once the door was firmly closed, he unfolded the paper, stared at it, then handed it to Storey, whose mouth broke open in a gleaming grin.

Finally, the paper was passed to Rebus. It contained a description of the red BMW, along with its licence plate. Below it, written in capitals, were the owner's details.

The owner was Stuart Bullen.

Storey snatched the note back from Rebus and planted a kiss on it. Then he did a little shuffle of a dance.

The high spirits seemed infectious. Davidson was grinning too. He patted Felix Storey on the back. 'Not often surveillance brings a result,' he offered, looking to Rebus for his agreement.

But it wasn't the surveillance, Rebus couldn't help thinking. It was another mysterious tip-off.

That, and Storey's own intuition about the BMW's ownership. If intuition was indeed all it had been . . .

25

When they arrived at the Nook, they met another raiding party –
Siobhan and Les Young. Offices were emptying for the day, and a
few suits were heading past the doormen. Rebus was asking
Siobhan what she was doing there when he saw one of the doormen
place a hand to the mouthpiece of his radio headset. The man was
turning his face to one side, but Rebus knew they'd been clocked.

'He's telling Bullen we're here!' Rebus called out to the others.
They moved quickly, pushing past the businessmen and into the
premises. The music was loud, the place busier than on Rebus's
first visit. There were more dancers, too: four of them on the stage.
Siobhan held back, studying faces, while Rebus led the way
towards Bullen's office. The door with the keypad was locked.
Rebus looked around, saw the barman – recalled his name: Barney
Grant.

'Barney!' he yelled. 'Get over here!'

Barney put down the glass he was filling, came out from behind
the bar. Punched in the numbers. Rebus shouldered the door and
immediately felt the ground fall away beneath him. He was in the
short corridor leading to Bullen's office, only now the cover of a
trapdoor had been lifted and it was through this opening that he'd
fallen, landing awkwardly on the wooden steps which led down into
darkness.

'What the hell's this?' Storey yelped.

'Sort of tunnel,' the barman offered.

'Where does it lead?'

He just shook his head. Rebus hobbled down the steps as best he
could. His right leg felt like he'd grazed it all the way from ankle to
knee, and he'd managed to twist his left ankle for good measure. He

peered up at the faces above him. 'Go outside, see if you can work out where it might lead.'

'Could be anywhere,' Davidson muttered.

Rebus peered along the tunnel. 'It's heading down towards the Grassmarket, I think.' He closed his eyes, trying to get them accustomed to the dark, and started moving, keeping his hands against the side walls to steady himself. After a few moments, he opened his eyes again, blinking a few times. He could make out the damp earthen floor, the curved walls and sloping ceiling. Probably man-made, going back centuries: the Old Town was a warren of tunnels and catacombs, mostly unexplored. They had sheltered the inhabitants from invasion, made assignations and plots possible. Smugglers might have used them. In more recent times, people had tried growing everything from mushrooms to cannabis in them. A few had been opened as tourist attractions, but the bulk were like this: cramped and unloved and filled with stale air.

The tunnel was veering left. Rebus took out his mobile, but there was no signal, no way of letting the others know. He could hear movement ahead of him, but nothing visible.

'Stuart?' he called out, voice echoing. 'This is bloody stupid, Stuart!'

And kept moving, seeing a faint glow in the distance, a body disappearing into it. Then the glow was gone. It was another door, this time in the side wall, and Bullen had closed it after him. Rebus placed both hands to the right wall, fearing he'd miss the opening. His fingers hit something hard. A doorknob of all things. He turned and pulled, but the door opened the other way. Tried again, but something heavy had been placed against it. Rebus called out for help, pushed with his shoulder. A noise from the other side: someone attempting to slide a box out of the way.

Then the door opened, leaving a space of only a couple of feet Rebus crawled through. The door was at floor level. As he stood up, he saw that a box of books had been used for the barricade. An elderly man was staring at him.

'He went out of the door,' was all he said. Rebus nodded and limped in that direction. Once outside, he knew exactly where he was: West Port. Emerging from a second-hand bookshop not a hundred yards from the Nook. He had his mobile in his hand. It had picked up a signal again. Glanced back towards the traffic lights at Lady Lawson Street, then to his right, down towards the Grassmarket. Saw what he'd been hoping for.

Stuart Bullen being marched up the middle of the road towards him. Felix Storey behind him with Bullen's right arm twisted upwards. Bullen's clothes torn and dirty. Rebus looked down at his own. They didn't look much better. He pulled up his trouser leg, glad to see there was no blood, just scrape marks. Shug Davidson was emerging at a jog from Lady Lawson Street, face red from running. Rebus bent at the waist, hands on his knees. Wanted a cigarette, but knew he wouldn't have the breath to smoke one. Stood up straight again and was face to face with Bullen.

'I was gaining,' he told the young man. 'Honest.'

They took him back to the Nook. Word had gone around, and the place was empty of punters. Siobhan was quizzing some of the dancers, who sat in a line at the bar, Barney Grant pouring soft drinks for them.

A solitary customer emerged from behind the VIP curtain, puzzled by the sudden lack of music and voices. He seemed to sum up the situation and tightened the knot in his tie as he made to exit. Rebus's limp caused him to bump shoulders with the man.

'Sorry,' the man muttered.

'My fault, councillor,' Rebus said, watching him as he left. Then he walked over to Siobhan, nodding a greeting to Les Young. 'So what's all this about?'

It was Young who answered. 'We need to ask Stuart Bullen a few questions.'

'About what?' Rebus's eyes were still on Siobhan.

'In connection with the murder of Donald Cruikshank.'

Now Rebus's attention shifted to Young. 'Well, intriguing as that sounds, you're going to have to wait in line. I think you'll find *we've* got first dibs.'

'*We* being . . . ?'

Rebus gestured towards Felix Storey, who was finally – and reluctantly – letting go of Bullen, now that his hands had been handcuffed. 'That man's Immigration. He's had Bullen under surveillance for weeks – people-smuggling, white slavery, you name it.'

'We'll need access,' Les Young said.

'Then go plead your case.' Rebus stretched an arm out towards Storey and Shug Davidson. Les Young gave him a hard stare, then headed off in that direction. Siobhan was glowering at Rebus.

'What?' he asked, all innocence.

'It's me you're pissed off with, remember? Don't go picking on Les.'

'Les is a big boy; he can look after himself.'

'Problem is, in a scrap, he'd play fair . . . unlike some.'

'Harsh words, Siobhan.'

'Sometimes you need to hear them.'

Rebus just shrugged. 'So what's this about Bullen and Cruik-shank?'

'Homemade porn in the victim's home. Featuring at least one of the dancers from this place.'

'And that's it?'

'We just need to talk to him.'

'I'm willing to bet there are some on the inquiry who're wondering why. They reckon if a rapist gets topped, why bust a gut over it?' He paused. 'Am I right?'

'You'd know better than me.'

Rebus turned towards where Young and Davidson were in conversation. 'Maybe you're trying to impress young Les over there . . .'

She hauled on Rebus's shoulder, so she had his full attention again. 'It's a murder case, John. You'd be doing everything I'm doing.'

He gave the beginnings of a smile. 'I'm just teasing, Siobhan.' He turned to the open doorway, the one leading to Bullen's office. 'The first time we were here, did you notice that trapdoor?'

'I just thought it was the cellar.' She halted. 'You didn't spot it?'

'Forgot it was there, that's all,' he lied, rubbing his right leg.

'Looks sore, mate.' Barney Grant was studying the injury. 'Like you've been studded. Used to play a bit of footie, so I know what I'm talking about.'

'You might have warned us about the trapdoor.'

The barman offered a shrug. Felix Storey was pushing Stuart Bullen towards the hallway. Rebus made to follow, Siobhan trailing him. Storey slammed shut the trapdoor. 'Good place to hide any illegals,' he said. Bullen just snorted. The door to the office was ajar. Storey opened it with one foot. It was as Rebus remembered it: cramped and full of junk. Storey's nose wrinkled.

'Going to take us a while to empty all this into evidence bags.'

'Christ's sake,' Bullen muttered by way of complaint.

The door of the safe was slightly ajar, too, and Storey used the tip of a polished brogue to open it up.

'Well now,' he said. 'I think we'd better get those evidence bags in here.'

'This is a fit-up!' Bullen started to shout. 'It's a plant, you bastards!' He made to shake himself free of Storey's grip, but the

Immigration man was four inches taller and probably twenty pounds heavier. Everyone stood crowded in the doorway, trying for a better view. Davidson and Young had arrived, as had some of the dancers.

Rebus turned to Siobhan, who pursed her lips. She'd seen what he'd just seen. Lying in the open safe – a stack of passports held together with a rubber band; blank credit and debit cards; various official-looking stamps and franking machines. Plus other folded documents, maybe birth or marriage certificates.

Everything you'd need to create a new identity.

Or even a few hundred.

They took Stuart Bullen to Torphichen's Interview Room 1.

'We've got your pal next door,' Felix Storey said. He'd removed his jacket and was loosening his cuff links so he could roll up his shirt-sleeves.

'Who's that then?' Bullen's handcuffs had been removed and he was rubbing his reddened wrists.

'Peter Hill, I think his name is.'

'Never heard of him.'

'Irish guy . . . speaks very highly of you.'

Bullen caught Storey's eye. 'Now I know this is a fit-up.'

'Why? Because you're confident Hill won't talk?'

'I've already told you, I don't know him.'

'We've got photos of him coming in and out of your club.'

Bullen stared at Storey, as if trying to gauge the truth of this. Rebus himself didn't know. It was possible the surveillance had netted Hill; then again, Storey could be bluffing. He had brought nothing with him to this meeting: no files or folders. Bullen turned his gaze on Rebus.

'Sure you want him around?' he asked Storey.

'How do you mean?'

'Word is, he's Cafferty's man.'

'Who?'

'Cafferty – he runs this whole city.'

'And why should that concern you, Mr Bullen?'

'Because Cafferty hates my family.' He paused for effect. 'And *someone* planted that stuff.'

'You'll have to do better than that,' Storey said, almost sorrowfully. 'Try explaining away your connection to Peter Hill.'

'I keep telling you,' Bullen's teeth were gritted, 'there isn't any.'

'And that's why we found him in your car?'

306

The room went quiet. Shug Davidson was walking up and down with arms folded. Rebus stood in his favoured place by the wall. Stuart Bullen was making an examination of his own fingernails.

'Red BMW 7-series,' Storey went on, 'registered in your name.'

'I lost that car months back.'

'Did you report it?'

'Hardly worth the effort.'

'And that's the story you'll be sticking to – planted evidence and a misplaced BMW? I hope you've got a good lawyer, Mr Bullen.'

'Maybe I'll try that Mo Dirwan . . . he seems to win a few.' Bullen shifted his gaze to Rebus. 'I hear the two of you are good mates.'

'Funny you should mention it,' Shug Davidson interrupted, stopping in front of the table. 'Because your friend Hill has been seen out at Knoxland. We've got photos of him from the demo, same day Mr Dirwan was nearly attacked.'

'That what you do all day, take pictures of people without them knowing?' Bullen looked around the room. 'Some men do that and get called pervs.'

'Speaking of which,' Rebus said, 'we've got another inquiry waiting to talk to you.'

Bullen opened his arms. 'I'm a popular man.'

'And that's why you're going to be with us for quite some time, Mr Bullen,' Storey said. 'So make yourself comfortable . . .'

Forty minutes in, they took a break. The detained cockle-pickers were being held at St Leonard's, the only place with enough cells to take them all. Storey headed off to a telephone, to check on progress with the interviews. Rebus and Davidson had just got their hands on a tea apiece when Siobhan and Young found them.

'Do we get to talk to him now?' Siobhan asked.

'We'll be going back in soon,' Davidson told her.

'But all he's doing right now is kicking his heels,' Les Young argued.

Davidson sighed, and Rebus knew what he was thinking: anything for a quiet life. 'How long do you need?' he asked.

'We'll take what you can give us.'

'On you go then . . .'

Young turned to leave, but Rebus touched his elbow.

'Mind if I tag along, just out of interest?'

Siobhan gave Young a warning look, but he nodded anyway. Siobhan turned on her heels and started striding towards the interview room, so that neither man could see her face.

Bullen had his hands clasped behind his head. When he saw Rebus's tea, he asked where his own was.

'In the kettle,' Rebus replied, as Siobhan and Young began to introduce themselves.

'You're taking it in shifts?' Bullen growled, lowering his hands.

'Good tea this,' Rebus chipped in. The look he received from Siobhan told him she found the contribution not altogether helpful.

'We're here to ask you about a piece of homemade pornography,' Les Young kicked off.

Bullen let out a laugh. 'The sublime to the ridiculous.'

'It was found in the home of a murder victim,' Siobhan added coolly. 'Some of the performers might be known to you.'

'How's that then?' Bullen seemed genuinely curious.

'I recognised at least one of them.' Siobhan had folded her arms. 'She was pole-dancing that time I visited your premises with Detective Inspector Rebus.'

'News to me,' Bullen offered with a shrug. 'But girls come and go . . . I'm not their grandma, they're free to do what they like.' He leaned across the table towards Siobhan. 'Found that missing girl yet?'

'No,' she admitted.

'But the guy got himself topped, didn't he, the one who raped her sister?' When she made no answer, he shrugged again. 'I read the papers, same as anyone else.'

'That's whose house the film was found in,' Les Young added.

'I still don't see how I'm supposed to help.' Bullen turned to Rebus, as if for advice.

'Did you know Donny Cruikshank?' Siobhan asked.

Bullen turned back to her. 'Never heard of him till I saw the murder in the paper.'

'He couldn't have visited your club?'

'Course he could – there are times I'm not around . . . Barney's the one to ask.'

'The barman?' Siobhan said.

Bullen nodded. 'Or you could always ask Immigration . . . they seem to've been keeping a pretty close watch.' He smiled unconvincingly. 'Hope they took care to catch my good side.'

'You mean you've got one?' Siobhan asked. Bullen's smile vanished. He glanced at his watch. It looked expensive: chunky and gold.

'We about done here?'

'Not by a long chalk,' Les Young commented. But the door was

opening, Felix Storey entering the room, followed by Shug Davidson.

'The gang's all here!' Bullen exclaimed. 'If the Nook was this
busy, I'd be retiring to Gran Canaria . . .'

'Time's up,' Storey was telling Young. 'We need him again.'

Les Young looked to Siobhan. She was producing some polaroids
from her pocket, spreading them across the table in front of Bullen.

'You know *her*,' she said, stabbing one with her finger. 'What
about the others?'

'Faces don't always mean a lot to me,' he said, looking her up and
down. 'It's bodies I tend to remember.'

'She's one of your dancers.'

'Yeah,' he admitted at last. 'She is. What of it?'

'I'd like to talk to her.'

'She's got a shift this evening, as it happens . . .' He looked at his
watch again. 'Always supposing Barney can open up.'

Storey was shaking his head. 'Not until we've searched the place.'

Bullen gave a sigh. 'In that case,' he told Siobhan, 'I don't know
what to say.'

'You must have an address for her . . . a phone number.'

'The girls like to be discreet . . . I might have a mobile
somewhere.' He nodded towards Storey. 'Ask nicely and he might
find it for you when he's ransacking the premises.'

'Not necessary,' Rebus said. He'd walked over to the table to
study the photos. Now he picked up the one of the dancer. 'I know
her,' he said. 'Know where she lives, too.' Siobhan stared at him in
disbelief. 'Name's Kate.' He looked down at Bullen. 'That's right,
isn't it?'

'Kate, yeah,' Bullen admitted grudgingly. 'Likes to dance a bit,
does Kate.'

He said it almost wistfully.

'You handled him well,' Rebus said. He was in the passenger seat,
Siobhan driving. Les Young had left them to it, needing to get back
to Banehall. Rebus was sifting through the polaroids again.

'How so?' she eventually asked.

'Someone like Bullen, you have to be straight with them. They
clam shut otherwise.'

'He didn't give us much.'

'He'd have given young Leslie a lot less.'

'Maybe.'

'Christ, Shiv, accept some praise for once in your life!'

'I'm looking for the ulterior motive.'

'You won't find one.'

'That would be a first . . .'

They were heading for Pollock Halls. On the way out to the car, Rebus had filled her in on how he knew Kate.

'Should have recognised her,' he'd said, shaking his head. 'All that music in her room.'

'Call yourself a detective,' Siobhan had teased him. Then: 'Might have helped if she'd just been wearing a thong.'

They were on Dalkeith Road now, a stone's throw from St Leonard's with its cells full of cockle-pickers. Nothing as yet had come of the questioning – or nothing that Felix Storey was willing to share. Siobhan signalled left into Holyrood Park Road, and right into Pollock. Andy Edmunds was still manning the barrier. He crouched down by the open window.

'Back again so soon?' he asked.

'A few more questions for Kate,' Rebus explained.

'You're too late – saw her heading out on her bike.'

'How long ago?'

'No more than five minutes . . .'

Rebus turned to Siobhan. 'She's on her way to her shift.'

Siobhan nodded. No way Kate could know they'd pulled in Stuart Bullen. Rebus gave Edmunds a wave as Siobhan executed a three-point turn. She ignored the red light at Dalkeith Road, horns sounding all around her.

'I need to fix a siren to this car,' she muttered. 'Reckon we'll beat her to the Nook?'

'No, but that doesn't mean we won't catch her – she's going to want an explanation.'

'Are any of Storey's men there?'

'No idea,' Rebus admitted. They had passed St Leonard's and were heading for the Cowgate and the Grassmarket. It took Rebus some moments to work out what Siobhan already knew: this was the quickest route.

But also prone to tailbacks. More horns sounded, headlights alerting them to several illegal and bad-mannered manoeuvres.

'What was it like in that tunnel?' Siobhan asked.

'Grim.'

'No sign of any immigrants, though?'

'No,' Rebus admitted.

'See, if I was in charge of a surveillance, it would be *them* I'd want to watch.'

Rebus tended to agree. 'But what if Bullen never goes near them? He doesn't need to, after all – he's got the Irishman working as go-between.'

'The same Irishman you saw at Knoxland?'

Rebus nodded. Then he saw what she was getting at. 'That's where they are, isn't it? I mean, that's the best place to stash them.'

'I thought the place had been searched high and low?' Siobhan said, playing devil's advocate.

'But we were looking for a killer, looking for witnesses . . .' He broke off.

'What is it?' Siobhan asked.

'Mo Dirwan was beaten up when he went snooping . . . beaten up in Stevenson House.' He was reaching for his mobile, punched in Caro Quinn's number. 'Caro? It's John, I've got a question for you – where were you exactly when you were chased off Knoxland?' His eyes were on Siobhan as he listened. 'You're sure of that? No, no real reason . . . I'll talk to you later. Bye.' He ended the call. 'She'd just arrived at Stevenson House,' he told Siobhan.

'Now there's a coincidence.'

Rebus was staring at his mobile. 'I need to tell Storey.' Instead of which, he turned the mobile over and over in his hand.

'You're not calling him,' she commented.

'I'm not sure I trust him,' Rebus admitted. 'He gets all these useful anonymous tip-offs. That's how he knew about Bullen, the Nook, the cockle-pickers . . .'

'And?'

Rebus shrugged. 'And he got this sudden inspiration about the BMW . . . exactly what was needed to connect it to Bullen.'

'Another tip-off?' Siobhan guessed.

'So who's making the calls?'

'Has to be someone close to Bullen.'

'Could just be someone who knows a lot about him. But if Storey *is* being fed all this gen . . . surely he must have suspicions of his own?'

'You mean: "Why am I being fed all this great stuff?" Maybe he just isn't the type to look a gift horse in the mouth.'

Rebus pondered this for a moment. 'Gift horse or Trojan horse?'

'Is that her?' Siobhan said abruptly. She was pointing to an approaching cyclist. The bike passed them, heading downhill to the Grassmarket.

'I didn't really see,' Rebus admitted. Siobhan bit her lip.

'Hang on,' she said, hitting the brake hard, executing another

three-point turn, this time with traffic backing up in both directions. Rebus waved and shrugged by way of apology, then, when
one driver started yelling from his window, resorted to less
conciliatory gestures. Siobhan was driving them back into Grassmarket, the angry driver on her tail, lights on full beam, horn
sounding a tattoo.

Rebus turned in his seat and glared at the man, who kept
shouting and waving a fist.

'He's got a hard-on for us,' Siobhan said.

Rebus tutted. 'Language, please.' Then, leaning out of the
window, he yelled, 'We're fucking police officers!' at the top of his
voice, keenly aware that the man couldn't hear him. Siobhan burst
out laughing, then turned the steering wheel sharply.

'She's stopped,' she said. The cyclist was getting off her bike,
preparing to chain it to a lamp-post. They were in the heart of the
Grassmarket, all smart bistros and tourist pubs. Siobhan pulled up
on a double yellow and jogged from the car. From this distance,
Rebus recognised Kate. She was dressed in a frayed denim jacket
and cut-off jeans, long black boots and a silky pink neck-scarf. She
was looking confused as Siobhan introduced herself. Rebus undid
his seatbelt and was about to open the door when an arm snaked
through the window and caught his head in its vice-like grip.

'What's your game then, pal?' the voice roared. 'Think you own
the bloody highway, do you?'

Rebus's mouth and nose were muffled by the padded sleeve of the
man's oily jacket. He fumbled for the door handle and pushed with
all his might, tumbling from the car on to his knees, sending a fresh
jolt of pain through both legs. The man was still on the opposite
side of the car door from Rebus and showed no sign of releasing his
prey. The door acted as a shield, protecting him from Rebus's
swipes and punches.

'Think you're the big guy, eh? Giving me the finger . . .'

'He *is* the big guy,' Rebus heard Siobhan saying. 'He's police,
same as me. Now let him go.'

'He's what?'

'I said let him go!' The pressure eased on Rebus and he pulled his
head free, standing up straight and feeling the blood singing in his
ears, the world swirling around him. Siobhan had wrenched the
man's free arm halfway up his back and was now forcing him down
on to his knees, head stooped. Rebus brought out his warrant card
and held in front of the man's nose.

'Try that again and I'll do you,' he gasped.

Siobhan released her hold and took a step back. She, too, had her ID out by the time the man straightened up.

'How was I supposed to know?' was all he said. But Siobhan had already dismissed him. She was walking back towards Kate, who had watched the performance wide-eyed. Rebus made a show of noting the man's registration as he retreated to his car. Then he turned and joined Siobhan and Kate.

'Kate was just stopping off for a drink,' Siobhan explained. 'I've asked if we might join her.'

Rebus could think of nothing better.

'I'm meeting someone in half an hour,' Kate cautioned.

'Half an hour's all we need,' Rebus assured her.

They made for the nearest place, found a table. The jukebox was loud, but Rebus got the barman to turn it down. A pint for himself, soft drinks for the two women.

'I was just telling Kate,' Siobhan said, 'how good a dancer she is.' Rebus nodded agreement, feeling a jolt of pain in his neck. 'I thought it the first time I saw you at the Nook,' Siobhan went on, making the place sound like an upmarket disco. Smart girl, thought Rebus: no moralising, no making the witness nervous or embarrassed . . . He took a gulp from his glass.

'That's all it is, you know . . . dancing.' Kate's eyes flitted between Siobhan and Rebus. 'All these things they are saying about Stuart – that he is a people-smuggler – I did not know anything about it.' She paused, as if about to say something more, but instead sipped her drink.

'You're putting yourself through uni?' Rebus guessed. She nodded.

'I saw an advertisement in the newspaper: "Dancers wanted".' She smiled. 'I'm not stupid, I knew straight away what sort of place the Nook would be, but the girls there are great . . . and all I ever do is dance.'

'Albeit with no clothes on.' The sentence came out almost without thinking. Siobhan glared at Rebus, but too late.

Kate's face hardened. 'Are you not listening? I said I do not do any of the other things.'

'We know that, Kate,' Siobhan said quietly. 'We've seen the film.'

Kate looked at her. 'What film?'

'The one where you're dancing beside a fireplace.' Siobhan placed the polaroid on the tabletop. Kate snatched at it, not wanting it seen.

'That happened the one time,' she said, refusing to make eye contact. 'One of the girls told me it was easy money. I told her I wouldn't do anything . . .'

'And you didn't,' Siobhan agreed. 'I've seen the film, so we know that's true. You put on some music and you danced.'

'Yeah, and then they wouldn't pay me. Alberta offered me part of her money, but I would not take it from her. She had worked for that money.' She took another sip of her drink, Siobhan following suit. Both women placed their glasses down at the same time.

'The guy behind the camera,' Siobhan said, 'did you know him?'

'I had never met him until we walked into the house.'

'And where was the house?'

Kate shrugged. 'Somewhere outside Edinburgh. Alberta was driving . . . I did not really pay much attention.' She looked at Siobhan. 'Who else saw this film?'

'Just me,' Siobhan lied. Kate turned her attention to Rebus, who shook his head, letting her know he hadn't viewed it.

'I'm looking into a murder,' Siobhan continued.

'I know . . . the immigrant in Knoxland.'

'Actually, that's DI Rebus's case. The one I'm involved in happened in a town called Banehall. The man behind the camera . . .' She broke off. 'Do you happen to remember his name?'

Kate looked thoughtful. 'Mark?' she eventually offered.

Siobhan nodded slowly. 'No surname?'

'He had a big tattoo on his neck . . .'

'A spider's web,' Siobhan agreed. 'At one point, another man came in, and Mark handed him the camera.' Siobhan produced another polaroid, this time a blurred image of Donny Cruikshank. 'Do you remember him?'

'To be honest with you, I had my eyes closed most of the time. I was trying to concentrate on the music . . . it's how I do the job – by thinking of nothing but the music.'

Siobhan nodded again, to show she understood. 'He's the one who got murdered, Kate. Is there anything you can tell me about him?'

She shook her head. 'I just got the feeling the two of them were enjoying themselves. Like schoolkids, you know? They had that feverish look to them.'

'Feverish?'

'Almost as if they were trembling. In a room with three naked women: I got the feeling it was new to them, new and exciting . . .'

'You never felt scared?'

She shook her head again. Rebus could see she was thinking back on the scene, with no fond memories at all. He cleared his throat.

'You say this other dancer took you along with her to the shoot?'

'Yes.'

'Did Stuart Bullen know about it?'

'I do not think so.'

'But you can't be positive?'

She shrugged. 'Stuart has always played fair with the girls. He knows the other clubs are looking for dancers – if we don't like where we are, we can always move on.'

'Alberta must have known the man with the tattoo,' Siobhan said.

Kate shrugged again. 'I suppose so.'

'Do you know how she knew him?'

'Maybe he came into the club . . . that is how Alberta tended to meet men.' She rattled the ice in her tumbler.

'Want another?' Rebus asked.

She looked at her watch and shook her head. 'Barney will be here soon.'

'Barney Grant?' Siobhan guessed. Kate nodded.

'He's trying to talk to all the girls. Barney knows if we go a day or two without work, he'll lose us.'

'Meaning he intends keeping the Nook open?' Rebus asked.

'Just until Stuart comes back.' She paused. 'He *will* be coming back?'

In lieu of answering, Rebus finished his pint.

'We better leave you to it,' Siobhan told Kate. 'Thanks for talking to us.' She made to get up from the table.

'I'm sorry I cannot be more help.'

'If you remember anything else about those two men . . .'

Kate nodded. 'I'll let you know.' She paused. 'The film with me in it . . .'

'Yes?'

'How many copies do you think there are?'

'No way of telling. Your friend Alberta . . . does she still dance at the Nook?'

Kate shook her head. 'She left soon afterwards.'

'You mean, soon after the film was made?'

'Yes.'

'And how long ago was that?'

'Two or three weeks.'

They thanked Kate again and headed for the door. Outside, they faced one another. Siobhan spoke first. 'Donny Cruikshank must've just been out of jail.'

'No wonder he looked feverish. You going to try finding Alberta?'

Siobhan let out a sigh. 'I don't know . . . It's been a long day.'

'Fancy another drink someplace?' She shook her head. 'Got a date with Les Young?'

'Why? Have you got one with Caro Quinn?'

'I was just asking.' Rebus took out his cigarettes.

'Give you a lift?' Siobhan offered.

'I think I'll walk, thanks all the same.'

'Okay then . . .' She hesitated, watched him light the cigarette. Then, when he didn't say anything, she turned and headed for her car. He watched her go. Concentrated on smoking for a moment, then crossed the road. There was a hotel, and he loitered by its entrance. He'd just finished the cigarette when he saw Barney Grant walking downhill from the direction of the Nook. He had his hands in his pockets and was whistling: no sign that he was worried about his job or his boss. He entered the pub, and for some reason Rebus checked his watch, then noted down the time.

And stayed where he was, in front of the hotel. Looking in through the windows, he could see its restaurant. It looked white and sterile, the sort of place where the size of each plate is in inverse proportion to the amount of food served on it. There were only a few tables in use, the staff outnumbering clients. One of the waiters gave him a look, trying to shoo him away, but Rebus just winked back at him. Eventually, just as Rebus was getting bored and deciding to leave, a car drew up outside the pub, engine roaring as it idled, the driver playing with the accelerator. The passenger was talking into a mobile phone. The pub's door opened and Barney Grant came out, sliding his own mobile back into his pocket as the passenger folded his closed. Grant got into the back seat of the car, which was in movement again even before he'd closed the door. Rebus watched as the car raced up the hill, then began to follow on foot.

It took him a few minutes to reach the Nook, and he arrived just as the car was taking off again. He stared at the locked door of the Nook, then across the street towards the closed-down shop. No more surveillance, no sign of the parked van. He tried the door of the Nook but it was locked tight. All the same, Barney Grant had dropped in for some reason, the car waiting for him. Rebus hadn't recognised the driver, but he knew the face in the passenger seat, had known it ever since it had screamed at him when he'd wrestled its owner to the ground, cameras capturing the moment for tabloid posterity.

Howie Slowther – the kid from Knoxland, the one with the paramilitary tattoo and the race hate.

Friend of the Nook's barman . . .

Either that, or of its owner.

DAY NINE

Tuesday

26

Dawn raids in Knoxland, the same team who'd chased cockle-pickers along Cramond's seashore. Stevenson House – the one with no graffiti. Why so? Either fear or respect. Rebus knew he should have seen it right at the start. Stevenson House had looked different, and it had been treated differently, too.

The original door-to-door teams had encountered many unanswered knocks there – almost a whole floor of them. Had they gone back and tried again? They had not. Why? Because the murder squad had been stretched . . . and maybe because the officers hadn't been trying too hard, the victim a statistic to them, nothing more.

Felix Storey was being more thorough. This time doors would be pounded, letter-boxes peered into. This time they wouldn't take no for an answer. The Immigration Service – as with Customs and Excise – wielded more power than the police. Doors could be kicked in without the need for search warrants. 'Due cause' was the phrase Rebus had heard mentioned, and Storey was clear in his own mind that whatever else they might have, they had due cause aplenty.

Caro Quinn – threatened when she tried taking photos in and around Stevenson House.

Mo Dirwan – attacked when his door-to-door activities took him to Stevenson House.

Rebus had been awake at four, listening to Storey's pep-talk at five – surrounded by bleary eyes and the smells of breath-freshener and coffee.

In his car soon afterwards, heading to Knoxland, giving lifts to four others. They didn't say much, windows down to stop the Saab misting up. Passing darkened shops, then bungalows where a few bedroom lights were just starting to come on. A convoy of cars, not

321

all of them unmarked. Taxi-drivers staring at them, knowing something was up. The birds would be awake, but there was no sound of them as the cars pulled to a stop in Knoxland.

Only car doors opening and closing – quietly.

Whispers and gestures, a few muffled coughs. Someone spat on the ground. An inquisitive dog was shooed away before it could start barking.

Shoes moving up the stairwell, making a sound like sandpaper.

More gestures, whispers. Taking up position all along the third floor.

The floor where so few doors had been answered, first time the police had come calling.

They stood and waited, three to each door. Watches were checked: quarter to six, they'd start pounding and shouting.

Thirty seconds to go.

And then the stairwell door had opened, a foreign boy standing there wearing a long smock over his trousers, a grocery bag in one hand. The bag falling, milk bursting from it. One of the officers was just placing a finger to his lips as the boy filled his lungs.

Let out an almighty cry.

Doors pummelled, letter-boxes rattled. The boy lifted from his feet and carried downstairs. The cop who carried him left milky footprints.

Doors answered; others shoulder-charged. Revealing:

Domestic scenes – families gathered around the breakfast table.

Living rooms where people lay in sleeping-bags, or beneath blankets. As many as seven or eight to a room, sometimes spilling into the hallway.

Kids screaming in terror, wide-eyed. Mothers reaching for them. Young men pulling on clothes, or gripping the edges of their sleeping-bags, fearful.

Elders remonstrating in a clatter of languages, hands busy as if in mime. Grandparents inured to this new humiliation, half-blind without their spectacles but determined to muster whatever dignity the situation would allow.

Storey moving from room to room, flat to flat. He'd brought three interpreters, not nearly enough. One of the officers handed him a sheet of paper torn from a wall. Storey passed it on to Rebus. It looked like a work roster – addresses of food-processing factories. A roll-call of surnames with the shifts they'd be filling. Rebus passed it back. He was interested in the oversized polythene bags in one hallway, filled with headbands and wands. He switched one of the headbands on, its small twin spheres flashing red. He looked around but couldn't see the kid from Lothian Road, the one who'd been selling the same sort of stuff. In the kitchen, a sink full of decomposing roses, their buds still tightly closed.

The translators were holding up surveillance photos of Bullen and Hill, asking people to identify them. Shakes of the head and pointed fingers, but a few nods, too. One man – he looked Chinese to Rebus – was shouting in fractured English:

'We pay much money come here . . . much money! Work hard . . . send money home. Work we want to! Work we want to!'

A friend snapped back at him in their native language. This friend's eyes locked on Rebus, and Rebus nodded slowly, knowing the gist of his message.

Save your breath.

They're not interested.

Not interested in us . . . not for who we are.

This man started walking towards Rebus, but Rebus shook his head, gestured towards Felix Storey. The man stopped in front of Storey. The only way he could get his attention was to tug on the sleeve of his jacket, something the man probably hadn't done since he was a kid.

Storey glared at him, but the man ignored this.

'Stuart Bullen,' he said. 'Peter Hill.' He knew he had Storey's attention now. 'These are the men you want.'

'Already in custody,' the Immigration man assured him.

'That is good,' the man said quietly. 'And you have found the ones they murdered?'

Storey looked to Rebus, then back to the man.

'Would you mind repeating that?' he asked.

The man's name was Min Tan and he was from a village in central China. He sat in the back of Rebus's car, Storey alongside him, Rebus in the driver's seat.

They were parked outside a bakery on Gorgie Road. Min Tan took loud sips from a beaker of sugary black tea. Rebus had already ditched his own drink. It wasn't until he'd lifted the weak grey coffee to his lips that he'd remembered: this was the same place he'd bought the undrinkable coffee the afternoon Stef Yurgii's body had been found. Yet the bakery was doing good business: commuters at the nearby bus-stop all seemed to be holding beakers to their faces. Others munched on breakfast rolls of scrambled egg and sausage.

Storey had taken a break from the questioning, so he could hold another conversation with whoever was on the other end of his mobile phone.

Storey had a problem: Edinburgh's police stations could not accommodate the immigrants from Knoxland. There were too many of them, and not nearly enough cells. He'd tried asking the courts, but they had accommodation problems of their own. For now, the immigrants were being held in their flats, the third floor of Stevenson House blocked off to visitors. But now manpower was the issue: the officers Storey had commandeered were needed for their day-to-day duties. They couldn't play at being glorified guards. At the same time, Storey was in no doubt that without adequate provision, there was nothing to stop the illegals in Stevenson House charging past any skeleton crew and making a run to freedom.

He'd called his superiors in London and elsewhere, requested aid from Customs and Excise.

'Don't tell me there aren't a few VAT inspectors twiddling their thumbs,' Rebus had heard him say. Meaning the man was clutching at straws. Rebus wanted to ask why they couldn't just let the poor buggers go. He'd seen the fatigue on those faces. They'd been working so hard, it had drilled its way into the marrow of their bones. Storey would argue that most – maybe even all – had entered the country illegally, or had overstayed their visas and permits. They were criminals, but it was obvious to Rebus that they were victims, too. Min Tan had been talking about the grinding poverty of the life he'd left in the province, of his 'duty' to send money home.

Duty – not a word Rebus came across too often.

Rebus had offered the man some food from the bakery, but he'd wrinkled his nose, not being quite desperate enough to partake of the local cuisine. Storey, too, had passed, leaving Rebus to purchase a reheated bridie, most of which now lay in the gutter alongside the beaker of coffee.

Storey snapped shut his mobile with a growl. Min Tan was pretending to concentrate on his tea, but Rebus had no such scruples.

'You could always concede defeat,' he offered.

Storey's narrowed eyes filled the rearview mirror. Then he turned his attention to the man beside him.

'So we're talking about more than one victim?' he asked.

Min Tan nodded and held up two fingers.

'Two?' Storey coaxed.

'At least two,' Min Tan said. He seemed to shiver, and took another sip of tea. Rebus realised that the clothes the Chinaman was wearing weren't quite enough to ward off the morning chill. He turned on the ignition and adjusted the heat.

'We going somewhere?' Storey snapped.

'Can't sit in the car all day,' Rebus replied. 'Not without catching our death.'

'Two deaths,' Min Tan stressed, misunderstanding Rebus's words.

'One of them was the Kurd?' Rebus asked. 'Stef Yurgii?'

The Chinaman frowned. 'Who?'

'The man who was stabbed. He was one of your lot, wasn't he?' Rebus had turned in his seat, but Min Tan was shaking his head.

'I do not know this person.'

Which served Rebus right for jumping to conclusions. 'Peter Hill and Stuart Bullen, they didn't kill Stef Yurgii?'

'I tell you, I do not know this man!' Min Tan's voice had risen.

'You saw them kill two people,' Storey interrupted. Another shake of the head. 'But you just said you did . . .'

'Everyone knows about it – we all are told about it.'

'About what?' Rebus persisted.

'The two . . .' Words seemed to fail Min Tan. 'Two bodies . . . you know, after they die.' He pinched the skin of the arm which held his beaker. 'It all goes, none left.'

'No skin left?' Rebus guessed. 'Bodies with no skin. You mean skeletons?'

Min Tan wagged a finger triumphantly.

'And people talk about them?' Rebus went on.

'One time . . . man not want to work for so low pay. He was loud. He told people not to work, to go free . . .'

'And he was killed?' Storey interrupted.

'Not killed!' Min Tan cried in frustration. 'Just listen, please! He was taken to a place, and they showed him bodies with no skin. Told him this would happen to him – to everybody – unless he obeyed, did good work.'

'Two skeletons,' Rebus said quietly, talking to himself. But Min Tan had heard him.

'Mother and child,' he said, eyes widening in remembered horror. 'If they can kill mother and child – not arrested, not found out – they can do anything, kill anyone . . . anyone who disobeys!'

Rebus nodded his understanding.

Two skeletons.

Mother and child.

'You've seen these skeletons?'

Min Tan shook his head. 'Others saw. One a baby, wrapped in newspaper. They showed it in Knoxland, showed the head and hands. Then buried mother and baby in . . .' He sought the words he needed. 'Place underground . . .'

'A cellar?' Rebus suggested.

Min Tan nodded eagerly. 'Buried them there, with one of us watching. He told us the story.'

Rebus stared out through the windscreen. It made sense: using the skeletons to terrify the immigrants, keep them in fear. Stripping away the wires and screws to make them more authentic. And for a final flourish, pouring concrete over them in front of a witness, that man returning to Knoxland, spreading the story.

They can do anything, kill anyone . . . anyone who disobeys . . .

It was half an hour till opening when he knocked on the door of the Warlock.

Siobhan was with him. He'd called her from his car, after dropping Storey and Min Tan at Torphichen, the Immigration man armed with a few more questions for Bullen and the Irishman. Siobhan hadn't quite woken up, Rebus having to go over the story more than once. His central point – how many pairs of skeletons had popped up in recent months?

Her eventual answer: just the one that she could think of.

'I need to speak to Mangold anyway,' she said now, as Rebus kicked at the door of the Warlock, his polite knock having been ignored.

'Any particular reason?' he asked.

'You'll find out when I question him.'

'Thanks for sharing.' One final kick and he took a step back. 'Nobody home.'

She checked her watch. 'Cutting it fine.'

He nodded. Usually there'd be someone inside this close to opening – if only to prime the pumps and fill the till. Cleaner might have come and gone, but whoever was manning the bar should have been limbering up.

'What did you get up to last night?' Siobhan asked, trying for a conversational tone.

'Not much.'

'Not like you to refuse the offer of a lift.'

326

'I felt like walking.'

'So you said.' She folded her arms. 'Stop off at any watering-holes on route?'

'Despite what you think, I can go whole hours at a time without a drink.' He busied himself lighting a cigarette. 'What about you? Was it another rendezvous with Major Underpants?' She stared at him, and he smiled. 'Nicknames have a habit of travelling.'

'Maybe so, but you've got it wrong – it's Captain, not Major.'

Rebus shook his head. 'Might've been that originally, but I can assure you it's Major now. Funny things, nicknames . . .' He walked to the top of Fleshmarket Close, blew smoke down it, then noticed something. Walked to the cellar door.

The cellar door standing ajar.

Pushed it open with his fist and stepped inside, Siobhan following.

Ray Mangold was staring at one of the interior walls, hands in his pockets, lost in thought. He was on his own, surrounded by the half-finished building work. The concrete floor had been lifted in its entirety. The rubble had gone, but there was still plenty of dust in the air.

'Mr Mangold?' Rebus said.

Spell broken, Mangold swivelled his head. 'Oh, it's you,' he said, sounding less than thrilled.

'Nice bruises,' Rebus commented.

'Healing,' Mangold said, touching his cheek.

'How did you get them?'

'Like I told your colleague . . .' Mangold nodded towards Siobhan. 'I had a bust-up with a punter.'

'Who won?'

'He won't be drinking in the Warlock again, that's for sure.'

'Sorry if we're interrupting anything,' Siobhan said.

Mangold shook his head. 'Just trying to think what this'll look like when it's finished.'

'Tourists will lap it up,' Rebus told him.

Mangold smiled. 'That's what I'm hoping.' He removed his hands from his pockets, clapped them together. 'So what can I do to help you today?'

'Those skeletons . . .' Rebus gestured towards the patch of earth where the find had been made.

'I can't believe you're still wasting your time . . .'

'We're not,' Rebus broke in. He was standing next to a wheelbarrow, presumably belonging to the builder, Joe Evans. There was a

327

toolbox lying open inside it, a hammer and stone-chisel uppermost. Rebus lifted the stone-chisel, impressed with its weight. 'Do you know a man called Stuart Bullen?'

Mangold considered his answer. 'I know *of* him. Rab Bullen's son.'

'That's right.'

'I think he owns some sort of strip joint . . .'

'The Nook.'

Mangold nodded slowly. 'That's it . . .'

Rebus let the chisel clatter back into the barrow. 'He also does a nice sideline in slavery, Mr Mangold.'

'Slavery?'

'Illegal immigrants. He puts them to work, probably holds back a decent cut for himself. Looks like he might be providing them with new identities, too.'

'Christ.' Mangold looked from Rebus to Siobhan and back again. 'Hang on, though . . . what's this got to do with me?'

'When one of the immigrants started acting up, Bullen decided to scare him off. Showed him a couple of skeletons being buried in a cellar.'

Mangold's eyes widened. 'The ones Evans dug up?'

Rebus just shrugged, eyes boring into Mangold's. 'Cellar door always kept locked, Mr Mangold?'

'Look, I told you right at the start, that concrete was laid before I came here.'

Rebus offered another shrug. 'We've only got your word for that, seeing how you've not been able to supply any paperwork.'

'Maybe I could take another look.'

'Maybe you could. Careful, though: the brain-boxes at the police lab are dab hands . . . they can pinpoint how far back something was written or typed – can you believe that?'

Mangold nodded to show that he could. 'I'm not saying I *will* find anything . . .'

'But you'll take another look, and we appreciate that.' Rebus lifted the chisel again. 'And you don't know Stuart Bullen . . . never met him?'

Mangold shook his head vigorously. Rebus let the silence lie between them, then turned towards Siobhan, signalling her turn to enter the ring.

'Mr Mangold,' she said, 'can I ask you about Ishbel Jardine?'

Mangold seemed nonplussed. 'What about her?'

'That sort of answers one of my questions – you do know her then?'

'Know her? No . . . I mean . . . she used to come to my club.'

'The Albatross?'

'That's right.'

'And you knew her?'

'Not really.'

'Are you telling me you remember the name of every punter who came to the Albatross?'

Rebus snorted at this, adding further to Mangold's discomfort.

'I know the name,' Mangold stumbled on, 'because of her sister. She's the one who killed herself. Look . . .' He glanced at his gold wristwatch. 'I should be upstairs . . . we're due to open in a minute.'

'Just a few more questions,' Rebus said resolutely, still holding the chisel.

'I don't know what's going on. First it's the skeletons, then it's Ishbel Jardine . . . what's any of it got to do with me?'

'Ishbel's disappeared, Mr Mangold,' Siobhan informed him. 'She used to go to your club, and now she's disappeared.'

'Hundreds of people came to the Albatross every week,' Mangold complained.

'They didn't all disappear, though, did they?'

'We know about the skeletons in your cellar,' Rebus added, letting the chisel drop again with a deafening clang, 'but what about the ones in your cupboard? Anything you want us to know, Mr Mangold?'

'Look, I've got nothing to say to you.'

'Stuart Bullen's in custody. He'll be wanting to do a deal, telling us more than we ever needed to know. What do you think he'll tell us about those skeletons?'

Mangold was making for the open doorway, passing between the two detectives as if starved of oxygen. He burst out into Fleshmarket Close and turned to face them, breathing hard.

'I have to open up,' he gasped.

'We're listening,' Rebus said.

Mangold stared at him. 'I mean I have to open the bar.'

Rebus and Siobhan emerged into daylight, Mangold turning the key in the padlock after them. They watched him march to the top of the lane and disappear around the corner.

'What do you think?' Siobhan asked.

'I think we still make a good team.'

She nodded agreement. 'He knows more than he's telling.'

329

'Just like everyone else.' Rebus shook his cigarette packet; decided he'd save the last one for later. 'So what's next?'

'Can you drop me at my flat? I need to pick up my car.'

'You can walk to Gayfield Square from your flat.'

'But I'm not going to Gayfield Square.'

'So where *are* you headed?'

She tapped the side of her nose. 'Secrets, John . . . just like everyone else.'

27

Rebus was back at Torphichen, where Felix Storey was in the midst of a heated debate with DI Shug Davidson over his urgent requirement for an office, desk and chair.

'And an outside line,' Storey added. 'I've got my own laptop.'

'We've no *desks* to spare, never mind offices,' Davidson replied.

'My desk's going free at Gayfield Square,' Rebus offered.

'I need to be *here*,' Storey insisted, pointing down at the floor.

'Far as I'm concerned, you're welcome to stay there!' Davidson spat, walking away.

'Not a bad punchline,' Rebus mused.

'Whatever happened to cooperation?' Storey asked, sounding suddenly resigned to his fate.

'Maybe he's jealous,' Rebus offered. 'All these nice results you've been getting.' Storey looked as if he was getting ready to preen. 'Yes,' Rebus went on, 'all these nice, easy results.'

Storey looked at him. 'What do you mean by that?'

Rebus shrugged. 'Nothing at all, except that you owe your mystery caller a case or two of malt, the way he's come through for you on this one.'

Storey was still staring. 'That's none of your business.'

'Isn't that what the bad guys usually tell us when there's something they don't want us to know?'

'And what is it exactly that you think I don't want you to know?' Storey's voice had thickened.

'Maybe I won't know till you tell me.'

'And why would I do a thing like that?'

Rebus gave an open smile. 'Because I'm one of the good guys?' he offered.

'I'm still not convinced of that, Detective Inspector.'

'Despite me jumping down that rabbit-hole and flushing Bullen out the other end?'

Storey gave a cool smile. 'Am I supposed to thank you for that?'

'I saved your nice, expensive suit from getting scuffed . . .'

'Not *that* expensive.'

'And I've managed to keep quiet about you and Phyllida Hawes . . .'

Storey scowled. 'DC Hawes was a member of my team.'

'And that's why the two of you were in the back of that van on a Sunday morning?'

'If you're going to start making allegations . . .'

But Rebus smiled and slapped Storey's arm with the back of his hand. 'I'm just winding you up, Felix.'

Storey took a moment to calm down, during which Rebus told him about the visit to Ray Mangold. Storey grew thoughtful.

'You think the two of them connect?'

Rebus offered another shrug. 'I'm not sure it's important. But there's something else to consider.'

'What?'

'Those flats in Stevenson House . . . they belong to the council.'

'So?'

'So what names are on the rent books?'

Storey studied him. 'Keep talking.'

'More names we get, the more ways we have of jabbing away at Bullen.'

'Which means making an approach to the council.'

Rebus nodded. 'And guess what? I know someone who can help . . .'

The two men sat in Mrs Mackenzie's office while she laid out for them the convolutions of Bob Baird's illicit empire, an empire which included, it seemed, at least three of the flats raided that morning.

'And maybe more,' Mrs Mackenzie stated. 'We've found eleven aliases so far. He's used his relatives' names, ones he seems to have picked out of the phone book, and others belonging to the recently deceased.'

'You'll be taking this to the police?' Storey asked, marvelling at Mrs Mackenzie's paperwork. It was a huge family tree, comprising sheets of copy paper sellotaped together, and covering most of her desk. Beside each name were details of its provenance.

'The wheels are already in motion,' she said. 'I just want to make sure I've done as much at this end as I can.'

Rebus gave a nod of praise, which she accepted with a reddening of the cheeks.

'Can we assume,' Storey was saying, 'that most of the flats on the third floor of Stevenson House were being sub-let by Baird?'

'I think we can,' Rebus replied.

'And can we further assume that he had full knowledge his tenants were being supplied by Stuart Bullen?'

'That would seem logical. I'd say half the estate knew what was going on – that's why the local youths didn't even dare tag the walls.'

'This Stuart Bullen,' Mrs Mackenzie said, 'he's a man people have reason to fear?'

'Don't worry, Mrs Mackenzie,' Storey assured her, 'Bullen's in custody.'

'And he won't know how busy you've been,' Rebus added, tapping the diagram.

Storey, who had been leaning over the desk, now pushed himself upright. 'Maybe time for a little chat with Baird.'

Rebus nodded his agreement.

Bob Baird had been escorted by two uniforms to Portobello police station. They'd made the journey on foot, Baird spending most of that time bellowing in outrage at the humiliation of it all.

'Which just made people notice us all the more,' one of the constables reported, with a certain amount of contentment.

'But it does mean he's likely to be in a foul temper,' his colleague warned.

Rebus and Storey looked at one another.

'Good,' they said in unison.

Baird was pacing what space there was in the cramped interview room. As the two men walked in, he opened his mouth to utter another list of grievances.

'Shut it,' Storey spat. 'The trouble you're in, I'd advise you to do absolutely nothing in this room but answer any questions we might see fit to put to you. Understood?'

Baird stared at him, then snorted. 'Bit of advice, pal – ease up on the sun lamp.'

Storey met the smile with one of his own. 'I take it that's a reference to the colour of my skin, Mr Baird? I suppose it helps to be a racist in your game.'

'And what game's that?'

Storey had reached into his jacket for his ID. 'I'm an Immigration official, Mr Baird.'

'Going to do me under Race Relations, are you?' Baird snorted again, reminding Rebus of a pig that had missed a meal. 'All for renting flats to your fellow tribesmen?'

Storey turned to Rebus. 'You told me he'd be entertaining.'

Rebus folded his arms. 'That's because he still thinks this is about diddling the council.'

Storey turned back to Baird, allowed his eyes to widen a little. 'Is that what you think, Mr Baird? Well, I'm sorry to be the bearer of bad news.'

'Is this one of those hidden-camera shows?' Baird said. 'Some comedian pops out to let me in on the joke?'

'No joke,' Storey said quietly, shaking his head. 'You let Stuart Bullen use your flats. He stashed his illegal immigrants there, when he wasn't working them like the slaves they were. I dare say you met his associate a few times – nice guy by the name of Peter Hill. Tasty connections with the Belfast paramilitaries.' Storey held up two fingers. 'Slavery and terrorism: now there's a combination, eh? And that's before I get to the people-smuggling – all those fake passports and National Health cards we found in Bullen's possession.' Storey held up a third finger, close to Baird's face. 'So we get to charge you with conspiracy . . . not just to defraud the local council and the honest, hard-working taxpayer, but smuggling, slavery, identity theft . . . sky's the limit really. Nothing Her Majesty's lawyers like better than a nice, tight-fitting conspiracy, so if I were you I'd try to retain that sense of humour – you're going to need it in jail.' Storey dropped his hand. 'Mind you . . . ten, twelve years, the joke might have worn a bit thin.'

There was silence in the room; so quiet, Rebus could hear a watch ticking. He reckoned it was Storey's: probably a nice model, classy without being showy. It would do the job asked of it, and do it with precision.

A bit, Rebus was forced to admit, like its owner.

The colour had disappeared completely from Baird's face. He looked calm enough on the surface, but Rebus knew strategic damage had been done. His jaw was set, lips pursed in thought. He'd been in situations before; knew his next few decisions might be the most crucial of his life.

Ten, twelve years, Storey had said. No way would Baird serve anything like that, even with guilty verdicts ringing in his ears.

But Storey had pitched it just right: if he'd said fifteen-to-twenty, chances were Baird would have known he was lying and called his bluff. Or would have decided he might as well take the fall, tell them nothing.

A man with nothing to lose.

But ten-to-twelve . . . Baird would be doing the calculations. Say Storey was exaggerating for effect, maybe meaning he'd actually get seven-to-nine. He'd still have to serve four or five, maybe even a little more. Years became all the more precious when you got to Baird's age. It had been explained to Rebus once: the great cure for repeat offenders was the ageing process. You didn't want to die in prison, wanted to be around for kids and grandkids, doing things you'd always wanted to do . . .

All of this Rebus thought he could read in Baird's deeply lined face.

And then, finally, the man blinked a few times, stared up at the ceiling and sighed.

'Ask me your questions,' he said.

So they asked.

'Let's be clear on this,' Rebus said. 'You were allowing Stuart Bullen to use some of your flats?'

'Correct.'

'Did you know what he was doing with them?'

'I had an inkling.'

'How did it start?'

'He came to see me. He already knew I was sub-letting to needy minorities.' As he uttered these last two words, Baird's gaze shifted to Felix Storey.

'How did he know?'

Baird shrugged. 'Maybe Peter Hill told him. Hill was hanging around Knoxland, wheeling and dealing – mostly the latter. Chances are, he'd started hearing things.'

'And you were ready to oblige?'

Baird smiled sourly. 'I knew Stu's old man. I'd already met Stu a few times – funerals and what have you. He's not the sort of fellow you want to say no to.' Baird lifted the mug to his lips, smacked them afterwards as if savouring the taste. Rebus had made tea for all three of them, poaching from the station's tiny kitchenette. Only two tea-bags remaining in the box: he'd squeezed the life out of them and into three mugs.

'How well did you know Rab Bullen?' Rebus asked.

'Not that well. I was a bit of a wheeler-dealer myself back then. Thought Glasgow might have something to offer . . . Rab soon put me right. He was pleasant enough – like any other businessman. He just explained the way the city was carved up, and that there was no room for a new boy.' Baird paused. 'Shouldn't you be taping this or something?'

Storey leaned forward in his chair, hands pressed together. 'This is by way of a preliminary interview.'

'Meaning there'll be others?'

Storey nodded slowly. 'And those will be recorded, videotaped. For now, you might say we're feeling our way.'

'Fair enough.'

Rebus had taken out a fresh pack of cigarettes and was offering it round. Storey shook his head, but Baird accepted. There were No Smoking signs on three of the four walls. Baird blew smoke towards one of them.

'We all break a few rules from time to time, eh?'

Rebus ignored this, asked a question of his own instead. 'Did you know that Stuart Bullen was part of a people-smuggling operation?'

Baird shook his head emphatically.

'I find that hard to believe,' Storey said.

'Doesn't alter the truth.'

'Then where exactly did you think all these immigrants were coming from?'

Baird shrugged. 'Refugees . . . asylum-seekers . . . it wasn't really my business to ask.'

'You weren't curious?'

'Isn't that what killed the cat?'

'Even so . . .'

Baird just shrugged again, examining the tip of his cigarette. Rebus broke the silence with another question.

'You knew he was using all those people as illegal workers?'

'I couldn't have told you if they were illegal or not . . .'

'They were breaking their backs for him.'

'So why didn't they leave?'

'You've said yourself – *you* were scared of him . . . what makes you think they weren't?'

'That's a point.'

'We've got evidence of intimidation.'

'Could be he's a product of his genes.' Baird flicked ash on to the floor.

'Like father like son?' Felix Storey added.

Rebus stood up and walked around Baird's chair, stopping and leaning down, so his face was next to the other man's shoulder.

'You say you didn't know he was a people-smuggler?'

'No.'

'Well, now that we've enlightened you, what do you think?'

'How do you mean?'

'Are you surprised?'

Baird thought for a moment. 'I suppose I am.'

'And why's that?'

'I don't know . . . maybe it's that Stu never gave any inkling that he could play on that size of stage.'

'He's essentially small-time?' Rebus offered.

Baird thought for another moment, and then nodded. 'People-smuggling . . . you're playing for high stakes, right?'

'Right,' Felix Storey agreed. 'And maybe that's why Bullen did it – to prove he was a match for his old man.'

This gave Baird pause, and Rebus could see he was thinking of his own son Gareth: fathers and sons with things to prove . . .

'Let's just get this clear,' Rebus said, moving around the chair again so that he was eye-to-eye with Baird. 'You didn't know anything about the fake IDs, and it surprises you that Bullen was a big enough player to get involved in something like that?'

Baird nodded, keeping eye contact with Rebus.

Now Felix Storey rose to his feet. 'Well, that's what he was doing, whether we like it or not . . .' He held out a hand, meaning for Baird to shake it, which entailed Baird standing up.

'You're letting me go?' Baird asked.

'As long as you promise not to do a runner. We'll call you – might be in a few days. You'll do another interview, taped this time.'

Baird just nodded, letting go of Storey's hand. He looked at Rebus, whose hands were staying in his pockets – no handshake on offer there.

'Can you see yourself out?' Storey asked.

Baird nodded and turned the door-handle, hardly able to believe his luck. Rebus waited till the door was closed again.

'What makes you think he won't run?' he hissed, not wanting Baird to hear.

'Gut feeling.'

'And if you're wrong?'

'He's not given us anything we don't already have.'

'He's a piece of the jigsaw.'

'Maybe so, John, but if he is, he's a bit of sky or cloud – I can see the picture clearly enough without him.'

'The whole picture?'

Storey's face hardened. 'You don't think I'm using up enough Edinburgh police cells as it is?' He switched on his mobile, started checking for messages.

'Look,' Rebus argued, 'you've been working this case for a while, right?'

'Right.' Storey was studying his phone's tiny screen.

'And how far back can you trace the line? Who else do you know about except Bullen?'

Storey glanced up. 'We've got a few names: an Essex-based haulier, a Turkish gang in Rotterdam . . .'

'And they definitely connect to Bullen?'

'They connect.'

'And all this is from your anonymous caller? Don't tell me that doesn't make you wonder . . .'

Storey held up a finger, asking for quiet so he could listen to a message. Rebus turned on his heels and walked to the far wall, switched on his own phone. It started ringing almost immediately: not a message but a call.

'Hello, Caro,' he said, recognising her number.

'I just heard on the news.'

'Heard what?'

'All those people they've arrested in Knoxland . . . those poor, poor people.'

'If it's any consolation, we've arrested the bad guys, too – and we'll be keeping them behind bars long after the others have been sent on their way.'

'But on their way to where?'

Rebus glanced over at Felix Storey; no easy way to answer her question.

'John . . . ?' A split-second before she asked, he knew what her question was going to be. 'Were you there? When they kicked down the doors and rounded them all up, were you watching?'

He thought of lying, but she deserved better. 'I was there,' he said. 'It's what I do for a living, Caro.' He dropped his voice, realising that Storey's own conversation was ending. 'Did you hear me telling you we caught the people responsible?'

'There are other jobs out there, John.'

'It's what I am, Caro . . . take it or leave it.'

'You sound so angry.'

He glanced towards Storey, who was pocketing his own phone. Realised his issue was with Storey, not Caro. 'I've got to go . . . can we talk later?'

'Talk about what?'

'Whatever you like.'

'The looks on their faces? The babies crying? Can we talk about that?'

Rebus pressed the red button, folded the phone shut.

'Everything okay?' Storey asked solicitously.

'Hunky-dory, Felix.'

'Jobs like ours can play havoc . . . That night I came to your flat, I didn't sense a Mrs Rebus.'

'We'll make a detective of you yet.'

Storey smiled. 'My own wife . . . well, we stay together for the kids.'

'You don't wear a ring, though.'

Storey held up his left hand. 'That's right, I don't.'

'Does Phyllida Hawes know you're married?'

The smile disappeared, eyes narrowed. 'None of your business, John.'

'Fair enough . . . let's talk about this "Deep Throat" of yours instead.'

'What about him?'

'He seems to know a hell of a lot.'

'So?'

'You've not asked yourself what his motive is?'

'Not really.'

'And you've not asked him?'

'You want me to scare him off?' Storey folded his arms. 'Now why would you want that?'

'Stop twisting things round.'

'Know what, John? After Stuart Bullen mentioned that man Cafferty, I did a bit of background reading. You and Cafferty go back a long way.'

It was Rebus's turn to scowl. 'What are you saying?'

Storey held up his hands in apology. 'That was out of line. Tell you what . . .' He checked his watch. 'I think we deserve some lunch – my treat. Anywhere local you'd recommend?'

Rebus shook his head slowly, keeping his eyes on Storey. 'We'll drive into Leith, find something down by the shore.'

'Shame you're driving,' Storey said. 'Means I'll have to drink for both of us.'

'I dare say I could manage a glass,' Rebus assured him.

Storey held the door open, gesturing for Rebus to walk ahead of him. Rebus did so, eyes unblinking, thoughts churning. Storey had been rattled, using Cafferty to turn the tables on Rebus. What was it he was afraid of?

'Your anonymous caller,' Rebus said, almost casually, 'you ever tape your conversations with him?'

'No.'

'Any idea how he came by your number?'

'No.'

'You've no way of calling him back?'

'No.'

Rebus glanced over his shoulder at the glowering figure of the Immigration man. 'He's hardly real at all, is he, Felix?'

'Real enough,' Storey growled. 'Else we wouldn't be here.'

Rebus just shrugged.

'We've got him,' Les Young told Siobhan as she walked into Banehall Library. Roy Brinkley was on the desk, and she'd smiled at him as she passed. The murder room was buzzing, and now she knew why.

They'd caught Spider Man.

'Tell me,' she said.

'You know I sent Maxton to Barlinnie to ask about any friends Cruikshank might have made? Well, the name Mark Saunders came up.'

'Spider's-web tattoo?'

Young nodded. 'Served three years of a five for indecent assault. He got out the month before Cruikshank. Moved back to his home town.'

'Not Banehall?'

Young shook his head. 'Bo'ness. It's only ten miles north.'

'Is that where you found him?' She watched Young nod again. She couldn't help being reminded of the toy dogs she used to see on the back shelves of cars. 'And he's confessed to Cruikshank's murder?'

The nodding came to an abrupt halt.

'I suppose that was asking too much,' she admitted.

'The thing is, though,' Young argued, 'he didn't come forward when the story broke.'

'Meaning he has something to hide? Couldn't be he just thinks we'd try fitting him up for it . . .'

Now Young frowned. 'That's pretty much exactly the excuse he gave.'

'You've talked to him then?'

'Yes.'

'Did you ask him about the flick?'

'What about it?'

'Why he made it.'

Young folded his arms. 'He has this idea he's going to be some kind of porn baron, selling over the internet.'

'He obviously did a lot of thinking in the Bar-L.'

'That's where he studied computers, web design . . .'

'Nice to see we're offering such useful skills to our sex offenders.'

Young's shoulders slumped a little. 'You don't think he did it?'

'Give me a motive and ask me again.'

'Guys like that . . . they fall out all the time.'

'I fall out with my mum every time I talk to her on the phone – I don't think I'm going to go for her with a hammer . . .'

Young noticed the look which suddenly came to her face. 'What's wrong?' he asked.

'Nothing,' she lied. 'Where's Saunders being held?'

'Livingston. I've got another session with him in an hour or so, if you fancy sitting in . . .'

But Siobhan was shaking her head. 'Few things I need to do.'

Young was studying his shoes. 'Maybe we can hook up later then?'

'Maybe,' she allowed.

He made to move off, but seemed to think of something. 'We're interviewing the Jardines, too.'

'When?'

'This afternoon.' He shrugged. 'Can't be helped, Siobhan.'

'I know – you're doing your job. But go easy on them.'

'Don't worry, my strongarm days are behind me.' He seemed pleased by the smile he received. 'And those names you gave us – Tracy Jardine's friends – we're finally getting round to them, too.'

Meaning Susie . . .

Angie . . .

Janet Eylot . . .

Janine Harrison . . .

'You think there's a cover-up?' she asked.

'Let's just say Banehall's not exactly been cooperative.'

'They're letting us use their library.'

It was Les Young's turn to smile. 'That's true.'

341

'Funny,' Siobhan said, 'Donny Cruikshank died in a town full of enemies, and the one person we've zoned in on is just about the only friend he had.'

Young shrugged. 'You've seen it yourself, Siobhan – when friends fall out, it can be uglier than any vendetta.'

'That's true,' she said quietly, nodding to herself.

Les Young was playing with his watch. 'Got to get going,' he told her.

'Me too, Les. Good luck with Spider Man. I hope he spills his guts.'

He was standing in front of her. 'But you wouldn't bank on it?'

She smiled again and shook her head. 'Doesn't mean it won't happen.'

Mollified, he gave her a wink and headed for the door. She waited until she heard a car starting outside, then headed for the reception desk, where Roy Brinkley was sitting at his computer screen, checking a title's availability for one of his customers. The woman was tiny and frail-looking, hands gripping her walking-frame, head twitching slightly. She turned towards Siobhan and gave a beaming smile.

'*Cop Hater*,' Brinkley was saying, 'that's the one you want, Mrs Shields. I can order it by inter-library loan.'

Mrs Shields nodded that this was satisfactory. She started shuffling away.

'I'll give you a bell when it comes in,' Brinkley called after her. Then, to Siobhan: 'One of my regulars.'

'And she hates cops?'

'It's Ed McBain – Mrs Shields likes the hard-boiled stuff.' He finished typing in the request, adding a flourish to his final keystroke. 'Was there something you wanted?' he asked, standing up.

'I've noticed you keep newspapers,' Siobhan said, nodding towards the circular table where four pensioners were swapping tabloid sections between them.

'We get most of the dailies, plus some magazines.'

'And when you're finished with them?'

'We chuck them.' He saw the look on her face. 'Some of the bigger libraries have room to keep them.'

'But not you?'

He shook his head. 'Something you were looking for?'

'An *Evening News* from last week.'

'Then you're in luck,' he said, emerging from behind his desk. 'Follow me.'

He led her to a locked door. The sign said 'Staff Only'. Brinkley punched numbers into the keypad and pushed the door open. It led to a small staff room with kitchen sink, kettle and microwave. Another door led to a toilet cubicle, but Brinkley went to the door next to it, turning the handle.

'Storage,' he said.

It was a place where old books went to die – shelves of them, some missing their covers or with loose pages seeping from within.

'Every now and again we try to flog them off,' he explained. 'If that doesn't work, there are charity shops. But then there are some that even the charities don't want.' He opened one to show Siobhan that the last few pages had been torn out. 'Those we recycle, along with old magazines and papers.' He tapped his shoe against a bulging carrier-bag. There were others next to it, filled with newsprint. 'As luck would have it, our recycling run's tomorrow.'

'You're sure "luck" is the right word?' Siobhan said sceptically. 'I don't suppose you've any idea which of these bags might hold last week's papers?'

'You're the detective.' The faint sound of a buzzer came from outside: a customer was waiting at Brinkley's desk. 'I'll leave you to it,' he said with a smile.

'Thanks.' Siobhan stood there, hands on hips, and took a deep breath. The air was musty, and she considered her alternatives. There were a few, but they all involved a drive back into Edinburgh, after which she'd just have to come back out to Banehall.

Decided, she crouched down and pulled a paper from the first bag, checking the date. Kept it out and tried another from further back. Kept that one out, too, and tried another. Same procedure with the second and third bags. In the third, she found papers from a fortnight back, so she cleared a space and pulled out the whole lot, sifting through them. She usually took an *Evening News* home with her at night, sometimes flicking through it over the next morning's breakfast. It was a good way to find out what the councillors and politicians were up to. But now the recent headlines seemed stale to her. Most of them she couldn't recall from first time around. Finally she found what she was looking for and tore the entire page out, folding it and sliding it into her pocket. The papers wouldn't all fit back in the bag, but she did her best. Then stopped

343

at the sink for a mug of cold water. Making to leave, she gave Brinkley the thumbs-up, and headed to her car.

Really, it was walking distance to the Salon, but she was in a hurry. She double-parked, knowing she wouldn't be long. Went to push the door open, but it wouldn't budge. She peered through the glass: nobody home. The opening hours were posted on a sign behind the window. Closed Wednesday and Sunday. But this was Tuesday. And then she saw another sign, hastily hand-written on a paper bag. It had been stuck to the window but had come loose and now lay on the floor – 'Closed due to un4seen'. The next word had started out as 'circumstances', but the spelling had proved a problem to the writer, who'd crossed it out, leaving the message unfinished.

Siobhan cursed herself. Hadn't Les Young himself told her? They were being interviewed. Officially interviewed. Meaning a trip to Livingston. She got back in her car and headed that way.

Traffic was light and it didn't take long. Soon, she was finding a parking spot outside F Division HQ. Went inside and asked the Desk Sergeant about the Cruikshank interviews. He pointed her in the right direction. She knocked on the door of the interview room, pushed it open. Les Young and another CID suit were inside. Across the table from them sat a man covered in tattoos.

'Sorry,' Siobhan apologised, cursing once more beneath her breath. She waited in the corridor a moment to see if Young would emerge, wondering what she was up to. He didn't. She released the breath she'd been holding and tried the next door along. Two more suits looked up at her, frowning at the intrusion.

'Sorry to disturb you,' Siobhan said, walking in. Angie was looking up at her. 'Just wondered if anyone knew where I could find Susie?'

'Waiting room,' one of the suits said.

Siobhan gave Angie a reassuring smile and made her exit. Third door lucky, she was thinking.

And she was right. Susie was sitting with one leg crossed over the other, filing her nails and chewing gum. She was nodding at something Janet Eylot was telling her. The two women were alone, no sign of Janine Harrison. Siobhan saw Les Young's reasoning – bring them together, get them talking, maybe nervous. No one felt entirely at ease in a police station. Janet Eylot looked particularly twitchy. Siobhan remembered the wine bottles in her fridge. Janet probably wouldn't say no to a drink right this minute, something to take the edge off . . .

'Hello there,' Siobhan said. 'Susie, mind if I have a word?'

Eylot's face fell further. Perhaps she was wondering why she alone was being excluded, why the others were all talking to the police.

'Won't be a minute,' Siobhan assured her. Not that Susie was in a hurry to leave. First, she had to open her leopard-spot shoulder bag, take out her make-up bag, and tuck the nail-file back beneath its little elasticated band. Only then did she stand up and follow Siobhan into the corridor.

'My turn for the inquisition?' she said.

'Not quite.' Siobhan was unfolding the sheet of newspaper. She held it up in front of Susie. 'Recognise him?' she asked.

It was the photo accompanying the Fleshmarket Close story: Ray Mangold in front of his pub, arms folded and smiling genially, Judith Lennox next to him.

'He looks like . . .' Susie had stopped chewing her gum.

'Yes?'

'The one who used to pick up Ishbel.'

'Any idea who he is?'

Susie shook her head.

'He used to run the Albatross nightclub,' Siobhan prompted.

'We went there a few times.' Susie studied the photo more closely. 'Yes, now you come to mention it . . .'

'Ishbel's mystery boyfriend?'

Susie was nodding. 'Might be.'

'Only "might"?'

'I told you, I never really got a good look at him. But this is close . . . might well be him.' She nodded slowly to herself. 'And you know the funny thing?'

'What?'

Susie pointed at the headline. 'I saw this when it came out, but it never dawned on me. I mean, it's just a picture, isn't it? You never think . . .'

'No, Susie, you never do,' Siobhan said, folding the page closed. 'You never do.'

'This interview and everything,' Susie was saying, dropping her voice a little, 'do you reckon we're in trouble?'

'For what? You didn't gang up and kill Donny Cruikshank, did you?'

Susie screwed up her face in answer. 'But that stuff we wrote in the toilets . . . that's vandalism, isn't it?'

'From what I saw of the Bane, Susie, a decent lawyer would

345

argue it was interior design.' Siobhan waited till Susie smiled. 'So don't worry about it . . . any of you. Okay?'

'Okay.'

'And make sure you tell Janet.'

Susie studied Siobhan's face. 'You've noticed then?'

'Looks to me like she needs her friends right now.'

'Always has done,' Susie said, regret creeping into her voice.

'Do your best for her then, eh?' Siobhan touched Susie on the arm, watched as she nodded, then gave a smile and turned to leave.

'Next time you need a restyle, it's on the house,' Susie called to her.

'Just the kind of bribe I'm open to,' Siobhan called back, giving a little wave.

28

She found a parking space on Cockburn Street, and walked up Fleshmarket Close, turning left on to the High Street and left again into the Warlock. The clientele was mixed: workmen on a break; business types poring over the daily papers; tourists busy with maps and guidebooks.

'He's not here,' the barman informed her. 'Hang around twenty minutes, he might be back.'

She nodded, ordered a soft drink. Made to pay for it but he shook his head. She paid anyway – some people she'd rather not owe a favour to. He shrugged and pushed the coins into a charity tin.

She rested on one of the high stools at the bar, took a sip of the ice-cold drink. 'So where is he, do you know?'

'Just out somewhere.'

Siobhan took another sip. 'He's got a car, right?' The barman stared at her. 'Don't worry, I'm not fishing,' she told him. 'It's just that parking's a nightmare round here. I was wondering how he managed.'

'Know the lock-ups on Market Street?'

She started to shake her head, but then nodded instead. 'All those arch-shaped doors in the wall?'

'They're garages. He's got one of those. Christ knows how much it cost him.'

'So he keeps his car there?'

'Parks it and walks here – only exercise I've ever known him take . . .'

Siobhan was already heading for the door.

Market Street faced the main railway line south from Waverley Station. Behind it, Jeffrey Street curved steeply towards the

Canongate. The lock-ups sat in a row at pavement level, tapering in size depending on Jeffrey Street's incline. Some were too small to fit a car inside, all but one were padlocked shut. Siobhan arrived just as Ray Mangold was pulling his own doors closed.

'Nice bit of kit,' she said. It took him a moment to place her, then his eyes followed hers to the red Jaguar convertible.

'I like it,' he said.

'I've always wondered about these places,' Siobhan went on, studying the lock-up's arched brick roof. 'They're great, aren't they?'

Mangold's eyes were on her. 'Who told you I owned one?'

She smiled at him. 'I'm a detective, Mr Mangold.' She was walking around the car.

'You won't find anything,' he snapped.

'What is it you think I'm looking for?' He was right, of course: she was taking in every inch of the interior.

'Christ knows . . . more bloody skeletons maybe.'

'This isn't about skeletons, Mr Mangold.'

'No?'

She shook her head. 'It's Ishbel I'm wondering about.' She stopped in front of him. 'I'm wondering what you've done with her.'

'I don't know what you mean.'

'How did you get those bruises?'

'I've already told you . . .'

'Any witnesses? As far as I recall, when I asked your barman he said he wasn't involved. Maybe an hour or two in an interview room would help him tell the truth.'

'Look . . .'

'No, you look!' She'd straightened her back so that she was barely an inch shorter than him. The doors were still a few feet ajar, a passer-by pausing for a moment to take in the argument. Siobhan ignored him. 'You knew Ishbel from the Albatross,' she told Mangold. 'You started seeing her, picked her up a few times from work. I've got a witness who saw you. I dare say if I go showing photos of you and your car around Banehall, a few more memories would be jogged. Now Ishbel's gone missing, and you've got bruises on your face.'

'You think I've done something to her?' He'd reached for the doors, was about to pull them shut. But Siobhan couldn't have that. She kicked one of them, so it swung wide open. A tour bus was rumbling past, the passengers staring. Siobhan gave them a wave and turned to Mangold.

'Plenty of witnesses,' she warned him.

His eyes widened further. 'Christ . . . look . . .'

'I'm listening.'

'I haven't done *anything* to Ishbel!'

'So prove it.' Siobhan folded her arms. 'Tell me what's happened to her.'

'Nothing's happened to her!'

'You know where she is?'

Mangold looked at her, lips clamped shut, jaw moving from side to side. When he finally spoke, it was like an explosion.

'Yes, all right, I know where she is.'

'And where's that?'

'She's fine . . . she's alive and well.'

'And not answering her mobile.'

'Because it would only be her mum and dad.' Now that he'd spoken, it was as if a weight had been lifted from him. He leaned back against the Jaguar's front wheel-arch. 'They're the reason she left in the first place.'

'So prove it – show me where she is.'

He looked at his watch. 'She's probably on a train.'

'A train?'

'Coming back to Edinburgh. She's been shopping in Newcastle.'

'Newcastle?'

'Better shops, apparently, and more of them.'

'What time are you expecting her?'

He shook his head. 'Some time this afternoon. I don't know what time the trains get in.'

Siobhan stared at him. 'No, but *I* do.' She took her phone out and called Gayfield CID. Phyllida Hawes answered. 'Phyl, it's Siobhan. Is Col there? Put him on, will you?' She waited a moment, her gaze still on Mangold. Then: 'Col? It's Siobhan. Listen, you're the man with the plan . . . What time do the trains from Newcastle arrive . . . ?'

Rebus sat in the CID office at Torphichen and stared once more at the sheets of paper on the desk in front of him.

They represented a thorough job. The names from the roster in Peter Hill's car had been checked against those arrested on the beach at Cramond, then cross-checked against the residents of the flats on the third floor of Stevenson House. The office itself was quiet. With the interviews finished, vans had headed off towards Whitemire, bearing a cargo of fresh inmates. As far as Rebus knew,

Whitemire had been near capacity as it was – how they would cope with this influx he could only imagine. As Storey himself had put it:

'They're a private company. If there's profit in it, they'll manage.'

Felix Storey had not compiled the list on Rebus's desk. Felix Storey hadn't paid much attention to it when it had been presented to him. He was already talking about heading back down to London. Other cases crying out for his attention. He would return from time to time, of course, to oversee the prosecution of Stuart Bullen.

In his own words, he would 'stay in the loop'.

Rebus's comment: 'Like a hamster on its wheel.'

He looked up now as Rat-Arse Reynolds came into the room, looking around as though seeking someone. He was carrying a brown paper bag, and seemed pleased with himself.

'Can I help you, Charlie?' Rebus asked.

Reynolds grinned. 'Got a going-away present for your pal.' He lifted a bunch of bananas from the bag. 'Trying to figure the best place to leave them.'

'Because you've not got the guts to do it to his face?' Rebus had risen slowly to his feet.

'Just a bit of a laugh, John.'

'For you maybe. Something tells me Felix Storey won't be quite so easy to please.'

'That's true, actually.' The speaker was Storey himself. As he came into the room he was checking the knot in his tie, smoothing it down against his shirt front.

Reynolds slid the bananas back into their bag, clutching it to his chest.

'Those for me?' Storey asked.

'No,' Reynolds said.

Storey got right into his face. 'I'm black, therefore I'm a monkey – that's your logic, is it?'

'No.'

Storey had started opening the bag. 'As it happens, I like a nice banana ... but these look past it to me. A bit like yourself, Reynolds: going rancid.' He closed the bag again. 'Now off you go and try playing detective for a change. Here's your challenge – to find out what everyone around here calls *you* behind your back.' Storey patted Reynolds's left cheek, then stood with arms folded to indicate that he was dismissed.

After he'd gone, Storey turned to Rebus and winked.

'Tell you another funny thing,' Rebus said.

'I'm always up for a laugh.'

'This is more funny-peculiar than funny-ha-ha.'

'What is?'

Rebus tapped one of the sheets of paper on his desk. 'Some of the names, we don't have bodies for.'

'Maybe they heard us coming and did a runner.'

'Maybe.'

Storey rested his backside against the edge of the desk. 'Could be they were working a shift when the raid went down. If they got wind of it, they're not likely to turn up in Knoxland, are they?'

'No,' Rebus agreed. 'Chinese-looking names, most of them ... And one African. Chantal Rendille.'

'Rendille? You think that sounds African?' Storey frowned, craned his neck to study the paperwork. 'Chantal's a French name, isn't it?'

'French is the national language of Senegal,' Rebus explained.

'Your elusive witness?'

'That's what I'm wondering. I might show it to Kate.'

'Who's Kate?'

'A student from Senegal. There's something I need to ask her anyway ...'

Storey eased himself upright from the desk. 'Best of luck then.'

'Hang on,' Rebus said, 'there's something else.'

Storey let out a sigh. 'And what's that?'

Rebus tapped another of the sheets. 'Whoever did this went the extra yard.'

'Oh yes?'

Rebus nodded. 'Every single one we interviewed, they were asked for an address prior to Knoxland.' Rebus looked up, but Storey just shrugged. 'Some of them gave Whitemire.'

Now he had Storey's attention. 'What?'

'Seems they were bailed.'

'Bailed by who?'

'A variety of names, probably all of them fake. Fake contact addresses, too.'

'Bullen?' Storey guessed.

'That's what I'm thinking. It's perfect – he bails them out, puts them to work. Any of them complain, Whitemire's hanging over them like a noose. And if that doesn't work, he's always got the skeletons.'

Storey was nodding slowly. 'Makes sense.'

'I think we need to talk to someone at Whitemire.'

'To what end?'

Rebus shrugged. 'Lot easier to pull something like this off with a friend . . . how can I put it?' Rebus pretended to search for the phrase. 'In the loop?' he suggested at last.

Storey just glared at him. 'Maybe you're right,' he conceded. 'So who is it we need to talk to?'

'Man called Alan Traynor. But before we get started with all that . . .'

'There's more?'

'Just a little bit.' Rebus's eyes were still on the sheets of paper. He'd used a pen to draw lines connecting some of the names, nationalities and places. 'The people we found in Stevenson House – and the ones on the beach for that matter . . .'

'What about them?'

'Some came from Whitemire. Others hold expired visas, or the wrong kind . . .'

'Yes?'

Rebus shrugged. 'A few don't have any paperwork at all . . . leaving just a tiny handful who seem to've arrived here on the back of a lorry. A tiny handful, Felix, and no fake passports or other IDs.'

'So?'

'So where's this vast smuggling operation gone to? Bullen's this master criminal with a safe full of dodgy documents. How come nothing's turned up outside his office?'

'Could be he'd only just received a fresh consignment from his friends in London.'

'London?' Rebus frowned. 'You didn't tell me he had friends in London.'

'I said Essex, didn't I? Same thing essentially.'

'I'll take your word for it.'

'So are we going to visit Whitemire or what?'

'One last thing . . .' Rebus held up a finger. 'Just between the two of us, is there anything you're not telling me about Stuart Bullen?'

'Such as?'

'I'll only know that when you tell me.'

'John . . . it's case closed. We got a result. What more do you want?'

'Maybe I just want to make sure I'm . . .'

Storey held a hand up in mock warning, but too late.

'In the loop,' Rebus said.

*

352

Back to Whitemire: passing Caro at the side of the road. She was talking into her mobile, didn't so much as glance up at them.

The usual security checks, gates unlocked and locked again behind them. The guard escorting them from the car park to the main building. There were half a dozen empty vans in the car park – the refugees had already arrived. Felix Storey seemed interested in everything around him.

'I'm assuming you've not been here before?' Rebus asked. Storey shook his head.

'Been to Belmarsh a few times, though – heard of it?' Rebus's turn to shake his head. 'It's in London. A proper prison – high security. That's where the asylum-seekers are kept.'

'Nice.'

'Makes this place look like Club Med.'

Waiting for them at the main door: Alan Traynor. Not bothering to hide his irritation.

'Look, whatever this is, can't it wait? We're trying to process dozens of new arrivals.'

'I know,' Felix Storey said, 'I'm the one who sent them.'

Traynor didn't seem to hear; too preoccupied with his own problems. 'We've had to commandeer the canteen ... even so, it's going to take hours.'

'In which case, sooner you're rid of us the better,' Storey suggested. Traynor let escape a theatrical sigh.

'Very well then. Follow me.'

In the outer office, they passed Janet Eylot. She looked up from her computer, eyes boring into Rebus's. She got as far as opening her mouth to say something, but Rebus spoke first.

'Mr Traynor? Sorry, but I need to use the ...' Rebus had seen a toilet in the corridor. He was pointing a thumb in its direction. 'I'll catch you up,' he said. Storey's eyes were on him, knowing he was up to something but unsure what. Rebus just gave a wink and turned on his heels. Retraced his steps through the office and into the corridor.

And waited there until he heard Traynor's door close. Popped his head into the doorway and gave a little whistle. Janet Eylot left her desk, came to meet him.

'You lot!' she hissed. Rebus put a finger to his lips and she lowered her voice. It still trembled with rage. 'I haven't had a minute's peace, not since I first spoke to you. I've had police at my door ... in my kitchen ... and now I'm just back from Livingston police headquarters and here you are again! And we've got all these new arrivals – how are we supposed to cope?'

'Easy, Janet, easy.' She was shaking, eyes red-rimmed and watery. There was a pulse fluttering behind her left eyelid. 'It'll soon be over, nothing for you to worry about.'

'Not even when I'm a suspect in a murder?'

'I'm sure you're not a suspect; it's just something that has to be done.'

'And you've not come here to talk to Mr Traynor about me? Isn't it bad enough that I had to lie to him about this morning? Told him it was a family emergency.'

'Why not just tell him the truth?'

She shook her head violently. Rebus leaned past her and peered into the office. Traynor's door was still closed. 'Look, they'll be getting suspicious . . .'

'I want to know why this is happening! Why is it happening to *me*?'

Rebus held her by both shoulders. 'Just hang in there, Janet. Not much longer.'

'I don't know how much more I can take . . .' Her voice was dying away, eyes losing focus.

'One day at a time, Janet, that's the best way,' Rebus offered, dropping his hands. He held eye contact for a moment. 'Take it one day at a time,' he repeated, walking past her, not looking back.

He knocked on Traynor's door, entered and closed it behind him.

The two men were seated. Rebus lowered himself into the empty chair.

'I've just been telling Mr Traynor about Stuart Bullen's network,' Storey said.

'And I'm incredulous,' Traynor said, throwing up his hands. Rebus ignored him, met Felix Storey's stare.

'You haven't told him?'

'Waiting for you to come back.'

'Told me what?' Traynor asked, trying for a smile. Rebus turned to him.

'Mr Traynor, quite a few of the people we detained had come from Whitemire. They'd been bailed out by Stuart Bullen.'

'Impossible.' The smile had gone. Traynor looked at both men. 'We wouldn't have let him do it.'

Storey shrugged. 'There would've been aliases, false addresses . . .'

'But we interview the applicants.'

354

'You personally, Mr Traynor?'

'Not always, no.'

'He'd have had people fronting for him, respectable-looking people.' Storey produced a sheet of paper from his pocket. 'I've got the Whitemire list here . . . easy enough for you to check it.'

Traynor took the piece of paper and studied it.

'Any of the names ring a bell?' Rebus asked.

Traynor just nodded slowly, thoughtfully. His phone rang, and he picked it up.

'Oh yes, hello,' he said into the mouthpiece. 'No, we can cope, it's just going to take a bit of time. Might mean increasing the workload for the staff . . . Yes, I'm sure I could do a spreadsheet, but it might not be for a few days . . .' He listened, eyes on his two visitors. 'Well, of course,' he said at last. 'And if we could take on some new staff, or poach a few from one of our sister facilities . . . ? Just until the new intake's bedded in, so to speak . . .'

The conversation lasted only another minute, Traynor jotting something down on a sheet of paper as he dropped the receiver back into its cradle.

'You can see what it's like,' he told Rebus and Storey.

'Organised chaos?' Storey guessed.

'Which is why I really must cut this meeting short.'

'Must you?' Rebus said.

'Yes, I really must.'

'And that wouldn't be because you're scared of what we'll say next?'

'I don't quite catch your drift, Inspector.'

'Want me to do you a spreadsheet?' Rebus gave an ice-cold smile. 'A lot easier to pull something like this off with someone on the inside.'

'What?'

'Some cash changing hands, over and above the bail money.'

'Look, I really don't like the tone you're taking.'

'Take another look at the list, Mr Traynor. Couple of Kurdish names there – Turkish Kurds, same as the Yurgiis.'

'So what?'

'When I asked you, you said no Kurds had been bailed from Whitemire.'

'Then I made a mistake.'

'Another name on the list – I think it says she's from the Ivory Coast.'

Traynor looked down at the sheet of paper. 'That appears to be what it says.'

'Ivory Coast – official language: French. But when I asked you about Africans in Whitemire, you said the same thing – none had been bailed.'

'Look, I've had a lot on my plate . . . I really don't remember saying that.'

'I think you do, and the only reason I can think for you to lie is that you had something to hide. You didn't want me to know about these people, because then I might have gone looking for them and found out about their sponsors' fake names and addresses.' It was Rebus's turn to hold his hands up. 'Unless you can think of another reason.'

Traynor slammed both hands against the desktop and rose to his feet, face darkening. 'You've got no right to make these accusations!'

'Convince me.'

'I don't think I need to.'

'I think you do, Mr Traynor,' Felix Storey said quietly. 'Because the allegations are serious, and they'll have to be investigated, which means my men going through your files, checking and cross-checking. They'll swarm all over this place. And we'll be looking at your personal life, too – bank deposits, recent purchases . . . maybe a new car or expensive holiday. Rest assured, we'll be thorough.'

Traynor had his head bowed down. When the phone started ringing again, he swept it from his desk, sending a framed photo flying at the same time. The glass smashed, dislodging the photograph: a woman smiling, arm around her young daughter. The door opened, Janet Eylot's head appearing.

'Get out!' Traynor roared.

Eylot squeaked as she retreated.

Silence in the room for a moment, broken eventually by Rebus. 'One more thing,' he said quietly. 'Bullen's going down, no two ways about it. Reckon he'll be keeping his mouth shut about anyone else involved? He'll take down whoever he can. Some of them he might be scared of, but he won't be scared of you, Traynor. Once we start doing deals with him, I'd say your name's going to be the first one out of his mouth.'

'I can't do this . . . not now.' Traynor's voice was close to breaking. 'I have all these new arrivals to take care of.' He looked up at Rebus, appeared to be blinking back tears. 'These people need me.'

Rebus just shrugged. 'And afterwards, you'll speak to us?'

'I'll have to think about that.'

'If you *do* talk,' Storey confided, 'there's less reason for us to come crawling all over your little domain.'

Traynor gave a twisted smile. 'My "domain"? The minute you make your allegation public, I'll lose this place.'

'Maybe you should have thought of that before.'

Traynor said nothing. He came out from behind his desk, picked up the telephone, putting the receiver back in place. Immediately, it started ringing again. Traynor ignored it, bent down to pick up the photo frame.

'Will you leave now, please? We'll talk again later.'

'But not much later,' Storey warned him.

'I need to see to the new arrivals.'

'Tomorrow morning?' Storey prompted. 'We'll be back first thing.'

Traynor nodded. 'Check with Janet that there's nothing in my diary.'

Storey seemed content with this. He stood up, buttoning his jacket. 'Then we'll leave you to it. But remember, Mr Traynor – this isn't going to go away. Best that you speak to us before Bullen does.' He held out his hand, but Traynor ignored it. Storey opened the door and made his exit, Rebus staying behind an extra moment before joining him. Janet Eylot was flicking through a large desk diary. She found the relevant page.

'He's got a meeting at ten fifteen.'

'Cancel it,' Storey ordered. 'What time does he start work?'

'Around eight thirty.'

'Book us in for then. We'll need a couple of hours minimum.'

'His next meeting's at noon – should I cancel that, too?'

Storey nodded. Rebus was staring at the closed door. 'John,' Storey said, 'you'll be with me tomorrow, right?'

'I thought you were keen to get back to London.'

Storey shrugged. 'This ties everything into one neat bundle.'

'Then I'll be here.'

The guard who'd escorted them from the car park was waiting to show them out. Rebus touched Storey's arm. 'Can you wait for me at the car?'

Storey stared at him. 'What's going on?'

'Just someone I want to see . . . it won't take a minute.'

'You're locking me out,' Storey stated.

'Maybe I am. But will you do it anyway?'

Storey took his time deciding, then agreed.

Rebus asked the guard to take him over towards the canteen. It was only when Storey was out of earshot that he refined his request.

'Actually, I want the family wing,' he said.

When he got there, he saw what he needed to: Stef Yurgii's kids, playing with the toys Rebus had bought. They didn't notice him; too wrapped up in their own worlds, same as any other children. There was no immediate sign of Yurgii's widow, but Rebus decided he didn't need to see her. Instead, he nodded to the guard, who led him back towards the courtyard.

Rebus was halfway to the car when he heard the scream. It was coming from inside the main building, getting closer. The door burst open and a woman stumbled out, falling to her knees. It was Janet Eylot, and she was still screaming.

Rebus ran towards her, conscious that Storey was heading that way too.

'What's the matter, Janet? What is it?'

'He's . . . he's . . .'

But instead of answering, she slumped to the ground and started wailing, pulling her knees up, curving her body to meet them. Lying on her side, arms locked around herself.

'Oh God,' she cried. 'God have mercy . . .'

They ran inside, down the corridor and into the outer office. The door to Traynor's room was open, staff members filling the doorway. Rebus and Storey pushed past. A uniformed female guard was kneeling by the body on the floor. There was blood everywhere, soaking into the carpet and into Alan Traynor's shirt. The guard was pressing the palm of her hand against a wound on Traynor's left wrist. Another guard, male this time, was working on the slashed right wrist. Traynor was conscious, staring wide-eyed, chest rising and falling. There was more blood smeared across his face.

'Get a doctor . . .'

'An ambulance . . .'

'Keep pressing . . .'

'Towels . . .'

'Bandages . . .'

'Just keep the pressure on!' the female guard yelled to her male colleague.

Keep the pressure on indeed, Rebus thought: wasn't that exactly what he and Storey had done?

There were shards of glass on Traynor's shirt. Shards from the cracked photo frame. The shards he'd used to cut open his wrists.

Rebus realised that Storey was looking at him. He returned the stare.

You knew, didn't you? Storey's look seemed to be saying. *You knew it would come to this . . . and yet you did nothing.*

Nothing.

Nothing.

And the look Rebus gave him back, it said nothing at all.

When the ambulance arrived, Rebus was just inside the perimeter fence, finishing a cigarette. As the gates were opened, he stepped out on to the road, walking past the guardhouse and down the slope towards where Caro Quinn was standing, watching the ambulance disappear into the compound.

'Not another suicide?' she asked, appalled.

'An attempt anyway,' Rebus informed her. 'But not one of the inmates.'

'Who then?'

'Alan Traynor.'

'What?' Her whole face seemed to crease itself into the question.

'Tried slashing his wrists.'

'Is he all right?'

'I really don't know. Good news for you, though.'

'What do you mean?'

'Next few days, Caro, a lot of shit's going to start flying. Maybe even enough to see this place shut down.'

'And you call that good news?'

Rebus frowned. 'It's what you've been wanting.'

'Not like this! At the cost of another man's life!'

'I didn't mean it like that,' Rebus argued.

'I think you did.'

'Then you're paranoid.'

She took half a step back. 'Is that what I am?'

'Look, I just thought . . .'

'You don't know me, John. You don't know me *at all* . . .'

Rebus paused, as if considering his answer. 'I can live with that,' he said at last, turning to head back to the gates.

Storey was waiting for him at the car. His only comment: 'You seem to know a lot of people around here.'

Rebus gave a snort. Both men watched as one of the paramedics jogged back to the ambulance for something he'd forgotten.

'Reckon we should have made that *two* ambulances,' Storey said.

'Janet Eylot?' Rebus guessed.

Storey nodded. 'Staff are worried about her. She's in another of the offices, lying on the floor wrapped in blankets, shaking like a leaf.'

'I told her everything would be all right,' Rebus said quietly, almost to himself.

'Then I won't go depending on you for an expert opinion.'

'No,' Rebus said, 'you definitely shouldn't do that . . .'

29

The train was fifteen minutes late.

Siobhan and Mangold were waiting at the end of the platform, watching the doors slide open, the passengers start spilling out. There were tourists with suitcases, looking tired and bewildered. Business travellers emerged from the first-class compartments and headed briskly towards the taxi rank. Mothers with kids and buggies; elderly couples; single men swaggering, light-headed after three or four hours of drinking.

No sign of Ishbel.

It was a long platform, plenty of exit points. Siobhan craned her neck, hoping they wouldn't miss her, aware of tuts and looks from the new arrivals as they were forced to move around her.

And then Mangold's hand was on her arm. 'There she is,' he said.

She was closer than Siobhan had realised, laden with carrier bags. Seeing Mangold, she lifted these and opened her mouth wide, excited by the day's expedition. She hadn't noticed Siobhan. Moreover, without Mangold's prompting, Siobhan might have let her walk straight past.

Because she was the old Ishbel again: hair restyled and back to its natural colour. No longer a copy of her dead sister.

Ishbel Jardine, large as life, throwing her arms around Mangold and planting a lingering kiss on his lips. She had her eyes screwed shut, but Mangold's stayed open, looking over Ishbel's shoulder towards Siobhan. Eventually Ishbel took a step back, and Mangold turned her a little by the shoulder, so she was facing Siobhan.

And recognising her.

'Oh, Christ, it's you.'

'Hello, Ishbel.'

'I'm not going back! You have to tell them that!'

'Why not just tell them yourself?'

But Ishbel was shaking her head. 'They'd make me . . . they'd talk me into it. You don't know what they're like. I've let them control me for way too long!'

'There's a waiting room,' Siobhan said, pointing towards the concourse. The crowd had thinned, taxis labouring up the exit ramp towards Waverley Bridge. 'We can talk there.'

'There's nothing to talk about.'

'Not even Donny Cruikshank?'

'What about him?'

'You know he's dead?'

'And good riddance!'

Her whole attitude – voice, posture – was harder than when Siobhan had last met her. She was armoured, toughened by experience. Not afraid of letting her anger show.

Probably capable of violence, too.

Siobhan turned her attention to Mangold. Mangold with his bruised face.

'We'll talk in the waiting room,' she said, making it sound like an order.

But the waiting room was locked, so they walked across the concourse and into the station bar instead.

'We'd be better off at the Warlock,' Mangold said, examining the tired-looking decor and tireder clientele. 'I need to be getting back anyway.'

Siobhan ignored him, ordered the drinks. Mangold got out a roll of notes, said he couldn't let her pay. She didn't argue the point. There was no conversation in the place, yet it was noisy enough to cover anything the three of them might say: TV tuned to a sports channel; piped music drifting from the ceiling; extractor fan; one-armed bandits. They took a corner table, Ishbel spreading her bags out around her.

'A good haul,' Siobhan said.

'Just some bits and pieces.' Ishbel looked at Mangold again and smiled.

'Ishbel,' Siobhan said soberly, 'your parents have been worried about you, which in turn means the police have been worried.'

'That's not my fault, is it? I didn't ask you to stick your noses in.'

'Detective Sergeant Clarke's only doing her job,' Mangold said, playing the peacemaker.

362

'And I'm saying she needn't have bothered . . . end of story.' Ishbel lifted her glass to her lips.

'Actually,' Siobhan informed her, 'that's not strictly true. In a murder case, we need to speak to every single suspect.'

Her words had the desired effect. Ishbel stared from above the rim of her glass, then put it down untouched.

'I'm a suspect?'

Siobhan shrugged. 'Can you think of anyone who had more reason to thump Donny Cruikshank?'

'But he's the whole reason I left Banehall! I was scared of him . . .'

'I thought you said you left because of your parents?'

'Well, them too . . . They were trying to turn me into Tracy.'

'I know, I've seen the photos. I thought maybe it was your idea, but Mr Mangold put me right on that.'

Ishbel squeezed Mangold's arm. 'Ray's my best friend in the whole world.'

'What about your other friends – Susie, Janet and the rest? Didn't you think they'd be worried?'

'I was planning to phone them eventually.' Ishbel's tone was turning sullen, reminding Siobhan that despite the outward armour she was still a teenager. Only eighteen, maybe half Mangold's age.

'And meantime you're off spending Ray's money?'

'I want her to spend it,' Mangold countered. 'She's had a tough life . . . time she had a bit of fun.'

'Ishbel,' Siobhan said, 'you say you were scared of Cruikshank?'

'That's right.'

'Scared of what exactly?'

Ishbel lowered her eyes. 'Of what he'd see when he looked at me.'

'Because you'd remind him of Tracy?'

Ishbel nodded. 'And I'd *know* that's what he was thinking . . . remembering the things he'd done to her . . .' She placed both hands over her face, Mangold sliding an arm around her shoulders.

'And yet you wrote to him in prison,' Siobhan said. 'You wrote that he'd taken your life as well as Tracy's.'

'Because Mum and Dad were turning me *into* Tracy.' Her voice cracked.

'It's all right, kid,' Mangold said quietly. Then, to Siobhan: 'You see what I mean? It's not been easy for her.'

'I don't doubt it. But she still needs to speak to the investigation.'

'She needs to be left alone.'

'Left alone with you, you mean?'

363

Behind the tinted glasses, Mangold's eyes narrowed. 'What are you getting at?'

Siobhan just shrugged, pretending to busy herself with her glass.

'It's like I told you, Ray,' Ishbel was saying. 'I'll never be free of Banehall.' She started shaking her head slowly. 'The other side of the world wouldn't be far enough.' She was clinging to his arm now. 'You said it would be all right, but it's not.'

'A holiday's what you need, girl. Cocktails by the pool . . . room service and a nice sandy beach.'

'What did you mean just then, Ishbel?' Siobhan interrupted. 'About it not being all right?'

'She didn't mean anything,' Mangold snapped, moving his arm further around Ishbel's shoulders. 'You want to ask any more questions, make it official, eh?' He was rising to his feet, picking up some of the bags. 'Come on, Ishbel.'

She picked up the rest of the shopping, took a final look around to see if she'd missed anything.

'It *will* be made official, Mr Mangold,' Siobhan said warningly. 'Skeletons in the cellar are one thing, but murder's quite another.'

Mangold was doing his best to ignore her. 'Come on, Ishbel. We'll take a taxi to the pub . . . no sense walking with all this lot.'

'Call your parents, Ishbel,' Siobhan said. 'They came to me because they were worried about *you* . . . nothing to do with Tracy.'

Ishbel said nothing, but Siobhan called out her name, louder this time, and she turned.

'I'm glad you're safe and well,' Siobhan told her with a smile. 'Really I am.'

'Then *you* tell them.'

'I will if you want me to.'

Ishbel hesitated. Mangold was holding open the door for her. Ishbel stared at Siobhan and gave an almost imperceptible nod. Then she was gone.

Siobhan watched from the window as they headed for the taxi rank. She shook her glass, enjoying the sound of the ice cubes. Mangold, she felt, really did care about Ishbel, but that didn't make him a good man. *You said it would be all right, but it's not . . .* Those words had spurred Mangold to his feet. Siobhan thought she knew why. Love could be an even more destructive emotion than hate. She'd seen it plenty of times: jealousy, mistrust, revenge. She considered all three as she shook her glass again. At some point, it must have started annoying the barman.

He upped the volume on the TV, by which time she'd whittled the three down to one.

Revenge.

Joe Evans was not at home. It was his wife who answered the door of their bungalow on Liberton Brae. There was no front garden as such, just a paved parking space, an empty trailer sitting there.

'What's he done now?' his wife asked, after Siobhan had identified herself.

'Nothing,' Siobhan assured the woman. 'Did he tell you what happened at the Warlock?'

'Only a couple of dozen times.'

'It's just a few follow-up questions.' Siobhan paused. 'Has he been in trouble before?'

'Did I say that?'

'As good as.' Siobhan smiled, telling the woman it didn't matter to her in any case.

'Just a couple of fights in the pub . . . drunk and disorderly . . . but he's been pure gold this past year.'

'That's good to know. Any idea where I could find him, Mrs Evans?'

'He'll be in the gym, love. I can't keep him away from the place.' She saw the look on Siobhan's face and gave a snort. 'Just messing with you . . . He's same place as every Tuesday – quiz night at his local. Just up the hill, other side of the road.' Mrs Evans gestured with her thumb. Siobhan thanked her and headed off.

'And if he's not there,' the woman called after her, 'come back and let me know – means he's got a fancy piece tucked away somewhere!'

The hacking laugh followed Siobhan all the way back to the pavement.

The pub boasted a tiny car park, already full. Siobhan parked on the street and headed in. The drinkers all looked seasoned and comfortable: sign of a good local. Teams sat around every available table, one of their number writing the answers down. A question was being repeated as Siobhan walked in. The quizmaster seemed to be the landlord. He stood behind the bar with microphone in hand, the question sheet gripped in his free hand.

'Final question, teams, and here it is again: "Which Hollywood starlet connects a Scottish actor to the song 'Yellow'?" Moira's coming round now to collect your answers. We'll have a wee break, and then we'll let you know which team's come out top. Sandwiches are on the pool table, so help yourselves.'

Players started to rise from their tables, some handing their completed sheets to the landlady. There was a sudden blare of conversation as people asked each other how they'd done.

'It's the bloody arithmetic ones that get me . . .'

'And you a book-keeper!'

'That last one, did he mean "Yellow Submarine"?'

'Christ's sake, Peter, there's been music made since the Beatles, you know.'

'But nothing to come close to them, and I'll fight any man that says otherwise.'

'So what *was* the name of Humphrey Bogart's partner in *The Maltese Falcon?*'

Siobhan knew the answer to this one. 'Miles Archer,' she told the man. He stared at her.

'I know you,' he said. He was holding the dregs of a pint in one hand, pointing at her with the other.

'We met at the Warlock,' Siobhan reminded him. 'You were drinking brandies then.' She gestured towards his glass. 'Get you another?'

'What's this about?' he asked. The others were giving Siobhan and Joe Evans space to themselves, as if an invisible force-field had suddenly been activated. 'Not still those bloody skeletons?'

'Not really, no . . . To be honest, I'm after a favour.'

'What sort of favour?'

'The sort that begins with a question.'

He thought about this for a moment, then considered his empty glass. 'Better get me a refill then,' he said. Siobhan was happy to oblige. At the bar, questions flew at her – nothing to do with the quiz, but locals curious as to her identity, how she knew Evans, was she his parole officer maybe, or his social worker? Siobhan handled these deftly enough, smiling at the laughter, and handed Evans a fresh pint of best. He raised it to his mouth and took three or four long gulps, coming up for breath eventually.

'So go ahead and ask your question,' he said.

'Are you still working at the Warlock?'

He nodded. 'That's it?' he asked.

She shook her head. 'What I'm wondering is, do you have a key for the place?'

'For the pub?' He snorted. 'Ray Mangold wouldn't be that daft.'

Siobhan shook her head again. 'I meant the cellar,' she said. 'Can you let yourself in and out of the cellar?'

Evans looked at her questioningly, then took a few more gulps of beer, wiping his top lip dry afterwards.

'Maybe you want to ask the audience?' Siobhan suggested. His face twitched in a smile.

'The answer's yes,' he said.

'Yes, you've got a key?'

'Yes, I've got a key.'

Siobhan took a deep breath. '. . . is the correct answer,' she said. 'Now, do you want to go for the star prize?'

'I don't need to.' There was a twinkle in Evans's eye.

'And why's that?'

'Because I know the question. You want me to lend you my key.'

'And?'

'And I'm wondering how far in the manure that would get me with my employer.'

'And?'

'I'm also wondering why you want it. You reckon there are more skeletons down there?'

'In a manner of speaking,' Siobhan admitted. 'Answers to be provided at a later date.'

'If I give you the key?'

'It's either that or I tell your wife I couldn't find you at the quiz night.'

'That's a hard offer to refuse,' Joe Evans said.

Late night in Arden Street. Rebus buzzed her up. He was waiting in his doorway by the time she reached his landing.

'Happened to be passing,' she said. 'Saw your light was on.'

'Bloody liar,' he said. Then: 'Feeling thirsty?'

She held up the carrier bag. 'Great minds and all that.'

He gestured for her to enter. The living room was no messier than usual. His chair was by the window, phone, ashtray and tumbler next to it on the floor. Music was playing: Van Morrison, *Hard Nose the Highway*.

'Things must be bad,' she said.

'When are they not? That's pretty much Van's message to the world.' He lowered the volume a little. She lifted a bottle of red from the bag.

'Corkscrew?'

'I'll fetch one.' He started heading for the kitchen. 'I suppose you'll be wanting a glass, too?'

'Sorry to be fussy.'

She took off her coat, was resting on the arm of the sofa when he returned. 'A quiet night in, eh?' she said, taking the corkscrew from him. He held the glass for her while she poured. 'You having any?'

He shook his head. 'I'm three whiskies in, and you know what they say about the grape and the grain.' She took the glass from him, made herself comfortable on the sofa.

'Been having a quiet night yourself?' he asked.

'On the contrary – up until forty minutes ago, I was hard at it.'

'Oh, aye?'

'Managed to persuade Ray Duff to burn the midnight oil.'

Rebus nodded. He knew Ray Duff worked forensics at the police lab in Howdenhall; by now they owed him a world of favours.

'Ray finds it hard to say no,' he agreed. 'Anything I should know about?'

She shrugged. 'I'm not sure . . . So how's your day been?'

'You heard about Alan Traynor?'

'No.'

Rebus let the silence lie for a moment between them; picked up his glass and took a couple of sips. Took his time appreciating the aroma, the aftertaste.

'Nice to sit and talk, isn't it?' he commented at last.

'All right, I give in . . . You tell me yours and I'll tell you mine.'

Rebus smiled, went to the table where the bottle of Bowmore sat. Refilled his glass and returned to his chair.

Started talking.

After which, Siobhan told him her own story. Van Morrison was swapped for Hobotalk and Hobotalk for James Yorkston. Midnight had come and gone. Slices of toast had been made, buttered, and consumed. The wine was down to its last quarter, the whisky to its final inch. When Rebus checked that she wouldn't be trying to drive home, Siobhan admitted that she'd come by cab.

'Meaning you assumed we were going to do this?' Rebus teased.

'I suppose.'

'And what if Caro Quinn had been here?'

Siobhan just shrugged.

'Not that that's going to happen,' Rebus added. He looked at her. 'I think I may have blown it with the Lady of the Vigils.'

'The what?'

He shook his head. 'It's what Mo Dirwan calls her.'

Siobhan was staring at her glass. It looked to Rebus as though she had a dozen questions waiting, a dozen things to say to him. But in the end, all she said was: 'I think I've had enough.'

'Of my company?'

She shook her head. 'The wine. Any chance of a coffee?'

'Kitchen's where it's always been.'

'The perfect host.' She got to her feet.

'I'll have one too, if you're offering.'

'I'm not.'

But she brought him a mug anyway. 'The milk in your fridge is still useable,' she told him.

'So?'

'So that's a first, isn't it?'

'Listen to the ingratitude!' Rebus put the mug on the floor. Siobhan returned to the sofa, cupping hers between her hands. While she'd been out of the room, he'd opened the window a little, so she wouldn't complain about his smoke. He saw her notice what he'd done; watched her decide to make no comment.

'Know what I'm wondering, Shiv? I'm wondering how those skeletons ended up in Stuart Bullen's hands. Could he have been Pippa Greenlaw's date that night?'

'I doubt it. She said his name was Barry or Gary, and he played football – I think that's how they met . . .' She broke off as a smile started spreading across Rebus's face.

'Remember when I grazed my leg at the Nook?' he said. 'That Aussie barman told me he could sympathise.'

Siobhan nodded. 'Typical football injury . . .'

'And his name's Barney, isn't it? Not quite Barry, but close enough.'

Siobhan was still nodding. She'd reached into her bag for her mobile and notebook, flicked through it for the number.

'It's one in the morning,' Rebus warned her. She ignored him. Pushed buttons and held the phone to her ear.

When it was answered, she started talking. 'Pippa? It's DS Clarke here, remember me? You out clubbing or something?' Her eyes were on Rebus as she relayed the answers to him. 'Just waiting for a taxi home . . .' She nodded. 'Been to the Opal Lounge or somewhere? Well, I'm sorry to bother you so late at night.' Rebus was walking towards the sofa, leaning down to share the earpiece. He could hear traffic sounds, drunken voices close by. A screech of *Taxi!* followed by swearing.

'Missed that one,' Pippa Greenlaw said. She sounded breathless rather than drunk.

'Pippa,' Siobhan said, 'it's about your partner . . . the night of Lex's party . . .'

'Lex is here! Do you want to talk to him?'

'It's you I want to talk to.'

Greenlaw's voice grew muffled, as though she were trying not to let someone hear. 'I think we might be starting something.'

'You and Lex? That's great, Pippa.' Siobhan rolled her eyes, giving the lie to her words. 'Now, about the night those skeletons went missing . . .'

'You know I kissed one of them?'

'You told me.'

'Even now it makes me want to puke . . . *Taxi!*'

Siobhan held the phone further from her ear. 'Pippa, I just need to know something . . . the guy you were with that night . . . could he have been an Australian called Barney?'

'What?'

'Australian, Pippa. The guy you were with at Lex's party.'

'Do you know . . . now you come to mention it . . .'

'And you didn't think it worth telling me?'

'I didn't think much of it at the time. Must've slipped my mind . . .' She spoke to Lex Cater, filling him in. The phone changed hands.

'Is that Little Miss Matchmaker?' Lex's voice. 'Pippa told me you set the pair of us up that night . . . it was meant to be you, but she was there instead. Female solidarity and all that, eh?'

'You didn't tell me Pippa's guest at your party was an Aussie.'

'Was he? Never really noticed . . . Here's Pippa again.'

But Siobhan had ended the call. 'Never really noticed,' she echoed. Rebus was heading back to his chair.

'People like that, they seldom do. Think the world revolves around *them*.' Rebus grew thoughtful. 'Wonder whose idea it was.'

'What?'

'The skeletons weren't stolen to order. So either Barney Grant had the idea of using them to scare off any uppity immigrants . . .'

'Or Stuart Bullen did.'

'But if it was our friend Barney, that means he knew what was going on – not just barman, but Bullen's lieutenant.'

'Which might explain what he was doing with Howie Slowther. Slowther's been working for Bullen too.'

'Or more likely for Peter Hill, but you're right – the end result's the same.'

'So Barney Grant should be behind bars, too,' Siobhan stated. 'Otherwise, what's to stop the whole thing starting up again?'

'A little bit of proof might be useful right about now. All we've got is Barney Grant in a car with Slowther . . .'

'That and the skeletons.'

'Hardly enough to convince the Procurator Fiscal.'

Siobhan blew across the surface of her coffee. The hi-fi had gone quiet; might have been that way for some time.

'Something for another day, eh, Shiv?' Rebus eventually conceded.

'Is that me getting my marching orders?'

'I'm older than you . . . I need my sleep.'

'I thought you need less sleep as you get older?'

Rebus shook his head. 'You don't *need* less sleep; you just take it.'

'Why?'

He shrugged. 'Mortality closing in, I suppose.'

'And you can sleep all you like when you're dead?'

'That's right.'

'Well, I'm sorry to keep you up so late, old-timer.'

Rebus smiled. 'Not too long now till there's a younger cop sitting opposite *you*.'

'Now there's a thought to end the night with . . .'

'I'll call you a cab, unless you want to crash here – there's a spare bedroom.'

She started putting on her coat. 'We don't want tongues wagging, do we? But I'll walk down to the Meadows, bound to find one there.'

'Out on your own at this time of night?'

Siobhan picked up her bag, slung it over her shoulder. 'I'm a big girl, John. I think I can manage.'

He shrugged and showed her out, then returned to the living-room window, watching her walk down the pavement.

I'm a big girl . . .

A big girl afraid of wagging tongues.

DAY TEN

Wednesday

30

'I've got a lecture,' Kate said.

Rebus had been waiting for her outside her hall of residence. She'd given him a look and kept walking, heading for the bicycle rack.

'I'll give you a lift,' he said. She didn't respond, unlocking the chain from her bike. 'We need to talk,' Rebus persisted.

'There's nothing to talk about.'

'That's true, I suppose . . .' She looked up at him. 'But only if we choose to ignore Barney Grant and Howie Slowther.'

'I've got nothing to say to you about Barney.'

'Warned you off, has he?'

'I've got nothing to say.'

'So you said. And Howie Slowther?'

'I don't know who he is.'

'No?'

She shook her head defiantly, hands gripping her bike's handle-bars. 'Now, please . . . I'm going to be late.'

'Just one more name then.' Rebus held up a forefinger. He took her sigh as permission to ask. 'Chantal Rendille . . . I'm probably pronouncing it wrong.'

'It's not a name I know.'

Rebus smiled. 'You're a terrible liar, Kate — your eyes start fluttering. I noticed it before when I was asking about Chantal. Of course, I didn't have her name then, but I have it now. With Stuart Bullen locked up, she doesn't need to hide any more.'

'Stuart did not kill that man.'

Rebus just shrugged. 'All the same, I'd like to hear her say it for herself.' He slid his hands into his pockets. 'Too many people running scared recently, Kate. Time for it to stop, wouldn't you agree?'

'It's not my decision,' she said quietly.

'You mean it's Chantal's? Then have a word with her, tell her she doesn't have to be scared. It's all coming to an end.'

'I wish I had your confidence, Inspector.'

'Maybe I know things you don't . . . things Chantal should hear.'

Kate looked around. Her fellow students were heading off to classes, some with the glazed eyes of the newly roused, others curious about the man she was talking to – so obviously neither student nor friend.

'Kate?' he prompted.

'I need to speak to her alone first.'

'That's fine.' He gestured with his head. 'Do we need the car, or is it walking distance?'

'That depends on how much you like walking.'

'Seriously now, do I look the type?'

'Not really.' She was almost smiling, but still edgy.

'Then we'll take the car.'

Even having been coaxed into the passenger seat, it took Kate a while to pull the door closed, and longer still to fasten her seatbelt, Rebus fearing that she might bale out at any time.

'Where to?' he asked, trying to make the question sound casual.

'Bedlam,' she said, just audibly. Rebus wasn't sure he'd heard her. 'Bedlam Theatre,' she explained. 'It's a disused church.'

'Across the road from Greyfriars Kirk?' Rebus said. She nodded, and he started to drive. On the way, she explained that Marcus, the student across the corridor from her, was active in the university's theatre group, and that they used Bedlam as their base. Rebus said he'd seen the playbills on Marcus's walls, then asked how she had first met Chantal.

'This city can seem like a village sometimes,' she told him. 'I was walking towards her along the street one day, and I just knew when I looked at her.'

'You knew what?'

'Where she came from, who she was . . . It's hard to explain. Two Senegalese women in the middle of Edinburgh.' She shrugged. 'We just laughed and started talking.'

'And when she came to you for help?' She looked at him as if she didn't understand. 'What did you think? Did she tell you what had happened?'

'A little . . .' Kate stared from the passenger-side window. 'This is for her to tell you, if she decides to.'

'You realise I'm on her side? Yours, too, if it comes to it.'

'I know this.'

Bedlam Theatre stood at the junction of two diagonals – Forrest Road and Bristo Place – and facing the wider expanse of George IV Bridge. Years back, this had been Rebus's favourite part of town, with its weird bookshops and second-hand record market. Now Subway and Starbucks had moved in and the record market was a theme bar. Parking had not improved either, and Rebus ended up on a double yellow, trusting to luck that he'd be back before the tow truck could be called.

The main doors were locked tight, but Kate led him around the side and produced a key from her pocket.

'Marcus?' he guessed. She nodded and opened the small side door, then turned towards him. 'You want me to wait here?' he guessed. But she stared deep into his eyes and then sighed.

'No,' she said, decided. 'You might as well come up.'

Inside, the place was gloomy. They climbed a flight of creaky steps and emerged into an upstairs auditorium, looking down on to the makeshift stage. There were rows of former pews, mostly stacked with empty cardboard boxes, props, and pieces of lighting rig.

'Chantal?' Kate called out. '*C'est moi*. Are you there?'

A face appeared above one row of seats. She'd been lying in a sleeping-bag, and was now blinking, rubbing sleep from her eyes. When she saw that there was someone with Kate, her mouth and eyes opened wide.

'*Calmes-toi*, Chantal. *Il est policier.*'

'Why you bring?' Chantal's voice sounded shrill, frantic. As she stood up, sloughing off the sleeping-bag, Rebus saw that she was already dressed.

'I'm a police officer, Chantal,' Rebus said slowly. 'I want to talk to you.'

'No! This will not be!' She waved her hands in front of her, as though he were smoke to be wafted away. Her arms were thin, hair cropped close to her skull. Her head seemed out of proportion to the slender neck atop which it sat.

'You know we've arrested the men?' Rebus said. 'The men we think killed Stef. They are going to prison.'

'They will kill me.'

Rebus kept his eyes on her as he shook his head. 'They're going to be spending a lot of time in jail, Chantal. They've done a lot of bad things. But if we're going to punish them for what they did to Stef . . . well, I'm not sure we can do it without your help.'

'Stef was good man.' Her face twisted with the pain of memory.

'Yes, he was,' Rebus agreed. 'And his death needs to be paid for.' He'd been moving towards her by degrees. Now they stood within arm's reach. 'Stef needs you, Chantal, this one final time.'

'No,' she said. But her eyes were telling him a different story.

'I need to hear it from you, Chantal,' he said quietly. 'I need to know what you saw.'

'No,' she said again, her eyes pleading with Kate.

'*Oui, Chantal,*' Kate told her. 'It is time.'

Only Kate had eaten breakfast, so they headed for the Elephant House café, Rebus driving them the short distance, finding a parking bay on Chambers Street. Chantal wanted hot chocolate, Kate herbal tea. Rebus ordered a round of croissants and sticky cakes, plus a large black coffee for himself. And then bottles of water and orange juice – if no one else drank them, he would. And maybe a couple more aspirin to go with the three he'd swallowed before leaving his flat.

They sat at a table at the very back of the café, the window next to them giving a view of the kirkyard, where a few winos were starting the day with a shared can of extra-strong lager. Only a few weeks back, some kids had desecrated a tomb, using a skull like a football. 'Mad World' was playing quietly over the café's loud-speakers, and Rebus was forced to agree.

He was biding his time, letting Chantal wolf down her breakfast. The pastries were too sweet for her, but she ate two croissants, washed down with one of the bottles of juice.

'Fresh fruit would be better for you,' Kate said, Rebus unsure of her target as he finished an apricot tart. Then it was time for a coffee refill, Chantal saying she might manage more hot chocolate. Kate poured herself more raspberry-coloured tea. As Rebus queued at the counter, he watched the two women. They were talking conversationally: nothing heated. Chantal seemed calm enough. That was why he'd chosen the Elephant House: a police station would not have had the same effect. When he returned with the drinks, she actually smiled and thanked him.

'So,' he said, lifting his own mug, 'finally I get to meet you, Chantal.'

'You very persistent.'

'It may be my only strength. Do you want to tell me what happened that day? I think I know some of it. Stef was a journalist, he knew a story when he saw one. I'm guessing it was you who told him about Stevenson House?'

'He knew already a little,' Chantal said haltingly.

'How did you meet him?'

'In Knoxland. He . . .' She turned to Kate and let out a volley of French, which Kate translated.

'He'd been questioning some of the immigrants he met in the city centre. This made him realise something bad was happening.'

'And Chantal filled in the gaps?' Rebus guessed. 'And became his friend in the process?' Chantal understood, nodding with her eyes. 'And then Stuart Bullen caught him snooping . . .'

'It was not Bullen,' she said.

'Peter Hill then.' Rebus described the Irishman, and Chantal sat back a little in her seat, as though recoiling from his words.

'Yes, that is him. He chased . . . and stabbed . . .' She lowered her eyes again, placing her hands on her lap. Kate reached out and covered the nearest hand with her own.

'You ran away,' Rebus said quietly. Chantal started speaking French again.

'She had to,' Kate told Rebus. 'They would have buried her in the cellar, with all the other people.'

'There weren't any other people,' Rebus said. 'It was just a trick.'

'She was terrified,' Kate said.

'But she went back once . . . to place flowers at the scene.'

Kate translated for Chantal, who gave another nod.

'She travelled across a continent to reach somewhere she'd feel safe,' Kate told Rebus. 'She's been here almost a year, and still she does not understand this place.'

'Tell her she's not the only one. I've been trying for over half a century.' As Kate translated this, Chantal managed a weak smile. Rebus was wondering about her . . . wondering at her relationship with Stef. Had she been something other than a source to him, or had he simply used her, the way many journalists did?

'Anyone else involved, Chantal?' Rebus asked. 'Anyone there that day?'

'A young man . . . bad skin . . . and this tooth . . .' She tapped at the centre of her own immaculate teeth. 'Not there.' Rebus reckoned she meant Howie Slowther, might even pick him out from a line-up.

'How do you think they found out about Stef, Chantal? How did they know he was about to go to the newspapers with the story?'

She looked up at him. 'Because he tell them.'

Rebus's eyes narrowed. 'He *told* them?'

She nodded. 'He want his family brought to him. He know they can do this.'

'You mean bailing them out of Whitemire?' More nodding. Rebus found himself leaning across the table towards her. 'He was trying to *blackmail* the whole lot of them?'

'He will not tell what he know . . . but only in return for his family.'

Rebus sat back again and stared from the window. Right now, that extra-strong lager looked pretty good to him. A mad, mad world. Stef Yurgii might as well have penned himself a suicide note. He hadn't met with the *Scotsman* journalist because it had been a bluff, letting Bullen know what he was capable of. All of it for his family . . . Chantal just a friend, if that. A desperate man – husband and father – taking a fatal gamble.

Killed for his insolence.

Killed because of the threat he posed. No skeletons were going to put *him* off.

'You saw it happen?' Rebus asked quietly. 'You saw Stef die?'

'I could do nothing.'

'You phoned . . . did what you could.'

'It was not enough . . . not enough . . .' She had started crying, Kate comforting her. Two elderly women watched from a corner table. Their faces powdered, coats still buttoned almost to the chin. Edinburgh ladies, who probably had never known any life but this: the taking of tea, and a serving of gossip on the side. Rebus glared at them till they averted their eyes, going back to the spreading of butter on scones.

'Kate,' he said, 'she'll have to tell the story again, make it official.'

'In a police station?' Kate guessed. Rebus nodded.

'It would help,' he said, 'if you were there with her.'

'Yes, of course.'

'The man you'll talk to will be another inspector. His name's Shug Davidson. He's a good guy, does the sympathy thing even better than me.'

'You will not be there?'

'I don't think so. Shug's the man in charge.' Rebus took a mouthful of coffee and savoured it, then swallowed. 'I was never supposed to be here,' he said, almost to himself, staring out of the window again.

*

He called Davidson from his mobile, explained the set-up, said he'd bring both women to Torphichen.

In the car, Chantal was silent, staring at the passing world. But Rebus had a few more questions for her companion in the back seat.

'How did your talk with Barney Grant go?'

'It was all right.'

'You reckon he'll keep the Nook going?'

'Until Stuart comes back, yes. Why do you smile?'

'Because I don't know if that's what Barney wants . . . or expects.'

'I'm not sure I understand.'

'Doesn't matter. That description I gave Chantal . . . the man's called Peter Hill. He's Irish, probably with paramilitary connections. We reckon he was helping Bullen out, on the understanding that Bullen would then back him up when it came to dealing drugs on the estate.'

'What has this got to do with me?'

'Maybe nothing. The younger man, the one with the missing tooth . . . his name's Howie Slowther.'

'You said his name this morning.'

'That's right, I did. Because after your little chinwag with Barney Grant in the pub, Barney climbed into a car. Howie Slowther was in that car.' In the rearview mirror, his eyes connected with hers. 'Barney's in this up to his neck, Kate . . . maybe even a little further. So if you were planning on relying on him . . .'

'You do not have to worry about me.'

'That's good to hear.'

Chantal said something in French. Kate spoke back to her in the same language, Rebus picking up only a couple of words.

'She's asking about being deported,' he guessed, then watched in the rearview as Kate nodded. 'Tell her I'll pull every string I can. Tell her it's carved in stone.'

A hand touched his shoulder. He turned and saw that it was Chantal's.

'I believe you,' was all she said.

31

Siobhan and Les Young watched as Ray Mangold got out of his Jag.
They were sitting in Young's car, parked across the road from the
Market Street lock-up. Mangold unlocked the garage doors and
started pulling them open. Ishbel Jardine sat in the passenger seat,
applying make-up as she checked her face in the rearview mirror.
Having lifted the lipstick to her mouth, she hesitated a fraction too
long.

'She's clocked us,' Siobhan said.

'You sure?'

'Not a thousand per cent.'

'Let's wait and see.'

Young wanted the car garaged. That way, he could drive up in
front of it, blocking any exit. They'd been sitting there the best part
of forty minutes, Young going into too much detail about the
rudiments of contract bridge. The ignition was off, but Young's
hand was on the key, ready for action.

With the garage doors wide open, Mangold had returned to the
idling Jag. Siobhan watched as he got in, but couldn't tell whether
Ishbel had said anything. When she saw Mangold's eyes meet hers
in one of the side mirrors, she had her answer.

'We need to move,' she told Young. Then she opened her
passenger door – no time to waste. But the Jag's reversing lights
were on. It moved past her at speed, heading for New Street, engine
whining with the effort. Siobhan got back into the passenger seat,
the door closing of its own accord as Young's car surged forward.
The Jag meantime had reached the New Street junction and was
braking into a slide, facing uphill towards the Canongate.

'Get on the radio!' Young shouted. 'Call in a description!'

Siobhan called it in. There was a queue of traffic heading up the Canongate, so the Jag turned left, downhill towards Holyrood.

'What do you reckon?' she asked Young.

'You know the city better than I do,' he admitted.

'I think he'll head for the park. If he stays on the streets, he'll hit a snarl-up sooner or later. In the park, there's a chance he can put his foot down, maybe lose us.'

'Are you besmirching my car?'

'Last time I looked, Daewoos didn't sport four-litre engines.'

The Jag had pulled out to overtake an open-topped tourist bus. The street was at its narrowest, and Mangold clipped the wing mirror of a stationary delivery van, the driver emerging from a shop and shouting after him. Oncoming traffic stopped Young passing the bus as it continued its slow descent.

'Try using your horn,' Siobhan suggested. He did, but the bus paid no heed until it came to a temporary stop outside the Tolbooth. Drivers coming the opposite way protested as Young swept into their lane and past the obstruction. Mangold's car was way ahead. As it reached the roundabout outside Holyrood Palace, it took a right, making for Horse Wynd.

'You were right,' Young admitted, while Siobhan called in this new information. Holyrood Park was crown property, and as such had its own police force, but Siobhan knew protocol could wait for later. For now, the Jag was racing away, rounding Salisbury Crags.

'Where next?' Young asked.

'Well, he either circles the park all day, or else he comes off. That means Dalkeith Road or Duddingston. My money's on Duddingston. Once he's past there, he's within a gear-change of the A1 – and he'll *definitely* outrun us there, all the way to Newcastle if need be.'

There were a couple of roundabouts to be negotiated first, however, Mangold nearly losing control on the second, the Jaguar mounting the kerb. He was passing the back of Pollock Halls, engine roaring.

'Duddingston,' Siobhan commented, calling it in again. This part of the road was all twists and turns and they finally lost sight of Mangold completely. Then, from just past a stone outcrop, Siobhan could see dust billowing upwards.

'Oh, hell,' she said. As they rounded the bend, they saw tyre tracks veering crazily across the carriageway. There were iron railings on the right-hand side of the road, and the Jaguar had crashed through these, rolling down the steep slope towards

Duddingston Loch. Ducks and geese were flapping out of harm's way, while swans glided across the water's surface, seemingly unworried. The Jaguar kicked up stones and old feathers as it bounced downhill. The brake lights glowed red, but the car seemed to have other ideas. Finally it slewed sideways and then another ninety degrees, its back half plunging into the water, resting there, the front wheels hanging in the air, spinning slowly.

There were people further along the water's edge: parents and their offspring, feeding bread crusts to the birds. Some of them started running towards the car. Young had pulled the Daewoo up on to what pavement there was, so as not to block the carriageway. Siobhan skidded down the slope. The doors of the Jaguar were open, figures emerging from either side. But then the car jerked backwards again and started to sink. Mangold was out, up to his chest in water, but Ishbel had been thrown back into her seat, and the pressure was pushing her door closed again as the interior started to fill with water. Mangold saw what was happening and reached inside, starting to haul her across to the driver's side. But she was caught somehow, and now only the windscreen and roof were showing. Siobhan waded into the foul-smelling water. Steam was rising from the submerged and super-heated engine.

'Give me a hand!' Mangold was yelling. He had hold of both Ishbel's arms. Siobhan took a deep breath and plunged beneath the surface. The water was murky and bubbling, but she could see the problem: Ishbel's foot was wedged between the passenger seat and the handbrake. And the harder Mangold pulled, the faster it would hold. She surfaced again.

'Let go!' she told him. 'Let her go or she'll drown!' Then she took another breath and ducked back beneath the surface, where she came face to face with Ishbel, whose features had taken on an unexpected calmness, surrounded by the loch's flotsam and jetsam. There were tiny bubbles escaping from her nostrils and the sides of her mouth. Siobhan reached past her to release the foot, and felt arms wrap around her. Ishbel was drawing her closer, as if determined that the two of them should stay there. Siobhan tried wriggling free, all the time working on the trapped foot.

But it was no longer trapped.

And still Ishbel stayed there.

And held her.

Siobhan tried grabbing at the hands, but it was difficult: they were locked behind her back. The last of her air was leaving her lungs. Movement was growing almost impossible, Ishbel trying to draw her further into the car.

Until Siobhan kneed her in the solar plexus, and felt the embrace loosen. This time she was able to wrench herself free. She grabbed Ishbel by the hair and kicked upwards, hands immediately finding her – not Ishbel's this time, but Mangold's. With her face above water, Siobhan's mouth opened to suck in air. Then she spat water from her mouth, wiped it from her eyes and nose. Pushed the hair back out of her face.

'You stupid bloody bitch!' she screamed, as Ishbel, gasping and spluttering, was led to the bank by Ray Mangold. Then, to a gawping Les Young: 'She was going to take me with her!'

He helped her out of the water. Ishbel was lying a few yards away, a group of onlookers gathering around her. One of them had a video camera out, recording the event for posterity. When he pointed it at Siobhan, she slapped it away and bore down on the prone, drenched figure.

'What the hell did you do that for?'

Mangold was kneeling, trying to cradle Ishbel in his arms. 'I don't know what happened,' he said.

'I don't mean you, I mean *her*!' She prodded Ishbel with a toe. Les Young was trying to lead her away by the arm, mouthing words she couldn't hear. There was a raging in her ears, a fire in her lungs.

Ishbel eventually turned her head to look up at her rescuer. Her hair was plastered to her face.

'I'm sure she's grateful,' Mangold was saying, while Young added something about it being an automatic reflex . . . something he'd heard about before.

Ishbel Jardine, however, didn't say anything. Instead, she bowed her head and spewed a mixture of bile and water on to damp earth stained white with feather-down.

'I was bloody well fed up of you lot, if you want to know.'

'And that's your excuse, is it, Mr Mangold?' Les Young asked. 'That's your whole explanation?'

They were seated in Interview Room 1, St Leonard's police station – no distance at all from Holyrood Park. A few of the uniforms had expressed surprise at Siobhan's return to her old stomping-ground, her humour not improved by a call on her mobile from DCI Macrae at Gayfield Square, asking where the hell she was. When she'd told him, he'd started a long complaint about attitude and teamwork and the apparent disinclination of former

St Leonard's officers to show anything other than contempt for their new billet.

All the time he was talking, Siobhan was having a blanket wrapped around her, a mug of instant soup pressed into her hand, her shoes removed to be dried on a radiator . . .

'Sorry, sir, I didn't catch all of that,' she was forced to admit, once Macrae had stopped talking.

'You think this is funny, DS Clarke?'

'No, sir.' But it was . . . in a way. She just didn't think Macrae would share her sense of the absurd.

She sat now, bra-less in a borrowed T-shirt, and wearing black standard-issue trousers three sizes too large. On her feet: a pair of men's white sports socks, covered by the polythene slip-ons used at crime scenes. Around her shoulders: a grey woollen blanket, the kind provided in each holding-cell. She hadn't had a chance to wash her hair. It felt thick and dank, and smelled of the loch.

Mangold was wrapped in a blanket, too, hands cupped around a plastic beaker of tea. He'd lost his tinted glasses, and his eyes were reduced to slits in the glare of the strip-lighting. The blanket, Siobhan couldn't help noticing, was exactly the same colour as the tea. There was a table between them. Les Young sat next to Siobhan, pen poised above an A4 pad of paper.

Ishbel was in one of the holding-cells. She would be interviewed later.

For now, they were interested in Mangold. Mangold, who hadn't said anything for a couple of minutes.

'That's the story you're sticking with,' Les Young commented. He'd started doodling on the pad. Siobhan turned to him.

'He can give us any drivel he feels like; it doesn't alter the facts.'

'What facts?' Mangold asked, feigning only the faintest interest.

'The cellar,' Les Young told him.

'Christ, are we back to that again?'

It was Siobhan who answered. 'Despite what you told me last time round, Mr Mangold, I think you *do* know Stuart Bullen. I think you've known him for a while. He had this notion of a mock burial – pretending to bury those skeletons to show the immigrants what would happen to them if they didn't toe the line.'

Mangold had pushed back so that the front two legs of his chair were off the floor. His face was angled ceilingwards, eyes closed. Siobhan kept talking, her voice quiet and level.

'When the skeletons were concreted over, that should have been the end of that. But it wasn't. Your pub's on the Royal Mile, you see

386

the tourists every day. Nothing they like better than a bit of atmosphere – that's why the ghost walks are so popular. You wanted some of that for the Warlock.'

'No secret there,' Mangold said. 'It's why I was having the cellar renovated.'

'That's right . . . but think what a boost you'd get if a couple of skeletons were suddenly discovered under the floor. Plenty of free publicity, especially with a local historian stoking the fires . . .'

'I still don't see what you're getting at.'

'The thing is, Ray, you weren't seeing the bigger picture. Last thing Stuart Bullen wanted was those skeletons coming to light. People were bound to start asking questions, and those questions might lead back to him and his little slave empire. Is that why he slapped you about a bit? Maybe he got the Irishman to do it for him.'

'I've told you how I got the bruises.'

'Well, I'm choosing not to believe you.'

Mangold started laughing, still facing the ceiling. 'Facts, you said. I'm not hearing anything you can even *begin* to prove.'

'The thing I'm wondering is . . .'

'What?'

'Look at me and I'll tell you.'

Slowly, the chair returned to the ground. Mangold fixed his slitted eyes on Siobhan.

'What I can't decide,' she told him, 'is whether you did it out of anger – you'd been beaten up and shouted at by Bullen, and you wanted to mete that out on someone else . . .' She paused. 'Or whether it was more in the nature of a gift to Ishbel – not wrapped in ribbons this time, but a gift all the same . . . something to make her life that bit easier.'

Mangold turned to Les Young. 'Help me out here: do *you* have any idea what she's on about?'

'I know exactly what she's on about,' Young told him.

'See,' Siobhan added, shifting slightly in her chair, 'when DI Rebus and I came to see you that last time . . . found you in the cellar . . .'

'Yes?'

'DI Rebus started playing around with a chisel: you remember that?'

'Not really.'

'It was in Joe Evans's toolbox.'

'Hold the front page.'

Siobhan smiled at the sarcasm; knew she could afford to. 'There was a hammer there too, Ray.'

'A hammer in a toolbox: what will they think of next?'

'Last night, I went to your cellar and removed that hammer. I told the forensics team it was a rush job. They worked through the night. It's a bit soon for the DNA results, but they found traces of blood on that hammer, Ray. Same group as Donny Cruikshank.' She shrugged. 'So much for the facts.' She waited for Mangold's reply, but his mouth was clamped shut. 'Now,' she went on, 'here's the thing ... If that hammer was used in the killing of Donny Cruikshank, then I'm thinking there are three possibilities.' She held up one finger at a time. 'Evans, Ishbel, or yourself. It had to be one of you. And I think, realistically, we can leave Evans out of it.' She lowered one of the fingers. 'So it's down to you or Ishbel, Ray. Which is it to be?'

Les Young's pen was poised once more above the pad.

'I need to see her,' Ray Mangold said, voice suddenly dry and brittle-sounding. 'Just the two of us ... five minutes is all I need.'

'Can't do it, Ray,' Young said firmly.

'I'm giving you nothing till you let me see her.'

But Les Young was shaking his head. Mangold's gaze shifted to Siobhan.

'DI Young's in charge,' she told him. 'He calls the shots.'

Mangold leaned forward, elbows on the table, head in hands. When he spoke, his words were muffled by his palms.

'We didn't catch that, Ray,' Young said.

'No? Well, catch this!' And Mangold lunged across the table, swinging a fist. Young jerked back. Siobhan was on her feet, grabbed the arm and twisted. Young dropped his pen and was around the table, putting a headlock on Mangold.

'Bastards!' Mangold spat. 'You're *all* bastards, the whole bloody lot of you!'

And then, a minute or so later, and with back-up arriving, restraints at the ready: 'Okay, okay ... I did it. Happy now, you shower of shite? I stuck a hammer in his head. So what? Doing the world a huge bloody favour, that's what it was.'

'We need to hear it from you again,' Siobhan hissed in his ear.

'What?'

'When we let go of you, you'll need to say it all again.' She released her grip as the officers moved in.

'Otherwise,' she explained, 'people might think I'd twisted your arm.'

*

388

They took a coffee break eventually, Siobhan standing with eyes closed as she leaned against the drinks machine. Les Young had opted for the soup, despite her warnings. He now sniffed the contents of his cup and winced.

'What do you think?' he asked.

Siobhan opened her eyes. 'I think you chose badly.'

'I meant Mangold.'

Siobhan shrugged. 'He wants to go down for it.'

'Yes, but did he do it?'

'Either him or Ishbel.'

'He loves her, doesn't he?'

'I get that impression.'

'So he could be covering for her?'

She shrugged again. 'Wonder if he'll end up on the same wing as Stuart Bullen. That would be a kind of justice, wouldn't it?'

'I suppose so.' Young sounded sceptical.

'Cheer up, Les,' Siobhan told him. 'We got a result.'

He made a show of studying the drinks machine's front panel. 'Something you don't know, Siobhan . . .'

'What?'

'This is my first time leading a murder team. I want to get it *right*.'

'Doesn't always happen in the real world, Les.' She patted his shoulder. 'But at least now you can say you've dipped a toe in the water.'

He smiled. 'While you headed for the deep.'

'Yes . . .' she said, voice trailing off, 'and nearly didn't come up again.'

389

32

Edinburgh Royal Infirmary was sited just outside the city, in an area called Little France.

At night, Rebus thought it resembled Whitemire, the car park lit but the world around it in darkness. There was a starkness to the design, and the compound seemed self-contained. The air as he stepped from his Saab felt different from the city centre: fewer poisons, but colder, too. It didn't take him long to find Alan Traynor's room. Rebus himself had been a patient here not so long ago, but in an open ward. He wondered if someone was paying for Traynor's privacy: his American employers maybe.

Or the UK's own Immigration Service.

Felix Storey sat dozing by the bedside. He'd been reading a women's magazine. From its frayed edges, Rebus guessed it had come from a pile in another part of the hospital. Storey had removed his suit jacket and placed it over the back of his chair. He still wore his tie, but with the top button of his shirt undone. For him it was a casual look. He was snoring quietly as Rebus entered. Traynor, on the other hand, was awake but looked dopey. His wrists were bandaged, and a tube led into one arm. His eyes barely focused on Rebus as he entered. Rebus gave a little wave anyway, and kicked one of the chair legs. Storey's head jerked up with a snort.

'Wakey-wakey,' Rebus said.

'What time is it?' Storey ran a hand down his face.

'Quarter past nine. You make a lousy guard.'

'I just want to be here when he wakes up.'

'Looks to me like he's been awake a while.' Rebus nodded towards Traynor. 'Is he on painkillers?'

'A hefty dose, so the doctor said. They want a shrink to look at him tomorrow.'

'Get anything out of him today?'

Storey shook his head. 'Hey,' he said, 'you let me down.'

'How's that?' Rebus asked.

'You promised you'd go with me to Whitemire.'

'I break promises all the time,' Rebus said with a shrug. 'Besides, I had some thinking to do.'

'About what?'

Rebus studied him. 'Easier if I show you.'

'I don't . . .' Storey looked towards Traynor.

'He's not fit to answer any questions, Felix. Anything he gives you would be thrown out of court . . .'

'Yes, but I shouldn't just . . .'

'I think you should.'

'Someone has to keep watch.'

'In case he tries topping himself again? Look at him, Felix, he's in another place.'

Storey looked, and seemed to concede the point.

'Won't take long,' Rebus assured him.

'What is it you want me to see?'

'That would spoil the surprise. Do you have a car?' Rebus watched Storey nod. 'Then you can follow me.'

'Follow you where?'

'Got any trunks with you?'

'Trunks?' Storey's eyebrows furrowed.

'Never mind,' Rebus said. 'We'll just have to improvise . . .'

Rebus drove carefully, keeping an eye on the headlights in his rearview. Improvisation, he couldn't help thinking, was at the heart of everything he was about to do. Halfway, he called Storey on his mobile, told him they were nearly there.

'This better be worth it,' came the tetchy reply.

'I promise,' Rebus said. The city outskirts first: bungalows fronting the route, housing schemes hidden behind them. It was the bungalows visitors would see, Rebus realised, and they'd think what a nice, upright place Edinburgh was. The reality was waiting somewhere else, just out of their eye-line.

Waiting to pounce.

There wasn't much traffic about: they were skirting the southern edge of the city. Morningside was the first real clue that Edinburgh might have some night life: bars and takeaways, supermarkets and students. Rebus signalled left, checking in his mirror that Storey did the same. When his mobile sounded, he knew it would be Storey: irritated further and wondering how much longer.

'We're here,' Rebus muttered under his breath. He pulled into the kerb, Storey following suit. The Immigration man was first out of his car.

'Time to stop with the games,' he said.

'I couldn't agree more,' Rebus answered, turning away. They were on a leafy suburban street, large houses silhouetted against the sky. Rebus pushed open a gate, knowing Storey would follow. Instead of trying the bell, Rebus headed for the driveway, walking purposefully now.

The jacuzzi was still there, its cover removed once more, steam billowing from it.

Big Ger Cafferty in the water, arms stretched out along its sides. Opera music on the sound system.

'You sit in that thing all day?' Rebus asked.

'Rebus,' Cafferty drawled. 'And you've brought your boyfriend: how touching.' He ran a hand over his matted chest-hair.

'I'm forgetting,' Rebus said, 'the two of you have never actually met in person, have you? Felix Storey, meet Morris Gerald Cafferty.'

Rebus was studying Storey's reaction. The Londoner slid his hands into his pockets. 'Okay,' he said, 'what's going on here?'

'Nothing.' Rebus paused. 'I just thought you might want to put a face to the voice.'

'What?'

Rebus didn't bother answering straight away. He was staring up at the room above the garage. 'No Joe tonight, Cafferty?'

'He gets the odd night off, when I don't think I'll be needing him.'

'Number of enemies you've made, I wouldn't have thought you ever felt safe.'

'We all need a bit of risk from time to time.' Cafferty had busied himself with the control panel, turning off jets and music both. But the light was still active, still changing colour every ten or fifteen seconds.

'Look, am I being fitted up here?' Storey asked. Rebus ignored him. His eyes were on Cafferty.

'You bear a grudge a long time, I'll give you that. When was it you fell out with Rab Bullen? Fifteen . . . twenty years ago? But that grudge gets passed down the generations, eh, Cafferty?'

'I've nothing against Stu,' Cafferty growled.

'Wouldn't say no to a bit of his action though, eh?' Rebus paused to light a cigarette. 'Nicely played, too.' He blew smoke into the night sky, where it merged with the steam.

'I don't want any of this,' Felix Storey said. He made as if to turn and leave. Rebus let him, betting he wouldn't carry through. After a few paces, Storey stopped and turned, then retraced his steps.

'Say what you want to say,' he challenged.

Rebus examined the tip of his cigarette. 'Cafferty here is your "Deep Throat", Felix. Cafferty knew what was going on because he had a man on the inside – Barney Grant, Bullen's lieutenant. Barney feeding info to Cafferty, Cafferty passing it along to you. In return for which, Grant would get Bullen's empire handed to him on a plate.'

'What does it matter?' Storey asked, brow furrowing. 'Even if it *was* your friend Cafferty here . . .'

'Not *my* friend, Felix – *yours*. But the thing is, Cafferty wasn't just passing you information . . . He came up with the passports . . . Barney Grant planted them in the safe, probably while we were chasing Bullen down that tunnel. Bullen would take the fall and all would be well. Thing was, how did Cafferty *get* the passports?' Rebus looked at both men and shrugged. 'Easy enough if it's Cafferty who's smuggling the immigrants into the UK.' His gaze had rested on Cafferty, whose eyes seemed smaller, blacker than ever. Whose entire rounded face glistened with malice. Rebus gave another theatrical shrug. 'Cafferty, not Bullen. Cafferty feeding Bullen to you, Felix, so he could bag all that business for himself . . .'

'And the beauty is,' Cafferty drawled, 'there's no proof, and absolutely nothing you can do about it.'

'I know,' Rebus said.

'Then what's the point of saying it?' Storey snarled.

'Listen and you'll learn,' Rebus told him.

Cafferty was smiling. 'With Rebus, there's always a point,' he conceded.

Rebus flicked ash into the tub, which put a sudden stop to the smile. 'Cafferty is the one who knows London . . . he has contacts there. Not Stuart Bullen. Remember that photo of you, Cafferty? There you were, with your London "associates". Even Felix here let slip that there's a London connection involved in all of this. Bullen didn't have the muscle – or anything else – to put together something as meticulous as people-smuggling. He's the fall guy, so things ease up for a while. Thing is, putting Bullen in the frame

393

becomes a whole lot easier if someone else is on board – someone like you, Felix. An Immigration officer with an eye for an easy score. You crack the case, it means a big fillip. Bullen's the only one who's being shafted. Far as you're concerned, he's scum anyway. You're not going to worry about who's behind the shafting or what might be in it for them. But here's the thing – all the glory you're going to get, it adds up to the cube of bugger-all, because what you've done is smoothed Cafferty's path. It'll be *him* in charge from now on, not only bringing illegals into the country, but working them to death too.' Rebus paused. 'So thanks for that.'

'This is bullshit,' Storey spat.

'I don't think so,' Rebus said. 'To me, it makes perfect sense . . . it's the only thing that does.'

'But like you said,' Cafferty interrupted, 'you can't make any of it stick.'

'That's true,' Rebus admitted. 'I just wanted to let Felix here know who he'd really been working for all this time.' He flicked the rest of his cigarette on to the lawn.

Storey lunged at him, teeth bared. Rebus dodged the move, grabbing him in a chokehold around the neck, forcing his head into the water. Storey was maybe an inch taller . . . younger and fitter. But he didn't have Rebus's heft, his arms flailing, uncertain whether to search for purchase on the side of the tub, or try to unlock Rebus's grip.

Cafferty sat in his corner of the pool, watching the action as if he were ringside.

'You haven't won,' Rebus hissed.

'From where I'm sitting, I'd say you're wrong.'

Rebus realised that Storey's resistance was lessening. He released his grip and took a few steps back, out of range of the Londoner. Storey fell to his knees, spluttering. But he was soon up again, advancing on Rebus.

'Enough!' Cafferty barked. Storey turned towards him, ready to channel his anger elsewhere. But there was something about Cafferty . . . even at the age he was, overweight and naked in a tub . . .

It would take a braver – or more foolish – man than Storey to stand up to him.

Something Storey knew immediately. He made the right decision, shoulders untensing, fists unclenching, trying to control his coughs and splutters.

'Well, boys,' Cafferty went on, 'I think it's past both your bedtimes, isn't it?'

'I'm not finished yet,' Rebus stated.

'I thought you were,' Cafferty said. It sounded like an order, but Rebus dismissed it with a twitch of the mouth.

'Here's what I want.' His attention was on Storey now. 'I said I can't prove anything, but that might not stop me trying – and shit has a way of making a smell, even when you can't see it.'

'I've told you, I didn't know who "Deep Throat" was.'

'And you weren't just a tiny bit suspicious, even when he gave you a tip such as who owned the red BMW?' Rebus waited for an answer, but got none. 'See, Felix, the way it'll seem to most people, either you're dirty or else incredibly stupid. Neither looks good on the old CV.'

'I didn't know,' Storey persisted.

'But I'm betting you had an inkling. You just ignored it and concentrated on all those brownie points you'd be getting.'

'What do you want?' Storey croaked.

'I want the Yurgii family – the mother and kids – released from Whitemire. I want them housed somewhere you'd choose for yourself. By tomorrow.'

'You think I can do that?'

'You've blown an immigrant scam apart, Felix – they owe you.'

'And that's it?'

Rebus shook his head. 'Not quite. Chantal Rendille . . . I don't want her deported.'

Storey seemed to be waiting for more, but Rebus was finished.

'I'm sure Mr Storey will see what he can do,' Cafferty said levelly – as if his was always the voice of reason.

'Any of your illegals turn up in Edinburgh, Cafferty . . .' Rebus began, knowing the threat to be empty.

Cafferty knew it too, but he smiled and bowed his head. Rebus turned to Storey. 'For what it's worth, I think you just got greedy. You saw a golden chance and you weren't going to question it, far less turn it down. But there's a chance to redeem yourself.' He jabbed a finger in Cafferty's direction. 'By pointing your guns at *him*.'

Storey nodded slowly, both men – locked in combat just moments before – now staring at the figure in the tub. Cafferty had half turned, as if he'd already dismissed them from his mind and his life. He was busy with the control panel, jets suddenly gushing into the tub again. 'You'll bring your trunks next time?' he called as Rebus started heading for the driveway.

'And an extension cable,' Rebus called back.

For the two-bar electric fire. Watch the lights change colour when *that* hit the water . . .

Epilogue

The Oxford Bar.

Harry poured Rebus a pint of IPA, then told him there was a 'journo' in the back room. 'Fair warning,' Harry said. Rebus nodded and took his drink through. It was Steve Holly. He was perusing what looked like the next morning's paper, folded it closed at Rebus's approach.

'Jungle drums are going mental,' he said.

'I never listen to them,' Rebus replied. 'Try never to read the tabloids either.'

'Whitemire's approaching meltdown, you've got a strip-club owner in custody, and there's a story the paramilitaries have been muscling in on Knoxland.' Holly raised his hands. 'I hardly know where to start.' He laughed and hoisted his glass. 'Actually, that's not strictly true . . . want to know why?'

'Why?'

He wiped foam from his top lip. 'Because everywhere I look, I come across your dabs.'

'Do you?'

Holly nodded slowly. 'Given the inside gen, I could make you the hero of the piece. That would put you on the fast track out of Gayfield Square.'

'My saviour,' Rebus offered, concentrating on his beer. 'But tell me this . . . Remember that story you wrote about Knoxland? The way you twisted it so the refugees became the problem?'

'They *are* a problem.'

Rebus ignored this. 'You wrote it that way because Stuart Bullen told you to.' It sounded like a statement, and when Rebus looked into the reporter's eyes, he knew it was true. 'What did he do –

397

phone you? Ask a favour? Pair of you scratching one another's backs again, just like when he used to give you tip-offs on any celebs leaving his club . . .'

'I'm not sure what you're getting at.'

Rebus leaned forward on his chair. 'Didn't you wonder why he was asking?'

'He said it was a matter of balance, giving the locals a voice.'

'But *why*?'

Holly shrugged. 'I just reckoned he was your everyday racist. I'd no idea he had something he was trying to hide.'

'You know now though, don't you? He wanted us focusing on Stef Yurgii as a race crime. And all the time, it was him and his men . . . with slime like you at their beck and call.' Though Rebus was staring at Holly, he was thinking of Cafferty and Felix Storey, of the many and various ways in which people could be used and abused, conned and manipulated. He knew he could unload it all on Holly, and maybe the reporter would even do something with it. But where was the proof? All Rebus had was the queasy feeling in his gut. That, and a few embers of rage.

'I only report the stuff, Rebus,' the reporter said. 'I don't make it happen.'

Rebus nodded to himself. 'And people like me try to clean up afterwards.'

Holly's nostrils twitched. 'Speaking of which, you've not been swimming, have you?'

'Do I look the type?'

'I wouldn't have thought so. All the same, I can definitely smell chlorine . . .'

Siobhan was parked outside his flat. As she emerged from the driver's side, he could hear bottles chiming in her carrier bag.

'We can't be working you hard enough,' Rebus told her. 'I heard you'd taken time off for a dook in Duddingston Loch.' She managed a smile. 'You're okay, though?'

'I will be after a couple of glasses . . . Always supposing you're not expecting different company.'

'You mean Caro?' Rebus slid his hands into his pockets and gave a shrug.

'Was it my fault?' Siobhan asked into the silence.

'No . . . but don't let that stop you taking the blame. How's Major Underpants?'

'He's fine.'

Rebus nodded slowly, then brought the key from his pocket. 'No cheap plonk in that bag, I hope.'

'The finest bin ends in town,' she assured him. They climbed the two flights together, finding comfort in the silence. But at Rebus's landing, he stopped short and uttered a curse. His door was ajar, the jamb splintered.

'Bloody hell,' Siobhan said, following him inside.

Straight to the living room. 'TV's gone,' she stated.

'And the stereo.'

'Want me to phone it in?'

'And provide punchlines for Gayfield all next week?' He shook his head.

'I'm assuming you're insured?'

'I'll need to check I kept the payments up . . .' Rebus broke off as he noticed something. A scrap of paper on his chair by the bay window. He crouched down to peer at it. Nothing but a seven-digit number. He picked up his phone and made the call, staying in a crouch as he listened. An answering machine, telling him all he needed to know. He ended the call, stood back up.

'Well?' Siobhan asked.

'A pawn shop on Queen Street.'

She looked puzzled, even more so when he smiled.

'Bloody Drugs Squad,' he told her. 'Pawned the stuff for the price of that bloody torch.' Despite himself, he laughed, pinching the skin at the bridge of his nose. 'Go fetch the corkscrew, will you? It's in the kitchen drawer . . .'

He picked up the scrap of paper and fell into his chair, staring at it, the laughter subsiding by degrees. And then Siobhan was standing in the doorway, holding another note.

'Not the corkscrew?' he said, face dropping.

'The corkscrew,' she confirmed.

'Now *that's* vicious. That's more than flesh and blood can stand!'

'Maybe you could borrow one from the neighbours?'

'I don't know any of the neighbours.'

'Then this is your chance to get acquainted. It's either that or no booze.' Siobhan shrugged. 'Your decision.'

'Not to be taken lightly,' Rebus drawled. 'You better sit yourself down . . . this might take a while.'